Castles in the Clouds

MYRA JOHNSON

Franciscan
MEDIA
Cincinnati, Ohio

Cover design and illustration by Candle Light Studios
Book design by Mark Sullivan

LIBRARY OF CONGRESS CATALOGING-IN-PUBLICATION DATA
Names: Johnson, Myra, 1951-, author.
Title: Castles in the clouds / Myra Johnson.
Description: Cincinnati, Ohio : Franciscan Media, [2016] | Series: Flowers of Eden ; 2
Identifiers: LCCN 2016018753 | ISBN 9781632530028 (paperback)
Subjects: LCSH: Man-woman relationships—Fiction. | BISAC: FICTION / Christian / Romance. | FICTION / Christian / Historical. | GSAFD: Christian fiction. | Love stories.
Classification: LCC PS3610.O3666 C37 2016 | DDC 813/.6—dc23
LC record available at https://lccn.loc.gov/2016018753

ISBN 978-1-63253-002-8

Published by Franciscan Media
28 W. Liberty St.
Cincinnati, OH 45202
www.FranciscanMedia.org

Printed in the United States of America.
Printed on acid-free paper.
16 17 18 19 20 5 4 3 2 1

For all the teachers in my family—especially Jack, Ben, Judy, Jim, Joel, and Helen—and remembering those special teachers from my youth who encouraged creativity and instilled a love of story. There is no way to quantify the far-reaching ways you have touched students' lives.

Acknowledgments

In 2013, when our pastor announced a photo safari through Kenya as the next church group travel excursion, my husband and I jumped at the chance. Our daughter Julena and her husband were serving as missionaries in Ethiopia at the time (look at a map and you'll find Kenya right next to Ethiopia), so what better opportunity to tack on a visit to see them in their working environment, something we'd always wanted to do! Not to mention Julena had already filled our imaginations with visions of Kenya following her college mission trip there in the mid-1990s.

Experiencing both Ethiopia and Kenya firsthand? This was indeed the trip of a lifetime, and we came home with wonderful memories and close to a thousand photographs. I also knew that someday, somehow, I had to work these adventures into a story. As the character of Larkspur Linwood began to form in my mind, ideas about sending her to Africa soon followed.

For friends John and Diana Lasater who arranged our trip, thank you for making sure all the travel details were handled just right—even those crazy, unpredictable glitches! Who knew the Nairobi international terminal would catch fire the day we were supposed to fly in! John, your calming presence helped tremendously, as did Diana's reassuring e-mails from back in the States. Diana, it's a delight singing next to you in our church choir soprano section, and thank you so much for your joyful enthusiasm in support of my novels!

I'm amazed at how "small" our world has become in the age of jet travel and the Internet. And I'm grateful God has blessed my husband and me with the good health and financial resources to enjoy these kinds of travel adventures (although *enjoy* isn't exactly the word I'd choose to describe ten to fifteen hours in a cramped airplane seat). I'm truly thankful for this amazingly diverse and beautiful world God has entrusted to us, and I pray that we never take a single one of his blessings for granted.

I must also express my gratitude for this opportunity to work once again with the excellent editorial staff of Franciscan Media, especially my brilliant editor, Ericka McIntyre. Your keen eye, gentle guidance, and utmost professionalism have made working on these novels a pleasure.

For my agent, Natasha Kern, I am ever blessed to be counted among your clients—even more so, to call you friend. Thank you for being such an energetic champion for my stories and for the personal interest you take in each one of your clients.

As always, I must mention my treasured "Seekerville sisters," at www.seekerville.net. Thank you for the daily laughs, prayers, and encouragement, but most especially for your enduring friendship. I don't even want to imagine what this journey would be like without you!

And last but certainly not least, thanks to my beloved family. Jack, my dear husband, your rock-solid support never wavers, even when I give you "the eye" for invading my writing space with a question about the grocery list or to ask my opinion on your current home-maintenance project. Daughters Johanna and Julena, both busy moms and active servants of God, you still find time to cheer your mother on, and I can't begin to express how much that means to me! Hugs to you, your loving husbands, and our seven cherished grandchildren.

I can't leave out Shadow and Poppy, our precious rescue dogs and my daily writing companions. You bring joy to my heart, you keep my toes warm on chilly days, and you never fail to remind me when quitting time rolls around.

Through family, friends, colleagues, and calling, I am truly blessed!

"Rejoice always, pray without ceasing,
give thanks in all circumstances; for this is the
will of God in Christ Jesus for you."
—1 Thessalonians 5:16–18

"For we walk by faith, not by sight."
—2 Corinthians 5:7

Chapter One

May 1932
Henderson State Teachers College
Arkadelphia, Arkansas

A bad case of jitters had Larkspur Linwood by the scruff of the neck. She'd passed all her exams, hadn't she? With flying colors, every one. Then why this curt summons to Professor Keene's office?

She halted outside his closed door, a stack of library books due back today clutched firmly against her chest. Professor Keene hadn't specified a time, only that she must see him this afternoon at her earliest convenience.

Perhaps she should deliver the books first and come back later. *Much* later, when he'd likely be anxious to get home to his supper and wouldn't lecture her overly long about...whatever this was about!

The bald truth was the man both enchanted and terrified her. His smile could change in an instant from warm invitation to a sanctimonious smirk. In her two years at Henderson State Teachers College, Lark had been the unwitting victim of both.

Eyes squeezed shut, mouth in a twist, she prepared for a hasty escape.

The door swung open.

"Miss Linwood. Please come in."

He would look so fine today, dark hair slicked back and shiny, broad shoulders tugging against the fabric of his starched white shirt. With a gentlemanly sweep of his arm, Professor Keene motioned Lark into the office. He relieved her of the library books and plopped them on a low bookshelf by the door, then held a chair while she sat.

As he took his seat behind the desk, Lark tried to decipher which smile he wore today. A little like Alice's Cheshire cat, or perhaps the Mona Lisa? In other words, utterly inscrutable. "Sir, have I left some course work unfinished? If I've overlooked anything—"

"Don't be ridiculous!" Professor Keene tipped his chair back and crossed one leg, hands folded at his svelte waist. "Surely you realize you're one of the top undergraduates at Henderson."

Lark relaxed, but only slightly. The professor didn't call a student to his office without good reason. A wayward wisp of blond hair had dipped across her temple, and she nervously thrust it behind her ear. "Then why…"

His smile twitching higher at one corner, Professor Keene straightened. "Miss Linwood—Lark, if I may, since I hope over the past two years our acquaintance has moved beyond merely that of professor and student."

Prickles of awareness raced up her spine. "Sir?"

"What I'm trying to say, and not very well, obviously, is that both your intellect and your dedication have greatly impressed me. Your participation in my literature discussion circle has revealed a maturity I don't often find in underclassmen." The professor lowered his gaze momentarily, and the pause gave Lark a chance to discreetly inhale a flustered breath. "For this reason, I have come to admire you as a colleague, a fellow seeker after knowledge, someone whose perspectives and insights I hold in the highest regard."

Lark would require several more steadying breaths, or quite possibly an oxygen tank, to survive this conversation. Her heart threatened to hammer right out of her chest. Surely—*surely!*—these remarks couldn't mean what she hoped they might. Yet his words flattered her. His admiration buoyed her. His attention thrilled her.

Clutching her handbag, she tried to swallow, her throat as dry as the crumbling soil of Grandpa's farm back home in Eden. "I hardly know what to say, Professor Keene."

"Say you'll come to my home on Saturday evening for a special gathering. I guarantee you'll find it intriguing, the opportunity of a lifetime." He rose and rounded the desk, then took her hand and helped her to her feet. The persuasive quirk of his lips did strange things to her insides. "Seven o'clock. You remember where I live, right?"

"Cherry Street, near Riverside." Last December, Professor Keene had hosted a Christmas tea for his students, and Lark well remembered his charming brick bungalow and its decidedly masculine decor. She edged past him to gather up her library books, then paused at the door. "May I ask who else will be in attendance?"

The professor's gaze shifted. "I've invited two other young ladies, both recent graduates. You'll recall meeting them at a few of our discussion circles last year."

Two other young ladies, but closer in age to the professor than Lark's twenty-one years. Her spirits sank just a little. Perhaps she wasn't as special to the handsome Professor Keene as she'd foolishly dared to imagine.

"Don't be concerned about appearances, though. Mrs. Eck from the campus health clinic is attending, along with a gentleman who will present some illuminating—and I daresay quite compelling—information."

Lark certainly wouldn't worry about any improprieties with prim and proper Mrs. Eck in attendance. "And you can give me no hint as to the nature of this gathering?"

With one hand braced casually against the doorframe, Professor Keene grinned. "As I said, it'll be a grand opportunity in which I hope you'll be eager to take part."

Clearly, he intended to reveal nothing further, and Lark couldn't begin to imagine what this presentation might entail.

"I'll have to ask Mr. O'Neill. I'm working at the grocer's all day, and on Saturdays we do inventory after the store closes."

The professor laid his hand lightly upon Lark's shoulder, just for a moment, but in that moment she felt special again, uniquely important in his eyes. "Please come, Lark. I promise you, this will mean immensely more to your future than counting tins of string beans."

*   *   *

Lark went straight from Professor Keene's office to the library, hardly aware of her feet touching the ground. If she had passed any other students along the way, she'd be hard pressed to recall a single one. After dropping the books into the return bin, she dashed the six blocks to O'Neill's Grocery and slipped in through the loading dock door. She grabbed a work apron with one hand and punched her time card with the other, then relieved Mr. O'Neill behind the cash register.

The plump, balding grocer moved down the counter and pulled out an accounts ledger. "Busy day on campus?"

"Very." Still breathless, Lark scooted onto one of the tall stools her employer kept behind the counter. "Sorry I'm running late, but with the spring term just ending, I had several stops to make on my way over."

"Not a problem." Mr. O'Neill winked over the top of his wire-rimmed glasses. "You still planning to spend some time at home before the summer term begins?"

"Just a few days. I'll leave Sunday and be back Thursday." Since jobs were scarce and this one helped pay her way through school, she couldn't afford to take any more time off than necessary. On the other hand, Grandpa and Rose, Lark's younger sister, had been working the farm pretty much by themselves for the past couple of years. They deserved a brief respite from what chores Lark could help with. She'd never much cared for life on the farm, even less the toil and sweat for little return, but she did love her family.

A customer brought her basket to the register, and Lark rang up the purchases. "That'll be four dollars and sixty-three cents, Mrs. Dimity."

The white-haired woman clucked her tongue as she opened her wallet. "Next I s'pose you'll be asking an arm and a leg. Lord help us if the cost of groceries rises any higher."

"I know, ma'am. Everyone's struggling." Lark slipped a peppermint stick into Mrs. Dimity's bag. "For your grandson," she said with a smile.

Mr. O'Neill glanced over and nodded his approval. He did his best to keep his prices down, but times were hard all over, and the drought that had held Arkansas in its grip since the summer of 1930 was slow to relent. Lark prayed every day that Grandpa would pull in a decent cotton harvest this year—and wouldn't kill himself in the process.

When Mrs. Dimity left, Lark straightened a few things on the shelves, then sidled over to Mr. O'Neill's end of the counter. "I hate to ask, but is there any chance you can do inventory without me tomorrow evening?"

He looked up with an arched brow and a curious grin. "Now don't tell me, Lark Linwood, that after two whole years at Henderson, you've finally found yourself a beau?"

"Oh, no! Nothing like that." She held both hands aloft and hoped her face wasn't as red as it felt. "My faculty advisor is having an important meeting, and he's asked me to attend."

"Professor Keene? Well, then, it *must* be important." Mr. O'Neill rubbed his jaw. "I can ask Bobby to come in and help with inventory. He'll be glad for the extra hours."

Bobby was another student working part-time for the grocer, and he needed the work as badly as Lark. Perhaps more so, since he had five brothers and sisters at home. "If you're sure. Because I'll work if you need me."

"Lark." Mr. O'Neill gave her hand a fatherly pat. "I don't want you worrying for a moment about your job. It's yours as long as you want it. So you take the time you need for this meeting with your professor, and I'll ask Bobby if he'll trade some hours with you when you get back next week. Then you'll both come out even."

With a quiet sigh of relief, Lark thanked her boss and returned to her duties. Slow as business had been since Lark first hired on, she suspected the kind man made do with minimal profit for the sole purpose of helping impoverished college students like her and Bobby.

And while the lulls between customers usually allowed Lark plenty of time for keeping up with her studies, with the spring term at an end, she had far too much time to ponder Professor Keene's mysterious invitation.

*   *   *

Friday and Saturday dragged by, helped only by the unnecessary work Lark made for herself at the grocer's. By the time she clocked out late Saturday afternoon, every shelf had been dusted clean, the floors swept and mopped until they shone, and tally sheets prepared for when Bobby arrived to do inventory.

"My goodness, you're in a state," Mr. O'Neill said as Lark fumbled with her apron strings. "Wish you weren't leaving directly for Eden in the morning so's I'd see you in church and you could tell me what all the excitement's about."

"It's probably nothing more than a visiting academic Professor Keene thinks we'd enjoy conversing with." If only Lark could convince herself of such. By now, she had the apron ties in a knot, and her nervous fingers wouldn't cooperate to work it loose. A most unchristian curse word begged for release, but she bit it back.

Stepping behind her, Mr. O'Neill grasped both her wrists and firmly placed them at her sides, then deftly freed the knot. He eased the apron bib over her head. "There. Now take a deep breath and stop your fretting. Whatever's on the docket for tonight, you just remember who you are and keep your wits about you. You'll come out just fine."

Lark offered a grateful smile as she tidied her bun. "You sound like my grandpa."

"And I'm most flattered by the comparison." He took her handbag from its cubbyhole and thrust it into her hands. "Best get going. You don't want to be late. And I'll expect a full report when I see you at the end of the week."

Lark had scarcely enough time to hurry back to the dormitory, make herself a quick sandwich, and freshen up after a long day at the grocer's. Next came the decision about which dress to wear, not that she had many choices. Too bad Lark's roommate had already gone home for the break. She had the fashion sense—and the attractive wardrobe—Lark did not. In the end, Lark decided on her light blue shirtwaist with white polka dots and wide lace collar. Silly, but it always seemed Professor Keene smiled a little more admiringly when she wore this dress to class.

And, oh, if she couldn't kick herself for such fanciful thoughts!

By ten of seven she raced out the door and headed toward Cherry Street. At the end of Professor Keene's block, she slowed her steps and strove for calm. If the man thought her mature, she certainly mustn't arrive at his front door with her hair in a tangle and her chest heaving as if she were a flighty schoolgirl. She adjusted the tortoise-shell combs at her temples and smoothed the bun coiled at her nape.

Continuing on, she noted the two automobiles parked in the professor's driveway. Obviously, she wasn't the first to arrive. She wished now she hadn't wolfed down the sandwich, because if her nerves didn't settle quickly, she might be making a mad dash for the lavatory as soon as she stepped through the door.

It opened before she reached the top step. Professor Keene, in shirtsleeves, vest, and tie, smiled a welcome. "You made it. I'm so glad." He took her hand and drew her into the entryway. "Come in, and I'll introduce you to my other guests. And may I say," he ventured, lowering his voice in a way that raised chill bumps on Lark's neck, "you're looking especially lovely this evening."

She managed a quavering "Thank you."

With a hand at the small of her back, Professor Keene guided her through an archway and into the cozily furnished living room. "Everyone, this is my student Lark Linwood. Lark, you remember Debra McCarrick and Sandra Nott from our literature circles."

"Yes, of course. Delighted to see you again." Lark acknowledged the two graduates on the sofa with a polite nod. She'd always thought Debra both smart and beautiful, an ivory complexion complementing her jet-black hair and regal bearing. Sandra, equally intelligent, lacked Debra's height and stark coloring but made up for her petite stature with a voice that could cut through the noisiest classroom.

"You know Mrs. Eck." The professor indicated the middle-aged woman primly perched in a wing chair opposite the sofa. "And it's my privilege to introduce Dr. Irwin Young, our special guest for this evening." He nodded toward the gray-haired gentleman who'd just hefted his bulk from the overstuffed armchair across the room.

The man stepped forward and offered his hand. "That would be PhD, not MD. Pleased to make your acquaintance, Miss Linwood. Franklin speaks very highly of you."

For a moment, Lark couldn't imagine who Franklin might be, until she remembered it was Professor Keene's first name. "How do you do."

"Please, make yourself comfortable." The professor steered

Lark to a spot at the end of the sofa next to Sandra, then settled into the armchair at Dr. Young's right. "I'm sure you ladies are curious about why I've asked you here, so without further ado, I'll allow the esteemed Dr. Young to explain."

"Thank you, Franklin." The older man cleared his throat and sat forward, his gaze intense and his smile intriguing. "Ladies, I'm here to invite you on an adventure."

Lark exchanged puzzled glances with Sandra, who seemed as ignorant of the purpose of this meeting as she. Debra's expression remained serenely unreadable, but across the room, the twinkle in Mrs. Eck's eyes suggested she had an inkling or two and now anxiously awaited further details.

Sandra removed her gold-framed glasses and held them in her lap with nervous fingers. "Having only completed my first year of teaching, I'm not certain I'm ready for any adventures. Besides, considering our nation's current economic conditions, I can ill afford to jeopardize my career."

Dr. Young shared a look with Professor Keene, and the glimmer of anticipation in both their expressions sent a shiver up Lark's spine.

"Not even," Dr. Young began, "if this adventure I speak of could turn the tide of your teaching careers and provide a unique form of postgraduate study unavailable at any American university?"

Sandra grew silent, her lips drawn into a tight line. She shifted her gaze to Debra, whose expression reflected guarded interest.

"Sounds intriguing," Debra stated. "Please, Dr. Young, continue."

Lark inched forward on the sofa, preparing to rise, make her excuses, and leave. "Since I have two more years to complete my college studies, I'm not sure I should even be here."

Professor Keene lifted one hand. "Hear us out, Lark. This could be a tremendous opportunity for you as well."

Irritation bristled, and Lark couldn't hold her tongue a moment longer. "I've spent the past two days on pins and needles wondering what this meeting could possibly be about. And now, with you both looking as if you're sitting on the secrets of the cosmos, I'm even more apprehensive than before I arrived."

Dr. Young had the decency to look chagrined. "Please forgive us, ladies. It was never my intent to engender so much anxiety. However, Franklin personally recommended each of you for this opportunity, so whether or not you decide to come on board with us, I do ask your discretion."

Lark chewed her lip. Then, with a quick glance at the others, she nodded and leaned back into the sofa. "Very well."

After retrieving some papers from the briefcase beside his chair, Dr. Young passed them to Professor Keene, who distributed copies to Lark, Mrs. Eck, and the other two ladies. "The pictures in the brochures you're holding are of a mission school established several years ago in the Great Rift Valley of Kenya. However, due to recent developments between the Christian missionaries running the school and the indigenous population, the school is undergoing some necessary staff changes." He looked pointedly at Lark, Sandra, and Debra in turn. "I hope to fill the openings with the talent right here in this room."

Lark stared at the photograph depicting a long, two-story brick building with a wide porch and thick pillars. Two women in nun's habits and a tall, angular man wearing a bow tie and white straw fedora flanked a motley class of about twenty black-skinned children sitting in rows along the porch steps. The children's eager faces tugged at Lark's heart. "But...but I'm not a teacher."

"Not yet," Professor Keene said softly. "But imagine what this experience could mean for your future, Lark. Even in your teaching practicum here at Henderson, you'll never get this level of immersion in what it truly means to bring enlightenment to a child hungry to learn."

The sound of her pulse loud in her ears, Lark scarcely heard the conversations suddenly bursting to life around her. She did recognize the fervor in their voices, though, an excitement to match her own.

"Ladies, ladies," Dr. Young interrupted with a chuckle. "I'm thrilled by your enthusiasm, and if you'll give me a chance, all the essential questions will be answered before you leave tonight."

Lark couldn't believe she'd even consider accepting this call, but only one question came to mind: "How soon can we go?"

* * *

"How soon will they arrive?" Anson Schafer lowered the cool compress from his stinging eyes and sought out Sister Mary John.

From her smaller desk catercornered to Anson's, the plump woman looked up, only a blur to him in her white habit. "You know as well as I do how long ship travel takes. Don't expect any relief before mid-July at the earliest."

Anson released a muted groan. Irwin had promised months ago that while back in the States he would actively recruit new teachers and staff. Established nearly forty years ago by Anson's parents, Catholic missionaries from Little Rock, Arkansas, Matumaini School had brought the hope its name implied to countless families in this spectacularly beautiful section of Kenya's Great Rift Valley.

But as Kenyans grew increasingly resistant both to British colonization and the intolerance of certain missionary groups toward long-standing ethnic customs, local support for the school had dwindled. The only way Anson and the few remaining staff believed the school could survive was to bring in teachers who were more concerned with practical education than pros-elytizing. In addition, they wanted to train Kenyan men and women as teachers so that as more independent schools were established, there would be no lapse in the children's education. And in Anson Schafer's mind, education offered the only true hope for any society.

Returning his attention to the open science textbook on his desk, he blinked several times, to no avail. The words ran together in jumbled lines of fading black ink. How was he supposed to prepare tomorrow's lesson if he couldn't see to read?

Sister Mary John clucked her tongue and marched over, snatching up the compress. She dipped it in the washbasin, wrung it out, and thrust it into his hands. "Do you want to go blind? Close the book and rest your eyes. You know these texts by heart anyway."

She wasn't far from wrong. Anson had been teaching the same subjects from the same ragged set of textbooks since his return to the school after finishing his graduate studies seven years ago. "Maybe you're right. I'll put more drops in my eyes and go to bed."

Sister Mary John stayed him with a hand upon his shoulder, her voice lowering to a concerned whisper. "Be sparing, though. You've been too generous with the infected children. If we're not careful, there won't be enough to last until our supply is replenished."

Apprehension stabbed Anson's gut. Copper sulfate solution was the only thing saving him from permanent blindness as a result of this tenacious eye infection. The condition was not uncommon in this part of the world, but Anson had avoided treating it until a month ago.

All the more reason he needed those new teachers and the nurse Dr. Young had promised. Sister Mary John, capable though she was, had stretched herself thin enough after most of the others had abandoned them.

Was he fighting a losing battle, attempting to keep the school going despite increasing opposition from all sides? While he might personally abhor certain ethnic traditions, he took umbrage at the missionaries who summarily excommunicated Christian Kenyans for continuing their centuries-old cultural practices. Didn't St. Paul himself address such sectarianism? *To the weak I became weak, so that I might win the weak*, he wrote to the Corinthians. *I became all things to all people, that I might by all means save some.*

Anson sometimes wondered if perhaps they'd be better served to leave religion out of it entirely. Not that he didn't still hold firmly to his faith. As a boy, he'd envisioned joining the priesthood, as two of his uncles had done. But somewhere between his parochial upbringing here at the school and earning his master's degree at Loyola back in the States, he'd come to believe his calling lay in teaching.

But now, if Irwin's recruitment efforts failed—and more important, if the American missions society funding the school didn't agree to the necessary operational changes—everything Anson and his staff yet hoped to accomplish could fall to ruin.

Retiring to his Spartan living quarters above the school, Anson decided against using more of the precious copper sulfate solution to treat his eyes. He'd rather save the sight of those children he'd dedicated his life to educating, for they were the future of Kenya.

After changing into his pajamas, he crawled beneath the mosquito netting surrounding his narrow bed. Here on the lower southwestern slopes of Mount Kenya, the days were warm and pleasant, but the evenings quickly grew chilly. The rainy season would last another week or two, and dampness permeated everything, even his blankets and pillow. He burrowed deeper under the covers, then reached through an opening in the netting for the envelope he'd left lying on his nightstand.

The lantern light was too dim and Anson's vision too blurry to make out the words of Irwin's telegram, but since its arrival six days ago, he'd asked Sister Mary John repeatedly to read the message aloud, as if he needed to be convinced of the assurance it held: *Take heart. Recruitment meetings in progress. Expect help by summer's end.*

With a tired sigh, Anson extinguished the lantern, then lay back with the telegram clutched to his breastbone. Closing his burning eyes, he crossed himself and sent up a prayer that the promised relief would come soon.

Chapter Two

As the bus pulled to a stop in front of Eden's general store, Lark glimpsed Grandpa's rusty old black pickup parked beside the building. Her heart fluttered. She'd promised herself not to say a word about Kenya right away. But how would she manage to contain her excitement until the ideal moment arrived?

The bus driver shot her a scowl through the rearview mirror. "Hey, Miss Larkspur, you gettin' off here or not? Don't forget I got a schedule to keep."

"Just collecting my things." Handbag looped over one arm, train case tucked beneath the other, Lark muscled her suitcase from the overhead rack and lugged it toward the front. "Thanks, Jasper. You take care, all right?"

The driver tipped his cap. "See you in a few days for the return trip?"

One foot on the lower step, Lark glanced back with an uncertain smile. "Guess I'll see you when I see you."

"Larkspur Jane Linwood!"

At the sound of her sister Rose's jubilant cry, she whirled around and would have toppled face-first to the pavement if Rose hadn't been right there to sweep her into a hug. The suitcase and train case dropped to the ground, and she wrapped both arms around her sister, as much in self-defense as in greeting. "Gracious sakes alive, Rosie! I'm glad to see you, too, but give a girl a chance to breathe."

Rose's russet curls vied for freedom from a messy braid as she jauntily snatched up Lark's suitcase. Behind them, the bus pulled away, and they started for the pickup. "Grandpa's still jawing with the pastor over yonder at the church, but I didn't want to miss your bus. We're going from here over to Brinkley to have

Sunday dinner with Bryony and Michael. They can't wait to see you again."

Just over a year ago, Bryony, the eldest Linwood sister, had married Michael Heath, son of the plantation owner Grandpa leased his farm from. "Is Bry in a family way yet?"

Rose's smile dimmed, and she shook her head. "Don't say anything about it. She gets sad if you do."

"It'll happen in God's timing." With a light laugh, Lark set her handbag and train case inside the pickup cab. "Bryony's been too much of a mother hen to us for the Lord to deny her children of her own."

"I'm never gonna have kids." Rose plopped the suitcase into the pickup bed. "Too much trouble."

"And you're too young to be making such pronouncements. Once you and Caleb—"

"You hush right now!" Rose yanked open the driver's-side door and glared as Lark settled into the passenger seat. "I'm never getting married either. You're off at college, Bry's left home to start her own family, so somebody's got to stick around to help Grandpa on the farm."

Lark couldn't help chuckling to herself over Rose's unmistakable blush at the mention of Caleb Wieland's name. She could deny it all she wanted, but the day would come when Rose Linwood would lose her tomboy ways and appreciate the attentions of a good man like Caleb.

As you've come to appreciate Professor Keene's attentions? Lark shifted her gaze toward the open window to hide the heat creeping up her own cheeks. "There's Grandpa walking over from the church. We should get going."

Rose started the motor and headed up the road to meet Grandpa. With an ear-to-ear grin, he yanked open Lark's door and smothered her in a hug before climbing in beside her. "Ain't you a sight for sore eyes! Lordy, if you don't look more grown up every time we see you."

Easter had been Lark's last visit home, so while they drove over to Brinkley, a larger town about twenty miles away, both Grandpa and Rose peppered Lark with questions about school. Easy enough to steer the conversation toward her studies and campus life while avoiding mention of the meeting at Professor Keene's house last evening. Lark still couldn't believe she was actually considering this leap of faith, for that's what it amounted to, since she knew so little of what lay ahead.

What she did know, and what compelled her as much as anything else, was that Professor Keene himself had already requested a leave of absence from Henderson and would be making the journey to Kenya with the others Dr. Young had recruited. It appeared both Sandra and Debra were going, and Mrs. Eck as well, for her nursing skills would be a highly valued asset to the mission.

When Rose pulled into the driveway beside a small, white-washed bungalow, Lark drew her wandering thoughts back to the present. As Lark clambered from the pickup with Grandpa and Rose, the screen door flew open. Bryony darted down the porch steps, her dark hair flying, and once again, Lark found herself smothered in a welcoming embrace.

"Our college girl's home at last." Bryony finally released Lark and ushered her toward the house. "Come on inside. Chicken and dumplings are on the stove."

Lark slid her arm around Bryony's waist. "I can't tell you how I've been craving my big sister's fine home cooking."

Bryony's husband, Michael, held the door for them, offering Lark a brotherly kiss on the cheek. "Aced your exams again, I hear. All signed up for the summer term?"

A tremor started in Lark's belly. She avoided her brother-in-law's question with a noncommittal twist of her lips. "Last week my biology professor showed me the science journal with your latest illustrations. Are you working on anything new?"

"Don't get him started," Bryony interrupted, "or we'll be talking botany the rest of the afternoon, when what I *really* want to hear about is how school's going." She ordered everyone to wash up and then get seated in the dining room.

By the time Lark took her place at the table, Bryony had ladled generous servings of chicken and dumplings in a thick, savory sauce. The aroma alone was enough to make Lark's stomach rumble. Michael invited Grandpa to offer thanks, and for the next several minutes the clicks of silverware against china eclipsed conversation.

When Bryony rose to clear the table and bring dessert, Michael stopped her. "Stay and visit. I'll take care of the dishes and put some coffee on."

"Let me help." Lark reached for Rose's and Grandpa's plates and stacked them atop her own. Anything to stall a bit longer before she broke the news about Kenya.

Michael snatched up the plates before Lark could push back her chair. "Nonsense. You're the guest of honor."

With a halfhearted smile, Lark meticulously folded her napkin and laid it on the table. "I do have something important to tell you," she began, "about school and...other things. Michael, you might want to stay."

Arching a brow, he set the stack of dishes on the sideboard, then went to stand behind Bryony's chair. "This sounds serious."

"It does," Bryony agreed. She reached up to take Michael's hand, then turned a concerned look toward Lark. "You're not thinking of dropping out of college because of the expense, are you? Because Michael and I would do anything to help—"

"Please, just let me say this." Lark clasped her hands beneath the edge of the tablecloth and swallowed over the nervous tremor in her throat. "I—I've volunteered to go to Kenya."

"Kenya!" Rose's mouth fell open. "In *Africa*?"

Lark sat a little straighter but avoided Grandpa's mute stare. "Yes, Africa."

Bryony gasped. "Wait—what do you mean, you *volunteered*? Lark, I don't understand."

"It's the opportunity of a lifetime," Lark stated, echoing Professor Keene's description. "I'll be working at a school there and gaining valuable teaching experience."

"But what about college?" Bryony shook her head in confusion.

"I'm only committing for a year. I'll finish school when I return to the States." Lark finally dared a look at her grandfather, whose expression had grown thoughtful.

"Whose idea was this?" he asked. "You ain't going off on a whim 'cause of some handsome fella's sweet-talking, are you?"

The tiniest shiver of guilt tickled Lark's nape. She couldn't escape the fact that Professor Keene's "sweet-talking" had most certainly swayed her decision. But it wasn't only his flattery and praise. She'd truly been moved by the children's eager faces pictured in Dr. Young's brochure. "The name of the school is Matumaini, which means *hope* in Swahili. And that's what they bring to the people there—hope for a better life through education."

Without releasing Bryony's hand, Michael slipped around to his chair. "Offering hope is a wonderful thing," he said softly, "and you're to be admired for such a noble ambition. But to travel so far away, and for so long…I'm sure you can understand your family's concerns."

Leave it to Michael to be the voice of calm perspective. Lark smiled her gratitude. "Of course I understand. And if you all weren't concerned about me, I'd really start to worry. Yes, this has come up suddenly, but it's more than just a whim."

Bolstered by her passion for this calling, Lark spoke with growing confidence as she offered more details from the meeting at Professor Keene's, careful to emphasize that other teachers and a nurse would also make the journey, and that the travel costs were being funded by the missions aid society in Little Rock. She jumped up from her chair and fetched Dr. Young's brochure from her handbag. She handed it to Grandpa, who read it over thoroughly and then passed it to Bryony.

"You can see the need, can't you?" Lark turned to Rose, who'd grown teary-eyed, and squeezed her hand. "My heart aches at the thought of leaving you behind, but I feel deep down that I'm meant to go."

"Then you must," Bryony stated, her voice trembling. "When will you leave?"

This was the truly hard part. "I need to be packed and on the train to Charleston by Wednesday."

Bryony cried out. "Oh, Lark, so soon?"

"I'm afraid so. Dr. Young is booking passage on a tramp steamer that leaves port next Saturday."

"Excuse me, I—I can't—" Stifling a sob, Bryony bolted from the room.

With an apologetic glance, Michael hurried after her.

Remorse swelled into a giant ache beneath Lark's breastbone. She looked from Rose to Grandpa, her own eyes filling. "Will Bry forgive me? Will *you*?"

"Come here, you." Grandpa tugged her onto his lap as if she were still a confused and frightened seven-year-old, just as she'd been when Mama had brought her and her sisters to live on the farm after Daddy was killed in the Great War. "Ain't nothin' to forgive about obeying the Lord's call on your life. If the Holy Spirit told you to go to Africa to teach them young'uns over yonder, then he'll take care of you every step of the way."

"And look after you while I'm gone, right?" With her arms firmly clasped around Grandpa's neck, Lark peered at him expectantly.

Before he could answer, Rose came over and wrapped her arms around both of them. "Like he always does. I'll pray for you every morning and every night, Lark, till you're back safe and sound."

Only in that moment did Lark fully appreciate all she'd leave behind.

* * *

Anson scanned the two rows of students seated on benches before him, his gaze settling on an eight-year-old boy, easily recognizable because he squirmed more than all the rest. "Kanja, please read the sentence Sister Mary John has written on the chalkboard."

Kanja stood and tugged at the hem of his faded blue shirt, an American-style school uniform donated by the missions aid society. "The...brown...b-b-bear...roared—*Mwalimu* Schafer, what is a bear? Is it like a lion?"

Anson tried not to laugh, not so much at Kanja's question, but at Sister Mary John's continual disregard of the children's unfamiliarity with so many things Westerners took for granted. With a wink at the flustered nun, Anson went to the board, erased the word *bear*, and replaced it with *lion*. "Try again now, Kanja."

The boy beamed a gap-toothed smile. "The...brown...*lion*...roared...l-l-loudly."

"Excellent!" Anson returned to his chair behind a wobbly wooden desk. Picking up his pencil, he blinked several times in a vain attempt to find Kanja's name in the grade book.

Sister Mary John came up beside him. Looking over his shoulder, she casually rested her finger alongside a name and held it there while Anson placed a checkmark in the adjoining column. Returning to the chalkboard, she cast him a chiding glance.

Before Anson could call on the next student, Sister Angelica peeked into the room and signaled for him. He turned the class over to Sister Mary John and stepped outside. "What did you need, Sister?"

"Another telegram, sir." Atremble with excitement, the bespectacled nun, a bit younger than Anson's thirty-two years, held out a wrinkled envelope.

He reached for it, then changed his mind. "Please, read it to me."

Sister Angelica tore open the flap and unfolded the message. "It's from Dr. Young. He writes, 'Success! Ship left port Saturday 4 June. Expect us mid-July.'" She looked up with a wide grin. "The teachers are coming—hallelujah!"

Anson suspected her elation stemmed not so much from the fact that new teachers were on the way, but because she could soon return to the States. Sister Angelica hadn't adapted well to life in Africa.

"Oh, and a delivery came from Nairobi. I think it's the medicines you sent for."

Holding back a relieved sigh, Anson asked Sister Angelica to assist Sister Mary John for the remainder of the school day. He hurried around the corner to his office and found a package wrapped in brown paper sitting on his desk. When he'd torn aside the paper and inspected the contents, his knees went weak with gratitude. At long last, fresh vials of copper sulfate. Two days ago, he'd instructed Sister Mary John to use their remaining supply to treat the infected eyes of three students. Now he could resume treating his own infection.

Filling a dropper, he stretched out on the cot in the corner and applied the solution, then lay with his eyes closed and prayed. If he lost his sight, he'd be useless here. He already relied too heavily on the nuns when his eyes grew continually more tired throughout the day. By evening, his vision sometimes became so clouded that he could barely see his way up the stairs to bed.

He awoke sometime later to find Sister Mary John gently

jostling his shoulder. "I see the medicines arrived," she said. "Praise God!"

He sat up. "Did you see the telegram?"

"Indeed." She turned a chair around and sat facing him. Anson didn't need perfect vision to recognize the concerned downturn of her lips. "I'm still not certain it's of any use to bring in new teachers. Two more villagers came this afternoon to say their children will not return. If they go to school at all, it will be to the new independent Kikuyu school."

"We saw this coming," Anson said tiredly. "They've had enough of us Westerners imposing our Christian standards upon them."

Sister Mary John hiked her chin. "You know what Christ has to say about lukewarm Christians. If we do not stand for our beliefs, we stand for nothing."

"And *nothing* is all that will be left if we flout the cultural underpinnings of the people we serve. No, Sister," he said, rising and crossing to his desk, "if we're to bring the benefits of education to the Kenyans, we must do so respectfully and without prejudice. No offense to you or the Church, but I sincerely hope these teachers Dr. Young has recruited are laypeople and not from any religious order."

Lips flattened in a scowl, Sister Mary John stood. "Removing Christ from the schoolroom will be a terrible mistake."

"I am by no means removing Christ from anywhere—as if I could." Anson had to clamp his teeth together to rein in his temper. Eyes burning, he pinched the bridge of his nose. "Can't you see what a fine line we're treading here? If we want this school to remain relevant, we must be willing to adapt—not to compromise our Christian beliefs, mind you, but to meet these people in a spirit of humble service, not superiority."

Whether he'd gotten through to her or not, he couldn't tell. But once the new teachers arrived and Sister Angelica arranged her passage home to the States, Sister Mary John would be Matumaini School's only Church representative on staff, and Anson needed her support now more than ever. Since he had first taken over as director at the school, she'd been his right hand, confidant, and most trusted advisor. Now, with his vision impaired, she'd become his eyes as well.

*   *   *

Bryony sat on the porch swing, her calico cat, Honey, curled up beside her and a letter from Larkspur spread across her lap. As she gazed across the sun-dappled lawn, a tear slid down her cheek. When the screen door creaked, she hurriedly brushed the wetness away.

"There you are." Michael crossed the porch and joined Bryony on the swing. Unhappy to be disturbed, Honey arched her back and leapt off. "Sorry, kitty, but no one comes between me and my wife. Not even you."

Chin quivering, Bryony couldn't help but laugh. She welcomed her husband's tender kiss, then wiped away another tear. "I can't believe she's gone."

"Honey? I think she'll come around as soon as she smells supper."

Bryony gave Michael's arm a playful slap. "You know I'm not talking about the cat."

"I know, and I hate to see *my* honey so sad." Michael drew her close and brushed his lips across her temple. "Lark is doing what she feels called to do. She sounds happy, doesn't she?"

With another glance at the letter, Bryony had to agree. Lark had mailed the letter the same morning she boarded the ship in Charleston. Every word spoke excitement and anticipation as she described an uneventful train trip with Professor Keene, Mrs. Eck, and the two Henderson State graduates, along with Dr. Irwin Young, the missions aid society representative who'd arranged everything.

"I can't help worrying, though." Bryony released a sharp sigh. "Lark speaks so much about her professor, and in such glowing terms. I'm afraid the *real* reason she's going to Africa is because of her attraction to him."

Michael grew silent for several moments. "Lark has never seemed the type to be so capricious, at least in the short time I've known her."

"Capricious? No. But always a dreamer, always had her nose buried in a book. From the time she was a little girl, she aspired to greater things than growing up on a farm."

"Then maybe that's all this is, Lark's chance to do something meaningful and lasting with her life."

"Maybe." Even so, Bryony couldn't shake the niggling worry that her sister was diving into waters too far over her head. Lark might well be the smartest of the Linwood sisters, but falling in love could do crazy things to one's sensibilities. Besides, what did any of them really know about this Professor Keene? He might be an utter cad, and if anything went wrong, Lark would be an ocean and a continent away.

Michael stroked Bryony's arm. "You're not convinced, are you?"

Honey had wandered back. With a plaintive mew, she jumped onto Bryony's lap, crumpling the letter and looking up with her marble eyes as if to say, *Enough already. Pay attention to me!*

After giving the cat a scratch behind the ears, Bryony rescued Lark's letter, smoothed the wrinkles, and folded it neatly into thirds. "I know it's a waste of time and energy to fret over the things I can't control."

"I couldn't agree more." Michael slid the letter from Bryony's hand and tucked it away in his shirt pocket. "And now, if we can persuade this cat who thinks she owns us to give us some time alone, I'd sincerely enjoy taking your mind off *all* your worries."

* * *

Lark began to wonder if she'd ever get past the seasickness and grow accustomed to the ship's continual rise and fall. She'd spent the first three days shut away in the cabin she shared with Mrs. Eck, each of them taking turns retching in the tiny lavatory and turning away all offers of food except soda crackers and dill pickles.

On the fourth day, Dr. Young coaxed them out on deck for some fresh air, and after a turn about the deck, Lark found Professor Keene chatting amiably with Dr. Young and the ladies. She couldn't help feeling envious that neither of the younger women looked the least bit sickly. Lark tried to smile and join in the conversation, but soon had to make a beeline for the cabin before she humiliated herself at the rail.

By the middle of the second week, she could eat normally without feeling queasy. Able to move about in relative comfort, she began exploring the ship and enjoying the expansive views of the Atlantic. The days took on a placid sameness but gave her ample opportunities to get better acquainted with her companions. She quickly grew to admire Debra and Sandra for their intellect and maturity, as well as their selfless commitment to serve as teachers at Matumaini School.

Matumaini. Lark repeated the name over and over in her mind, memorizing the spelling and pronunciation. Often when she retired for the night, she lay in her bunk browsing the brochure about the school and studying each photograph. She imagined standing in front of a classroom with those eager faces looking back at her, all those minds ready to be filled to the brim with the learning she'd impart. This was her own *matumaini*...her hope, her lifelong dream.

By the third week of June, the ship had passed through the Strait of Gibraltar and steamed into the Mediterranean Sea. Lark couldn't contain her elation at the very thought of traveling so near the cities and countries she'd only experienced through books. Morocco and Spain, Italy and Greece, Libya and Egypt. One afternoon as the ship made its way through Port Said via the Suez Canal, Professor Keene joined Lark at the rail. "Isn't it spectacular?"

At the brush of his arm against hers, Lark's heart skittered. She fixed her attention on the busy shoreline. "I can hardly believe I'm here."

"You've led a pretty sheltered life, haven't you?" The professor chuckled softly. Angling his body to face her, he rested one elbow on the rail. With his other hand, he brushed aside a lock of her hair that the breeze had loosened from her bun.

The intimacy of the gesture made Lark shiver. With a self-conscious laugh, she edged away and pinned the strand back in place. "I was born in Memphis but haven't traveled outside Arkansas since my mother brought us to Eden when I was seven years old." Again, she looked toward the shore, where boats of all sizes wove among the piers and automobiles passed each other on the tree-lined roadway. A dreamlike sigh slipped between her lips. "Until now, anyway. This is the most exciting—and the most frightening—thing I've ever done."

"There's nothing to be afraid of, Lark." Professor Keene moved nearer, his smile warmly inviting. "I truly am glad you're on this adventure with us."

His attentions shouldn't thrill her so, and yet she could no more control her reactions to his nearness than she could alter the ship's course. Besides, hadn't he been equally attentive to Sandra and Debra? Lark had often seen him strolling along the deck with one or the other of them, their heads bent together in animated conversation. He'd shown no favoritism during meal-times in the dining room either, making sure to vary the seating arrangement each time.

Of course, where their socializing was concerned, Mrs. Eck exerted no small amount of influence. She rarely tolerated inter-mixing of the genders without her explicit supervision.

Speaking of whom, here she came now on her afternoon stroll around the deck. "Good day, Professor. Miss Linwood." Mrs. Eck peeked through green-tinted sunglasses from beneath the brim of a floppy straw hat. "Isn't this the loveliest weather? Careful not to get burnt, you two." Both her tone and her expression implied she referred to more than just the angle of the sun.

"Thank you, madam," Professor Keene replied with a mock salute. "Enjoy your walk."

Lark turned away from the rail. "I suppose I should go in for a bit. I've never been able to take the sun like my sister Bryony. And poor Rose with her red hair and freckles!"

"Bryony, Larkspur, and Rose—what a lovely 'bouquet.' Of the three, though, I think I'd always choose larkspur. Such a lovely blue, just like your eyes."

The heat rising in Lark's cheeks had nothing to do with the Egyptian sun. She dipped her chin and hurried across the deck.

The professor followed her to the door and held it for her. "Think I'll see if Irwin is up to a game of shuffleboard. See you at dinner?"

She swallowed her discomfiture long enough to glance up with a smile. "I look forward to it, Professor Keene."

He wagged a finger at her. "How many times must I ask you to call me Franklin? Actually, just plain Frank would be fine. We're colleagues now, after all."

Pausing in the doorway, Lark gave a shrug and tipped her head toward Mrs. Eck as the woman neared the stern. "When our esteemed chaperone insists on formal address, I have difficulty doing otherwise."

"I see your point." Professor Keene rolled his eyes. "What would we do without our dear Mrs. Eck to keep us on our toes?"

Lark was tempted to reply that she might not have come on this journey at all, because without the assurance of Mrs. Eck's matronly presence, Grandpa would probably have locked Lark in her room at the farm until long after the ship had sailed.

With nothing much else to do besides find another good book to read, Lark made her way to the ship's small library. There, she found Debra with a book on her lap gazing out the porthole. The dark-haired woman glanced up with a crooked smile. "I was reading this book about Africa but decided the scenery is much more fascinating."

"Isn't it, though?" Lark took the chair beside her, only to realize Debra would have had an almost perfect view of where Lark and Professor Keene had been standing on the deck.

"There you go blushing again." Debra shook her head. "Honestly, honey, your feelings for Frank are written all over your face."

Lark fisted her hands while silently cursing her fair skin. "My feelings for *Professor Keene* are purely a student's admiration for her teacher."

"But he isn't your teacher now." Shifting slightly, Debra reached for Lark's arm. "Believe me, I've been in your shoes, and I know how charming he can be. Guard your heart, honey. I wouldn't want you getting hurt."

"Thank you for your advice. I'm sure it's well meant." Resentment nipped at Lark's spine. She rose stiffly, careful to offer a polite smile before striding out of the library.

Sandra met her in the corridor. "Oh, hi, Lark. Have you seen Frank? There are Egyptian men riding camels across the way, and I wanted to make sure he saw them." She seized Lark's hand. "Isn't this the most exciting adventure ever?"

"It certainly is." An unwelcome surge of nausea churned Lark's stomach. She covered her mouth. "Please excuse me, Sandra, but I suddenly don't feel so well."

Alone in the cabin a few minutes later, she lay down on her bunk with a cool cloth on her forehead. *When are you going to be honest with yourself, Larkspur Jane Linwood?* It wasn't merely the call to serve at a mission school that had enticed her on this journey. It was convincing herself that Franklin Keene saw her as someone special, someone he could care for as more than just a student or even a colleague.

But romance? Lark thought herself too cerebral to be swayed by dreamy eyes and sweet talk. All the same, a part of her did long for the kind of settled love her sister Bryony had found with Michael Heath. And they'd had so little in common as well, what with Bryony's working as a housemaid for Michael's wealthy, plantation-owning family.

Well, if anything could come of a relationship between Lark and her professor, she'd have an entire year in a distant land during which they might become more personally acquainted.

"Franklin," she said aloud, sitting up and laying aside the washcloth. "Frank." Using his given name would definitely place them on more equal terms. It would take some getting used to, but practice made perfect, didn't it? "Hello, Frank. Lovely day, isn't it? Frank, perhaps you can recommend a good book from the library. Oh, Frank, do let's take a stroll on deck while the stars are out."

Oh, please. Lark had never in her life had the knack for flirting that other girls seemed to master so easily. Better to be her bookish, idealistic self and entrust the future to God. After all, God had made her this way, and how could she love a man who didn't accept her just as she was?

Chapter Three

"Stubborn, stubborn man." Sister Mary John reached across Anson's desk to turn up the lantern light. "What you need is a wife to look after you, because you certainly don't look after yourself."

He tilted his head to offer a smirk. "Are you volunteering?"

"Humph. I am consecrated to Christ, as you well know." The round-faced nun straightened the hem of her starched white veil. "Not to mention I'm twice your age. On the other hand," she continued while rearranging a stack of textbooks, "you may find a suitable match in one of the new teachers arriving tomorrow."

"I am *not* looking for a wife." Anson heaved a groan and squinted at the daily record book open before him. Blast these eyes of his! The medicine had done much to clear up the infection, but the blurriness remained.

Sister Mary John clucked her tongue. "Go up to bed. I will finish today's notations."

"I'm not sleepy. I just—"

"You're not this, you're not that. Saints preserve us from a man who pretends to know his own mind." She bumped his shoulder with her well-padded hip, and he grudgingly got up from the chair.

Halfway across the room, he turned with an exasperated glare, which Sister Mary John, with her back to him, took no notice of. "I suppose as long as I have you, I have no reason to think at all."

"That would be best," she said without looking up from the journal. "Good night, Anson. Sleep well."

He could do nothing but laugh to himself and shake his head. Sister Mary John had been looking after him since his boyhood, both teacher and mother since his own mother died when he was barely twelve years old. Her grave, alongside Anson's father's, lay not fifty yards away in the cemetery behind the small chapel where Sister Mary John conducted prayers each morning before classes began.

Indeed, as the son of devoted missionary teachers and now the director of the school the Schafers had founded, Anson had quite a legacy to uphold. He only hoped he could honor the spirit of his parents' vision while positioning the school to fit into Kenya's evolving future.

Before retiring, he turned in the opposite direction down the upstairs hallway and peeked into the vacant rooms the new staff would occupy. In Irwin's latest communication, he had included more details about his recruiting efforts at Henderson State Teachers College. He would bring a college professor well qualified for both instructional and supervisory duties, along with a nurse, two accredited teachers, and a bright young teaching student who had completed two years at Henderson.

The rooms weren't large, but each contained two narrow beds, a highboy, and a small desk beneath a single window. Anson hoped the women wouldn't mind doubling up. Irwin planned to stay only a month before returning to the States, so he and the professor could share quarters temporarily. Sister Angelica would also leave with Irwin, which would free up another room.

One of the Kenyan women who cooked and cleaned for the school had swept, dusted, and made the beds in preparation for the new arrivals, but the rooms smelled damp and musty. With the rainy season at an end, it wouldn't hurt to open the windows and give the rooms a good airing overnight. Shoving up the sash in the bedroom nearest his own, Anson breathed in the cool evening air. From somewhere in the surrounding woodlands came the yips of hyenas, probably scavenging the remains of a leopard kill. Anson hoped Dr. Young had made clear to his recruits the untamed nature of the country in which they'd soon reside.

With the windows thrown open in the other rooms, Anson readied himself for bed. His tired eyes welcomed the darkness, and before falling asleep, he offered up his usual prayer for the success of the school and the safety of the travelers.

The morning brought a new level of hustle and bustle as anticipation grew for the new staff's arrival. The ship should have docked in Mombasa early yesterday, after which the group would board the train to Nairobi, then take another train to Nyeri. From there, Irwin would hire a car to drive them the rest of the way. They'd arrive tired, disoriented, and hungry, so Sister Mary John had the kitchen help preparing a hearty meal that could be heated up as soon as everyone got settled.

It was close to four in the afternoon by the time two rumbling vehicles pulled up at the base of the porch steps. Anson straightened his bow tie and smoothed back his hair before following Sister Mary John out the front door. Sister Angelica was nowhere to be found, and Anson suspected she was already packing her bag.

"Anson, my boy, so good to see you again!" Irwin heaved his bulk from the lead automobile and greeted Anson with a back-thumping hug.

"You, too, my friend. I trust you had an uneventful trip?"

"A few rough days at sea but otherwise quite passable." Stepping back, Irwin took a hard look at Anson. "A little more gray at the temples than when I saw you last. How's the eye infection?"

"Improving." Anson blinked and turned his attention to the others gathering their things from the cars. "Please, introduce me to our new staff."

"Most definitely. And I know you'll find them to be real assets to the school." While their drivers moved the luggage onto the porch, Irwin made quick introductions.

Sister Mary John was already acquainting herself with the four women. "And you must use only boiled water for drinking and brushing your teeth," she explained. "If you think seasickness was bad, it doesn't compare to what you'll have to worry about here."

The fair-haired young woman in blue—Lark Linwood, if Anson heard correctly—visibly paled. She shot the other women a worried glance.

Anson stepped forward. "Sister, there's no reason to frighten everyone the moment they arrive. You have my assurance, ladies, we take every necessary precaution with both drinking water and food preparation. Now, please come inside, and Sister Mary John will show you to your quarters. Your luggage will be brought up momentarily."

While the women and the professor followed Sister Mary John upstairs, Anson called for two of the Kenyan hired men to get the bags. Then Irwin accompanied him to the office, where the cook had laid out tea and sandwiches.

"I meant it earlier," the older man stated as he helped himself to a cup of tea. "This work is aging you. I've never seen you look so tired."

"I *am* tired." One elbow resting on his desk, Anson massaged his forehead. "But it isn't the work. It's the worry over how much longer we can keep the school going. Three more families pulled out their children this week."

Irwin reached for a sandwich and nibbled thoughtfully. "I understand the independent schools are gaining a foothold. I do sympathize with your urging to secularize the school, but I'm afraid that doesn't sit well with the missions aid society. And I can't even imagine what your father, God rest his soul, would have to say on the matter. Why are we here if not to bring more souls to Christ?"

Anson's hand came down hard on the desktop and rattled the tea service. "We are here to educate the Kenyans so that they can hope for better lives right here on earth. At least that's why I'm here. If we can't agree—"

"Excuse me." A timid female voice sounded at the partly open door.

Gathering himself, Anson rose. Though his clouded vision made it hard to make out the face, he recognized the fair hair and blue dress. "Miss Linwood, isn't it? Did you need something?"

She sidled into the room. "It's just that everyone else is either settling in or resting. I'm rooming with Mrs. Eck, but she's already fallen asleep, and I didn't want to disturb her, so I wondered if it would be all right to explore a bit."

"Come in, come in," Irwin called from across the room. "Anson and I were having a spot of tea. You're welcome to join us."

"Yes, please," Anson agreed. Anything to put an end to this circular argument with his longtime friend. He loved the man dearly but doubted they'd ever agree on certain issues. "Afterward, I'd be happy to take you on a tour before the evening meal."

"Thank you, that's very kind." The young woman peered up at him and smiled, and he could see now that her eyes were the same cornflower blue as her dress. "You don't seem quite so tall in real life."

He cocked his head. "As opposed to…"

"Your photograph in the brochure."

"Ah, that." Behind him, Anson caught his companion's muted snicker. "Blame our esteemed Dr. Young, the photographer. He had me standing on a couple of bricks so I'd appear more—what was the exact word you used, Irwin?"

"Erudite, my boy. As the director of such a distinguished institution certainly should."

Hiding his own amusement, Anson turned to Miss Linwood. "And did you perceive me as such? Distinguished and erudite?"

At the young lady's nonplussed clearing of her throat, Irwin laughed out loud. "He's teasing you, my dear. Anson, pull over a chair for Miss Linwood while I fetch another teacup."

A few minutes later, the three of them sat in a semicircle near Anson's desk, sipping tea and munching on sandwiches. In response to Anson's questions, Miss Linwood spoke of her years growing up on a farm in central Arkansas and her life-long dream of becoming a teacher. She had an energy about her, mixed with a hefty dose of curiosity, that reminded him of his late mother, for she continually steered the conversation back to the school, the children, and the community they served.

Soon Irwin set his empty teacup aside and excused himself. "Miss Linwood, I'm afraid I don't possess your youthful stamina. I'm off for a nap before supper and must leave you two to carry on without me."

Suddenly conscious of being alone with a single woman who was *not* of the Catholic Sisterhood, Anson rose abruptly. "If you're ready, Miss Linwood, perhaps we should begin the tour I promised."

* * *

Though Mr. Schafer might not be quite as tall as he appeared in the photograph, after only a brief hour in his company, Lark definitely found him erudite. And though she knew full well that Dr. Young had intended the word *distinguished* to describe Matumaini School, she decided it also easily applied to Mr. Schafer. His slightly mussed sandy-brown hair, angular jaw, and narrow build gave him a professorial air, far more so than Franklin Keene, who sometimes seemed much too debonair for a college professor.

At the inappropriate direction of her thoughts, Lark hid a grimace and tried to pay closer attention as Mr. Schafer showed her around the school. They stood inside one of the classrooms now, and Lark couldn't resist sliding onto a bench in the first row behind a long, narrow table. The room itself wasn't so different from American classrooms, if one didn't notice the bare walls and scarcity of books, maps, and other teaching aids. A chalkboard took up the central area of the front wall, with an empty table and chair positioned off to the left.

"Not quite what you were expecting?" Mr. Schafer asked softly.

Lark ran her hand across the roughly planed surface of the table. "I wasn't sure what to expect. Not that Dr. Young didn't do his best to prepare us, but no description ever fully compares to the reality, does it?"

The director stepped closer, hands tucked in his pockets and a quirky smile twisting his lips. "Is that the voice of experience I hear?"

Lark's mind raced through the long list of disappointments in her life. Losing her daddy in the war. Barely starting second grade in Memphis when Mama said they had to move to Eden and live with Lark's grandfather on his tenant farm. Then in 1926 her mother's death in the savage Thanksgiving Day tornado outbreak that ripped through Arkansas. Most recently, the lingering effects of the drought that would have devastated her family if Bryony hadn't taken the maid's job at the Heaths'. That part of the story had a happy ending, at least. Now Bryony and Michael were married and deeply in love.

But sometimes Lark couldn't help wondering how their reality compared to the dream of a happily-ever-after.

The bench shifted, and Lark came out of her drifting thoughts to find Mr. Schafer sitting at the other end. "I must be more tired than I thought," she said with a self-conscious laugh. "My mind was a thousand miles away."

"More like eight or nine thousand miles, would be my guess." His kindly eyes showed a hint of concern. "I hope you won't be too homesick here."

A melancholy sigh slipped from Lark's lips. "I'm not even sure where home is anymore. I spent most of the past two years living in my college dormitory, and now here I am halfway around the world. But that's what life is all about, isn't it? Always changing, always adapting—and I will." She sat a little straighter. "I've looked forward to this moment from my first meeting with Dr. Young. It's thrilling beyond measure to think of actually getting to teach, and so much sooner than I ever imagined I would."

Mr. Schafer glanced away. "Then I hope this won't be one more reality that doesn't live up to your expectations. I'm afraid class attendance has dwindled appreciatively over the past several months. We're hoping to turn things around eventually, but it could take time."

Lark listened uneasily as the director explained about Kenya's shift toward independently run local schools and the clash between Christian missionary teachings and ethnic traditions. "But I believe there is room for compromise and cooperation," he went on to say, "and I still believe we can make a difference here."

The man had been quite tactful in his mention of the most troubling cultural practice that had created divisions between Christian missionaries and the Kenyan people, but Lark got the gist of it. She kept her gaze averted while nearly biting through her lower lip. The thought of what those young girls must suffer in such rites of passage—no wonder the missionaries took exception.

"So my intent," Mr. Schafer went on, "is to initiate a training program for Kenyans who desire to become teachers. At least it's one way we can pass along the benefits of quality education."

The younger nun Lark had met upstairs earlier peeked into the room. "They're serving supper now, Mr. Schafer. Everyone is gathering in the dining hall."

"Thank you, Sister Angelica." He rose and extended his hand to Lark. "Shall we?"

As he helped her from the bench, Lark decided she would very much enjoy working under Anson Schafer's direction. He had a quiet self-assurance about him that gave her a feeling of confidence. Though the school might be struggling, he had a clear vision for what he wanted to accomplish here, and Lark was grateful for the chance to be a part of it.

*   *   *

Nearly two weeks had passed since Lark's arrival at Matumaini School and she had yet to perform any task remotely akin to teaching. She supposed she shouldn't be surprised, since with class attendance down and both Debra and Sandra already full-fledged teachers, there was little need for Lark's help. Instead, she'd been relegated to supervising two half-hour recess periods each day, helping to serve the noon meal, and then cleaning chalkboards and wiping down desks after classes ended.

A shame Dr. Young hadn't informed her of the student situation before enticing her across the Atlantic.

Late one afternoon as she emptied a pail of wash water along the rows of corn in the vegetable garden, Professor Keene wandered out to stretch his legs. Since their arrival, he'd spent most of his time conferring with Mr. Schafer and Dr. Young about developing the teacher training program Mr. Schafer wanted to establish.

Her heart lifting at the prospect of spending a little time with Franklin—she much preferred the sophistication of his full given name over the shortened version—Lark was about to call a greeting when Debra appeared on the back steps. The lithe, dark-haired teacher glanced around briefly. When she spotted the professor, her eyes lit up with the unmistakable look of attraction. She darted down the steps to join him.

"Finally, a few minutes alone," Debra cooed, entwining her arm with his.

Lark slipped deeper into the corn rows as the ugly green monster of jealousy wrapped its tentacles around her throat. She watched unwillingly as the professor hurried Debra to the far corner of the building, pinned her against the wall, and teased her neck with languorous kisses.

The memory of Lark's brief conversation with Debra in the ship's library came rushing back. *Guard your heart?* Less a word of caution for Lark's benefit than a subtle warning to stay away from the man Debra already had her sights set on.

Backing away silently, Lark clamped a hand over her mouth to hold back the bile. When she reached the far end of the garden, she dropped her pail in the soft earth and ran toward the forest, stopping only when she recalled Mr. Schafer's clear warning about venturing too far from the compound. All she needed was to get herself good and lost and end up being eaten by a wild animal.

Reluctantly, she turned toward the school. Spine stiff, head erect, she determined to make her way around to the front door as if she'd just been out for a walk. She'd pretend she never noticed the couple spooning at the other end of the building.

She made it as far as the front steps before angry tears gushed forth. Swiveling, she sank onto the top step with a thud.

"Miss Linwood?" Anson Schafer's voice sounded behind her. "Is everything all right?"

Embarrassed, Lark scraped the wetness from her cheeks with the back of her hand. "I—I suppose homesickness is catching up with me after all."

He sat down next to her and gently took her hand. "It catches up with all of us at one time or another."

"You too?" Lark sniffled, glad for the distraction of his company. And his kindness. "But I thought you grew up in Kenya."

"I did, and I love it here. But there are...difficulties. Attending college in the States, I grew far too accustomed to the creature comforts of living in America. A well-stocked grocer. A library brimming with books." Mr. Schafer paused, and his voice dropped to a frustrated murmur. "A real doctor only a telephone call away."

"Your eyes—I'm so sorry." Lark had seen him struggle to read anything but the largest print.

He gave her hand a quick squeeze and then released it. "Yes, and I'm afraid I've allowed the situation to drag on too long. Which brings me to some news I must share, and you'll be the first to know, besides Irwin and Frank, with whom I've just been discussing this matter."

At the mention of Professor Keene's name, Lark bristled. She hiked her chin and tried not to think about what she'd witnessed behind the school. "You look so serious. Is it bad news?"

"I suppose it depends on your point of view." Mr. Schafer breathed deeply and braced his forearms on his knees. "When Irwin and Sister Angelica leave for the States next week, I'll be going with them."

A surprising surge of disappointment rocked Lark backward. "Oh, no—*why?*"

"Mrs. Eck has been examining my eyes every day since her arrival. She is convinced that without more sophisticated options than what is available here, it'll only be a matter of time before I go completely blind."

Lark couldn't resist reaching for Mr. Schafer's hand. He turned his gaze upon her, and she looked deeply into his clouded, red-rimmed eyes. The discouragement she saw there brought a catch to her throat. "I'm so sorry," she repeated. "So very, very sorry."

"Please," he said, forcing a laugh, "I'm not a hopeless case yet." His glance fell to her hand clutching his. "I'm the one who should be sorry, leaving my brand new teachers without a director, and the future of the school in such uncertainty."

"We'll manage, I'm sure. Will you leave Sister Mary John in charge?"

"She's quite capable of giving orders, no doubt about that." An amused grin turned up the left corner of his mouth. "But no, I'm turning over the directorship to Professor Keene. He has the impressive educational background the school needs, plus he understands my vision for adapting Matumaini as a teacher training institution."

"I see." Lark quietly slid her hand into her lap and faced forward.

Mr. Schafer slanted her a curious look. "You don't agree?"

"It isn't that." Why, oh why, had she ever come here? So much for working alongside Franklin Keene as a colleague as he'd so charmingly suggested all those weeks ago when inviting her to the information meeting. Now she would report to him once more, this time not as a student but as an underling, all the while living with the undeniable fact of his attraction to another woman.

"Miss Linwood—Lark. Clearly I've said something to upset you. If you'll tell me what it is—"

"It's not anything to do with you. You've been nothing but kind to me since I arrived. Thank you, more than I can say." She stumbled to her feet. "Please excuse me. I should freshen up before they call us to supper."

* * *

Anson didn't care for the troubled tone of Miss Linwood's voice. She'd been crying when he found her on the steps, and he suspected she was on the verge of tears again as she hurried inside just now. Her distress seemed more than a simple case of homesickness.

"There you are, Anson." Irwin met him on the porch as he rose to return to the office. "If you haven't changed your mind about traveling back to the States, I thought I'd borrow the school's Land Rover and drive over to Nyeri in the morning to book your passage."

"Haven't changed my mind and don't intend to. I'd be very grateful." Anson pressed his eyes shut for a moment. "I doubt I'll be doing much driving from now on."

Irwin clapped him on the shoulder. "Chin up, old man. Doctors back in the States are doing miraculous things these days."

At the rate his vision was deteriorating, Anson figured it would take a miracle to save his sight. He only hoped he hadn't waited too long to salvage what vision remained. For the moment, though, concern for the young teaching student eclipsed his own problems. "You didn't happen to see Miss Linwood just now, did you?"

"She rushed right past me heading upstairs. I said hello, but she seemed in rather a hurry."

Anson clamped his teeth together and strode to the porch rail. In the distance, the surrounding forest became one broad smudge of a hundred shades of green. "I'm concerned she's terribly unhappy, and as busy as we've been in our discussions, I've neglected to spend enough time assimilating her into the work we're doing here."

"You can't be blamed for that. We've had our hands full acclimating Miss Nott and Miss McCarrick to their teaching roles, and their services are much more essential at the moment." Irwin braced his hands on the rail. "I wondered if pulling an undergraduate out of school might turn out to be a mistake, but Franklin spoke quite highly of Miss Linwood and seemed particularly interested in bringing her on board."

"Really?" Doubt tinged Anson's tone. Angling his stance toward Irwin, he kept his voice low and asked, "How well did you know Franklin Keene before you signed him on?"

"He came to my attention a couple of years ago, when a Little Rock newspaper printed an article recognizing several outstanding educators from Arkansas colleges. His qualifications impressed me, so I initiated several informal conversations about what we're doing here, and I could see I'd piqued his interest." After a quick glance over his shoulder, Irwin dropped his voice even more. "You're not having second thoughts about him, I hope? With you returning to the States, we need him now more than ever."

Concerned about being overheard, Anson suggested they go for a walk, and they followed the path to the chapel. "It isn't that I question Frank's credentials," Anson said, "but sometimes he comes across a little too glib for my tastes. I have to wonder whether it was your recruiting efforts or Franklin Keene's charm that most enticed Miss Linwood and the other ladies to join us in this mission."

Irwin laughed, but there was something off about it. "If it's his charm you're worried about where our new teachers are concerned, I suspect it won't last. Besides, Sister Mary John will make sure nothing untoward ensues."

"Of that, I have no doubt." Still, Anson couldn't shake a sense of unease about Miss Linwood.

When they reached the chapel, Anson paused to look toward the main building. A motion near the back veranda caught his attention. He couldn't see well enough to recognize faces, but he could make out two people, one definitely a dark-haired woman. He tugged on Irwin's sleeve and pointed. "Who is that?"

After a brief hesitation, Irwin said stiffly, "It appears to be Frank and Miss McCarrick, locked in a clinch."

Suddenly Anson knew exactly the source of Lark Linwood's tears, and he wished more than ever that he didn't have to leave the school—and more specifically, one very impressionable young staff member—in Frank's hands.

On a Wednesday morning the following week, the students and staff at Matumaini School turned out to bid a tearful farewell to Anson Schafer, Dr. Young, and Sister Angelica. Lark had met them barely three weeks ago, but she would miss them, Mr. Schafer most of all. Since the afternoon she'd practically cried on his shoulder, he'd been especially considerate of her, asking often about her well-being and suggesting ways she might serve at the school that *didn't* involve wash water, brooms, or serving spoons.

One assignment she found especially rewarding was tutoring a nine-year-old student in reading. Jata, who said her name meant *star*, certainly had a sparkle about her, and spending time with the bright little girl helped keep Lark's mind off…other things.

Like the fact that Professor Keene, most definitely *not* Franklin in her mind any longer, had been appointed director in Mr. Schafer's absence. Everyone spoke as if Mr. Schafer would return once his eyes were better, but that could be months, possibly not even before Lark's one-year commitment ended.

If she survived that long. Mr. Schafer hadn't been away a full week before Professor Keene began reassigning duties, and Lark found herself once again relegated to more menial tasks.

The professor came looking for her one afternoon as she began to wipe down a chalkboard. "Lark, after supper tonight, I need you to straighten things up in the dining room. And see about some refreshments we can serve."

Anticipation welled in Lark's breast. "Are we expecting guests?"

"I announced it during Saturday's staff meeting," Professor Keene replied, an irritated edge to his tone. "A delegation from the surrounding villages is coming this evening to hear more about our teacher training initiative."

"I see." Indignation swallowed up Lark's momentary excitement over the prospect of visitors. "Well, since I was occupied elsewhere during Saturday's meeting, this is the first I've heard of your plans."

He had the decency to look remorseful. "Lark, I completely forgot." Striding across the room, he pried the wet cloth from her grip and dropped it into the water pail, then pressed both her hands in his. "I'm a heel. Please forgive me. I had you doing inventory on classroom supplies on Saturday, didn't I?"

The warmth of his touch, the sincerity in his dusky brown eyes, the slightly crooked smile of apology—against all her common sense, Lark felt her resentment melting away. "It's—it's all right," she heard herself say. "After two years working at Mr. O'Neill's grocery, I'm quite skilled at doing inventory, and I did come here to serve, after all."

"I knew I could count on you." He tweaked her chin. "Much to do. See you at supper." He spun on his heel and marched from the room.

Berating herself for feelings she seemed unable to control, Lark fished the cloth from the water pail and wrung it out. With long, determined swipes, she cleared the board of chalk residue and wished she could wipe away her attraction for the charming professor half so easily. As the days had passed, she'd tried to convince herself she'd been mistaken about what she'd seen between Professor Keene and Debra McCarrick.

But it was hard to mistake those amorous looks and steamy kisses for anything but what they were. When she couldn't deny the reality of what happened that afternoon, she rationalized that it was all Debra's doing, enticing Professor Keene with her full lips, long lashes, and sultry voice. Hard for any warm-blooded male to resist the lure of a woman bent on snagging his affection.

Finishing the board, Lark rinsed out the cleaning cloth and made a final check of the room before moving on to the next one. In the hallway, she halted outside the closed door of the second classroom. From the other side came hushed voices and muted laughter.

Then a high-pitched giggle. "Frank, stop it! She'll be coming in here to clean any minute now."

"And we'll tell her we were just looking for…a mathematics book or something. Honestly, the girl is such an innocent."

Nausea climbed into Lark's throat. They were talking about *her*! She wanted to run away, but her shoes seemed glued to the floor, and she couldn't stop herself from listening to every painful word.

"You know she's infatuated with you. We should tell her the truth. Her heart's going to be broken in too many pieces as it is."

"Lark?" Sandra's voice sounded behind her, and Lark spun around. "It's almost time for supper. What are you—" Sandra's brows drew together in a concerned frown, and she rushed forward. "Honey, what on earth is the matter?"

The words wouldn't come, and Lark could only stand frozen like a statue as tears spilled down her face.

Then the classroom door opened, and the laughter from inside stilled suddenly. Lark found herself staring into the startled faces of Debra and Professor Keene.

Sandra stepped forward, hands on her hips. "I don't even want to ask what's going on here."

"Nothing, nothing at all," Professor Keene insisted with his usual charming grin. "We were, uh…"

Somehow Lark found her voice. "Looking for a mathematics textbook?"

Debra paled. "Lark, this isn't—"

"What it appears? Really, do you think me so naïve that I can't recognize a romantic tryst when I see one?" Teeth clamped together, Lark slowly shook her head. "Just tell me, *Franklin*, did you bring me to Kenya only to ensure you'd always have someone around who's gullible enough to fall for your flattery?"

The professor stretched out his hand to her, his tone placating. "Lark, listen to me—"

"Not another word, please, because I can no longer trust anything you say." She backed away and stumbled into Sandra. The pail toppled, spilling filmy water across the floor.

"It's all right," Sandra soothed, bracing Lark with an arm around her shoulders. "We'll get one of the kitchen helpers to mop it up. In the meantime"—she cast a haughty glare at the couple in the doorway—"I believe we should have a nice, long talk with Sister Mary John and Mrs. Eck."

Debra darted toward them, remorse etching her face. "Sandra, please don't. We just need a chance to explain."

"I don't care to hear your excuses. I know how you operate, Frank, and though I'm immune to your charms, it galls me to realize how you've been leading Lark on all this time." Sandra scoffed, "And carrying on with Debra behind our backs? You both should be ashamed."

Unable to look at them a moment longer, Lark allowed Sandra to steer her toward the office. The room was empty, and Sandra sat Lark down in a chair, then poured a glass of water. "Here, honey. Pull yourself together while I fetch Sister Mary John and—"

"No, don't. Not now." Lark wrapped her hands around the cool glass. "I need some time to think."

"Of course you do. This must have come as quite a shock."

Lark uttered a harsh laugh. "Actually, it didn't—or at least it shouldn't have. More than anything, I'm angry with myself for reading more into Professor Keene's attentions than was meant."

She took a sip of water and let it soothe her aching throat. "As I said, I have some thinking to do. Would you make my apologies to…to anyone who matters? I'm going to walk over to the chapel for a bit."

Maybe after some intense prayer and a good night's sleep, though she doubted sleep would come easily, she'd know how to unravel the horrible mess her naïveté had landed her in.

* * *

"Oh, no. No, no, no!" Standing in the middle of the cotton field, Rose Linwood looked west toward the darkening sky.

Not rain clouds, which would have been bad enough this close to the cotton harvest. Not clouds at all, but a roiling reddish-brown mass of topsoil blown in from the drought-parched farm-lands of Texas and Oklahoma.

"Get to the house!" Grandpa yelled. Waving his arms, he jogged toward her along an adjacent row. "Get them windows shut fast as you can!"

Rose didn't need to be told. How many times already this summer had she swept out the grit that managed to find its way inside their house through even the tiniest cracks? How many meals had they eaten that grated between their teeth and left their mouths tasting like a sandy creek bed?

She made it to the house only minutes before the dust storm hit. With the windows bolted shut and the curtains drawn, Rose raced for the door to make sure Grandpa had made it back. He stumbled across the screen porch and into the kitchen, and Rose slammed the door behind him.

"Lord have mercy!" Grandpa whipped off his dusty straw hat, revealing a face coated with dirt and sweat. "How much more we gotta put up with?"

"Here, Grandpa." Rose handed him a wet cloth as he sank into a chair. She wet another one for herself, not so much to wipe the dirt from her face as to have something moist and cool to breathe through.

They sat in silence to wait out the storm. Not much use trying to talk over the whining wind and the constant *tap-tap-tap* of grit against the windowpanes.

Ten minutes later, the worst of it had blown by, and Rose steeled herself for another afternoon of sweeping out the house. She could only hope the cotton had held up okay. It already looked to be another poor harvest, what with the lingering effects of the drought and cotton prices bottoming out. They'd be in a terrible fix indeed if Miranda Heath Vargas, their landlord's daughter, hadn't worked out rent extension plans with all the tenants. Miranda was a whole lot more generous and forgiving than her father. But then, it didn't hurt that Rose's family had taken Miranda two years ago when she first returned home starving and pregnant.

No forty-seven ways to Sunday about it, this was an awful bad time for Arkansas farmers. For folks all over, so Rose had heard. And things weren't likely to improve until this drought broke, not just in Arkansas but throughout the Midwest, where all these dust storms blew in from.

Soon as the sky cleared, Grandpa went out to check on the crops, and Rose got busy with the broom and dustpan. As she carried another pail of grime out the back door, a dirty brown pickup came rattling up the lane.

"Hey, Miss Rosie!" Joe, the clerk from Eden's general store, waved out his window as he pulled up in front of the barn. "Hoo-eee, that was another bad'un, wasn't it?"

"Hey, Joe." Rose heard the fatigue in her voice. She set down the pail and sauntered over to the pickup. "What brings you out our way?"

He reached for something on the seat and handed it out the window. It was a Western Union envelope. "This came for y'all early this morning. First chance I had to run it out, 'specially with the storm and all."

"A telegram? Who from?" Without waiting for an answer, Rose peeled back the flap and unfolded the flimsy paper. "Oh, it's from Lark!"

"What's she say? Not that it's any of my business, but I'd sure like to hear how she's likin' Africa."

Ignoring him, Rose scanned the message: *Coming home. Expect to arrive in Brinkley late Sept. Details to follow. Miss you. Love, Lark*

This couldn't be good. Barely a month had gone by since Lark should have arrived in Kenya, and already she was coming home? It wasn't like Lark to give up on anything so easily, not when she'd set her heart on it. Was the school not what she'd expected? Had she taken ill?

Rose waved absently at the general store clerk. "Thanks, Joe. I gotta show this to Grandpa. See you in town."

She found Grandpa cleaning things up in the barn. Though he'd gotten the barn door secured before the dust storm hit, dirt aplenty had found its way through the spaces between the boards. Hermione and Daisy, the milk cow and mule, stood in their stalls blinking grit from their eyes.

"Look here what Joe just delivered." Rose handed Grandpa the telegram. "Lark's coming home."

Lips mashed together, Grandpa finished reading and gazed out the barn door. "Can't say as I'm sorry."

"I'm worried about her, Grandpa. There can't be any good reason she's leaving Kenya so soon."

"No, but if going was a mistake, better to find out sooner than later." He folded the telegram and stuffed it into the pocket of his overalls. "When you get done in the house, head on over to the Wielands'. See if Caleb wants to trade off helping with the cotton harvest again this year. Ours should be ready in another couple weeks."

Rose would oblige, but she was more concerned about her sister at the moment than thinking about the cotton crop. Maybe she'd detour through town on her way over to the Wielands' and ask Joe if she could borrow his telephone. Bryony should be told about the telegram, and once Lark came home, Bryony would know how best to help their sister through whatever mishap had brought on this sudden change of plans.

* * *

When the ship docked in Norfolk, Virginia, Irwin Young insisted Anson not wait a day longer to see a physician about his eyes. The doctor on board the ship had continued treatment but agreed Anson should see a specialist as soon as possible.

Now he sat in an examination room awaiting the ophthalmologist's verdict.

"You're not saying anything," Anson said as the doctor hovered inches away to peer through his scope. He should be glad the doctor hadn't eaten onions for lunch.

The doctor rolled his stool back and frowned. "The infection has healed, but the scarring on your cornea is permanent. I'm afraid you'll always have significantly impaired vision."

Anson released an agonized breath. "Will it worsen over time?"

"Not the scarring itself. But the infection has weakened your eyes and left you quite nearsighted. Glasses will help for the short term." The doctor shrugged. "Long term? Only time will tell. In the meantime, you must rest your eyes frequently and always wear dark glasses outdoors."

While the doctor scribbled something in his notes, Anson braved the question that had been on his mind since he set foot in the office. In truth, since he'd left Kenya five weeks ago. "Doctor, I need an honest answer. Is there anything about my eyes that would prevent my returning to Africa?"

Even with hazy vision, Anson recognized the doctor's doubtful frown. "Another infection could blind you permanently. If you don't want to lose what sight you have, I strongly recommend you remain in the States, or at least avoid travel to lesser developed countries where such infections proliferate."

Anson nodded his understanding. It wasn't what he wanted to hear, but he couldn't say he was surprised. He left the examination room in a state of numb acceptance.

An assistant escorted him into an adjoining room, where he fitted Anson with two pairs of glasses, one regular and one for wearing outdoors. "You should be able to pick these up day after tomorrow," the assistant said. "Leave the receptionist a number where we can reach you."

Irwin met him in the reception area. "Bad news. I can tell from your expression."

"Not now, Irwin." Jaw clenched, Anson headed for the exit. When they stepped into the bright afternoon, Anson pressed his fedora low over his eyes.

Pausing on the sidewalk, Irwin glanced right and left. "Are you hungry? There's a café up the street. You were with the doctor so long we missed lunch."

"Get something for yourself if you like. I'm ready to go back to the hotel, if you'll flag a cab for me." Anson hated feeling so helpless. It was hard to keep the bitterness out of his tone.

"No, it's all right. I'll accompany you to the hotel, and we can grab a bite there." Irwin nonchalantly slipped his hand around Anson's elbow and steered him to the curb. "Here's a cab now."

By the time they reached the hotel, Anson had regained a semblance of control. In the dining room, he sat across from Irwin at an out-of-the-way table, and while they waited for their club sandwiches, Anson relayed what the ophthalmologist had told him.

"Oh, my boy, I am truly sorry." Irwin wagged his head. "I'm sure you're devastated, but you must consider your own well-being. And there's no reason you can't continue in a supervisory role from afar."

"No, but it won't be the same." Squinting toward the window, Anson followed the indistinct forms of passersby. "Are you fully satisfied that Frank is suitably qualified to assume the directorship?"

"Qualified? Immensely. But we've had this conversation before. I don't believe it's his qualifications you're really concerned about."

A sharp exhalation whistled between Anson's lips. "I need to be assured my vision for the school—the school my parents founded and gave their lives for—isn't forgotten. I need to know Professor Keene will love and care for Matumaini School with that same dedication."

Irwin didn't reply immediately. He fingered his coffee cup. "There isn't another person alive," he said slowly, "who will ever match your devotion to Matumaini School. But that isn't to say the school won't thrive under someone else's leadership. I have the utmost confidence in Frank. And should it ever seem expedient, I will personally return to Kenya on your behalf and see to it that everything is running smoothly. You have my word."

Anson had his concerns about Franklin Keene, especially after what he'd witnessed between Frank and Miss McCarrick behind the school. On the other hand, Anson trusted Irwin Young implicitly. Besides, what choice did he have? He'd be of no use to the school or to anyone else if he ended up permanently blind.

The waiter brought their meals, then refilled their coffee cups. After a few bites, Irwin asked, "Have you thought about where you'll go from here?"

"On to Little Rock, I suppose. I'll need to give the missions aid society a report." Anson added another dollop of mustard to his sandwich. "After that, I have no idea. With these eyes, I doubt I'll be teaching again."

Irwin harrumphed. "Don't start talking like an old horse

ready to be put out to pasture. There's a lot of good you can still accomplish."

"Maybe." Although at the moment, Anson couldn't see it, either literally or figuratively. For one thing, his heart remained in Kenya.

Stirring more cream into his coffee, Irwin cocked his head. "You're still having doubts about Frank, aren't you?"

Anson laid aside his sandwich. "I can't forget what we saw that evening, and I can't help worrying about Lark Linwood. I'm afraid she's doomed to have her heart broken by her handsome professor, and now there's not a blasted thing I can do about it."

Inhaling deeply, Irwin opened his mouth to speak, then shut it again. After another short pause, he said, "There's something I should have told you a long time ago. And would have, had I not been sworn to secrecy."

Anson sat forward, his tone clipped. "I didn't realize we had secrets between us."

"Just this one, which I'm certain I'll live to regret." With a pained sigh, Irwin continued, "Despite what everyone assumed, nothing improper occurred between Frank and Miss McCarrick—or, more accurately, *Mrs.* Keene."

"They're *married*? For how long?"

"They wed a few months before Miss McCarrick finished college. But because Frank was her professor and academic advisor, they kept the marriage a secret to avoid any scandal at the school."

Crumpling his napkin, Anson nudged his chair back. "When, exactly, were they planning to make a public announcement?"

"Frank wanted to be certain they'd be continuing at Matumaini School long term, at which point he would make his resignation from Henderson official." Irwin lifted both hands in a shrug. "No professorship, no scandal."

"And in the meantime, Frank could go on toying with the affections of impressionable young women like Miss Linwood."

"If it's any consolation, I don't believe Frank intentionally led her on. It's just his personable nature."

"You call it 'personable.' I call it flagrantly irresponsible." Anson shoved to his feet. "I'll be at the front desk. I'm going to send a telegram to Sister Mary John."

* * *

Two days by train from Nyeri to Mombasa, then a little over a month at sea, gave Lark plenty of time to ponder what to do with her life. She wouldn't make it back to the States in time to register for classes at Henderson, but taking the fall term off might not be such a bad thing. She could help Grandpa and Rose at the farm while getting over her heartbreak.

No, make that her foolish attraction to a man who had been toying with her from the start.

She supposed she should thank Professor Keene for finally admitting the truth, if a little too late for it to matter. On her last day at the school, he'd asked for a private word with her.

"Please don't think ill of me, Lark," he'd said as they stood on the back porch looking out over the vegetable garden. "Or Debra either. We both felt there was too much risk to our careers if the fact of our marriage came out at an inopportune time."

At that moment, Lark hadn't been able to think of a single thing to say in reply. But during the long days at sea, she relived the afternoon time and time again, each time inventing new and more impassioned retorts.

"So keeping your secret took priority over keeping others from being hurt?"

"I'm sure you and Debra were quite entertained while laughing at me behind my back."

"I shall be eternally grateful to you for demonstrating how utterly untrustworthy men can be."

Not all men, though. Or so Lark sincerely hoped. She was in

no hurry to risk her heart again, but someday, after she finished college and taught for a while—after she'd grown immune to smooth-talking men and their flirtatious ways—maybe then she'd consider giving love another chance.

When the ship docked in Charleston, Lark spent one night at a rooming house for single women before boarding the train that would take her back to Arkansas. Another two days by rail and she arrived in Brinkley.

Bryony and Michael met her at the depot. Running up to her, Bryony scooped her into a hug. "Lark, honey, I'm so glad you're back!"

Nothing had ever felt so wonderful as being wrapped in her sister's love. Lark squeezed tighter, melting into Bryony's embrace. "I missed you so much. So much!"

When Lark had claimed her luggage, Michael found a porter to help them get everything to the car. Lark settled into the back-seat of the green Chevrolet and hoped Bryony would wait awhile to bring up the questions everyone surely wanted to ask.

"I'm going to be selfish and have you spend the night at our house," Bryony said as Michael drove away from the depot. "It's almost suppertime anyway, and I've got a roast in the oven. Then you can soak in the tub for a while to get the travel kinks out before you climb into bed for a good night's sleep."

Bryony always did have a keen sense for mothering. "Thank you, Bry. That sounds wonderful."

At the house, Michael took Lark's overnight case to the guest room while Bryony went to check on supper. "If you need anything, just ask," Michael said.

"I was wondering…" Lark bit her lip, unsure how to bring up such a delicate subject. "Is Bryony…"

As if reading her thoughts, Michael glanced away and shook his head. "Not yet."

"I'll keep praying."

With a sad smile, Michael excused himself so that Lark could freshen up. A few minutes later, Bryony called them to the dining room. All through the meal, Lark could see the silent questions in Bryony's eyes, so when they'd finished eating and Michael volunteered for kitchen cleanup, Lark invited Bryony out to the porch swing and told her the truth about Franklin Keene.

Brow furrowed, Bryony gazed across the lawn. "I was afraid you'd developed feelings for him."

"You mean because he's too old for me?" Lark bit back a twinge of resentment. "Michael's a full ten years older than you, and look how happy you are."

"It wasn't the age difference that concerned me." Bryony tucked her arm around Lark's shoulder. "As your professor, he should have discouraged any attraction on your part, or at least not fostered those feelings."

Lark sighed. As the hurt and anger lessened, she'd begun to see another side of Franklin Keene. "I don't think he can help himself. I wouldn't call him a womanizer, just a man who enjoys female attention." She pursed her lips. "And who doesn't know when it's time to turn off the charm."

Her gaze turning thoughtful, Bryony tilted her head and smiled. "My little sister is growing up."

Lark gave a wry laugh. "Why did it have to take crossing an ocean—not once, but twice?"

"Because some of us are more hardheaded than others?"

"Well, at least the long voyage renewed my perspective. I might have more readily endured Franklin Keene's duplicity if only my work there had been educationally fulfilling instead of his treating me like a glorified servant."

Resting her temple against Lark's, Bryony whispered, "I'm sorrier about that than anything, because I know how much this opportunity meant to you."

Lark closed her eyes as fatigue began to catch up with her. If she weren't careful, the gentle sway of the swing would lull her to sleep right here. Drowsily, she said, "Have I told you lately how much I love you, Bry? What would I ever do without my big sister?"

"I love you, too, Lark. More than you know." With a contented sigh, Bryony snuggled closer.

When something warm and wet brushed Lark's cheek, she turned slightly and smudged away her sister's tear with the edge of her thumb. "Don't cry, Bryony. I'm home now, back where I belong."

* * *

The next morning, Lark repacked her small overnight case and rode with Michael and Bryony over to Eden, where they met Grandpa and Rose for Sunday worship. Lark was glad they'd all arrived early and could have a few minutes together before the service began. There would be plenty of time to explain her sudden return to Grandpa and Rose after they got back to the farm.

But first, Lark had to endure greetings and questions from their pastor and church friends. She kept her replies as vague as possible, saying little more than that the situation in Kenya hadn't turned out quite as described and that she had quickly realized she wasn't a good fit for the school.

At home later, she gave Grandpa and Rose the full story, or at least most of it. No reason to belabor her utter lack of good judgment where Franklin Keene was concerned.

"What will you do now?" Rose asked as they washed up the dishes from Sunday dinner. "Will you go back to college?"

"Not until the spring term. I'm afraid you're stuck with me until then."

"Well, good." Rose snapped the dishtowel playfully against Lark's arm. "Then you can take over the housework and cooking so I can spend more time with Grandpa in the fields."

Emptying the dishpan down the drain, Lark made sure Grandpa had gone to the parlor for his nap, then lowered her voice. "Tell me, Rosie, how bad was the cotton harvest?"

"Downright awful. We were doing good to get a couple hundred pounds to the acre. When they're paying barely five cents a pound, the hole we're in just gets deeper and deeper."

Lark wasn't sure why she thought things would have drastically improved while she'd been away. Wishful thinking maybe? She draped the wet dishcloth over the edge of the sink and gazed out the window toward acres of stubbly fields beyond. "If I went back to Arkadelphia, Mr. O'Neill would probably let me work more hours at the store. Since I won't be paying fall tuition, I could send extra money home to you and Grandpa."

"I'd much rather have you here. Especially now that Bryony's over in Brinkley, I miss you more than ever."

Giving a smirk, Lark tugged on her sister's braid. "I think you really miss having somebody else do the cooking."

"Well…that too," Rose said with a simpering grin. Her expression grew wistful. "I love Grandpa with all my heart, but the truth is I miss having my sisters around to share girl talk with."

"Girl talk? As in a certain boy who only has eyes for you?"

"Don't start teasing me about Caleb!" Rose sashayed over to the table and plopped down. "I want you to tell me every single exciting thing that happened on your trip. What did you see? Who did you meet? What's Africa like? Were there lions and elephants and rhinoceroses—rhinoceri—whatever you call them?"

Laughing out loud, Lark joined Rose at the table. "I wish I'd had a camera or at least could draw as well as Michael." She sighed as the memories of all she'd experienced came rushing back. "Even with all that *didn't* go as I'd hoped, it truly was the adventure of a lifetime."

Chapter Five

Anson had been back in Little Rock less than a month before restlessness set in. Without a reason to go elsewhere, he'd accepted the offer of a room in Irwin Young's home. A widower for more than ten years, Irwin was glad to have a friend and colleague share his abode. Even more convenient, Irwin's house was within walking distance of the missions aid society offices, where Anson spent the better part of each day helping out as needed. But the tedium of answering telephones and attempting to file correspondence he could barely read without severe eye strain was wearing on him. He missed Matumaini School—the staff, the students, and, most of all, the sense he was making a difference.

He also hadn't considered he'd be returning to a country foundering in economic depression. It was both humbling and upsetting to realize how uninformed he'd remained during his years away. Irwin had always brought the latest newspapers whenever he visited, but while Anson dealt daily with the changes taking place in Kenya, he'd found it hard to take much interest in affairs half a world away.

Now he wished he'd paid more attention. Banks had failed or teetered on the brink. Millions of Americans remained unemployed, many resorting to living in their cars or in flimsy cardboard shanties. Both children and adults were succumbing to malnourishment. The world he'd come back to seemed a sad place indeed.

But perhaps this was Anson's chance to find new meaning for his life. He might not have the resources to provide food and housing for the needy, but the one thing he could offer was education. As he'd sought to bring hope through learning to the people of Kenya, couldn't he do the same for the uneducated children right here in Arkansas?

With plans to meet Irwin for supper that evening, Anson decided to share his thoughts. When the missions office closed for the day, he walked the two blocks to a nearby café and found Irwin already holding a table for them.

After they ordered, Anson got straight to the point. "I'm beyond frustrated, Irwin. I need to feel useful again." He described his ideas, vague as they remained, about creating educational opportunities for Arkansas's needy children. "It's a vicious cycle. They drop out of school to look for work or because they're needed on the farm, but without an education, they can never aspire to anything better, even when someday economic conditions are on the rise again."

"Very worthwhile aims," Irwin said as he buttered a roll. "Of course, funding is always an issue, and the missions aid society is stretched pretty thin already."

"So I've come to realize." Anson sliced off a bite of meatloaf. So often of late, he suffered twinges of guilt over his enjoyment of three square meals every day when so many went hungry. He might have to rethink his own financial situation soon. The missions aid society, his sole means of support for all these years, continued to pay him a small stipend while he transitioned to civilian life, but for the income to continue, he'd either have to return to the foreign mission field—which his doctors had strongly cautioned against—or prove valuable to the organization in a more significant capacity than clerical work.

"Let's both think on it some more. In the meantime," Irwin went on, crumpling his napkin beside his plate, "you may be interested in the letter I received from Sister Mary John this morning."

Anson perked up. "News from the school? What does she say?"

Irwin took the letter from his pocket, glancing through it as if to refresh his memory. He cleared his throat. "The teacher training initiative had a slow beginning, but she is hopeful interest will pick up as word spreads. There has been a fair amount of cooperation—or at least no real resistance—from the Kenyan school administrators."

"That's good news." Anson sipped his coffee. "Anything in the letter about Frank?"

"Says he's coping quite handily with the day-to-day management and that everyone on staff is gaining respect for him."

A quick, relieved breath shot from Anson's lungs. "Praise God."

"And one more bit of news." Irwin flipped to the next page, and Anson easily made out his concerned frown. "I'm afraid Miss Linwood left Kenya barely two weeks after we did."

"What? No!" Coffee splashed over the rim of Anson's cup as he smacked it down upon the saucer. Realization dawning, he closed his eyes briefly and shook his head. "I had the sense she wouldn't be happy there. Bad enough to learn Frank and Miss McCarrick were secretly married. Worse had to be her disillusionment over duties that had less to do with teaching than housekeeping."

"Which couldn't entirely be helped, as things have turned out. Yet I do feel for the girl, too inexperienced in the ways of the world, and too starry-eyed for her own good. I wish now Frank had never invited her to our informational meeting."

Anson sniffed. "As a man who's been on the missions board for decades, you're the last person I'd expect to turn up his nose at idealism."

"Maybe I'm just getting old," Irwin said with a weak laugh. "Or maybe it's the sad state of this country. There comes a time when practicality must take precedence."

Glancing out the window, Anson glimpsed a raggedly dressed man shuffling along the sidewalk. Gaunt and hollow-eyed, shoulders slumped, he looked as if he'd lost all hope. When the man paused to peer in the window, a fresh wave of guilt swept through Anson. He split open the last roll from the bread basket and spread it with butter, then laid his leftover meatloaf between the halves and wrapped the sandwich in a napkin. Excusing himself, he hurried out the door and handed the bundle to the surprised vagrant.

"Thank you, sir! God will bless you for your kindness." The man's eyes filled with tears. He handed Anson a wrinkled slip of paper before continuing on his way.

Adjusting his glasses, Anson struggled to make out the painstakingly printed message: *Hebrews 10:24–25. And let us consider how to provoke one another to love and good deeds, not neglecting to meet together, as is the habit of some, but encouraging one another, and all the more as you see the Day approaching.*

It was a verse Anson had pondered often, and one he hoped his own life reflected.

It also seemed like God's confirmation at the perfect time, a promise of blessing upon the next chapter in Anson's call to servanthood.

* * *

On Election Day, November 8, 1932, Lark marched into the general store with Grandpa and proudly marked her ballot for Franklin Delano Roosevelt. This was her first year to vote in a presidential election, and she was glad for the chance to kick Hoover out of office.

"You think Roosevelt will win?" Rose asked after Lark and Grandpa had deposited their ballots in the locked box by the door.

"He sure as shootin' better." The scowl on Grandpa's face left no doubt he believed Hoover had failed miserably to bring the country out of the depression.

Lark glanced toward the meat counter, where Joe was asking eleven cents a pound for ground hamburger. Last May, Mr. O'Neill had sold hamburger for three cents less than that, and everyone thought it was outrageous. About time America had a president who recognized the struggles of the poor and actually tried to do something about it.

Before Lark could follow Grandpa and Rose out to the pickup, Joe came bustling over. "Hey, y'all, don't forget your mail." He shoved some envelopes into Lark's hand. "Might be something important."

"Like bills?" Wrinkling her nose, Lark absently flipped through the small stack as she stepped through the door into the mild afternoon. Over her shoulder, she called, "Let us know when you hear the election results, okay, Joe?"

"You betcha."

Outside in the pickup, Rose waved from behind the steering wheel. "Hop in. Grandpa walked over to the feed-and-seed."

Lark finished sorting through the mail by the time Rose drove the short distance up the street and parked again. The only item of interest was a letter bearing Mr. O'Neill's return address. Lark had written to him a couple weeks ago asking if her job might still be available when she returned for the spring term. He'd written right back to say he'd always have a place for her, and also expressed his regret that the Kenya school situation hadn't worked out.

Today's letter included a clipping from the Arkadelphia newspaper. Mr. O'Neill wrote, *Is this the same fellow your letter mentioned from the Kenya school?*

Indeed it was. Anson Schafer's photograph appeared next to an article stating he was slated to speak at Henderson State Teachers College on Saturday, November 12.

Rose glanced over. "Whatcha got there?"

"It's Mr. Schafer, the director of Matumaini School." Lark's hand shook for no reason she could determine as she offered the letter and clipping to Rose. Then she blurted out, "I think I'm going to Arkadelphia this weekend."

Without pausing to explain, Lark jumped from the pickup and dashed back down the street to the general store. "I need to use your telephone, Joe. It'll be long distance, so just put it on our account."

Minutes later she had Mr. O'Neill on the line. The jolly man couldn't sound happier to hear from her, even more so when she presented her request. "Why, you get yourself right on over here, honey," he said. "Mrs. O'Neill will have the guest room spick and span for you."

Next, Lark had Joe issue her a ticket for the Friday bus to Arkadelphia, returning Sunday. By the time she met up with her family back at the feed-and-seed, Rose and Grandpa had already figured out what she was up to.

"You're not mad, are you?" Lark shuffled from foot to foot. "I'll pay for the phone call and bus ticket out of my own money, I promise."

"That ain't what we're worried about," Grandpa said with a frown. "I know how you are about building castles in the clouds. Just like this Africa thing, you're too quick with your leaps of faith without considering how far you might fall."

Feeling all fizzy inside, Lark drew her grandfather into a hug. "But if you're too focused on falling, it isn't a leap of faith at all, is it?" She squeezed harder, then inched back far enough to press Grandpa's cheeks between her palms. "I promise, I'm only going to hear Mr. Schafer speak. I will *not* make any fast or foolish decisions about anything."

* * *

On Saturday, Lark stood before the mirror in the O'Neills' guest room and straightened the collar of her blouse. The cuffs were a little frayed, and it wasn't the latest style, but Lark thought the ivory shade flattered her fair complexion.

And she wasn't about to wear the blue polka-dot dress she once thought Franklin Keene favored. Several times, she'd considered relegating the dress to the ragbag but couldn't afford to sacrifice one of the few nice things she owned.

Mrs. O'Neill peeked into the room. "Benjamin's ready to drive you over to campus whenever you're ready."

"Guess I'm ready as I'll ever be." With one more pat to her chignon, Lark snatched up her sweater and handbag.

Since the moment she'd laid eyes on Anson Schafer's picture in the news clipping, she hadn't been able to quell the excited tremors. Until then, she hadn't thought much about his being back in the States, figuring he'd probably get his eyes taken care of and be off to Africa again.

But now it appeared he planned to stay in Arkansas, and according to the newspaper article, he was in the process of launching an educational foundation to serve the neediest children around the state. If Lark could play some small role—if God had taken her all the way to Kenya just so she could meet Anson Schafer and become part of his outreach—then perhaps the last five months hadn't been an utter waste of her time and the missions aid society's investment in her.

Fifteen minutes later, Mr. O'Neill dropped her off in front of the lecture hall where Mr. Schafer would speak. On her way to find a seat, she said hello to several women she'd gotten to know over the past two years, and naturally they asked where she'd been since last spring. Only a few knew about her trip to Africa, and those friends wanted to know why she'd returned so soon. All she would say was that it turned out not to be a good fit.

An aisle seat in the third row remained unoccupied. Lark claimed it minutes before a silver-haired woman from the English department introduced Mr. Schafer. He stepped up to the podium with the same calm assurance and easy smile Lark remembered from Kenya. The only difference was the pair of round, gold-rimmed spectacles he now wore.

"Good afternoon," he began, "and thank you all for coming." The rich timbre of his voice immediately carried Lark back to the day she first met him in front of Matumaini School, and her heart surged in her chest. She leaned slightly toward the aisle in hopes he might recognize her. Soon, though, she could tell from the way he held his head and how often he fingered the temples of his glasses that his vision hadn't improved much. The thought brought a wave of sympathy and concern, along with even greater admiration as he described what he hoped to achieve on behalf of Arkansas's most neglected children.

At the conclusion of his talk, two volunteers passed out fliers with more information about his foundation and how to volunteer or contribute financially.

As the lecture hall emptied out, Lark made her way to the front. She waited off to one side as Mr. Schafer spoke with two other students. When they left, she stepped forward and shyly extended her hand. "Hello, Mr. Schafer. It's so good to see you again."

He cocked his head with an inquisitive smile as he closed his hand around hers. "Forgive me, these eyes aren't what they used to be. Your voice is familiar…" He squinted and bent closer, his face lighting up. "Miss Linwood!"

"Yes. When I found out you were speaking today, I had to come."

"I'm so glad you did." He motioned to someone beyond Lark's shoulder. "Irwin, look who's here."

Dr. Young strolled over. When he recognized Lark, his brows lifted in a concerned smile. "Miss Linwood. How are you? We heard from Sister Mary John that you'd returned home."

"Yes, I…decided it best." Lark would have offered to shake

Dr. Young's hand, but Mr. Schafer had yet to release hers. He now covered it with his left hand as well.

"Are you back at school here now?" Mr. Schafer asked.

"Not yet, but I plan to enroll for the spring term."

"But you're well?" He drew closer as if trying to see her better.

"I've been—that is, Irwin and I have both wondered..."

Stiffening her spine, Lark forced a smile and slid her hand free. "Last summer proved to be a valuable learning experience for me. I may have been disappointed in the outcome, but I'll always treasure my memories of Kenya."

After a moment of silence, Dr. Young gave a single nod. "I can see you have come through all the wiser for it."

Lark moistened her lips. "Well, I...I just wanted to say that if there's any way I can aid your cause—other than financially, I'm sorry to say—I hope you'll ask."

As she turned to go, Mr. Schafer took a giant step sideways and blocked her way. "Miss Linwood—Lark. Might you be free to join us for dinner this evening?"

* * *

If there was anything Anson cared more about seeing clearly than the books he so loved to read, it was Lark Linwood's face as she smiled at him across the dinner table. A halo of shiny blond hair framed her features, and her ice-blue eyes shone like pools in the lamplight.

"Dessert?" Irwin asked. "The cherry pie here is outstanding."

Lark shook her head. "None for me, thanks. I should get back to the O'Neills' before it gets any later. I have a bus to catch in the morning."

Anson's breath hitched. It felt as if they'd barely sat down to dinner, and he surprised himself with how reluctant he was for the evening to end. After all these years of bachelorhood and dedicating himself wholeheartedly to the school, seeing Lark again had stirred a longing he'd suppressed for far too long.

Irwin signaled for the bill. "Anson, you've had a long day. I'll drop you at the hotel on our way to take Miss Linwood to her friends' house."

"No," he replied too quickly. "I'd rather ride along."

With the bill taken care of, they walked out to Irwin's car. Irwin suggested Anson might prefer to sit in back with Miss Linwood so they could continue their conversation, and Anson gladly obliged.

When they arrived at the O'Neills' house, Anson stifled a sigh of regret. "It was good to see you again, Lark. Truly a welcome surprise."

"I wouldn't have missed it, Mr.—I mean…Anson." Even though he'd convinced her over dinner that they could drop the formalities, she spoke his given name with a certain amount of unease, for which Anson had no doubt he could blame Franklin Keene.

He made no move to open the car door. "I suppose with the holidays coming up, you'll have a lot of family things going on."

"Nothing fancy, but always special." Her expression was unreadable in the darkened car, but he sensed she was in no more of a hurry than he. "Will you be with family for the holidays?"

"I haven't much family left, and none I'm particularly close with. I expect it'll be just Irwin and me, two stick-in-the-mud bachelors making do." Anson ignored the sharp snort from Irwin in the front seat.

"You both would be more than welcome to come to Eden for Thanksgiving. I'd love for you to meet my family."

"That's a kind offer. We'll certainly consider it, won't we, Irwin?"

"Oh, most definitely." Irwin's sudden cough sounded more like a snicker to Anson's ears.

With no more excuses for stalling, he pushed open the door and stepped to the curb. He offered his hand to assist Lark.

On the O'Neills' front walk, she hesitated. "I was serious about Thanksgiving. If you decide to come, you can send word to General Delivery, Eden."

Anson filed the information away in his memory as he walked Lark to the door. "It was so good to see you again."

She laughed softly. "Yes, you said that already. And thank you so much for dinner. It was lovely to spend the evening with you. And with Dr. Young, too," she added quickly.

They were stalling again. Anson backed up a step. "Well, good night. Have a safe trip home."

"I'm sure I will. Good night." Lark set her hand upon the doorknob, then smiled over her shoulder. "By the way, I think your glasses make you look very distinguished."

A grin spread across Anson's face. "Well, good night."

"You said that already, too."

His face heating, Anson forced a swallow. "Then I think I'll just take my leave in silence."

At the car, he turned once more to find Lark still standing in the open front door. She waved, and he waved back, then climbed into the front seat next to Irwin.

Starting the motor, Irwin heaved an exaggerated groan. "Didn't realize I was chaperoning a couple of lovesick adolescents. My goodness, Anson, why didn't you kiss the girl while you had the chance?"

Only then did Anson realize how hard he'd been struggling to subdue that impulse. He couldn't even remember the last time he'd kissed a girl. Possibly when taking his roommate's sister home from a college dance eons ago, and only because it seemed expected. Too much of a bookworm, Anson had little experience courting the fairer sex, a fact he suddenly regretted immensely.

He scoffed. "Lovesick? Please. I'm thirty-two years old and half-blind. What woman in her right mind would want anything to do with me?"

"The woman we just deposited on the sidewalk back there, if I'm any judge." Irwin gave Anson a friendly poke in the arm. "So, shall we take her up on her Thanksgiving invitation? That'll give you not quite two weeks to hone your natural wit and charm."

"This isn't funny, Irwin. She's just a girl, and hurt once already because of her interest in an older man. She needs to meet someone her own age."

Irwin grunted his disagreement, then fell silent as they continued on to the hotel. In the corridor outside their separate rooms, Irwin suggested they attend eight o'clock Mass in the morning before driving back to Little Rock.

When he crawled into bed later, Anson missed once again the ability to draw his thoughts away from the day's activities by losing himself in a good book. The glasses did help him to read when necessary, but he had to shift his gaze slightly to use his peripheral vision, and the effort soon gave him a headache.

Tonight, his thoughts ran rampant. Bad enough his mind had been racing for weeks with ideas for his education campaign. Now he had to deal with the unexpected thrill of seeing Lark Linwood again. Hard as he tried to convince himself his interest in her was nothing more than friendly concern, he couldn't deny the appeal of accepting her Thanksgiving invitation.

But if he so much as hinted he was seriously considering it, there'd be no end to Irwin's teasing.

Maybe he wouldn't involve Irwin in the decision at all. Anson tossed aside the covers and switched on the bedside lamp. Before reason could stop him, he lifted the telephone receiver. "Yes, operator, can you help me place a local call, please? The name's O'Neill."

Within minutes, the operator connected him. When Lark came on the line, she sounded worried. "Mr. Schafer? Is anything wrong?"

"No, everything's fine. I, er...well, I've been thinking about your Thanksgiving invitation."

"Oh. If I was too forward—"

"Nothing of the kind. I only wanted to say that I—that is, Irwin and I *both*—would love to join you, provided you're absolutely certain your family won't mind."

"I'm sure they won't. So please, do come. Tell me your address, and I'll mail you the directions as soon as I get back to Eden."

Anson gave her Irwin's street number in Little Rock and then hurriedly said good night before he stammered any more foolishness. He hoped Irwin wouldn't mind if he napped in the car tomorrow on their drive back, because he could tell he'd get little sleep tonight.

Chapter Six

Since Bryony had married Michael, holidays hadn't been quite the same. Bryony understood having to divide her time between Michael's family and her own, but it didn't make the choices any easier. The Heaths lived a completely different lifestyle from what Bryony and her sisters had known. Even with the nation's economy floundering, Michael's father found ways to maintain an enviable standard of living at Brookbirch Plantation. Sebastian Heath was a shrewd businessman, despite humble beginnings of his own. His daughter, Miranda Heath Vargas, had inherited his head for business, and together their cautious financial strategies had helped to keep the plantation afloat while providing relief to Brookbirch's struggling tenants.

On Thanksgiving Eve, Bryony and Michael drove out to the farm with the sweet potato pies Bryony had baked. "Now you're not to have them all gone before we come back tomorrow evening," Bryony instructed as she and Lark set the pies on a pantry shelf.

Lark rolled her eyes. "Just don't eat yourselves so full at the Heaths' that you have no room left for the dinner Rose and I are making."

Easier said than done, considering the feast the Heaths' cook, Odette, already had well underway. Frowning, Bryony tucked her arm around Lark's waist. "I wish I could talk y'all into accepting Miranda's invitation to have dinner with us at the mansion."

Lark pursed her lips. "I've heard your stories of family get-togethers over there. Sebastian at one end of the room, Miranda and her family at the other."

"At least he's trying." No one expected Sebastian Heath would welcome his Mexican immigrant son-in-law with open arms, considering he'd disowned Miranda all those years ago for running away with Daniel Vargas. But since Miranda returned home two years ago, Sebastian had come a long way toward acceptance. For the past year, Daniel and his family, which included their teenage daughter, Callie, and their sixteen-month-old son, George, had lived near the mansion in a cozy brick house Sebastian had built for them.

"And what about you, Bry?" The bitterness in Lark's tone made Bryony flinch. "I still don't understand how you can hobnob with the Heaths after all those months you worked as their maid."

Bryony was thankful Michael had gone out to the barn to say hello to Grandpa and Rose. "Sometimes I still feel funny walking in the front door instead of going around back. But I'm not ashamed that I swept floors and cleaned toilets for the Heaths. And I'm certainly not sorry for whatever little part I've played in healing the wounds that family has suffered."

One hand pressed to her forehead, Lark sank into one of the kitchen chairs. "I'm sorry, Bry. It's my own frustration talking. The short time I spent in Africa, and now thinking about this new educational foundation Anson Schafer's hoping to launch—it's made me doubly aware of the awful prejudice in the world. Rich versus poor, white folk thinking they're better than everybody else—when will it ever end?"

"I know, honey. I know." Bryony stood behind her sister's chair and gently massaged Lark's shoulders. "It only ends one person at a time, and that's why I'm so proud of you for wanting to make a difference where you can."

"If only..." Lark sighed long and deep. "I feel like such a failure, Bryony. Maybe I gave up too easily. I've asked myself again and again whether I should have stayed in Kenya and made the best of things."

"Don't start second-guessing yourself." Taking the chair next to Lark's, Bryony reached for her hands. "Honey, don't you know how I've been praying for you? I'm claiming God's will over your life every single day, and I have faith he is placing you exactly where he wants you."

Michael came in just then, his curly brown hair mussed by the breeze and his lips drawn up in a merry grin. The sight of him never failed to give Bryony's heart a turn. "We should go, sweetheart," he said as he pressed in close to her side. "I need to get back to the buckthorn I found yesterday and finish the sketch before we lose the light."

Winking at Lark, Bryony heaved an exaggerated sigh. "That's the thing about being married to an artist. It's all about the light. Not enough, too much—he's never happy."

"On the contrary, my dear." Michael helped Bryony into her sweater. "The light of your love makes me the happiest man on earth."

"And you're full of blarney." With a playful slap on his arm, Bryony turned to give Lark a hug. "See you tomorrow, honey. Can't wait to meet your Mr. Schafer and his friend. And trust me," she added, dropping her voice to a whisper, "the Lord is holding your future secure, and I just know he's got wonderful things in store."

* * *

Lark wanted to believe Bryony, but she had to wonder how God intended to bring good out of a wasted summer and fall. Much further behind on her college credits than she'd planned, now Lark would have to wait even longer to complete her degree and earn teacher certification.

Little she could do about it until the spring term, though. She'd already made up her mind to take the maximum number of credit hours allowed, even if she had to trade sleep for study and work time. She'd survive...somehow.

At least being home the past few weeks meant spending more time with her family. On Thursday morning, she scurried around helping Rose get things ready for Thanksgiving dinner and the arrival of their guests. Lark wished she could host a meal even half as sumptuous as what Odette would serve at the Heath mansion. Instead, they'd make do with a small pork roast from the hog Grandpa butchered a few weeks ago. The Heaths had given each of their tenants a young pig last spring so they'd have meat to portion out through the coming winter. Lark would flavor the roast with onions and garlic, then use the drippings to make gravy for the mashed potatoes. String beans put up last summer and a pan of cornbread would complete the meal. They'd serve Bryony's pies for dessert.

As Lark pondered the meager menu, she had to remind herself how much better off they were than so many farm families across the state. Though the creeks were drying up and the river was down, Grandpa had been able to haul enough water to save the vegetable garden from the drought that just wouldn't let up.

Later, while the kitchen filled with mouthwatering aromas from the stove, Lark and Rose laid the table with Grandma's finest white tablecloth and china. Lark found a pair of beeswax candles and set them in the star-shaped crystal candleholders her parents had received as a wedding gift back in 1906. Then she found a few brightly colored autumn leaves and arranged them in the space between the candlesticks.

"Looks fit for royalty," Rose remarked. "I feel like I ought to put on my Sunday dress before our company comes."

Lark cast a critical eye over her sister's chambray shirt and denim overalls. "Unless you want to have your Thanksgiving dinner out in the chicken house, *I* feel like that would be a mighty good idea."

Deciding she could use some freshening up herself, Lark hung up her apron and joined Rose in the bedroom. Standing before the wardrobe, she wished she had something new and pretty to wear. And then she wanted to kick herself for entertaining such frivolous thoughts when so many did without even an extra shirt or a decent pair of shoes.

Across the room, Rose gave a loud "A-*hem*." At Lark's curious frown, she said, "Please don't tell me you're going to wear that ugly brown shift you've had for a hundred years. All you'll need is to knot your hair in a tight little bun and borrow Grandpa's reading glasses. Then you'll be the picture of the dull old schoolmarm."

Lark fisted her hips and tried to look irritated. "All right, Miss Know-It-All, what do *you* suggest I wear?"

Rose moseyed over to the wardrobe and flipped hangers back and forth. "This," she stated, pulling out the pale blue polka-dot dress Lark had tucked deep into the far corner.

Stomach clenching, Lark shook her head. "Too summery." She reached for the brown shift again. "This'll be fine. It's much more seasonal."

"All right, but..." Rose narrowed her eyes, then went to the bureau and rummaged through the top drawer. She pulled out a paisley scarf that had once belonged to their mother. "Wear this around the neckline like those Hollywood movie stars do. It'll add a little color and style."

Holding the dress and scarf in front of her, Lark studied her reflection with pursed lips. She shot a glance at Rose. "Since when has my tomboy sister taken such an interest in fashion?"

"Just 'cause I'm not much for getting all dolled up myself doesn't mean I don't appreciate what looks nice."

When Lark finished dressing, she had to admit her sister did have good taste. However, Rose failed to convince Lark to leave her hair loose about her shoulders. She wasn't some ingénue and didn't want to be seen as such, but she did allow Rose to give her some finger waves across her temples and twist her hair into a softer version of an updo.

A few minutes before three, an automobile rumbled up the lane. When Lark peeked out the parlor window, she recognized the car Dr. Young had driven in Arkadelphia. Her heart plummeted to the too-tight toes of her Sunday shoes, and she fired Grandpa a panicked look over her shoulder. "They're here!"

"Reckon so." He lumbered out of the easy chair where he'd been catching a quick nap. "Well, don't just stand there gapin' like a fish out of water, girlie. Invite your company in."

They so seldom used the front door that the harsh rap of the knocker nearly shot Lark to the ceiling. She straightened her scarf and smoothed her hands down the length of her dress, then opened the door to Anson Schafer and Dr. Young. "Hello, and welcome. I see you found us okay."

"Perfect directions," Dr. Young said, removing his hat and stepping inside. "And a lovely day for a drive."

Grandpa stepped into the tiny foyer. "How'do. I'm George Rigby, Lark's grandpa."

Lark introduced Dr. Young and Mr. Schafer, who repeatedly insisted on first names as they took turns accepting Grandpa's handshake. While Grandpa showed them into the parlor, Lark took their hats and overcoats to Grandpa's room and laid them across the bed.

By the time she returned to the parlor, Rose had peeked in from the kitchen to say hello. With her long red hair in a tidy braid down her back and wearing a neatly pressed green skirt and plaid middy blouse, Rose looked as pretty as Lark had ever seen her. It truly was a shame they couldn't get Rose into dresses more often.

As Rose excused herself to check on dinner, Lark couldn't resist a quick gibe under her breath. "Too bad we didn't invite the Wielands so Caleb could see you all prettied up for a change."

Rose's one-eyed glare said exactly what she thought of the idea.

When Lark returned her attention to the gentlemen's conversation, Anson was sharing his ideas about developing educational opportunities for disadvantaged Arkansas children. "I'm calling it the Charles and Lorena Schafer Educational Foundation in memory of my late parents. I've applied for grants, and we've already received donations from a few concerned philanthropists." He glanced briefly in Lark's direction, where she sat in a rocking chair across from the settee. "The next step will be to find qualified teachers willing to work under less than ideal circumstances and for little pay."

"Sounds like quite an undertaking," Grandpa mused. He also slid his gaze toward Lark. "Where do you s'pose you're gonna find those teachers?"

"Irwin and I are currently making the circuit to address church congregations, fraternal organizations, and colleges across the state." Anson sat forward, his enthusiasm evident. "Quite honestly, I wasn't sure what kind of response to expect, but we've been pleased with the initial outpouring of support. This is clearly a need that must be addressed, and soon."

Hearing another car, Lark looked out to see Michael's green Chevrolet drive past the window. She popped up from her chair. "That's my sister Bryony and her husband."

A few minutes later, more introductions had been made, and while Bryony helped Rose and Lark get dinner on the table, Lark could hear Michael and Anson getting acquainted. The two men were different in many ways—Anson with his master's degree in education, while Michael had joined the army and then spent years recovering from being gassed in the Great War—and yet alike in that they both owned a quiet intellect and love of learning.

Even more appealing, both remained oblivious to their own natural charm, a trait Lark resolved to keep high on her list of most sought-after qualities.

That is, should she ever decide to risk her heart again.

* * *

Anson's first Thanksgiving back in the States since his college days was proving even more enjoyable than he'd anticipated. His only regret was how little time he actually had to converse with Lark. She hovered in the background for most of the afternoon, while her more gregarious family peppered him with all kinds of questions about life in Kenya and his current support-raising efforts.

In Michael Heath, though, Anson had found a kindred spirit, a soft-spoken man with a keen mind and a generous heart. Michael promised to speak to his father and sister about making a donation to Anson's cause.

As the ladies served dessert following the simple but delicious meal, a pattering on the roof alerted them to the light rain beginning to fall. Both George Rigby and his granddaughter Rose hurried to the kitchen window, their faces filled with expectation.

"It's been a long dry spell," Lark murmured as she refilled Anson's cup with chicory-laced coffee.

The brief shower ended long before the dessert plates were cleared, and Anson sensed the disappointment settling around the table.

"That's all we been gettin' for two years." George Rigby rapped the table with an open palm. "A smidgen here, a dribble there, too little and too far between to do a mite of good."

Anson had been stunned at the desolation he'd seen during his recent excursions across the state. The dry and barren fields stood in stark contrast to the lush, green beauty on the slopes of Mount Kenya, yet the plight of the poorest was hauntingly similar. What British colonialism had effected in Kenya wasn't so different from Arkansas's system of tenant farming and sharecropping.

Returning from setting dishes in the sink, Bryony leaned down to plant a kiss on her grandfather's head. "Let's remember it's Thanksgiving and try to recall only the good in our lives." She smiled across the table toward Anson and Irwin. "Like the new friends Lark's invited to share our meal."

With a grateful nod, Irwin eased his chair back. "It has been our distinct pleasure. But we should be going soon. I don't want to get lost on these back roads after dark."

"You've at least another hour yet." Returning to the sink, Bryony snatched the dishtowel from Lark's hand. "Rose and I will finish up. Y'all should go out for a stroll and walk off some of that pie."

Lark offered a hesitant smile as she approached the table. "Who's interested?"

Anson glanced at Irwin. "How about it?"

"Go ahead, my boy. I'll be better served by one more cup of coffee for the road."

In the end, it was George, Michael, Lark, and Anson who bundled into their coats for a brisk walk around the property. Soon, though, George took Michael aside to ask his opinion about an unusual shrub he'd found growing behind the chicken house.

"They'll be awhile," Lark said. "Once you get Michael talking botany, there's no stopping him."

Anson fell into step with Lark as she started down the lane. "Michael is an interesting man. I like him."

"Me, too." Lark grew quiet, and the only sound was their footfalls on the hard-packed road.

After a few minutes, Anson remarked, "So you've lived here with your grandfather a long time?"

"Since I was seven. Memphis, where I was born, seems like someone else's life."

At her wistful sigh, Anson moved closer, his elbow brushing hers. "That's pretty much how I felt coming back to the States after so many years away. Kenya feels more like home than Arkansas."

Lark tilted her head to look up at him. "Are you sorry you came back? I mean, I understand you didn't have much choice because of your eyes, but it must be so hard."

"I have my moments of self-pity." Anson suppressed a cynical laugh. "But I've learned it doesn't do any good to argue with God. He's going to have his way no matter what."

"Then I'm sure you've prayed about God's direction for your new foundation."

She said it so matter-of-factly that Anson suffered a twinge of guilt. Had he asked the Lord's guidance for this next phase of his life? Or was he simply forging ahead along the only path he could see open to him? Truth be told, most days he left the praying to Irwin.

He didn't notice he'd stopped walking until Lark paused several steps ahead and glanced over her shoulder. "I'm sorry, are you ready to head back?"

"No, it's just...my thoughts were wandering." Anson caught up, and they continued at a leisurely pace.

"You're like Michael with his botanical sketches," Lark said with a chuckle. "One-track minds."

At the moment, though, Anson was content simply to enjoy Lark Linwood's company. All afternoon he'd hoped for an opportunity exactly like this, where they could talk together without the distraction of keeping up polite conversation with everyone else present. "Lark, I...I want you to know how grateful I am for today. You have a delightful family, and I'm sure I can speak for Irwin as well when I say how very welcome you've made us feel."

"I'm glad. What's a holiday without family and friends to share it with?"

Her remark brought back memories of growing up in Kenya. With no brothers or sisters of his own, and without the typical trappings of American celebrations, holidays there were quite different. "You're right. One could argue there are different kinds of families, but I don't suppose any are as special as your own flesh and blood."

They fell silent until they reached the main road. Lark halted abruptly, arms crossed and shoulders back. She looked left, then right, as if weighing which way to turn. Then with a long, tired sigh, she turned back toward the farmhouse. "It's late. I don't want you and Dr. Young getting lost."

Lost? Since returning from Kenya, Anson had never felt so lost in his life. The Schafer Foundation may be well on its way, but Anson obviously needed direction in his personal life. Otherwise, he'd never so much as consider what he was about to ask.

"Lark."

She glanced his way, a curious smile tilting her lips. "Yes?"

"Do you think perhaps we might see each other again after today?"

The smile faded. Anson didn't require perfect vision to notice the veil of reserve fall across her face. Steps quickening, she stated crisply, "It's barely over a month until the spring term begins at Henderson. Once classes start, I'll have little time for anything else."

"Lark." He spoke her name more firmly this time, then took her hand and drew her to a stop. When she hesitantly raised her chin to look at him, he said softly, "I am not Franklin Keene. I am nothing even remotely like him."

She blinked several times. "I—I know. Believe me, I know."

"Then also believe me when I say how very much I enjoy

your company." A light breeze toyed with her hair, and Anson couldn't resist smoothing it behind her ear. His fingertips tingled at the feel of the silky strands. When she stiffened, he abruptly lowered his hands to his sides. "I've been entirely too forward. Please forgive me."

"No...no," she murmured, staring off into the distance. "But it doesn't change the fact that I'll soon be in Arkadelphia, and you'll be traipsing all over Arkansas drumming up support for your foundation."

He chewed the inside of his lip. "It would mean a great deal to me if I could count on your involvement as well."

Now it was clear he'd misspoken. Lark's chin shot higher, and she started walking again. "I know I expressed interest after your lecture at Henderson, but since I'm not a teacher yet and have no money to donate to your cause, certainly you can appreciate how limited my support would be."

Anson didn't know what frustrated him more, the fortress Lark Linwood had erected around her fragile dignity, or his own ineptitude at voicing his true feelings. It would help tremendously if he could even identify those feelings. He only knew that the more time he spent with Lark, the dearer she became to him.

As they marched toward the farmhouse, he tried one last time. "Please, Lark, I know you need to finish school, but there's still so much you could do. I watched you in Kenya—your gentle way with the children, the joy on your face while you helped Jata with her reading."

Lark's steps faltered. "Those moments reminded me why I want so badly to be a teacher."

"And you know the need is equally great right here." Anson edged in front of her, forcing her to a stop once again. "But don't mistake this for one more recruitment speech. I'm asking you— *you*, Lark Linwood—not with words of idle flattery but because

I respect and admire you and want very much to have you join me in this important work."

Hands clasped, she glanced away. "I'm honored that you would ask, truly, but I don't see how—"

"I know there are complications," Anson interrupted, "but I'm confident we can work through them. Tell me you'll at least think about it."

Chapter Seven

In the weeks following Thanksgiving, Lark thought of little else but Anson's invitation to take an active role in his foundation. He wrote nearly every day to tell her about his travels and speaking engagements, with postmarks from all across Arkansas—from Fort Smith, Fayetteville, and Jonesboro in the north, all the way down to Texarkana and El Dorado in the south. He sounded optimistic that donations had begun to trickle in despite the struggling economy. It hadn't hurt that Roosevelt had won the election and promised new programs to increase employment and get the country back on its feet.

Roosevelt's promises couldn't alter the weather, though. The drought lingered on, dust storms from the Midwest continued to blow through, and Grandpa's worries about next year's crops intensified. These continual setbacks were aging him faster than Lark or her sisters wanted to admit.

Lark's dilemma haunted her. Every penny she spent on her college education took away from what she could contribute to her family's needs. But even taking the maximum course loads, she faced at least two more years to earn enough credits to graduate. Working for Anson's foundation would mean a small but steady income now, when her family most needed it. More important, just as she'd hoped to do in Kenya, she would be working toward the advancement of children who desperately needed the benefits education could offer.

With the deadline for spring registration looming, perhaps it was time to take her own advice and pray for God's direction—something she reluctantly admitted she'd done too little of during the initial rush of enthusiasm about Kenya.

Lord, I don't want to make another mistake.

She said as much to Bryony on a mid-December Sunday afternoon when Bryony and Michael came out for a visit after church. "And I must decide today, because if I'm going to register for spring classes, I've got to catch the bus to Arkadelphia first thing tomorrow or I'll miss the cutoff."

They sat together on Lark's bed, their backs to the wall and their heads together. "What's your heart telling you?" Bryony asked.

"Nothing. *Nothing!*" A growl rumbled deep in Lark's throat. She clenched her fists. "All my life, I've had a vision for my future. I *wanted* to go to college. I *wanted* to become a teacher. More than anything, I wanted to make a difference in this world. It was like a fire in my belly, and no matter how sad or hopeless things looked, that passion kept me going."

"And now?"

Lark wiped away a tear. "It's like the fire's gone out, and all that's left is darkness and confusion."

"But you were all agog to go hear Anson speak when he came to Henderson."

"I was. After he'd been so nice to me in Kenya, I truly looked forward to seeing him again. I need to be realistic, though. I need to start thinking more with my head instead of my heart."

With a thoughtful sigh, Bryony smoothed her skirt across her knees. "I suspect the real problem is you're afraid to trust your own feelings. The Holy Spirit often speaks to us through impressions on our hearts, but he can't reach a heart closed off by fear."

"Yes, I'm afraid." Lark's voice shook. "Weren't you the day you decided to go see Sebastian Heath about Grandpa's debt? Or when you first realized you were falling for Michael?"

Bryony laughed softly. "Oh, yes. Scared right down to my tippy-toes."

"Then how'd you know if you were hearing God's will?"

"I didn't always. Oh, honey, there were days I felt as deaf to God's direction as you do right now." Fingers woven through Lark's, Bryony gave a gentle squeeze. "But when you realize your fear is shouting louder than the voice of God, there's only one thing to do. You've got to muzzle that fear and lean into the Lord all the more."

Lark searched her sister's face. "And then what?"

"And then you do the next thing that needs doing and leave the results to the Lord."

The next thing. It sounded so simple. But quieting the worries about her family, the doubts about returning to college, and now the terror of committing her future to a new cause and risking the possibility of having her hopes dashed all over again? There was nothing simple about it.

One thing she believed to be true, though, whatever she decided: Anson Schafer was a good man, someone she could trust never to mislead or betray her.

The next thing. Without clear direction, she had only one choice: get on the bus to Arkadelphia in the morning and register for classes. If the Lord wanted something different for her, he'd have to show her before she handed her fees to the registrar.

*   *   *

Arriving in Arkadelphia shortly before noon on Monday, Lark had a niggling sense that she should stop by O'Neill's Grocery before registering for classes.

The moment she turned up Main Street and glimpsed the striped awning over the storefront, she knew something was amiss. The produce bins Mr. O'Neill usually set out on the walk each morning were nowhere in sight. As Lark drew nearer, she saw the shades were drawn, and a hand-lettered sign sat in the bare front window where Mr. O'Neill normally displayed the day's fresh baked goods.

"Going out of business," Lark read aloud slowly. Her stomach plummeted. This simply couldn't be! Mr. O'Neill had promised

to hold a job for her. Without it, how would she ever pay for her classes and dormitory?

She cupped a trembling hand to her temple and peered inside through a slit in the shade. Half the shelves stood empty. Racks and display tables had been shoved at odd angles toward the walls. The chalkboard announcing the daily specials hadn't been changed since the end of November.

Hearing sounds from the back of the store, Lark rapped on the glass. "Hello? Mr. O'Neill?"

A shadow passed behind the checkout counter, and Lark recognized Mrs. O'Neill's stocky form. The woman came to the window and lifted the shade. "Oh, Lark, it's you!" She twisted the lock and yanked open the door. "Come in, honey. I'm so sorry you had to find out like this."

Lark stumbled through the opening. "When—*how*—did this happen?"

"We lost too many customers, and too many others haven't been able to pay their bills. Then Benjamin—" Mrs. O'Neill's voice broke. "He's generous to a fault, you know. And worrying not only about our customers but young folks like you depending on the part-time work to get through school, well, it darned near gave him a heart attack."

"Oh, no! Is he all right?"

"We're hopeful, if he obeys doctor's orders." Heaving a tired breath, the plump woman found a handkerchief in her apron pocket and dabbed a tear from the corner of her eye. "He's not supposed to lift a finger around here until Doc gives him the okay. In the meantime"—she cast a glance about the store— "I'm doing what I can to sell off our stock and fixtures so we can be rid of this burden."

Lark hardly knew what to say. Her own worries seemed small compared to what Mr. and Mrs. O'Neill must be going through.

The store was their livelihood. "I'm so sorry. I wish I could help somehow."

"We'll get by. Benjamin's been putting money away for retirement. Just never expected to need it so soon." Pushing a limp strand of silver hair off her forehead, Mrs. O'Neill surveyed some canned goods on a nearby shelf. She nudged an empty cardboard crate closer and began moving the cans into the box.

"As long as I'm here, might as well make myself useful." Lark set her handbag on a table, then slipped out of her coat and joined Mrs. O'Neill in boxing up the canned goods.

A grateful smile lit the woman's round face. "Benjamin always said you were his best employee, always pitching in wherever you were needed." She set another can in the box, then straightened, her gaze filling with concern. "You're in town to register at school, aren't you? Oh, honey, that makes me feel a hundred times sorrier we don't have a job waiting for you. What will you do now?"

Bitter disappointment rising in her chest, Lark clutched a dented can of peas. The decision she'd been agonizing over had suddenly been made for her, because without the income from O'Neill's Grocery to supplement what little Grandpa insisted on providing—and could ill afford—Lark couldn't begin to cover her college expenses.

"Lark?"

She became aware of Mrs. O'Neill's hand on her arm. With a forced smile, she placed the peas in the box. "It's looking like the Lord has other plans for me than school. I was praying for a sign, and I think today he gave me one."

She'd just never expected it would be a real sign in the shuttered window of O'Neill's Grocery.

* * *

"Mail's here."

Anson glanced up from the desk in Irwin's study. "I hope there's a check or two in the pile."

Sinking into the chair on the opposite side of the desk, Irwin began sorting through the envelopes. "Here's something from the Baptist church we visited in Hot Springs." He shot it across the desk toward Anson. "And another from someone in Fayetteville."

Anson had already torn into the first envelope. Folded inside the typed letter on church stationery was a check. Adjusting his glasses, Anson squinted to make out the amount: twenty dollars. *We appreciate your cause and have taken up a collection*, the letter stated. *However, as you well know, folks are keeping a tight hold on their pocketbooks these days. We pray this donation will contribute in some small way toward your commendable efforts.*

"Not much, eh?" Irwin must have read the disappointment in Anson's expression. "We knew we were embarking on this at a difficult time."

"Yes, but this *difficult time* is exactly why what we're doing is so vital." Anson refolded the letter and slammed it down with the palm of his hand. "What else have you got there?"

"Here's ten dollars from the man in Fayetteville, a high school teacher who heard you speak at the Lions Club." After passing the letter and check over to Anson, Irwin picked up the next envelope. "Hmm, this one's postmarked Eden, Arkansas."

Anson's head snapped up. "Let's see it."

"Now, now, don't be in such a rush." Grinning, Irwin fanned the air with the envelope. "Maybe I should read it to you. Haven't you strained your eyes enough today already?"

In one swift motion, Anson bolted from his chair, stretched his body across the desk, and snatched the envelope from Irwin's hand. "Go make some coffee or something, why don't you? And shut the door on your way out."

Irwin snickered as he rose. "One would think—"

"One would think one's closest friend would know enough to mind one's own business."

Making a lock-and-key motion at his lips, Irwin quietly left the room. He did *not* close the door, however, and Anson heard him chuckling all the way to the kitchen.

All teasing aside, it was lunacy to let himself show so much interest in another letter from Lark Linwood. This would be only the second he'd received since Thanksgiving, a fact not lost upon him considering how many times he'd written to her. Maybe he'd been overplaying his hand by sending all those updates about his fundraising efforts. He'd tried to keep his letters strictly platonic, one friend informing another about a common interest. But she might easily have read between the lines and sensed his growing feelings for her, if only because of the galling frequency of his letters.

"You utter fool," he muttered to himself as he stared at the unopened envelope. In Lark's first letter, she'd thanked him for thinking of her during his travels and shared her hopes for his success. After a bit of news about her family and reminding him of her plans to continue college, she'd ended the letter with a polite "*Sincerely yours.*"

He should have gotten the message then. In this letter, she'd probably tell him enough was enough. Not in so many words, naturally—Lark was too polite to be so direct.

"Oh, hang it all," he said, tearing open the flap. No use torturing himself with maybes.

As before, Lark had written in large, clear cursive, a thoughtful gesture in consideration of Anson's eyes. He blinked several times, took a deep breath, and focused in on the words.

Dear Anson,
I hope your speaking engagements continue to prove fruitful and that you remain safe and healthy while

traveling across the state. No one is more deserving of success, nor a cause more worthy.

As for myself, unforeseen circumstances have altered my plans about returning to Henderson for the spring term. If your offer of a position, however small, within your foundation is still open, I do very much hope you will permit me to change my mind and accept.

Anson clenched a fist and stifled an exclamation that would surely have brought Irwin charging back in from the kitchen. Besides the fact that such outbursts of giddy delight were utterly out of character for Anson, nothing in the tone of Lark's letter sounded the least bit personal. He pressed his lips together and read on.

My first concern, however, is living arrangements, as I assume you remain headquartered in Little Rock. I shall have no other income than that which you have previously mentioned might be available from foundation funding. Therefore, I would require the most economical housing obtainable—and, naturally, it must be suitable for a single Christian woman.

Anson was already racking his brain for a place Lark could stay. Though Irwin had a spare bedroom here, Anson couldn't possibly suggest Lark room with two bachelors.

At Irwin's hesitant tap on the doorframe, Anson sighed and signaled for him to come in.

"Well? What news? I certainly can't tell from that smirk you're wearing." Irwin collapsed into the chair.

"Here, read it for yourself." Anson pushed the letter across the desk and sat back, hands loosely folded at his waist. "Don't worry, there's nothing of a confidential nature."

Picking up the page, Irwin arched a brow. "Which explains the obvious disappointment in your tone."

Anson waited while Irwin perused the letter, then asked, "Any thoughts?"

"My first thought is that Miss Linwood is even more adept at disguising her feelings than you."

"Disguising? It didn't seem to me that she was disguising anything." Anson cast a weary glance toward the ceiling. "I *meant* did you have any thoughts about where she might live if she comes to Little Rock."

"Of course you did." Tapping a finger to his lips, Irwin gazed at a spot on the wall behind Anson's head. "Actually, I've had another thought I've been meaning to bring up, and Lark's letter gives me exactly the opening I've needed. Since your intent is to bring educational opportunities to the poorest children in the state, shouldn't you go to where those children are? I realize you can't be everywhere at once, but with funding slow to come in, if you were to begin in one small area where there is great need... such as Eden, a community surrounded by tenant farming and sharecropping families..."

Anson slowly drew his lips into a smile. "I've always known we were friends for good reason. You're a wise man, Irwin Young. A very wise and perceptive man."

"Indeed." Irwin pushed up from the chair. "And now I shall fetch the coffee I just brewed and give you a few minutes to compose an appropriate reply to our dear Miss Linwood."

Taking stationery and a fountain pen from the drawer, Anson contemplated the wording. Should he remain as formal and detached as Lark had been, or simply blurt out in flowing prose how happy her letter had made him and how he couldn't wait to see her again?

Irwin took his time bringing the coffee—on purpose, no doubt—and by the time he brought in the tray, Anson had penned what he hoped was a cordial but appropriately business-like response.

If he did succeed in making Eden his base of operations, he'd have ample opportunity to grow his acquaintance with Lark from cordial to...

To what? *Courting?* Did he honestly believe a beautiful young woman like Lark Linwood could ever be romantically interested in a stodgy, visually impaired academic like himself? When he'd told Lark he was nothing like Franklin Keene, it was true in all the deleterious ways he'd intended.

It was equally true that Anson possessed neither Franklin Keene's engaging personality nor his debonair style and handsome features.

Irwin set a mug of coffee next to Anson's hand. "That's quite a dour look you're wearing. What happened to all the enthusiasm you exhibited before I left the room?"

"Just reality sinking in." Anson folded the letter and tucked it into an envelope. After penning Lark's address on the front, he found a stamp in the drawer.

Elbows propped on the armrests of his chair, Irwin sipped his coffee. "I know what you're thinking, and you should know you're dead wrong. Just because your work in Kenya kept you off the marriage market all these years doesn't mean it's too late for you."

"Marriage market?" Anson snorted. "You make it sound like a livestock auction, and me the cow who's past his prime."

"Don't you mean bull? If I'm not mistaken, *cow* refers to a female bovine."

"Fine, then—*bull.* Which certainly applies to this entire line of conversation." Anson shoved to his feet. "Now, if you will excuse me, I have a letter to mail."

* * *

After more than a week of frigid temperatures, by the Wednesday before Christmas, Lark no longer had to break up films of ice in the livestock's water pails each morning. She set a bucket under Hermione's udder, sat down on the milking stool, and reluctantly peeled off her wool gloves. Milking wasn't her favorite chore, but she kept reminding herself of two things: first and foremost, everyone's gratitude that the old milk cow had begun producing again after calving last spring; and second, that for as long as Lark remained at home, she was freeing up Grandpa and Rose for the heavier work.

She rested her forehead against Hermione's warm flank, her senses enveloped by earthy barn smells and the rhythmic splat of milk hitting the pail. When she'd returned from Arkadelphia with the news about Mr. O'Neill's grocery and her decision not to register for classes, she'd gotten quite an earful from both Rose and Grandpa. When Bryony found out, she'd been even more vocal with her disapproval, and considering all Bryony had sacrificed to send Lark off to college in the first place, Lark couldn't blame her. Bryony had even offered to approach Michael's family for help in paying Lark's tuition, but Lark refused to become even more indebted to the Heaths than her family already was.

"Hey, Lark." Rose peeked over the stall gate. "Soon as Grandpa finishes chopping wood, we're taking a few bales of forage over to the feed store to see what we can get for 'em. Need anything from town?"

"Maybe some cornmeal. Noticed yesterday we were getting low." Lark straightened and flexed her cramping fingers. Hermione was about emptied for the morning anyway. "And don't forget to pick up the mail."

Rose wiggled her brows and grinned. "Heaven forbid you should go a day without hearing from your beau."

Lark shot up so fast she nearly kicked over the milk pail. She quickly moved it to one side before Hermione could do the job for her. "Anson Schafer is *not* my beau."

"Really? I mean, considering he's written you a letter practically every single day since he came for Thanksgiving..." Curling her tongue around her upper lip, Rose slanted a thoughtful look toward the barn roof. "Yep, that spells B-E-A-U to me."

"Just go load your hay bales and leave me be." Lark snatched up the milk pail, shoved past Rose, and lumbered toward the house.

By the time she'd poured the fresh milk into clean glass jars, Grandpa had come in with a load of firewood. He dropped it into the metal bin next to the stove. "Rose tell you we're off to town?"

"Mm-hmm." Lark screwed down a jar lid. "Good luck at the feed store."

"Back by noon."

Grandpa had always been a man of few words, lately even more so. Apparently, once he'd used up everything he had to say about Lark's giving up on school, little else seemed worth the verbal effort.

She had yet to tell her family about the possibility of her moving to Little Rock to work for Anson's foundation. No use letting the cat out of the bag until there was actually a cat in the bag to worry about.

With the jars of milk cooling on the porch, Lark carried yesterday's milk inside and began separating the cream. Her arms were already tired from milking, and now she had to crank the butter churn. Cleaning chalkboards at Matumaini School might have been tedious work, but at the moment, it seemed far more attractive than repetitive farm chores. Not for the first time, Lark wondered how things might have gone if only she'd stayed in Kenya.

One thing was certain: She was no closer to becoming a real teacher here than she had been in Africa.

After scraping the meager amount of butter into a covered ceramic dish, Lark cleaned and put away the churn, then set yesterday's bean soup on the stove and started a batch of cornbread. By the time she finished, Grandpa and Rose returned from town. Glancing out the window, Lark noticed they'd brought back at least two of the hay bales. Neither Grandpa nor Rose looked happy when they trudged into the kitchen.

"Bad news at the feed store?" Lark asked as she set bowls and silverware on the table.

"Ever'body who had any kind of hay crop is trying to sell what they can spare." Grandpa moved stiffly as he tossed his dusty brown hat on a hook and shrugged out of his coat. "Ol' Ned took a couple bales in trade for grain, so's at least we can feed our own livestock."

"That's something, I guess." Using a folded dish towel, Lark took the cornbread from the oven. "Rose, can you dish up the soup?"

Breaking into a grin, Rose waved a thin handful of mail in front of Lark's face. "Sure you don't want to read the letter from your beau—excuse me, your handsome, charming, and scholarly *friend*?"

Lark slammed the cornbread pan on a trivet, then snatched the mail from Rose's hand. She refused to admit to anyone, least of all herself, the tiny thrill that shot through her every time one of Anson's letters arrived. She liked Anson just fine, respected him, too. But she'd learned her lesson about maintaining professional boundaries.

Slapping the mail onto the counter, she ordered everyone to the table. "Let's eat while it's hot."

It took no small amount of willpower to leave Anson's letter right where it was while they finished lunch and washed dishes afterward. Lark didn't miss Rose's sidelong glances and barely

disguised smirks. When Grandpa and Rose headed out to fix
something on the pickup, Lark grabbed the letter, pulled a
chair closer to the warmth of the stove, and tore back the flap.
The letter was dated last Friday. A tremor of anticipation shot
through her as she started to read.

My dear Lark,
I received your letter today and was disheartened to
learn about Mr. O'Neill's store closing, but even more so
your decision not to register for spring classes. I can only
imagine your extreme disappointment.
However, please forgive my own great pleasure at the
news of your interest in coming to work for my foundation. Yes, the offer is most definitely still open! I only wish
I had more positive news about the results of our fundraising efforts. As you are so very aware, money is tight
and few are able to give as freely as they would like.
As a result, Irwin and I are discussing the wisdom of
scaling back our initial outreach to a much smaller
geographical area. What would you think if we were to
begin our educational efforts right there in Eden?

Lark's heart climbed into her throat. She stopped and read the
paragraph again. *Right there in Eden.* Oh yes, the need was
great! Lark knew of many families who couldn't spare their children from farm work to send them to school. She'd have been in
the same situation herself if Bryony hadn't dropped out of high
school so that Lark could finish.

The letter continued with Anson's request for suggestions
about whom he might contact concerning both housing and
office arrangements. If anyone would know, it would be Pastor
Unsworth.

Lark grabbed her coat and darted outside. She found Rose
and Grandpa with their heads together under the hood of the

pickup muttering something about hoses and oil pressure. "Did you figure out what's wrong?"

Rose backed out and wiped her hands on an old rag. "Loose clamp. Should hold fine now."

"Good. I need to go into town."

"But we just came from town."

"And now I'm going back."

Grandpa slammed down the hood and dropped a wrench into the toolbox at his feet. "This anything to do with what came in the mail?"

After all the teasing she'd already endured about Anson, Lark wasn't in the mood to explain. "I've fed the chickens, milked the cow, churned butter, cooked y'all's lunch, and now I'm going to town. If you have a problem with that, then maybe I'll just let you fix your own supper tonight and see how you like it."

Grandpa and Rose shared a raised-eyebrow glance before lifting their hands in surrender and edging away. With a satisfied nod, Lark climbed in behind the wheel. As she steered the old pickup down the lane, it occurred to her that she really ought not to have left Anson's letter lying open on the kitchen table.

Chapter Eight

Preoccupied with foundation business, Anson barely acknowledged the advent of Christmas, and might not have marked it at all if Irwin hadn't insisted on attending the Christmas Eve Midnight Mass at Little Rock's Cathedral of St. Andrew. Then again, the church had contributed a sizable amount to Anson's foundation, along with the promise of monthly support for at least the next year. As an outward expression of gratitude, Anson felt obligated to make an appearance.

But his experiences in Africa had cooled him toward religion in general. Those hard-hearted missionaries who chose judgment over compassion seemed to have completely overlooked Christ's words in Luke 6:37: "Do not judge, and you will not be judged; do not condemn, and you will not be condemned. Forgive, and you will be forgiven."

Even so, the liturgy and pageantry, the candlelight and hymns, all combined to reach deep into Anson's heart and remind him that Christ's sacrificial love superseded every division. When worship ended, he made no move to exit the pew but sat and waited in silent contemplation while the cathedral emptied. He sensed Irwin's puzzled concern, but his friend wisely said nothing.

When almost everyone had gone, Irwin lightly rested a hand on Anson's arm. "Look there, lighting a candle—isn't that Lark's sister and her husband?"

Anson looked toward an alcove where rows of votive candles flickered. He glimpsed a man and woman standing there, but from this distance and with the dim lighting, he couldn't make out faces. "I can't tell. But would they have driven all the way over from Brinkley?"

"I'll find out." Irwin made his way to the side aisle and approached the couple.

As soon as Anson saw their initial surprise become a happy greeting, he rose and joined them. Michael offered a warm handshake, but Bryony enveloped him in an enthusiastic hug.

"I can't wait to see Lark tomorrow and tell her we ran into you," Bryony gushed. "Now I wish more than ever we could have brought her along."

Irwin looked at her askance. "Surely you aren't driving back tonight?"

"Oh, no, we have a hotel room." Linking her arm through Michael's, Bryony shared a smile with her husband. "We're reviving a Heath family tradition. When Michael was a boy, his parents would bring him and Miranda into Little Rock on Christmas Eve for Midnight Mass, then get a hotel for the night and have a sumptuous late breakfast on Christmas morning before returning home."

"Sounds like an enjoyable tradition." Anson shifted his overcoat to his other arm. "By chance do you know if Lark received a letter from me earlier this week?"

With a quick glance at Michael, Bryony said, "I'm not sure it's my place to say anything, but...yes, and I believe she's already mailed a reply."

"Oh?" An edge crept into Anson's tone. He suddenly felt unprepared for Lark's answer.

"I think you'll find it to be good news—"

Michael tugged on Bryony's arm. "As you said, darling, it isn't your place."

Smiling sheepishly, Bryony shrugged. "I'm sorry, Anson. Can you bear to wait until after Christmas?"

"Guess I'll have to." Anson nodded toward the exit. "It's late. We shouldn't keep you."

Michael offered farewell handshakes to Irwin and Anson in turn. "It was good to see you again. Merry Christmas."

"Merry Christmas to both of you as well." Anson accepted Bryony's quick kiss on the cheek and wondered that she should treat him so affectionately when Lark's letters sounded increasingly more aloof.

No doubt Bryony, like Irwin, assumed a closeness between Lark and Anson that did not exist, at least not to the level Anson had begun to hope for.

By the time he and Irwin made it home and crawled into bed, it was well past two in the morning. Anson slept until half past eleven on Christmas Day, awakened only by a commotion in the kitchen and the strident sound of a woman's voice. He dressed hurriedly without taking time to shave, but before he made it downstairs, their visitor had gone.

"I hope you're hungry." Irwin lifted the lid of a wicker picnic basket, releasing the tempting aromas of baked ham, candied yams, and cranberry sauce. "Compliments of Mrs. Herndale from the missions aid society. She feared we poor, helpless bachelors would starve."

Anson tore off a chunk of ham and stuffed it into his mouth, then groaned with pleasure. "Can we skip breakfast and go straight to dinner?"

"Seeing as how we both slept half the day away, I concur. You set the table, and I'll start coffee."

As they sat down to eat, Anson's thoughts kept drifting to Lark. He wondered what kind of Christmas she'd have, and if she thought of him at all. Monday's mail delivery seemed eons away. Eden was only seventy miles distant, and yet, because the Rigby farm didn't have a telephone, Anson's communication with Lark depended on the whims of the postal system.

Irwin's Christmas decorating amounted to a few greens draped along the mantel and a wreath on the door. He and

Anson had agreed not to exchange gifts, so they spent the rest of the afternoon alternating between chess games, coffee and Mrs. Herndale's pumpkin pie, and catnaps.

On Monday, Anson traipsed from the study to the mail slot in the front door more times than he could count. Irwin facetiously accused him of wearing away the finish on the oak flooring and threatened to bill him for repairs.

When the mail finally did arrive, Irwin beat him to it, then danced a wicked little jig while sorting the stack of letters well out of Anson's reach. Irwin's sudden triumphant laugh gave away his discovery. With a flourish, he laid the envelope in Anson's outstretched hand.

Marching to the staircase, Anson plopped down on the second step. He tore into the envelope and then couldn't bring himself to unfold the single page until he'd steadied both his breathing and his nervous fingers.

"Well? Don't keep me in suspense, boy." Irwin stood over him, hands on hips.

"Hold on, hold on…" Anson's grin widened as he continued reading.

In Lark's typical businesslike tone, she described a discussion with her pastor regarding a location in Eden where Anson could base his educational outreach. As it turned out, an elderly widow who lived on the edge of town had decided to move in with her son and daughter-in-law in Stuttgart. She hoped to sell her fifty-year-old farmhouse but would be willing to rent at a reduced rate if the tenant would agree to handle the necessary repairs. Lark was quick to add that, with the age of the house, there were many.

But my grandfather would be willing to help, Lark wrote, *and Pastor Unsworth is certain we can expect plenty of support from others in the community.*

The word *we* was not lost on Anson. He hauled in one long, slow breath and handed the letter to Irwin. "Read it, and then let's start packing."

* * *

After a chilly start, the day after Christmas quickly warmed to a balmy sixty degrees. Lark took advantage of the springlike afternoon, taking her sewing basket and a stack of mending to the screen porch while she waited for the wash she'd hung out earlier to dry.

Christmas Day had been a quiet holiday, with church in the morning and then finding ways to keep herself occupied until Bryony and Michael came by on their way home from Little Rock. It simply hadn't felt like Christmas until Lark had all her family around her.

In addition to the gifts Bryony brought—a new felt hat for Grandpa, cloud-soft wool sweaters for Rose and Lark—she'd picked up a delicious Boston cream pie from the Marion Hotel, where she and Michael had stayed following Midnight Mass. Later in the evening, Bryony and Michael had gone over to the Heath mansion to have Christmas with Michael's family and spend the night, and Bryony had promised to make another visit to the farm this afternoon before they drove back to Brinkley.

With the sun warm on her shoulders, Lark glanced up from her mending to check on Grandpa's progress. He'd started that morning repairing an old tractor Miranda's husband Daniel had brought over last week. Daniel had taken it off the hands of a farm family who'd given up and were selling off everything they could, and if Grandpa could get the thing running again, Daniel said it was his. Come time for spring plowing, their poor old mule, Daisy, would appreciate the relief. And it hadn't hurt Grandpa's optimism one bit that they'd had a fairly decent rain on Christmas Eve.

A shimmer of green and the rumble of tires along the main road caught Lark's attention. She poked her needle into the pincushion and plucked off her thimble before starting out the porch door to greet Bryony and Michael.

Climbing from the car, Bryony hurried over and threw her arms around Lark. "Isn't it a gorgeous day?"

"It is." Lark leaned away to shoot her sister a probing stare. "Gracious sakes, Bry, where's all this good cheer coming from? Christmas was yesterday!"

"Anything wrong with stretching out the season a bit?" With a catlike smile, Bryony seized Lark's hand and tugged her toward the screen porch.

Lark peeked over her shoulder at Michael, who grinned and sauntered over to where Grandpa had tractor parts strewn across an old tarp. She narrowed her eyes at Bryony. "Okay, something's up. And since you already told me you saw Anson and Dr. Young at the Christmas Eve service, there must be more news you haven't shared."

Inside the porch, the sisters sat next to each other in a pair of wooden rockers Grandpa had built years ago. Bryony's gaze swept the yard. "Where's Rose?"

"At the general store. Grandpa sent her to order a part for the tractor." Lark set the rocker in motion. "You're wearing my patience mighty thin, Mrs. Heath."

Then, as soon as the words left her mouth, Lark guessed the happy secret Bryony had been holding in. She shifted sideways to clasp her sister's arm. "Bryony...are you...?"

A tear rolled down Bryony's cheek as she smiled the biggest smile Lark had seen on her face in ages. "I wasn't completely sure until I talked to Dancy this morning." Dancy was a house-maid at the Heaths' who did some midwifing. "She said all the signs are there, and if we've figured right, the baby's due near the end of July."

"Oh, Bry! I'm so happy for you!" Clambering from the rocker, Lark crushed her sister in a hug, and they cried together until their tears turned to laughter. Out of breath, Lark sank back into the chair but didn't let go of Bryony's hand. "Who else knows?"

"Well, Michael, of course, and Dancy. And now you, because I just *had* to tell you or I'd burst." Bryony's expression grew serious. She stole a quick look across the yard. "But don't say a word to anyone else yet. Not even Rose or Grandpa. Once I see our doctor in Brinkley, I'll feel more comfortable sharing the news."

Worry snaked around Lark's heart. "You don't think anything could be wrong, do you?"

"No. No!" But Bryony's eyes told a different story. "It's just taken us so long that I need to be sure everything's all right with the baby."

"Of course you do, honey. And I know it will be." Lark brushed away another tear. "It'll be the most beautiful, most perfect baby ever in the world!"

Bryony nodded fiercely. "If it's a girl, I want to name her Iris, after Mama. I miss her now more than I ever thought possible."

"She'd be so thrilled. And now I'm gladder than ever that I didn't go back to school so I can be around to help with my new niece or nephew."

Bryony's big-sister frown furrowed her brow. "Well, that is one thing I am *not* pleased about. I wanted so badly for you to finish college."

"I will...someday." At least she fully intended to. But then, as these last several years had taught her, nothing in this life was certain. "In the meantime, I'll absorb all I can about teaching while helping Anson with his foundation." Looking off in the direction of Eden, Lark murmured, "I can't wait to hear back from him about the house I found. I wish now I'd gone to Little

Rock with you so I could have told him all about it in person."

When Lark recognized the meaningful glint in Bryony's eyes, she gave a huff. "Don't you dare start. Bad enough Rose hasn't let up since Thanksgiving. I'm telling you, I have absolutely no interest in Anson Schafer other than helping him bring education to Arkansas's needy children."

With a sad smile, Bryony smoothed aside a stray lock of Lark's hair. "Just because you were burned once doesn't mean it'll happen again."

"No, it certainly won't." Arms crossed, Lark faced forward and kicked the rocking chair into motion. "Because this time I'm going with my eyes wide open."

* * *

Anson didn't care to wait on mail service to respond to Lark's letter. That same afternoon he had the operator ring up the Eden general store. A fellow named Joe said he'd be happy to take a message out to the Rigby farm soon as he closed for the day. In the message, Anson said he would like very much to see the house Lark mentioned and asked if Thursday would suit her schedule. The next morning he telephoned Joe again to get Lark's reply, which was a happy yes.

True, at no time during their conversation had Joe used the word *happy* in regard to Lark's reaction, but Anson took pleasure in picturing her bright smile and imagining she might actually look forward to seeing him again. One might easily disguise one's true feelings behind the crisp wording of a letter, but face-to-face, the subtle tilt of a head, shuttering of the eyes, or quirk of one's lips could reveal myriad unspoken sentiments.

A truth that cut both ways, however. Would Lark see past his carefully guarded words to the deepening affection he felt for her? Or was it too late already? And how would he manage working alongside her every day if ever she told him outright to expect nothing from her beyond their mutual interest in bringing education to disadvantaged children? As he continually reminded himself, his myriad flaws guaranteed he was no woman's ideal catch.

Then why did the mere thought of Lark's smiling azure eyes and silky, straw-colored waves make his heart trip like that of a lovesick schoolboy?

"Anson, get your head out of the clouds. We're almost there." A touch of humor laced Irwin's sharp tone.

Anson had most definitely failed to hide his feelings from his friend. Shifting in the passenger seat of Irwin's Ford, he blinked several times and looked ahead as the town of Eden came into view. Lark had said to meet her at the parsonage next to the church—the only one in town, so not hard to find—and from there, Pastor Unsworth would take them to see the house.

As they turned into the driveway between the church and the parsonage, Anson made out Lark's slender form on the front porch of the brown cedar shake bungalow. Wearing a pale blue sweater over a gray dress, she waved and started down the steps, followed by a rotund, balding man in a black suit and clerical collar.

Anson was right—even through his dark glasses, there was no mistaking the happy glint in her eyes as she waited for him to step from the car. She hurriedly made the introductions and then said the widow's house was only a short walk down a side street. Pastor Unsworth led the way.

Anson fell in step beside Lark. "You seem as intrigued by the possibilities as I am."

"Why wouldn't I be? There's nothing I'd like more than bringing help to my own community." Her businesslike reserve was firmly back in place. "If you decide to take the house, how soon could we become operational?"

How he did love the word *we*! Smiling to himself, Anson pretended to ponder her question, and much longer than necessary, since after Lark's letter arrived on Monday, he and Irwin had done little else but prepare. "It would depend upon how soon we could take possession. Shouldn't take more than a week or two to settle in and set up an office. In the meantime, we can start getting the word out—a task I'll definitely rely on your help with."

"I've already begun a list of families we should contact. Miranda and Daniel—Bryony's sister-in-law and her husband—will be a big help, too." Lark grew quiet for a moment, then added hesitantly, "Have I mentioned Daniel Vargas is from Mexico?"

Anson's steps slowed as he tried to interpret Lark's thoughts on the matter, but her tone implied neither approval nor condemnation. "No, I don't believe it's come up."

"We all like him very much," she hurried to say, and Anson relaxed slightly. "But some people aren't very accepting of nonwhites. I'm sure you can imagine how hard it's been for him and Miranda, not to mention their children."

"No doubt." They'd reached a run-down two-story clapboard house. While Irwin and Pastor Unsworth continued on to the front door, Anson paused beside a rickety fence shot through with brambles. "Remember, Lark, I grew up in Africa. My boyhood playmates were all children of color, but to be honest, I never really noticed. If it weren't for the prevailing attitudes here in the South that have confronted me every day since my return, I still probably wouldn't give a second thought to the color of a person's skin. So if you're concerned about my openness to your friend Daniel, don't be. I look forward to meeting him."

She studied him for a long moment, and a tentative smile turned up one corner of her mouth. Then, glancing toward the house, she said, "There's Mrs. Jenkins. Let's go look around."

A stooped woman with iron-gray hair invited them in. "T'ain't much to look at, but I ain't had no help around this place since

Mr. Jenkins went to his heavenly reward nigh on four years ago."

"We are deeply sorry for your loss," Irwin offered. He ran his thumb across the peeling paint on the parlor doorframe but made no comment other than a short sniff.

Anson edged past Irwin into the parlor, aware of the floorboards giving under his feet. Dry rot, no doubt. Or termites. Yes, the house definitely had its problems. He scanned the room, where several boxes were stacked against the parlor walls and muslin sheets covered most of the furniture. Though not a large room, with the interior wall at one end where a blackboard could be mounted, the space could easily be converted into a classroom.

"Dinin' room's across the hall," Mrs. Jenkins said, then motioned vaguely over her shoulder. "Kitchen's back thataway. And upstairs is four bedrooms. We had indoor plumbing installed the year afore my husband died." She reached for a wall switch, and the room brightened. "Got electric lights, too. All the modern conveniences."

"Indeed." Irwin's smile belied the concerned glance he shot toward Anson before sidling into the hall. "May we look upstairs?"

The foursome traipsed after Mrs. Jenkins for a tour of the upper story. The creaking steps and wobbly banister must definitely be looked at, or someone would end up with a broken neck.

When the woman opened the door to one of the bedrooms, the knob fell off in her hand. She cast them an embarrassed grin. "Told ya the place needed work."

Anson peeked into each of the rooms, mostly bare of furniture except for the bedroom Mrs. Jenkins used, and all of them in desperate need of cleaning and a fresh coat of paint. While

Mrs. Jenkins had her back turned, he shot a questioning look at Irwin.

Irwin hiked his brows and shrugged. Aloud, he said, "Let's take another look downstairs and then talk, why don't we?"

After a perusal of the dining room, kitchen, and a small workroom at the rear of the house, Mrs. Jenkins took them back to the parlor. She whipped the sheets off two side chairs, taking one for herself and offering the other to Pastor Unsworth. Anson gingerly sat down on the dusty settee, with Lark in the middle and Irwin at the other end.

Pastor Unsworth rubbed his palms nervously along the creases in his slacks. "I can see you're worried about the amount of work this place needs. Mrs. Jenkins is more than willing to negotiate a fair arrangement, though."

Anson and Irwin had already agreed that with Irwin's sharper administrative skills, he would make the final decision. Yes, the old house needed significant repair work, but perhaps because of Anson's weakened eyesight, he could more easily see beyond the superficial to what the place *could* be. A schoolroom in the parlor, the foundation office in the dining room, living quarters upstairs, and a grassy expanse behind the house where children could run and play between lessons. He could almost smell the chalk dust and hear the sounds of children reciting their times tables or Longfellow's "The Song of Hiawatha."

He slid a glance toward Lark. She sat stock still, fingers knotted in her lap as she listened to the negotiations and scarcely breathed, as if what happened here today would decide not only Anson's future but hers as well. He'd give anything for the courage to reach for her hand and enfold it in his own.

Then he heard Irwin saying, "I believe we've come to an agreement. Will it be rushing you to move out by the end of next week?"

"Nope." Chin lifted, Mrs. Jenkins spoke firmly. "My son's coming this weekend with his pickup and a trailer. Anything we leave behind, you're welcome to use or pitch, as suits your fancy. Lord knows I ain't gonna have no more use for it."

They stood and shook hands all around, and the old woman showed them out. The pastor seemed as relieved as she, probably because if they hadn't come to terms, he'd have been stuck with the upkeep in Mrs. Jenkins's absence. On the walk back to the parsonage, Pastor Unsworth rattled on about different folks around town who'd be more than willing to hire themselves out for repair work.

This time, Lark took the lead in their conversation. "Lots of people are hurting for work, Pastor, and we'll keep the local folk in mind. First, though, I want my grandpa to give the house a once-over. We'll decide from there what we can do ourselves and what we might need to hire done."

Irwin nodded his approval. "Excellent idea, Lark." He thanked the pastor for his time, then offered Lark a ride back to the farm.

"Thanks, but I drove Grandpa's pickup. Y'all are welcome to come out and join us for supper if you've the time."

Without consulting Irwin, Anson replied, "We'd be delighted."

Chapter Nine

Rose was batting cobwebs from beneath the sagging porch roof when Caleb drove up to the Jenkins place. She propped the broom against the rail and sauntered down the steps to meet him. "Hey. Glad you could spare the time to come by."

"Anything for a dollar." Caleb winked. "And for you."

Heat raced up Rose's neck. Brows drawn together, she aimed a withering stare at the boy who'd been her best friend since grade school. "I'm not the one hiring you. This is strictly Mr. Schafer's operation."

"Uh-huh. But you're the one who drove all the way over to our place to ask if I wanted the work." Caleb ran an appraising eye across the front of the house. "Yep, the foundation's gonna need shoring up. And some of these window frames will have to be replaced."

"Ain't that what Grandpa already said?" Rose wedged irritation into her tone, because being irritated with Caleb Wieland was so much safer than admitting her admiration. When the drought hit, Caleb had given up college to look for work so his family wouldn't starve. Then his pa's heart started going bad, and they'd buried Nels Wieland about a year ago. Now Caleb took care of both his mother and their tenant farm, also part of the Heaths' Brookbirch Plantation.

"You should know by now I like to check things out for myself." Caleb kicked loose a piece of rotting wood at the base of one of the porch steps, then grinned at Rose, clearly giving *her* the once-over. "And don't you know *ain't* ain't a word?"

Rose harrumphed. "I'll use *ain't* whenever it suits me, thank you very much. Maybe you ought to get busy figuring out what supplies you're gonna need instead of giving me grief."

With a barely suppressed snicker, Caleb tossed his mop of honey-golden hair and pulled a pencil stub and water-stained notebook from his overalls pocket. From another pocket, he tugged out a folding carpenter's rule. "It'd sure help if you wrote while I measured."

"Fine." Rose held out her hand for the pencil and notebook. She pretended annoyance but couldn't deny the enjoyment she took in watching Caleb Wieland work. Except for maybe Lark, she'd never known anyone smarter. Whatever Caleb set his hand to, he managed right well. Until he'd dropped out of college, Rose had always believed he could have been a doctor or lawyer or maybe even president someday. Sure woulda done a better job than ol' Hoover.

Sad how hard times had compelled first Caleb and now Lark to set their college dreams aside. The world was a cruel place sometimes—the war that took Daddy from them, the tornado that killed their mother, the devastating floods of 1927, and now this endless drought. Rose wondered sometimes if they'd ever see better days again.

But she, like her sisters, was a fighter. More important, she had faith in a God who loved his children enough to go to the cross for them, a God who walked beside them—or carried them when necessary—through both trials and triumphs.

Caleb called out a measurement, and Rose scrawled the numbers in the notebook. Moving on down the porch, he glanced over his shoulder. "Can't figure how Schafer's gonna convince the families round these parts to send their kids here when they can't even make it to class at the county school."

"He's got a plan, that's all I know." Rose wrote down the next figure Caleb gave her. "Lark says he'll arrange his lesson schedules so the kids can do what's needed at home but still keep up with their learning."

Caleb snorted. "If they've got any energy left after working the fields all day."

"Yeah, but if they don't get educated, working in the fields all day is all they can ever aspire to."

"Somebody's got to raise the crops and livestock that put food on our tables." The abrupt stiffening of Caleb's shoulders told Rose she'd hit a nerve. He blew out long and slow as he measured a cracked windowpane. "Write down I'll need a ten-by-twelve-inch piece of glass."

Taking more notes, Rose followed him off the end of the porch and around to the side of the house. After a few minutes of silence, she said, "I didn't mean you, Caleb. I respect you more than I can say for taking care of your mom and the farm. And I know when things get better down the road someday, you and Lark both can go back to college. You'll get your degrees and do something amazing with your lives—"

"Stop. Just stop, Rosie." Caleb straightened and fixed her with a tired smile. "This is my life now, and I don't see it changing anytime soon. Sometimes we just have to accept things the way they are and make the best of it."

"So...you think Mr. Schafer's school is a wasted effort?"

"I didn't say that." He sighed again and ran his fingers through his hair. "It's all about hope, right? You'll never find me standing in the way of anything that gives people a little more reason to dream."

Rose only wished Caleb didn't seem to have given up on his own dreams.

*   *   *

The wretched brown wallpaper simply had to go. Balancing on the fourth step of Grandpa's stepladder, Lark worked the flat edge of her scraping tool beneath a seam and loosened the paper enough that she could peel back a wide strip. The plaster beneath would need some repair before they could begin painting, but

Lark already pictured how much brighter the room would look in eggshell white or possibly a sunny yellow.

She stepped down from the ladder and moved to the next section. With the windows open to a pleasantly mild afternoon, snatches of the conversation between Rose and Caleb drifted in. When Rose revealed her hopes that Lark and Caleb could both return to college someday, an ugly clump of self-pity lodged deep in Lark's abdomen. The teaching degree she'd always dreamed of now seemed more unreachable than the most distant star.

She couldn't let it slip away, though—she just *couldn't*. And Anson's plans for Schafer School had started an idea percolating. Perhaps she could borrow some college texts and catch up on what she'd been missing. Better yet, she could write to the dean at Henderson and ask about a home-study alternative—

The floorboards creaked behind her, and Lark whisked away a droplet of moisture that had escaped down her cheek. She turned to see Anson in the doorway, his shirtsleeves rolled up, his hair mussed, and ashy streaks across his forearms and face. The sight of him looking so different from his usually proper self banished her restless musings and brought a smile to her lips.

"What have you been doing?" she asked with arched brow. "Rolling around in a dustbin?"

Anson scoffed. "Might as well have been. It appears Mrs. Jenkins hadn't cleaned out her stove in months." He narrowed his eyes and surveyed the parlor, now empty except for Lark's ladder and a growing pile of wallpaper scraps. "I see you've been busy."

"I'd rather look at pitted plaster all day than *this* unsightly stuff." Lark cast a disdainful glance at the ragged section of paper she'd been battling. Then a twinge of guilt niggled at her. "Paint shouldn't cost much, should it?"

Cautiously pinching a piece of the discarded paper between

two fingers, Anson examined it more closely. "Whatever it costs to be rid of these hideous brown…whatever those swirly designs are supposed to be…will be money well spent."

"Then I'd better keep peeling." Reassured, Lark adjusted the ladder and started up the steps.

"I was about to clean up and have a cup of coffee and one of those oatmeal cookies Mrs. Unsworth brought over." Anson set one hand on the ladder, steadying it. "Take a break and join me. You've earned it."

Looking down, Lark realized how close Anson stood. She drew a tiny breath and swayed.

"Easy there." His free arm encircled her waist, and she was too wobbly to resist leaning into it.

"I'm all right now. Thank you." With a nervous laugh, she shrugged off his arm and inched down the ladder. "Yes, I—I think some coffee and cookies would hit the spot."

While Anson washed up at the sink, Lark filled two mugs from a vacuum flask and set them on the scarred table Mrs. Jenkins had left behind. When she pulled aside the napkin covering the plate of cookies, it was clear someone had already been feasting on them.

Dr. Young appeared in the doorway, grime coating the knees of his dungarees and a guilty look on his face. "Temptation got the best of me, I'm afraid."

Grinning, Anson accepted the coffee mug Lark handed him. "At least you maintained enough self-restraint to save some for the rest of us." He moved the plate farther out of Dr. Young's reach. "So, Irwin, what have you accomplished upstairs?"

"Scrubbed the bathroom top to bottom. Swept out the bedrooms and knocked a few cobwebs off the ceilings." Dr. Young helped himself to some coffee. "Have you decided when you want to move in?"

Anson bit into a cookie and chewed thoughtfully. "The sooner, the better. The house is livable, so we can continue with the refurbishing while we settle in."

"And classes?" Lark asked, her anticipation rising. "How soon before we open our doors to students?"

"Finishing the classroom is a top priority. I've ordered a chalkboard from Little Rock, and with your grandfather building us some simple desks and chairs, I'm hopeful we can begin lessons the first of February."

Dr. Young carried his mug to the window and looked out over the backyard. "Let's not get the cart before the horse, Anson. A school without students isn't worth much."

Here, at least, Lark could prove her worth in ways other than stripping wallpaper and scrubbing floors. "I've already talked with Daniel and Miranda Vargas about spreading the word among the Brookbirch Plantation tenant farmers. And with county schools resuming classes this week after the Christmas break, I'm planning to pay a visit to the superintendent and explain what we're doing here."

"Then I should go with you." Anson drained his coffee mug and set it in the sink. "Do you think he could see us tomorrow morning?"

His intention to accompany her struck an unexpectedly sour chord. Did he not think her capable of handling such a discussion on her own? "Superintendent Thornton goes to church here in Eden and has known me most of my life. I believe I stand a much better chance of gaining his support than you would as a newcomer."

Anson removed his glasses and silently began polishing them with a towel. "Of course, you're right," he said after a moment, and Lark winced at the hurt in his tone. "Irwin can provide you with our credentials and any other information you think might be helpful."

"I only meant it might be best for me to make the first contact," Lark hurried to explain. "Then I'm certain Superintendent Thornton will be most interested to meet you."

"Then I'll wait to hear how your meeting goes." Anson's smile seemed forced. "And now I'd better check with your friend Caleb and find out how much of a dent these repairs are going to make in our budget." Sliding on his glasses, he gave a curt nod and stepped outside through the back door.

Left alone with Dr. Young, Lark stared at her half-eaten cookie. "I've offended him."

"I perceive the feeling is mutual." Dr. Young offered her a kindly pat on the shoulder. "You two have more in common than you might think, you know."

"How do you mean?"

"For one thing, you're both idealists. For another..." With a sly grin, Dr. Young reached for another cookie. As he nibbled slowly, Lark curbed her growing curiosity. Finally, he winked and stated simply, "Perhaps I should let you both figure it out for yourselves."

"Wait, you can't leave it at that." Lark blocked his way as he started from the room. "In the past several months, I've altered the course of my life not once but twice. For reasons only God knows, Anson Schafer has ended up in the center of those changes, and now—"

"And now you're questioning the influence Anson has had on your choices."

"Shouldn't I? I mean—" She closed her eyes. It was true, she found Anson's gentle ways and solid sense of purpose beguiling. How could she ever be certain of choosing her path for the *right* reasons and not because of others' influence?

"My dear," Dr. Young murmured, lightly touching her arm. She looked up into his warm gaze. "In fact, God *does* know the reason you're here today and working alongside Anson for a noble cause. Our Lord never wastes an experience, but uses it to move us steadily deeper into his plan. Trust him to reveal his purposes in his own good time."

The only response Lark could manage was a quick nod. She stepped aside and allowed Dr. Young to pass. Alone in the silent kitchen, she had to wonder how her own faith had faltered so badly. Mama had raised Lark and her sisters to believe in a God of boundless love, and yet whose plans and purposes were so far above their own that human minds could never hope to comprehend them.

But Mama was dead now, in heaven with Daddy and Grandma, and Lark certainly couldn't comprehend a plan that would remove from her life the people she needed most—especially when she most needed their guidance.

* * *

After a restless night on one of the lumpy mattresses Mrs. Jenkins had left behind, Anson had decided to finish what Lark had begun in the parlor. By late yesterday she'd stripped the horrid brown wallpaper off two walls and part of a third. If he could finish while she met with the school superintendent this morning, they could prime the walls after lunch in preparation for painting.

And maybe when Lark saw the creamy yellow paint color Anson had sent Irwin to search for in Brinkley, it would smooth things over between them.

He still wasn't certain where they'd gotten off track yesterday. One minute they'd been laughing with each other about the wallpaper, and the next, Lark had seemed to take offense at his offer to accompany her to visit the superintendent.

And then *he'd* gotten offended that she didn't want him along.

What puzzled him even more was that this plucky and utterly fetching young woman could reduce him, a grown man in his thirties, to a mercurial bundle of adolescent angst.

"Making progress, I see." Irwin set two paint cans down just inside the parlor door.

"Back already? I didn't hear the car." Anson stepped off the ladder and tossed more wallpaper onto the steadily growing pile in the middle of the room. He glanced toward the front windows. "I don't suppose Lark's on her way back yet?"

"Not yet. But what say I help you get the rest of this ghastly paper down? I'm sure that'll please our young Miss Linwood to no end."

An hour later, they ripped down the last shred, and even with the scarred walls, the room looked a hundred times brighter. Anson gathered up the mess to carry it out to the waste bin, leaving Irwin to mix up plaster for filling the cracks and gouges.

On his way back to the house, he glimpsed a willowy, fair-haired figure striding up the driveway, and his pulse ramped up several notches.

He forced a calm breath. About time he accepted the fact that Lark didn't see their relationship as anything other than two people working for the same cause.

Still, when she waved and called his name, he felt lighter than air. Her cheery smile told him the meeting had gone well, and he couldn't wait to hear the details.

"Irwin picked up a few groceries this morning," he said, meeting her halfway. "Let's make some sandwiches and talk over lunch."

They started around to the back door, but then Lark's steps slowed. "Anson, I'm terribly sorry about yesterday. This is your foundation, and I had no right to assert myself as I did."

"No need to apologize. Your logic made perfect sense."

"Even so, there's no excuse for my defensiveness."

"Nor mine." Anson halted in front of her and offered his hand. "Still friends, right?"

"Yes." She gave his hand a firm shake. "Still friends."

A flicker of something else flashed across her expression, and once more Anson cursed his poor vision. What he wouldn't give for a clearer look into those cornflower-blue eyes to see what lay within.

Entering the kitchen, Anson called for Irwin. After they'd washed up and thrown together some pork roast sandwiches, the three of them sat down for lunch. While they ate, Lark described her meeting with the superintendent.

"He was hesitant at first, unsure why Eden needs a second school." Lark tore off a bread crust and nibbled on the end. "But after I explained the purpose, he thought it was a wonderful idea. He even offered to send out letters to those families to tell them about your program."

"*Our* program," Anson corrected. "We wouldn't have come this far without you, Lark."

Irwin cleared his throat. "Pardon me, but isn't Eden's school for whites only? Those children represent but a small portion of the families we hope to serve."

"That's true." After chewing a bite of sandwich, Anson sipped from his water glass. "I've made it clear from the outset, I don't want our doors closed to any child with the willingness and capacity to learn. We have to extend our reach."

Lark dabbed her lips with a napkin, then spoke carefully. "I understand, and I agree. But you keep forgetting this is Arkansas, not Kenya. There is little tolerance for the intermingling of races."

"*Intermingling?*" Anson shoved his chair back. "We're talking about educating children. Who cares what color—"

Irwin's hand shot out. "Anson. Calm down. We knew there'd be issues."

"I don't like it either," Lark said. "I think discrimination is abominable, and everyone in my family feels the same. But you'll risk reprisal if you attempt to put whites and blacks in the same classroom."

Unable to contain himself, Anson burst to his feet. He wasn't oblivious to the race problem in the South, but he clearly hadn't given it enough weight. He paced the small kitchen. "Then we'll hold separate classes, two evenings a week for the white children and two for the blacks."

Irwin and Lark exchanged tense glances. "It may not be enough," Lark said. "Some white folks will be opposed to allowing their children to use the same classroom—much less the same desks—as the colored children."

Anger flared in Anson's chest. "We're all human beings, aren't we? Beneath the color of our skin, what's different?"

"You're preaching to the choir." Irwin rose and briefly rested a hand on Anson's shoulder. "The three of us here aren't going to change a century of Southern prejudice. We'll have to settle for making small differences where we can."

Anson ground his teeth. "Then I suggest we get started. If a single classroom won't satisfy, we'll create two." He pulled open the door to the small workroom off the kitchen and peered at the cluttered space. "This will do for an office. It'll be crowded, but that way we can turn the dining room into a second classroom."

Satisfied, or at least mollified, he swung around and started for the front of the house. If he had any hope of welcoming students in the next few weeks, they still had much to accomplish. He hadn't planned to do much in the dining room except move in a couple of office desks and a worktable. Now he needed to reevaluate the space. Half the size of the parlor, it could still handle four small student desks and a slightly larger one for the teacher. He'd need to order another chalkboard as well.

His mind racing with adjusted plans, Anson snatched up the tin of wall plaster and a putty knife and set to work filling cracks in the parlor walls. He wasn't sure how much time had passed before Lark came up beside him with her own plaster and tools. She'd donned a muslin apron and had tied a kerchief over her hair.

She dabbed a spot with plaster and smoothed it out. "Dr. Young showed me the paint he bought. The color is perfect."

"Glad you like it." It took all his focus to pay attention to the wall in front of him and not to her nearness.

They worked in tandem, Anson patching the chinks along the upper part of the wall and Lark touching up the lower section.

After a few minutes, Lark said, "Caleb said he'd start tomorrow on the foundation repairs."

"Yes, I heard." Anson's next step brought an ominous creak from a floorboard. "I'll breathe a lot easier once that's done."

More silence followed. They reached a corner and started on the next wall.

Coming to a window, Lark paused and flicked a loose strand of hair off her forehead. "I hope our conversation over lunch didn't discourage you too badly."

The strain of squinting to see the holes and cracks had brought on a headache. Or maybe it was the result of confronting all the holes and cracks in his dream. With a stifled groan, Anson stepped away and set down his plaster tin. As complicated as the situation had become in Kenya, at least there he'd known what he dealt with. America presented a whole new set of challenges, and reminders like today's caused him to doubt he was up for them.

"Maybe I should just go back to Kenya."

He didn't realize he'd spoken aloud until he felt Lark's hesitant touch. "Tell me you don't mean it, not after all the work you've done to make this school happen."

When he raised his eyes to meet hers, he saw the confusion there. The disappointment. The dread. "No, no," he said, pushing two fingers up under his glasses to massage the bridge of his nose. "I'm frustrated, that's all. I've already been forced to admit my initial hopes for the Schafer Foundation were too grandiose. When we decided to scale back, I saw Eden as a stepping stone toward branching out into other communities. But now I'm faced with the reality that even here I may not be able to reach all the children who desperately need education."

"You can't think that way." Lark's grip on his arm tightened. "No matter how many children pass through these doors, or how few, every child you help is one more who'll have a better chance in life."

He heard her words, and he treasured them more than he could say. But in this moment, looking into her eyes, feeling the warmth of her hand on his arm, only one clear thought made its way to the surface: *I am falling in love with this woman.*

Chapter Ten

By Sunday, Lark was ready for a Sabbath rest. Anson and Dr. Young had cleaned out the workroom to use for office space, Caleb had made rapid progress on exterior repairs to the house, and the new schoolroom glistened in a pleasing shade of pale yellow.

Lark wasn't quite so pleased she'd ruined a perfectly good housedress with paint spatters, though.

Bryony and Michael attended church in Eden Sunday morning, and afterward Lark took her family over to the Jenkins house to show them all that had been accomplished. Stepping through the front door, though, she felt an inexplicable emptiness, then realized she'd been waiting for the sound of Anson's voice in greeting.

But he and Dr. Young had left yesterday afternoon for Little Rock and wouldn't return until later in the week, when they planned to bring some furnishings and personal belongings. Dr. Young would keep his residence but offer it for use by the missions aid society as temporary housing for missionaries home on furlough.

Bryony ran her hand along the freshly polished banister. "The house looks so much better than the last time I was here. It was definitely more than old Mrs. Jenkins could manage alone."

While Grandpa, Michael, and Rose wandered through the rooms, Lark lingered in the entryway with Bryony. "You're glowing, you know. I've never seen you happier."

Resting a hand on her abdomen, Bryony gave a tiny shiver. "I don't know how I can wait seven more months to meet our baby!"

"Hmm, doesn't seem as if you have much say in the matter."

Lark grabbed Bryony's hand and led her into the parlor. "I'm an experienced painter now, so when you're ready to decorate the nursery..."

Making a slow circle, Bryony nodded in admiration. "I don't suppose it's exactly been torture working alongside Anson this past week."

"Don't change the subject." Lark had to suppress a shiver of her own. Bryony's remark stirred unsettling reminders of the look in Anson's eyes last week right here in this room. Lark's hand tingled again at the memory of clasping his arm as she'd sought to encourage him in those troubling moments. For the next few days she'd kept a polite distance between them, and yet she missed him.

Missed him horribly.

"Why do you fight it, Lark?" Bryony's soft whisper severed the silence. "If love is meant to be, it will find a way. Trust me, I know."

"Don't be silly!" Hugging herself, Lark marched to the front windows. "I'm working for Anson's foundation because I care about his cause. We're friends and associates, that's all."

"The only one being silly here is you, baby sister. If you'd only—"

Footsteps echoed from the staircase, and Grandpa's voice rang out. "Yes, indeed, that Clyde Barrow's a bad'n. Done killed another lawman, this time somewhere near Dallas."

"Nowhere's safe, Grandpa," Rose stated. They reached the foot of the stairs and traipsed into the parlor. "Anyway, you don't need to be talking about scary stuff like that. It's giving me the heebie-jeebies."

"Same here," Bryony said with a shudder. "I don't care to hear about some bank robber shooting up half of Texas." She sauntered over and looped her arm through Lark's. "I'm ready for Sunday dinner. How about you?"

Lark was more than ready to leave the lonely Jenkins house behind. She rode back to the farm with Michael and Bryony, which turned out to be a mistake since Bryony wouldn't stop dropping hints about how Lark should be open to something more than friendship with Anson. Michael, sensibly, kept his opinions to himself and his eyes on the road.

Fortunately, Bryony let up once they got busy putting dinner on the table. Over fried ham, mashed potatoes, and turnip greens, Bryony prodded Michael to reveal his latest venture.

"It's nothing, really," he said with his typical reserve. "Just more botanical illustrations."

"Not *just*," Bryony insisted. "The journal editor Michael's been working with wants to publish his drawings in a book."

"That sounds exciting." Lark rose to fetch the water pitcher. She'd always felt a modicum of pride that she'd played a small part in connecting Michael with the university publisher.

"It's exciting...and also daunting," Michael said as Lark refilled his water glass. "I never imagined my drawings would matter to anyone besides myself."

Bryony squeezed his hand, her gaze filled with adoring love. "I always knew."

"You certainly did." When Michael leaned close for a kiss, Lark lowered her eyes.

"No smoochin' at the dinner table," Grandpa barked, but a snicker belied his gruff tone.

Grandpa had softened as much as anyone toward Bryony's husband. Michael and his sister might be heirs to Brookbirch Plantation, but they certainly never put on airs like their father, Sebastian Heath.

Thinking of Miranda Vargas, Lark made a mental note to visit with her later. It would be good to have some responses from the Brookbirch tenant families to share with Anson when he returned.

*   *   *

By Tuesday, Anson and Irwin had made substantial progress in packing for the move. Out of breath, Anson stacked another box in the front hallway. This one rattled with pots, pans, and utensils from Irwin's kitchen.

"Look out below!" came Irwin's shout from the upstairs landing.

Immediately afterward, an overpacked brown suitcase careened down the steps like a bobsled. Anson had to jump to one side to avoid being flattened.

Fists planted at his belt, he glared up at his friend. "You're supposed to carry things down, not toss them willy-nilly and risk killing someone in the process."

"You're young and agile. No harm done." Irwin heaved another suitcase closer to the top step. "Besides, there is a limited number of up-and-down trips these ancient legs can handle. I find my method far less taxing."

Anson burst out laughing as he dodged the next onslaught. He maneuvered Irwin's luggage into position next to the stacks of boxes, then returned to the kitchen to fill another container. The pantry and cupboards looked emptier by the hour. Irwin had already set aside a few kitchen items to leave behind for returning missionaries to use. Everything else they'd need to set up housekeeping in Eden.

He could hardly wait to get back. Caleb should be well along on repairs by now, and Lark had said she wanted to give the workroom a fresh coat of paint before they turned it into an office.

He wondered if she missed him even half as much as he missed her. Waking, sleeping...she was never far from his thoughts.

A touch at his elbow nearly shot him through the ceiling. "For pity's sake, Irwin, don't sneak up on me like that!"

"Daydreaming again? Shame, shame." Irwin snatched the spatula from Anson's hand and dropped it into the box. "Surely it's teatime. Put the kettle on. I'll make us some cheese and crackers."

"Food is all you think about."

"And a certain young lady is all *you* think about, so we're even."

"Not even close." Anson despised being so transparent. Unfortunately, his best friend and mentor knew him entirely too well. He filled the kettle and set it on the stove, then started for the front door. "I think I heard the mail arrive."

Weaving between the packing boxes, he made his way to the mail slot. Several letters lay scattered beneath. He gathered them up, pausing over a well-traveled envelope with a Kenyan postmark. He recognized Sister Mary John's handwriting and called the news to Irwin.

"What's she say?" Irwin set a plate of sliced cheese and saltines on the table.

Anson handed him the letter. "Your eyes are better than mine."

While Irwin read aloud, Anson set out cups and prepared the tea. Relief washed over him to learn that Matumaini School seemed to be holding its own despite the changes in Kenya. Franklin Keene had fostered good relations with the locals, and the teacher training program showed promise.

"See? You've left everything in good hands." Irwin laid the letter aside and handed Anson a slice of cheese. "Now you can turn your full attention to getting Schafer School up and running."

His full attention? How was that even possible, when a part of him would always remain in Kenya?

And then there was Lark. She distracted him in ways he'd never have imagined.

* * *

Early Friday morning, a small moving truck pulled into Irwin's driveway, and by midafternoon three muscled movers had loaded the truck with furniture and packing crates. Anson climbed into the passenger seat of Irwin's car, which was also weighed down with luggage and personal items, and the two-vehicle caravan set out for Eden.

When Irwin parked in front of the Jenkins house—no, now it was the Schafer Foundation House—Anson hardly recognized the place. The front yard had been spruced up, the porch didn't sag nearly as much, and someone had apparently started painting the siding because scaffolding had been erected along the exterior west wall.

"Impressive," Irwin murmured as he pushed open his car door. "Our friends have been busy."

"I'll say." Anson stepped out onto the driveway.

Then someone appeared at the front door and waved. Anson didn't need perfect vision to know it was Lark, and his heart gave a stutter.

Before he could make it to the porch, Caleb Wieland came around from the back, followed by two lanky, dark-skinned men in paint-speckled overalls. "Afternoon, Mr. Schafer. Hope you don't mind I engaged a couple of helpers." Caleb lowered his voice slightly. "I told 'em you couldn't pay much, but they're plenty happy to work for food and a little cash to take home to their families."

Anson wasn't sure the extra help was in the budget, but he nodded with a benign smile. The men hesitated at his offer of a handshake, almost as if they thought it was some kind of test. He had to remind himself again that this was Arkansas, not Kenya. He introduced himself and asked their names.

"I'm Zeke Jackson," the taller man stated. "This here's my brother Noah. We's sharecroppers on Ol' Man Pockett's farm. We's much obliged for the work, Mr. Schafer."

"And welcome to it." Anson glanced toward the house and saw that Irwin and Lark were showing the movers inside with the first load. Returning his attention to the Jackson brothers, he asked, "Do you men have families? Children of school age?"

"I got me three young'uns," Zeke replied. He scratched his chin. "They's mebbe twelve, ten, and seven, by my reckoning. But they ain't got time for schoolin'. Leastways, the colored school's too long a walk."

Anson nodded thoughtfully. "And you, Noah? Any children?"

"Two strappin' sons near grown to men—they's farmin' alongside me—and a purty little girl no bigger'n a bug." Noah flashed a wide grin. "She already learnin' to make cornpone good as her mama. Might cook for a rich family someday."

The pride in Noah's tone couldn't disguise an underlying sense of hopelessness…of inevitability. Anson inclined his head toward the house. "Did Mr. Wieland tell you what we're doing here?"

"'Deed he did, sir." Zeke shuffled his feet. "We best get on with the paintin', if that's all right with you, sir."

"Of course." But as they sidled away, Anson called after them, "I hope you'll think about sending your children here. I'm sure we can arrange lesson schedules to suit your family's needs."

The men tipped their hats in reply and continued around back, leaving Anson with the distinct sense that he wouldn't be seeing their children anytime soon.

He hoped Lark would have news of more positive responses from the Brookbirch Plantation tenants.

Caleb stepped into his line of vision. "I'm headed out to the Rigby farm to help George with your bookshelves and desks, but rest assured the Jackson brothers are reliable. They should finish up the house painting in a couple days, and then if there are any other odd jobs you can think of, I know they'd be obliged."

"I'll keep that in mind. Thank you, Caleb. For everything."

"See you tomorrow, then. And don't feel too bad about their standoffishness about sending their kids here. They're just wary is all. White folks haven't always treated them so kindly."

Anson's mouth flattened. "You don't have to explain."

Caleb went on his way, and with a tired sigh, Anson strode to the front porch. The movers were just carrying in the desk from Irwin's study. Anson waited while they maneuvered it through the door, then followed them to the workroom. Again, he was pleasantly surprised. The room seemed much brighter with a fresh coat of the same yellow paint they'd used for the parlor-turned-schoolroom.

"What do you think?" Lark had come up beside him.

"It seems larger with the light-colored walls and all the clutter gone." Their elbows brushed, and Anson savored the moment.

One of the movers yelped a curse as a leg of the desk slammed down on his toe. "Watch it, Clyde! I don't got but ten toes, and I need all of 'em!"

Anson grimaced at the man's foul language, but it gave him the perfect excuse to take Lark's arm and usher her out of earshot.

The dining room seemed like the safest vantage point for keeping an eye on things. The movers had already stacked several boxes along the walls, so Anson dusted one off and offered it to Lark as a seat.

As one of the movers passed by with a small chest of drawers strapped to his back, Lark glanced up with a smile. "With all the furniture arriving, it seems even more real."

Looking down at her, his breath catching at the back of his throat, all Anson could think was how utterly *unreal* it seemed that a woman should entrance him so completely.

He straightened abruptly. "I should find Irwin. He'll want a say about how the office is arranged."

"I think he took some things upstairs." Lark stood. "Should I start unpacking some of these boxes?"

"Good idea. Don't bother with the books, though. We'll wait on those until your grandfather brings the shelves he's building."

Another smile stretched brightly across Lark's face. "I can't wait for you to see the furnishings Grandpa and Caleb have been working on—ever so much nicer than the old church pews we sat on at the county school. Only the best for the Schafer Foundation students."

Recalling his conversation with Caleb and the Jackson brothers, Anson succumbed to more doubts. More to himself than to Lark, he said, "If only we can convince these families we're here to help them."

"They'll come, Anson. It may take time, but once the word gets out, they'll come."

He prayed she was right.

*   *   *

Another Sunday dinner with the Heath family and a year and a half after marrying Michael, Bryony still felt the awkwardness.

Odette, the Heath family's longtime cook, paused next to Bryony's chair with a tureen and ladle. "More soup, Bry—I mean, *Miz* Heath?"

"I have plenty, thanks." Bryony knew the plump woman's self-correction was nothing more than a friendly gibe. They'd forged a bond two years ago when Miranda, disinherited by her father years earlier for marrying Daniel who was the Heaths' groundskeeper at the time, had shown up at the mansion pregnant and near starvation. Bryony's offer to shelter Miranda at Grandpa's farm had earned her the respect and gratitude of the other Heath servants.

Now, against all odds, the entire clan regularly dined together at the same table. Sebastian had reinstated Miranda in his will and over time had gained a modicum of respect for Daniel. And though he hid it well, Bryony suspected he was developing a fondness for his grandchildren, Callie and little George, named for Bryony's grandpa.

Bryony swallowed another spoonful of Odette's delicious tomato soup, then laid aside her spoon. The morning sickness hadn't become too bothersome so far, but today her queasiness stemmed from a different source. This was the day she and Michael had agreed to break the news of her pregnancy to their families.

In truth, they hadn't really *agreed*. Bryony had begged Michael to wait another few weeks. "Just in case," she'd reasoned. They'd been waiting and hoping so long for this baby, and Bryony almost couldn't believe it was real. Neither could she shake the rising sense that something would happen to steal away their happiness.

But Michael kept insisting she had no basis for such fears. "Where's your faith, Bry? Look at all we've overcome already." Besides, as he often reminded her, she'd always been the one with unshakable faith, while he'd struggled to regain his after the bitterness that had almost destroyed his family and the war that nearly took his life.

Odette cleared the soup bowls and brought out the main course, roast chicken with rice and purple hull peas. Across the table, Callie seemed as uncomfortable as Bryony about being served. They exchanged helpless glances as if both fought the urge to rise from their seats and give Odette a hand. Bryony supposed she and Callie would always strain against the fit of their new positions in the Heath family.

Michael must have sensed Bryony's unease. Beneath the edge of the tablecloth, he reached for her hand. She loved this man with every fiber of her being, and she'd grown to love Michael's family, too, although perhaps *love* was rather too strong a word to describe her attitude toward Sebastian, except in the most Christian sense. But as a young girl dreaming of her future, she'd never envisioned her life this way, a complicated mix of simplicity and grandeur, openness and reserve.

Lost in her thoughts, Bryony scarcely heard the dinner table conversation going on around her. By the time Odette appeared

again to serve dessert and coffee, Bryony had barely touched
her meal. Arching a brow as she cleared Bryony's plate, Odette
smiled a secret smile, which Bryony quickly erased with a brisk
shake of her head. Odette's lips flattened in understanding, but
she couldn't hide the twinkle in her eyes.

Once again, Michael squeezed Bryony's hand. "Everyone, if I
could have your attention for a moment—"

A gasp sounded from the other end of the table as Michael's
mother, Fenella, toppled her water goblet. "Oh dear," she
muttered. "Oh dear, oh dear, I've made a mess."

Sebastian moved quickly to sop up the spill with both his and
Fenella's napkins. "It's all right, darling. No harm done."

"But it's all over everything! The tablecloth, the carpet, my
dress—" Tears streamed as Fenella's agitation grew, an increasingly troublesome aspect of her dementia.

Bryony scooted her chair back and motioned for Callie.
The two of them had always been the best at settling Fenella
during one of these episodes. "We'll take her upstairs," she told
Sebastian. "She'll be fine."

Except she wouldn't, not really, and Bryony's heart wrenched
at the love and despair filling Sebastian's eyes. When she glanced
Michael's way, the pain she saw there was just as deep. He
started to rise, a helpless grimace twisting his face, but Miranda
reached across the table to stop him. There was little any of
them could do, anyway, except let time run its course.

Yet as disturbing as it was to witness each new episode of
Fenella's decline, Bryony couldn't deny her relief that Michael's
announcement had been interrupted.

*　*　*

Lark knew the moment she saw Bryony step from the car
that something was wrong. Her thoughts flew immediately to
Bryony's pregnancy, and she dashed out the back door of the
farmhouse to meet her. "Oh, Bry, what's happened?"

"Stop your fussing. I'm fine." Bryony offered a weak smile as Michael held the porch door for them. "Fenella had a bad spell while we were finishing dinner. It took a while to settle her down."

"I'm so sorry." Lark cast Michael a sympathetic frown.

He shrugged. "We were going to tell my family the good news today, but with all the hubbub, it didn't seem like the best time."

"Well, you can still tell everyone here." Lark linked arms with Bryony as they strode through the screen porch. "Rose and Grandpa have a four-handed pinochle game going with Anson and Dr. Young. Grandpa and Rose are losing badly. I think they're ready to throw in the towel."

Bryony hung back. She swiveled her head toward Michael. "Let's wait. Please. I'm just not ready."

He shot her a despairing look, part confusion and part frustration. "What are you so worried about? The doctor says you couldn't be healthier. Everything's fine with the baby."

"I can't explain it. Can you please just accept that I need more time?"

Lark felt she should leave them alone to work this out, so she stepped quietly through the kitchen door and closed it behind her. It wasn't like Bryony to be so anxious, and that fact alone was enough to worry Lark. Since Mama died, Bryony had been the family's anchor, the one who held them fast when hard times came and hopes foundered.

Triumphant laughter burst out at the table, and Rose tossed down her cards with a groan. "That's the last game for me. They've humiliated us enough, Grandpa." She pushed back her chair. "Where's Bry? I thought they just drove up."

"They'll be in in a minute." Lark went to the stove. "I'll start fresh coffee."

Anson joined her. "Let me help." Lowering his voice, he asked, "Is everything all right?"

"I'm sure it will be." Surprised that he'd picked up on her concern, she couldn't help being touched. She'd hesitated to ask Anson and Dr. Young out to the farm for Sunday dinner, but since they had no other friends in Eden, it seemed the only polite thing to do. Besides, the men still had much to do to get their own kitchen organized and stocked. Lark had tried to help, but she'd barely made a dent in sorting through the boxes after the movers left.

With more chicory-laced coffee on to percolate, Lark suggested they move to the parlor. As the kitchen emptied, she tiptoed to the back door and peeked through the glass. Her heart clenched at the sight of Bryony quietly sobbing into Michael's chest. He caught Lark's eye and shook his head. Clearly, he was as bewildered as Lark.

"I'm taking her home," he mouthed, then guided Bryony out to the car.

Fingers to her lips, Lark watched them drive away. When she turned back to the kitchen, she found Anson standing behind her.

"Don't pretend with me," he said. "Something's wrong."

"I—I can't talk about it." She brushed past him to check the coffeepot.

"Is it your sister? Is she ill?"

"No, not ill." Lark began to wish Bryony had never confided in her about the pregnancy. But then she'd worry even more about Bryony's odd behavior. This surely was nothing more than a first-time mother-to-be's apprehension.

She decided she had to tell someone or burst. With a nervous glance toward the parlor, Lark motioned for Anson to follow her out to the porch. It was another mild afternoon, but even so, Lark shivered.

Anson clasped her upper arms, his touch tender but insistent. "You're scaring me, Lark. Tell me what's going on."

After a quick breath, she blurted it out: "Bryony is going to have a baby, and for some crazy reason, she's afraid that—" She hugged herself as tears of frustration slid down her cheek. "Honestly, I'm not sure what she's afraid of. This isn't like my sister at all."

She didn't know what she expected Anson to say or do, but his next action took her so by surprise that for a moment she couldn't breathe. Slowly, tenderly, he drew her into his embrace and kissed the top of her head.

"I'm sorry," he murmured. His encircling arms felt warmly comforting, a shelter from her torrent of emotions. "I wish I knew how to help."

Abruptly she pushed away, embarrassed by her lack of restraint. "I'm sure Bryony's worried for nothing, as am I." She marched to the kitchen door. "Excuse me, I should check the coffee."

By midweek, Lark had the Schafer School office in good order—books shelved, file cabinet organized, and her own small but comfortably arranged worktable settled in the corner, complete with a portable Royal typewriter. Serving as school secretary seemed the next best thing to actually teaching, and she intended to make the best of it.

The encouraging response she'd received from Henderson about the possibility of home study had also lifted her spirits. At some point she'd have to return to campus in order to complete her studies and graduate, but her advisor had agreed that certain basic courses could be handled through correspondence.

On Thursday, Anson's voice carried from the main classroom, where he directed the installation of the recently delivered chalkboard. "A little to the left and about a foot higher, please. I don't want the teacher's desk blocking the children's view."

Caleb Wieland and Daniel Vargas were doing the heavy lifting. The Jackson brothers had finished the exterior painting yesterday and now were doing some additional sprucing up in the yard. They seemed immensely grateful for the little Anson paid them, mostly in the way of cornmeal, flour, and canned goods from the general store.

However, Anson hadn't fully concealed his disappointment, at least from Lark and Dr. Young, about the Jacksons' lack of interest in sending their children for lessons.

After several more thumps and bangs, it sounded as if the men had successfully installed the chalkboard. A few minutes later, Daniel Vargas tapped on the office doorframe. "May I interrupt you, Miss Linwood?"

"Of course, Daniel." She shifted in her chair and shot him an accusatory smirk. "If I've told you once, I've told you a hundred times. Call me Lark. We're family, after all."

"Sorry." With a sideways glance, he stepped farther into the room. "Unfortunately, my in-laws still seem less like family than you."

"Bryony feels the same. I know it's hard." Motioning toward an empty chair, Lark invited Daniel to sit. "Thanks for coming over to help today."

"It was not my only reason. I have spoken with most of the Brookbirch tenants. Three families have expressed interest in your classes." Daniel tugged a slip of paper from his breast pocket and handed it to Lark. "Mr. Schafer said to give you the names."

"This is wonderful—thank you!" Lark scanned the list of children ranging in age from six to thirteen. She recognized two of the families as church acquaintances; the third must be new to the area. "And the other tenants? Any chance more will follow suit?"

"I cannot say. But as I make visits to the farms, I will encourage them."

"That's all we can ask."

Daniel started to rise, then sat again. "May I ask your advice on another matter?"

"Certainly. Anything." Laying aside the list, Lark looked up expectantly.

"Callie, my daughter—she is very bright and eager to learn. I would like to see her go to college someday, like you."

A surprised breath caught beneath Lark's breastbone. "I'm sure Callie would excel as a college student. Has she applied anywhere?"

Daniel's face hardened. "Her name is Vargas. I do not know what school would accept her."

"That's so unfair." Yet, sadly, all too true, and it made Lark's insides roil.

"Fair or unfair, to the Anglos we are nothing." Daniel's straw hat lay in his lap. He rolled the ragged brim between his fists. "It is only by an act of God that I have not already been deported. Last year my relatives in San Antonio were forced to return to Mexico."

"Daniel, I'm sorry. But how could they deport you? You're a legal citizen now."

"They would not care whether I have citizenship papers, only that my skin is brown." He heaved a pained sigh. "It is happening every day in Texas. The Anglos fear the Mexicans will take jobs that are rightfully theirs. Even when I went north two years ago to look for work, I found only the one employer willing to hire me, and he paid me practically nothing."

Lark ground her teeth. She looked again at the children's names Daniel had given her, all of them white. Anson would be glad for the students but disappointed they had yet to cross racial lines.

Remembering Daniel's question that had given rise to this discussion, she hiked her chin. "You asked for advice about Callie and college. I would do anything in my power to help, if only I knew how, but—"

"I thought perhaps if you were to instruct her…" Daniel sat forward and reached across the space between them to touch her arm. "At least it would be a start, and perhaps in a few years the ways of this world will change."

Lark glanced at his work-worn, nut-brown hand resting on her white sleeve, and her heart ached for the day when his vision for a more accepting future would become reality. "All right," she murmured. "Tell Callie I'll be happy to teach her what I can."

Daniel rose and clasped both Lark's hands. "Thank you, more than words can say."

When Daniel had said his good-byes, Lark took a moment to compose herself. Had she done the right thing in agreeing to tutor Callie? She'd kept all her college textbooks, too attached to part with them even for the money she might have sold them for. It would be lovely to revisit them with an intelligent young woman like Callie. Not to mention she could use this opportunity to further her own studies.

Yes, indeed, her dream of becoming a teacher could still become a reality.

With a satisfied nod, she opened the journal she'd designated for the school's student roster and began recording the children's names. As she entered the last one, Anson strode through the door. Sleeves rolled up and hair askew, he looked hot and disheveled.

Lark shut the journal and stood. "You look as if you could use a cold drink."

"I was thinking the same thing. It's warm for the middle of January."

"That's Arkansas for you. Unpredictable." Brushing past him into the kitchen, Lark asked, "How's the new chalkboard?"

"Looks fine. Nothing like a clean slate to start a new school semester." Coming up beside her, Anson took glasses from the cupboard.

Lark reached inside the refrigerator freezer for a tray of ice cubes. This was a luxury she didn't enjoy at the farm, where without electricity they still kept food chilled in an old-fashioned icebox. Old Mrs. Jenkins had used an icebox, too, but on Monday Dr. Young had had the electric refrigerator delivered from Brinkley. Electric appliances, electric lights, even a telephone in the office. Such conveniences made it hard to return home to the farm every evening.

After filling their water glasses, Lark sidled toward the office with hers. "I should get back to work."

"You've been at it all day, barely took ten minutes for lunch." Anson pulled out two chairs at the kitchen table. "Here, sit and rest awhile. I intend to." He plopped down and stretched out one leg.

Eying the empty chair so close to Anson's, Lark shook her head. "I have a few more things I want to finish in the office before I go home."

"Of course." Anson's agreeable reply didn't match the disappointment that flickered across his expression. Sipping his water, he shifted his gaze toward the window. "Irwin should be back from Brinkley soon with more classroom supplies. Let him know when you'd like him to drive you home."

"He doesn't have to. I can walk."

Anson set down his water glass with a thunk and rose to his feet. He stared hard at Lark, his mouth in a twist, and she waited for him to say something but no words came. Moments later, he strode past her and out of the kitchen, leaving her to wonder what she'd said or done to upset him so.

She couldn't worry about it. She had more important things with which to concern herself. Like office work. Farm chores. Teaching Callie. And most of all, which subject to choose for her first home-study college course. She couldn't afford to waste one single ounce of energy on anything extraneous to her immediate goals.

*　*　*

Anson stood on the front porch, hands thrust in his pants pockets and his chest heaving. Could Lark have made herself any plainer? She felt nothing for him but the respect and friendship of a colleague. Why did he imagine things could be otherwise?

He closed his eyes briefly while berating himself for wanting more, and when he opened them, one of the Jackson brothers stood before him at the bottom of the steps. Squinting against the slanting winter sun, Anson couldn't distinguish the man's features clearly. "Noah?"

"Yes, sir. We's done weedin' and trimmin', sir. The yard look to your satisfaction?"

Moving down the steps, Anson swept his gaze across the front lawn. He barely made out the neatly edged stepping stones leading to the street. The fence line appeared clear of weeds and the pickets newly whitewashed. The empty flowerbeds awaited spring planting, the soil lightly fragrant from yesterday's brief rain shower.

"Looks fine. I appreciate all you've done." Anson extended his hand. He held it there until Noah reluctantly took it, then gave a firm shake. "Come around back to the kitchen, and I'll pay you. Oh, and Mrs. Unsworth brought over two sweet potato pies this morning. Far more than we can eat, so I hope you'll take one off our hands and share it with your family."

"Most obliged, Mr. Schafer. You's treated us real fine." Noah walked with Anson around the side of the house. "If ever you got more work for me and Zeke, you just ask."

"I will." Anson stepped inside briefly to fetch the pie, then took a few bills from his wallet. As he passed the money and pie tin to Noah, he reminded him that classes would start soon. "It's no cost to you, and the schedule won't interfere with your children's chores at home. Please, just think about it."

Noah nodded thoughtfully as he stuffed the money into his shirt pocket. "I been thinkin' about it, yes indeed, and I can see how it might be a good thing." He looked off into the distance. "I just ain't sure it's a smart thing."

The reminder of those infernal Jim Crow laws set Anson's teeth on edge. "We'd take every precaution to avoid trouble. We'll have separate—" His throat closed that he even had to mention this. "Separate classrooms for your children, and we'll hold their lessons on different days than the white children. It'll all be handled very discreetly."

"Cain't say I know what that word means, Mr. Schafer." Noah gave a raspy laugh. "Maybe I oughta come to school, too."

"And you'd be most welcome." Anson immediately warmed to the idea of helping erase illiteracy among the children's parents.

"*Discreetly* simply means we intend to be wise and cautious in how things are run here. We don't plan to take any risks with your children's well-being."

"Good to know. I'll ruminate on it some more, and God bless you for your kindness, sir."

When Noah strode from the shaded back stoop into the bright afternoon, Anson had to look away. A dull ache had begun behind his eyes, and he pressed his thumb and forefinger deep into the hollows beneath his brows. He should be more mindful of keeping his dark glasses handy for these trips outdoors.

He turned to step inside, but the thought of encountering Lark again made him hesitate. Which was foolishness since their work at Schafer School would continue to throw them together on a daily basis. What had he done to himself, bringing this woman into his life, then daring to hope something might grow out of their friendship and shared commitment to education? Could he bear to be near her every day and keep things strictly platonic, when there were moments—too many of them lately—when all he could think about was how her lips would taste beneath his kisses?

So much for his confirmed bachelorhood. He'd thought himself immune to such feelings, or that at least he had reached an age where dreams of love and marriage and family could be permanently discounted. Lord help him, he was in trouble now!

He'd almost steeled himself to take his chances inside and get back to work when Irwin's car rumbled up the driveway.

Climbing from the car, Irwin called, "Anson, my boy, give an old man a hand, will you?"

"Old? How about ancient as the pyramids?" Anson strode over, glad for this distraction from the direction his thoughts had taken. "Did you find everything we needed?"

By now, Irwin had the trunk open. "Pencils, tablets, rulers, two copies each of those primers and mathematics books you asked for—enough to get us started, anyway."

Again, Anson wished for his dark glasses. The glare made it next to impossible to see much of what the boxes held. He lifted one from the trunk. "Maybe when a few more donations come in, we'll be able to purchase more textbooks."

Irwin reached for the second box and followed Anson into the house. They deposited everything in the larger classroom. Irwin shrugged out of his jacket, then set to work sorting the supplies and lining up the books in the bookcase George Rigby had delivered yesterday.

Picking up one of the texts, Anson struggled to focus on the cover page, but the printed words blurred before his eyes. Frustration burned beneath his sternum. Even his glasses weren't helping today.

He sensed Irwin studying him. "Your eyes are bloodshot," Irwin stated. "Go lie down and put a cool cloth on them for a bit. I'll finish in here."

"I'm all right. I'd rather keep working." Anson pulled another book from the box, its title no clearer than the one he'd just examined. His jaw muscles bunched.

Gently, Irwin slid the books from his grip and set them on the shelf. "What's going on, Anson?"

He sank onto a nearby chair, tugged off his glasses, and palmed his eye sockets. He refused to admit that his vision might be worsening. He couldn't afford to lose more of his sight, not now. Not when the school was days away from opening. He'd been compelled to relinquish Matumaini School to someone else's leadership. Would he now be forced to lay aside his hopes and plans for the Schafer Foundation?

He wouldn't. He couldn't...

"It's nothing," he said, pushing to his feet. "But you're right— I've been fighting a headache all day. A rest and a cool cloth might be just the ticket."

"Good idea. You go on upstairs." With a hand to Anson's shoulder, Irwin guided him to the front hall.

Reaching for the newel post, Anson paused. "I told Lark you'd drive her home when she's finished for the day."

"My pleasure. I'll check on her momentarily." Irwin stared at Anson a little longer than was comfortable, then gave a thoughtful nod before returning to the classroom.

Upstairs Anson found a clean washcloth in the bathroom and wet it under the faucet. With the shades drawn, he stretched out across his bed and laid the folded cloth over his eyes, letting the coolness soak through his lids.

What would it be like to be blind, to see nothing more than dim, hazy shadows, or worse, inky blackness? Could he remain a productive contributor to society...or would he become entirely dependent on others? Bad enough he already depended so heavily on Irwin. What would he do without his dear old friend?

But Lark—oh, Lark! Even if she were ever to return his affections, he couldn't inflict his disability on her. She deserved more, so much more.

*   *   *

By four thirty, Lark had finished typing the last of the thank-you letters to the foundation's most recent donors. As she affixed stamps to the envelopes, Dr. Young stepped into the office. "I thought I heard you come in," she said. "Did you need help putting away the supplies?"

"All taken care of." He circled behind the larger desk and plopped into the chair. A look of consternation skewed his expression as he glanced through a file folder.

Lark approached the desk. "I have these letters for Anson to sign. Is he..."

"I'll sign for him." Reaching for a pen, Dr. Young looked up with a weak smile. "He has a headache. I sent him upstairs to lie down."

A tiny sigh of relief slipped out. Lark didn't think she could bear to face Anson again today, not with so much hanging between them unspoken. She handed Dr. Young the letters, and he scrawled Anson's name at the bottom of each one. His ease at replicating Anson's signature made her suspect he'd done it many times before.

Dr. Young returned the pages to her, and as she folded them and inserted each one into its envelope, he said, "We can drop those at the post office on the way to your house."

"But I told Anson I'd walk. There's no need—"

His fatherly glare, laced with his natural good humor, silenced her. "There's every need, or I'll get an earful from Anson in the morning. Now get your things and let's be off. I don't know about you, but this old body's ready to call it a day."

A few minutes later, they stopped at the general store, and Lark ran in with the letters. She handed them to Joe, then waited while he checked her post office box.

"Yep, here's a couple things for your grandpa and somethin' for you, too, Miss Larkspur." Joe thrust the envelopes beneath the grate. "Oh, and here's some mail in the Schafer School's box if you don't mind taking it."

"Glad to. Dr. Young is waiting in the car." Lark thanked the clerk and started for the door while perusing the return addresses on Grandpa's mail and hers.

Seeing Mrs. O'Neill's name on one of the letters, she drew up short. She hadn't heard from her former boss since the day she'd learned the O'Neills were closing their grocery. It would be wonderful news if Mr. O'Neill's health had improved and he'd seen his way clear to reopen.

In the car, she passed the school's mail to Dr. Young, then pried open the flap of Mrs. O'Neill's letter. As they started toward the farm, Lark anxiously began reading. Halfway down the page, she sucked in a gasp.

Dr. Young glanced over briefly. "Not bad news, I hope?"

It was worse news than Lark could have imagined. She pressed shaking fingers to her lips. "Mr. O'Neill passed away on New Year's Day."

"I'm terribly sorry. This was your friend in Arkadelphia, wasn't it?"

"The kindest man ever. He gave me a job in his grocery while I was working my way through college." She blinked back tears, unable to finish the letter. "I can't believe he's gone!"

With a tender pat on her arm, Dr. Young drove on in silence. When they pulled up beside the farmhouse, Lark could only sit there and let the tears flow.

Dr. Young handed her his handkerchief. "It's clean, I assure you. There, there, my dear, cry all you need to."

She sniffled and handed him the letter. "Please read me the rest."

"Yes, yes, of course." Dr. Young scanned the page. "...*passed quietly...didn't suffer....* And here she writes, *You were always Benjamin's favorite of all the students who worked at the store. He loved you like a daughter.*"

A sob caught in Lark's chest, and she nodded firmly. "I loved him, too."

Dr. Young continued reading: "*He wanted with all his heart for you to finish college, so as his health failed, he made me promise to cash in the liberty bonds he bought during the war and give half the money to you.*"

"What?" Lark snatched the letter from Dr. Young's hands and read the words for herself. "Why? Why would he do such a thing?"

"His wife stated it quite clearly, I believe—because he thought so very highly of you." Dr. Young exhaled slowly and laid his hand on Lark's shoulder. When she met his gaze, he said, "My dear, I believe you have a decision to make."

*   *   *

With one ear cocked toward the back door, Rose scraped the last of the butter from the churn into a ceramic dish. She'd seen Dr. Young's car drive up several minutes ago and wondered why Lark hadn't come in yet. It was time to get supper on the stove, and Rose was plumb worn out from chores. Surely Lark hadn't used up near as much energy working in her cozy little school office. Anyway, it was Lark's turn to cook.

A full ten minutes later, Lark dragged herself inside. Rose could tell right away that her sister had been crying. She dropped the butter churn innards into the crock and rushed over. "What's wrong? Did something happen at the school?"

Tearfully, Lark relayed the news about her friend the grocer.

"Oh, Lark, I know how much you admired him."

"There's more. Read this." She handed Rose the letter and then collapsed at the kitchen table.

Seconds later, her thoughts in a dither, Rose joined her. "Oh, my. This is…" She swallowed, part of her thrilled that Lark had a chance to finish college and an even bigger part dreading another two years of just Rose and Grandpa left to work the farm. Even longer, if Lark got her degree and went off to teach somewhere besides Eden. "What are you going to do?"

"I don't know. I've hardly had time to let it all soak in." Lark mopped her cheeks with an oversized white handkerchief that already looked wet enough to wring out in the sink. "Can you manage supper without me? I'm not hungry, and I need some time alone to think."

"Sure, go on." Rose watched her sister trudge toward the bedroom.

She'd just fetched a couple of shriveled potatoes and a jar of beans from the root cellar when Grandpa came in from the barn. "Saw Dr. Young drive away. Where's Lark?"

"Resting. She had some upsetting news." While Rose peeled potatoes, she told him about Mrs. O'Neill's letter.

"Liberty bonds—if that don't beat all." Grandpa washed his hands at the sink. "Maybe Lark can register late and still get some classes in for the spring term."

Rose pursed her lips. "But what about Mr. Schafer and Dr. Young? They're just about to open the school."

"They'd understand. Anyways, in the long run, Lark would be more use to them if she was a real teacher, not just glorified office help."

"But that'd be a couple years down the road, and in the meantime, they'd be struggling along to run things without her."

Grandpa stood at Rose's elbow as she chopped the potatoes into chunks. "You sure you're worried about how they'd fare at the school, or are you just dreading being stuck here with your ol' grandpa and having to do all the cooking again?"

She frowned. "Maybe a little of both. You know I want the best for Larkspur, but I miss her something awful when she's gone. I almost couldn't let her go off to Africa thinking I might not see her for a year or more."

"But this ain't about you, is it, Rosie-girl? Much as I'd miss her, too, I know in my heart that each of my girls has to find her own way in this world." He released a low groan as he massaged his lower back. "I ain't gonna be around forever, so all's I want is to see each one of you make happy lives for yourselves."

"Don't talk like that, Grandpa." Rose's voice grew gruff. She fixed him with a hard stare that barely held back the tears suddenly pooling along her lower lids. "It's gonna be you and me working this farm for years to come. Promise me, okay?"

The corners of his eyes turned down in a sad smile. "Sure, Rosie. You and me, come what may."

Deep in her heart, she knew it was a hollow promise, but she'd hold on to it for as long as she could.

Chapter Twelve

Anson fumed in the passenger seat of Irwin's car the next day. "I don't have time for this, and you know it."

"But you have time to go completely blind, is that it?" They were halfway to Little Rock, headed to the ophthalmologist's appointment Irwin had insisted upon. "Lark will see to things at the school today."

"And you didn't tell her the real reason for this trip? You're certain she doesn't know?"

"I was very discreet, just as you ordered."

Even with impaired vision, Anson couldn't mistake his friend's scowl. Arms crossed, he watched the blurry scenery fly by. "I simply didn't see any point in causing her further concern until we know more."

"You mean until the doctor confirms you've overstrained your eyes and insists you take better care."

Anson blew out sharply through his nostrils. "You're worse at bossing me around than Sister Mary John ever was. Why do I put up with you?"

"Because no one else on God's green earth would put up with what I put up with from *you*!"

An hour later they arrived at the ophthalmologist's office. After a thorough exam and reviewing the records Anson had brought from the doctor he'd seen in Norfolk, the grim-faced man presented Anson with his conclusions. "The corneal scarring has spread but not significantly. However, your eyes have weakened enough that your current prescription isn't helping."

"So…a stronger pair of glasses should do the trick, right?"

"In the short term, perhaps." The doctor rubbed his chin. "But I suspect the deterioration is progressive. Are you wearing your dark glasses out of doors?"

"When I remember."

"Remember more often, then. With any eyestrain, whether from reading or exposure to bright light, you risk compromising your vision even more. And once you get past a certain point, not even glasses will help."

As they left the office, Irwin stated, "You've been warned. Now, what are you going to do about it?"

Halting in the middle of the sidewalk, Anson faced his friend, visible only as a shadow through the green-tinted lenses. "What would you have me do—give up the Schafer Foundation and all I've set out to accomplish? Besides, I believe it was you who insisted that even sightless, I could still make a valuable contribution to society. So I'm not crawling into a deep, dark cave never to read a good book or look into a sunlit blue sky again."

"And no one's asking you to." Irwin hooked his arm through Anson's and propelled him down the street toward where they'd left the car. "But maybe you need to step back—just a little, not entirely—and turn over more of the burden of the school to someone else."

"It isn't a burden; it's my calling. My life's mission." They'd reached the car. Anson slumped into the passenger seat, fatigue and frustration like lead weights upon his shoulders.

Irwin climbed in behind the wheel but didn't start the motor. "Yes, it's your mission, but you aren't in it alone. You know you have my complete and utter support. But perhaps it's time to bring a few others onboard. Some volunteer teachers, an office assistant..."

"I admit we could use another teacher on staff, but Lark is doing wonders organizing the office. She's also quite capable of tutoring younger students."

Irwin's prolonged silence spoke volumes.

Anson shot him a nervous glance. "What? What aren't you telling me?"

"I'm sorry, Anson, but my lips are sealed. If you want Lark to stay, you need to ask her yourself." He started the car and pulled into the street.

When Anson realized his friend would say nothing more on the subject, he gave up trying. They stopped by Irwin's house to check on things, then called on a pastor who had been collecting donations of money and school supplies for them. Preoccupied with other thoughts, Anson struggled to keep his mind in the conversation.

They arrived back in Eden long after Lark had gone home for the day. She'd clearly been busy, though. The six student desks her grandfather and Caleb had been crafting now sat in two straight rows facing the chalkboard. On each desktop Lark had placed two sharpened pencils and a lesson book. Across the top of the board she'd printed the alphabet, both capitals and lowercase, in large, neat letters. The globe Irwin had purchased in Brinkley sat on the corner of the teacher's desk.

The sight raised a lump in Anson's throat. He could imagine eager students filling the desks, primers open to the day's lesson. He could imagine the pride in their eyes when they conquered an arithmetic problem or learned a new spelling word. He could imagine them years down the road when what they'd achieved here propelled them to better lives than they'd ever dreamed possible.

What he couldn't imagine was not being part of it all. Being relegated to an advisory position at best—or worse, only the owner of the name over the door.

Irwin joined him in the doorway. "Our dear girl has been quite busy today. Wait until you see what she left us in the kitchen."

It turned out Lark had cooked up a pot of split pea soup earlier, and all they had to do was heat it up for their supper. She'd left a note on the kitchen table, which Irwin read aloud:

"Enjoy the soup. I won't be in tomorrow—much to catch up on at the farm this weekend."

The soup was delicious, but the prospect of going another entire day without seeing Lark took the edge off Anson's appetite—as if the day's events hadn't already taken their toll. Irwin had said Lark needed to be asked to stay, but why? She'd hardly spoken a word to Anson yesterday but had kept busy with typing letters, inventorying supplies, and arranging shelves and cupboards. Did her increasing coolness toward him mean she was contemplating her resignation? Had he done something, said something, to upset or offend her?

What would it take to win her back? And even if he could, after what the doctor had told him today, did he dare try?

* * *

A spate of warm days had led up to the weekend, and Lark took full advantage that Saturday. Shortly after Michael and Bryony were married, Michael had brought over iris rhizomes and daffodil bulbs from his mother's garden. With the drought still hanging on, they had sparingly hand-watered the plants, but when the first blooms appeared the following spring, the splashes of color had brightened Grandpa's eyes like nothing had in years.

"It's like your grandma's back," he'd said that day with a tear in his eye. "Special memories, yes, indeed."

Lark wanted to make sure the ground was ready for early-spring growth, so once the house was cleaned and laundry on the line, she slipped on her gardening gloves and knelt in the earth to loosen the soil and weed the beds.

The work also gave her time to think, not that she'd done much else since receiving Mrs. O'Neill's letter. She needed to send a reply soon, but how could she respond to such a generous gift when she wasn't yet certain whether she should accept? Lark longed to talk everything over with Bryony, but with her sister's worries over her pregnancy, Lark didn't want to trouble her further.

It was a relief on Sunday, though, to be met with a much calmer Bryony when Lark, Rose, and Grandpa arrived at church. Michael seemed relieved as well. He pulled Lark aside to tell her Bryony had had another checkup, and both the doctor's reassurance and encouragement from Dancy, Mrs. Heath's maid, seemed to have gotten through.

"New mama jitters, they called it," Bryony said with a tremulous laugh when she joined their conversation. "I'm doing my best to put all my worries on the Lord."

"Then are you ready to tell the rest of the family?" Lark asked.

"After church, when we come out for Sunday dinner." Then an uneasy look flickered in Bryony's eyes. "Will Anson and Dr. Young be there?"

Lark's throat shifted. "I didn't invite them this time. Figured they're settled enough to return to their normal routines."

Bryony's lopsided frown said she didn't put much stock in Lark's reasoning.

Overhead, the church bell pealed, and Lark started for the door. Before she made it up the steps, Bryony caught up and pinched her elbow. Close to Lark's ear, she murmured, "After Sunday dinner, you and I have some talking to do, little sister."

Lark almost regretted her earlier thoughts about missing Bryony's listening ear.

Then during worship, Pastor Unsworth preached on 1 Corinthians 13:12, the passage about seeing in a mirror dimly. The words reached deep, cutting to the heart of Lark's torment: *Now I know only in part; then I will know fully, even as I have been fully known.*

She needed wisdom. She needed clarity. She needed hope.

Over dinner at the farm later, Michael and Bryony made their announcement, and Lark endured the expected chiding over being the first to know and then keeping the news to herself. "What was I supposed to do?" she said with a feigned pout. "Bry swore me to secrecy. And let me tell you, *not* telling was one of the hardest things I've ever done."

Rose nearly choked Lark with a one-arm hug around the neck. "Well, all's forgiven since we're gonna be aunts—praise be!"

Happy as he was, Grandpa couldn't disguise the tremor of his lips nor the moisture pooling beneath his eyes. Lark suspected his thoughts had followed hers and her sisters' to the graves of Mama, Daddy, and Grandma, loved ones whose presence was always missed a little bit more at times like this.

Once the hubbub had died down and the table had been cleared, Bryony drew Lark aside. "Time for that talk you promised me."

Lark dried a plate and set it in the cupboard. "I didn't *promise* anything. You insisted."

Even so, she didn't resist when Bryony led her out to the porch and aimed her toward one of the weathered wooden rocking chairs. Bryony scooted one closer for herself. "All right, what's going on with you and Anson?"

"What kind of a question is that?"

"The kind that says I know good and well you have feelings for him. Yet when I asked about him earlier, you snapped shut faster than the door on one of Grandpa's rabbit traps."

Arms crossed, Lark stared straight ahead. "Well, you haven't exactly been real open to conversation lately, sister-dear."

"You're right, and I'm sorry." Bryony's voice softened. "But I'm here now, so talk."

"I'm just...confused, that's all." Rocking harder, Lark sniffed back a wave of emotion. "I have a chance to go back to college, and—"

"You do?" With a gasp, Bryony pivoted in her seat and pried Lark's hand from her side. "Honey, that's wonderful! Did you get a scholarship? Is Anson's foundation sending you?"

"No, no, nothing like that." Lark explained about Mr. O'Neill's bequest.

Now Bryony's eyes filled, and she gripped Lark's hand more tightly. "What a wonderful, kind, and thoughtful man God sent into your life."

"I know. I loved him dearly." Lark stared into her sister's eyes. "But is it the right thing to do?"

"Go back to college? It's your dream. It's what you've waited your whole life for. Why would you—" Then understanding darkened Bryony's expression. She bit her lip. "Anson."

"I made a commitment to him—to the foundation, I mean." Lark shared her news about being allowed to take certain courses via correspondence. "With that option now open to me, how can I just walk away from Schafer School?"

"But don't you think Anson would want you to finish college sooner rather than later? He knows what it means to you—what it would mean to the school in the long term."

Lark shook her head. "The money will always be there, so maybe next year, after the school gets established…"

Releasing Lark's hand, Bryony sat back and rocked, slow and steady. She didn't speak for what felt like forever, and Lark grew anxious about what must be going on inside her sister's head. Bryony had a way of seeing through to the truth of a situation, just like she'd recognized Michael's need to draw again after Sebastian Heath had destroyed his pictures. Just like she'd known exactly how to encourage the bond between Mrs. Heath and her granddaughter by having Callie read to her.

"Lark, I think you're in love with Anson." Bryony spoke the words so matter-of-factly that Lark flinched. "That's why you're having such a hard time with this decision."

"Don't be silly. I have neither the time nor the inclination for romance." Lark wrapped her fingers around the armrests and held herself rigid.

"The only one being silly here is you." Again, Bryony shifted to face Lark. "Oh, honey, don't I know what it's like to fear the promptings of your own heart! But this is a man who cares about you, who *wants* you to fulfill your dreams. If you keep shutting him out, you could lose him forever, and if that happens, you'll regret it to your dying day."

Suppressing a shiver, Lark gazed out across the dry and colorless backyard, then to the flowerbeds she'd been digging in yesterday. She'd peeked beneath the soil, thrilled to see the tiniest tips of green emerging from the daffodil bulbs, a promise of beauty soon to blossom.

She glanced at Bryony. "How did you know? How could you tell what you felt for Michael was love?"

Tears glistened in Bryony's eyes, and she smiled a tender, knowing smile. "I knew it was love when seeing him happy mattered more than my own life. I knew it was love when every moment apart from him felt like ten thousand years."

A tender spot beneath Lark's breastbone began to ache. She'd felt it before, chalked it up to indigestion or fatigue or her overactive imagination. But now she knew it was real, and she recognized it for what it was.

She needed to see Anson.

*   *   *

After Grandpa dropped Lark at the Schafer School Monday morning, she stood for a full minute at the front gate. No decision could be made about returning to college full-time until she settled in her own mind exactly where things stood between her and Anson.

A quiver raced up her spine. You didn't simply walk up to someone and blurt out, "I think I love you. Do you love me?"

No, she'd require a bit more tact, along with a huge measure of Bryony's keen insight.

Sending a quick prayer heavenward, she marched up the driveway. Anson and Dr. Young had told her she needn't bother knocking each morning but to use the kitchen door and let herself into the office.

The moment she stepped inside, she knew something was wrong. Broken glass covered the floor in front of the sink, and a blood-soaked cloth lay on the counter.

Heart thundering, she tossed her handbag on the table and raced through the house. "Anson? Dr. Young?"

"Right here, dear." Dr. Young met her at the foot of the stairs, his hands stained red, and blood streaking his cuffs and shirt front.

Lark rushed forward. "What happened? Are you hurt?"

"Not me. Anson." He grimaced. "He cut himself pretty badly, I'm afraid. I got him cleaned up and bandaged. He really should have stitches, but he won't let me drive him into Brinkley to see a doctor."

"Where is he? Maybe I can help."

"Lying down upstairs. Says he just needs to rest." Muttering a curse, Dr. Young shook his head. "Excuse my language, but sometimes I want to wring his neck."

Feeling her knees about to go limp, Lark clung to the banister and drew several tight breaths. "When I saw all the blood, I didn't know what to think. How did it happen?"

Dr. Young motioned her to the classroom and into a chair at a student desk. Looking none too steady himself, he nudged out another chair and sat down. He stared at his open hands as if studying the bloodstains. "We were making breakfast, and he reached for a glass in the cupboard. But he must not have seen it clearly and knocked it off the shelf. When he grabbed for it, it shattered against the counter. The shards sliced open his palm, and a small one flew up and nicked his face."

Lark covered her mouth to hold back the horror swelling her throat. "There was so much blood. Are you sure he'll be all right?"

"Not at all sure. He's got to be more careful or—" Dr. Young heaved a harsh sigh and looked away. Lark had never seen him so distressed.

Then certainty filled her. "It's his eyes, isn't it? They're getting worse."

Dr. Young nodded grimly. "But if you say I told you, I'll deny it. The boy has his pride, misguided as it may be." He stood slowly. "I need to wash up, and then I'll clean up the kitchen."

"No, let me. You've been through enough already."

He didn't argue, only smiled his gratitude. While he trudged upstairs, Lark returned to the kitchen, stepping gingerly around the broken glass. After hanging her sweater in the office, she used a broom and dustpan to gather up the glass she could see. To capture the tinier fragments, she wet an old towel and dragged it along the countertop then across the floor and into the corners. She took the towel and the bloody cloth out to the incinerator.

From the middle of the backyard, she paused to gaze upward to Anson's window, and her heart turned over in her chest. In that moment she knew, because it was exactly as Bryony had said. This feeling growing inside her, pushing and prodding and stretching her perceptions about every single aspect of her life...this feeling that made her want to align her every hope and dream with those of one gentle man...

It wasn't friendship.

It wasn't infatuation.

It was love.

Chapter Thirteen

Bryony snuggled close to Michael, the precious baby in her womb sheltered between their nestled bodies. "Lark's in love."

He released a knowing laugh and kissed her forehead. "What else is new?"

"You could tell?" She tipped her head back to see him better in the glow of morning. The sun had risen more than an hour ago, but Bryony tended to sleep longer than usual these days.

Although she hadn't minded at all when Michael woke her earlier with his tender kisses and gently persuasive touch.

He nuzzled her neck. "What's more, she's not the only one. Anson is quite smitten as well."

"He told you this?"

"He didn't have to. Having fallen madly in love not so long ago myself, I'm quite familiar with the signs." One arm cradling Bryony, the opposite hand tucked beneath his head, Michael gazed up at the ceiling. "I think he's too afraid to tell her, though."

"Then Lark may have to be the one to speak first." Bryony flopped onto her back next to Michael, their heads touching. "Of course, Lark may hold off on marriage until she finishes college in a couple of years. Then, with her teaching certificate, she and Anson can run Schafer School together. It'll become known far and wide as the place to send your children for a quality education."

"That's quite a vision, but I thought Lark had postponed college indefinitely."

Bryony confided in him about Mr. O'Neill and the liberty bonds. "If Anson truly cares for her, he'll want her to follow her dream and finish school as soon as she possibly can."

At Michael's silence, Bryony raised up on one elbow to look at him. "You don't think she should?"

"It isn't that." Michael sat up and reached for his flannel robe. Slipping it on, he stood and faced Bryony. "What I'm saying is that if they're truly in love, this is a decision they should make together, because when you make such a deep and lasting commitment, your life is no longer *only* about you."

A quiver started in Bryony's belly, a sudden, irrational fear about the sacrifices Michael had made for her. He was heir to Brookbirch Plantation. He could be living in luxury with servants at his beck and call, not in this tiny bungalow with hand-me-down furniture, a moody pregnant wife, and a temperamental cat he'd never really wanted in the first place.

He bent to kiss her forehead. "I'm starved. I'll get breakfast going."

"Michael." She snatched his hand before he could get away. "What dreams did you give up for me?"

"Give up?" His smile turned sadly disbelieving. "How can you ask such a thing, when you've brought so much more into my life than I ever dared to hope for?" He tweaked her nose. "Now get dressed, because I'm making waffles, and afterward, we're going to see my family and tell them our happy news."

Her husband doing the cooking—another sign of how his life had changed since they married, and yet he seemed to enjoy every minute of it.

"You foolish woman," Bryony chided herself aloud. It had to be the pregnancy putting all these worries and doubts in her head.

Worries and doubts she couldn't shake, despite the front she was putting up for the sake of her family. Michael had been so upset with her Sunday a week ago when she couldn't bring herself to share the news about the baby. Once he got her home, they'd talked long into the evening—or rather, Michael had done most of the talking, which was unlike him since he tended to be the quiet one.

But he'd worn himself down trying to convince her she had no cause to be so afraid, until she'd finally given in and agreed he should make her another doctor's appointment, if for no other reason than for reassurance that all was well.

Didn't anyone understand? Doctors couldn't predict the future. They couldn't know for sure Bryony's baby would be all right, that nothing would happen to rob her and Michael of this joy.

So she'd lied. Pretended she was over her fear. Put on a smile and tried hard as she could to make her emotions follow. Sometimes it worked, mostly it didn't. But this was *her* sacrifice for the sake of her loved ones. No reason they should know the forbidden paths her thoughts took, the specters of harm and misfortune constantly shadowing her steps.

She'd keep her eyes on Michael, that's what she'd do. His love, his faith, would hold the fears at bay.

She scrambled from the bed, pulled on a housedress, and scurried to the kitchen. "Need some help, honey?"

*   *   *

Hand throbbing, Anson clenched his jaw against the pain. Against his own idiocy and carelessness. Against the merciless infection that had come close to blinding him and had set all this misery in motion.

He generally despised any leanings toward self-pity, particularly in himself, but at the moment he felt like making an exception. He wanted to wallow in the depths of despondency, to moan and groan and bewail the utter injustice of his fate. He wanted—

"Anson, are you awake?" The door creaked open, and Irwin sidled into the bedroom.

"Of course I'm awake. It hurts too much to sleep." Anson rolled cautiously onto his side and sat up. "We have a mess to clean up, I imagine."

"All taken care of. Are you sure you won't let me take you in for stitches? You'll open the wound if you move your hand much."

"It'll be fine. Just hurts like the dickens."

Coming closer, Irwin used his fingertips to gently probe the area where the glass had nicked Anson's temple. He gave a disdainful sniff. "Any closer and—"

"And I'd be down one eye. No great loss, if you think about it." Anson shoved Irwin's hand away. "Quit fussing over me, for pity's sake. If we're going to be ready for students soon, I need to get back to work."

"I think you should take it easy today. Lark and I can handle things."

At the mention of Lark's name, Anson's stomach swooped. He certainly didn't need her seeing him in this state. "Is she here already?"

"Arrived shortly after your little accident. In fact, she's the one who disposed of the mess you made, bless her kind and noble heart."

Anson hung his head. The thought of Lark dealing with all that glass and blood made him never want to go downstairs again.

"Come now, she isn't going to think any less of you." Irwin marched to the bureau and began rifling through the drawers.

"Any less than she already does," Anson muttered. "And what on earth are you scrounging for. Keep your mitts off my things."

"Oh, quit your bellyaching. I'm just looking for—" Pulling something long and shapeless from the second drawer, Irwin turned in triumph. "This will do nicely. Here, hold still while I make you a sling."

"Wait! Is that my good wool scarf?" Anson tried to jerk his arm away, but Irwin held it firm. Not to mention the sudden movement shot fresh waves of pain all the way to his shoulder.

"I said, hold still!" After tying the scarf in a knot at the back of Anson's neck, Irwin carefully grasped his arm and slid it into the makeshift sling. "There, that'll keep your hand semi-immobilized. It'll also remind you not to use it when you shouldn't so it'll have a better chance of healing."

Stoical endurance was about the best Anson could offer his persistent friend. "You do remember you're a PhD, not a medical doctor, correct?"

"I won't tell if you won't." Taking Anson's good arm, Irwin helped him to his feet. "If you refuse to rest, you may as well come downstairs and make yourself useful."

"Doing what, exactly, since I am now essentially a one-armed blind man?"

Irwin made a rude noise in his throat. "There are none so blind as those that will not see."

Not in the mood for a lecture, Anson didn't dare ask what Irwin intended by quoting Matthew Henry. Instead, he gave himself up to being led downstairs and hoped Lark wouldn't heap more humiliation upon him with either her questions or her sympathy.

She emerged from the office as Anson and Irwin stepped into the kitchen. Anson didn't need twenty-twenty vision to see her glance fall at once to his bandaged hand.

He forced a casual laugh. "Don't be swayed by Irwin's over-zealous use of gauze and this"—he raised his elbow a few inches—"this outrageous sling he insisted upon."

"No, of course not. Hand injuries do bleed horribly." Lark crossed to the stove, where something sizzled in a skillet. "It appeared you never got around to breakfast, so I found some bacon in the refrigerator and thought I'd fry some up. Do you like your eggs over easy or scrambled?"

As if Lark's kindness alone hadn't cheered him, the aroma filling the kitchen was enough to drive all thoughts of the accident from Anson's mind. Mouth watering, he answered, "Either is fine."

Claiming she'd eaten at home, Lark declined to join them but served up plates of perfectly crisped bacon and the fluffiest scrambled eggs Anson had ever tasted. After pouring coffee for Anson and Irwin, she filled a mug for herself and carried it to the office.

At least eggs and bacon required only one hand and a fork. Anson should be thankful he'd injured his left hand and not the right, or he might prove even clumsier while he healed.

When they finished, Irwin rose to clear the table. With a firm nod toward the office, he suggested Anson check on their secretary. "And you might let her know how very much you appreciate and value her."

Interesting that Irwin quite specifically said *you* and not *we*. Slanting a look toward his inscrutable friend, Anson steeled himself and strode through the office door.

A moment later, Irwin came up behind him. "I'll just close this so I don't disturb you while I'm banging around at the sink."

The door clicked shut.

Anson swallowed.

Lark turned from her typing desk and peered up at him. He must have been grimacing, because she asked, "Does it hurt much?"

"Not as badly now." He shot a quick glance toward the closed door. "I, uh…wanted to thank you for…for everything."

"You're welcome." She wouldn't stop looking at him.

He palmed the back of his neck, his fingers catching on the scarf knot and jerking his injured hand. He winced.

Lark jumped up. "Are you sure you shouldn't—"

"Really, it's just a scratch." The air around him seemed suddenly suffocating, or was it only Lark's nearness? In this small room, the office furnishings left little space to maneuver.

"When I saw the broken glass, all the blood..." A shivery breath seeped between her parted lips.

At this moment, being nearsighted was a true blessing as he looked upon that sweet, sweet mouth. His own breath caught somewhere between his heart and his throat. "Lark..."

"Yes?"

"Your being here, working alongside me—I think you should know that I couldn't have done any of this without you."

"Anson, I need to tell you something." Was she crying? Had he bungled this moment so horribly?

"Anything. You can tell me anything." It took all his restraint to keep from reaching out to brush the tears from her cheek. "Have I asked too much of you? Counted on you too heavily?"

"No, not at all."

"Then what?" The tension in her posture, in her voice, seemed ominous. His good hand crept higher. He yearned to cup her cheek but made himself stop at her shoulder, its rounded softness filling up his palm and pulsing waves of longing through him. "Please, Lark, what is it?"

"I—it's just that—" She inhaled slowly and closed her eyes. When she opened them again, she stood a little taller, her face more composed. "I need to go to Arkadelphia. After your accident, I hate even asking, but it would only be for a couple of days. Can you spare me that long?"

A relieved sigh gushed from Anson's lungs. He'd been expecting so much worse! He gave her shoulder an awkward pat before reluctantly dropping his hand to his side. Now he was curious about her reason for this trip. "Certainly you may go. Is there a problem? Anything I can do?"

"I had a letter on Thursday. Mr. O'Neill passed away on New Year's Day." She sniffled but kept her head erect. "I—I want to express my condolences to Mrs. O'Neill in person."

"Lark, I'm so terribly sorry." This time, he couldn't refrain from caressing her tear-moistened cheek. She pressed into his touch, though so briefly he wasn't entirely certain he hadn't imagined it. "Why didn't you say something earlier?"

"I haven't really seen you since I got the news. Plus, it came as such a shock. You and Irwin were gone on Friday, and I needed the weekend to let it sink in, and then I arrived to find..." A weary smile creased her lips as she nodded toward his wounded hand.

He wanted to draw her closer, hold her, comfort her. His fingertips crept deeper into the silky hair at her nape. "You should go home right now. I'll give Irwin the news and ask him to drive you."

Her glance shifted sideways, but blessedly she didn't pull away. Her voice lowered to a hesitant murmur. "Dr. Young already knows. He was with me when I read the letter."

"I see."

"Anson..." There was sadness and hope and a plea all wrapped up in her tone. She covered his hand with her own.

And now he couldn't stop himself. His clasp firm at the back of her head, he feathered his lips across hers and tasted lightly of their inviting sweetness. She gave a tiny gasp and shuddered, but still she didn't move away. He took it as permission to kiss her again, more thoroughly this time, and hoped her moaning sigh was one of pleasure and not regret.

*   *   *

What have I done?

Alone now in the office, Lark sank into her chair and touched two fingers to her swollen lips. She'd wanted Anson's kiss— desperately! But giving herself over to it had terrified her more than anything she'd ever done in her life, even more than when she'd left on her ill-advised adventure to Kenya.

From the other side of the door, she could hear Anson speaking with Dr. Young, probably arranging for her ride back to the farm. Dr. Young knew about Mr. O'Neill's liberty bonds, but Lark hadn't told Anson and didn't intend to. If he thought for one minute she'd passed up this opportunity to return to college full-time for his sake, he'd never forgive her.

But after this morning's accident and what Dr. Young had told her about Anson's worsening eyesight, Lark felt more convinced than ever that, at least for now, her place was here.

It wasn't pity—not entirely anyway, because she did also feel immense sorrow, even anger, over the loss of Anson's sight.

And it wasn't only her dedication to Schafer School, though she'd come to believe wholeheartedly in Anson's vision of bringing education to the poorest of Arkansas's children.

No, it was time to be honest with herself. In the months she'd known and worked alongside Anson, first in Africa and now here in the States, she'd come to see him as more than a mentor, to care for him as more than a friend.

Bryony had been right. Love had swooped in and taken Lark completely by surprise.

She crumpled over, burying her face in her hands. Her whole body trembled with a barely suppressed mixture of laughter and tears. Never in her life had her emotions felt so completely out of control...and yet so perfectly, honestly *right*.

The door creaked open. Straightening, she dried her eyes with a quick swipe of her fingers.

Dr. Young smiled kindly. "Would you like me to take you home now?"

"Thank you," she said, rising to gather her things, "but I think I'd rather walk. I need to—need to—" A hiccup caught in her throat, and she shrugged helplessly.

"I understand." He held the door for her, his eyes saying he perceived more than he'd been told.

Anson leaned against the kitchen counter, his good hand tucked in his pocket. "Be safe, Lark. Please give Mrs. O'Neill our sympathies."

"I will." She gave an awkward nod and stepped toward the back door. "See you in a few days."

On the way out of town, she stopped at the general store and purchased a bus ticket for the following morning. With so much thinking and praying to do, it took her until nearly noon before her meandering route brought her home to the farm. Grandpa and Rose wondered at her early return, until she described Anson's accident and informed them of her change of plans—again—about college.

She left out the part about how she'd wantonly shared a kiss with Anson.

Grandpa hemmed and hawed while he reheated the chicory left over from breakfast. "You sure this is what you want?"

"I'm positive. I feel deep down in my soul that I'm doing the right thing." She showed him the correspondence course information from her Henderson State advisor. "See? I'll still make progress toward my teaching degree. It's just going to take a little longer this way."

Grandpa didn't look convinced, but that was his problem, not Lark's. She spent the afternoon helping Rose tend the vegetable garden, where they'd planted beans, onions, carrots, and beets for an early-spring harvest. They still had to tote water from the backyard pump or the creek, but at least the mild winter had brought a few light showers, which gave faint hope that the onset of summer wouldn't burn the garden to a crisp like the past couple of years had done.

Rose hadn't said much since Lark's announcement, but as she tossed another weed onto their growing pile, she looked over with a frown. "I'm not the least bit sorry you'll be sticking around, but why? I mean, *really* why?"

Her sister's question brought back in crystal clarity the ecstasy of Anson's kiss, and for a moment, Lark could only close her eyes and remember. In the tiniest whisper, she replied, "I think I'm in love with him."

"With Mr. Schafer?" Rose huffed and tugged another weed from the crumbling soil. "Shoulda known. Next you'll run off and get married like Bry."

The suggestion struck Lark like a blow to the chest. She sat back on her heels. "There's no wedding on the horizon, I can guarantee. I'm still—" Well, she couldn't exactly admit she was still reeling from the kiss, not to mention the overwhelming newness of feelings she'd resisted for so long.

Then the true meaning behind Rose's words sank in. Lark leaned sideways across the row of plants between them and pulled her sister into a hug. "Oh, Rosie-girl, don't you know I'll always be your big sister? Nothing can change how much I love you, or how hard I'll fight to keep you safe and well."

Rose squirmed a little but hugged Lark right back. "Careful, you're sounding more like Bry every day."

Which wasn't a bad thing at all, in Lark's mind. She could stand to get her head out of the clouds and do some growing up. It was well past time she started putting others' needs above her own plans and dreams.

Except one particular dream, maybe, because she did hope someday that this thing between her and Anson could blossom into something lasting. She could picture them already, husband and wife—yes, most certainly, someday down the road when things settled down. They'd work side by side at Schafer School, the classrooms filled to overflowing with eager students, and they'd share in the pride of each young man and woman who left their lowly circumstances behind and went on to better lives.

"Lark? Lark!" Rose poked her with the handle of a garden trowel. "There you go, off in dreamland again. Where does your mind wander off to, anyways?"

"Nowhere," Lark snapped, embarrassed at how easily her thoughts betrayed her. She whacked at another weed. "Better get busy if we're gonna finish by suppertime."

* * *

Lark's visit with Mrs. O'Neill proved as heartbreaking as she'd expected. It seemed so strange to talk of Mr. O'Neill in the past tense, to walk past the old grocery store and see the windows boarded up and a FOR RENT sign on the door. Almost as sad was noting how many other businesses had shut down as a result of the depression. Lark feared for all the Henderson State college students who relied on part-time work in town to help pay their way through school.

Mrs. O'Neill had been most understanding, though, when Lark described her involvement with Schafer School and her decision to continue her education via correspondence for the time being. "You do what you must, my dear," the woman told her. "Whether you're here at Henderson or studying from home, the money is yours to use for your college education."

They went together to the bank to add Lark's name to the savings account Mrs. O'Neill had opened, and Lark promised repeatedly that she'd use the money for college and nothing else. "And when I do finish my degree one day," she stated with tears in her eyes, "it will be because of dear folks like Mr. O'Neill who believed in me."

She stayed two nights with Mrs. O'Neill, listening to the woman's many stories about her late husband's life and reminiscing about both the joys and the trials of working at O'Neill's Grocery.

On Thursday before catching her bus home, Lark paid a visit to the college advisor she'd been in touch with and made arrangements to begin a home-study course in American history. Afterward, she took a nostalgic stroll across the Henderson State campus. She paused for a long time beneath Professor Keene's former office window and recalled with chagrin how she'd succumbed to his charming ways—and all the while he'd been secretly married to Debra McCarrick!

Then she finally turned away, choosing instead to remember the kiss she'd shared with Anson. She'd take things slowly, though. No more chasing those castles in the clouds, as her family so often teased her about. She'd keep her eyes open and her feet planted firmly on solid ground.

Chapter Fourteen

After a weekend of putting the finishing touches on the class-rooms, Anson grew anxious to open the school to their first students. Lark had returned to work on Friday after her trip to Arkadelphia, and Anson couldn't help noticing a certain... *settledness* about her, a level of confidence he hadn't seen before.

They didn't speak about the kiss, although more than once Anson entertained rash thoughts of pulling her aside for another. He determinedly refused to act on such impulses, however, for fear of spoiling the memory of that one moment, in case he'd completely misread Lark's response.

On Sunday, Anson and Irwin attended Mass in Brinkley. Afterward, they met with Daniel Vargas, who accompanied them on visits to several of the Brookbirch Plantation farm families. By the end of the day, they'd added four more children to the student roster, with plans to begin classes the following week. Since most of the children they'd enrolled so far were needed for farm chores during the day, lessons would be held from six to eight o'clock on Monday and Wednesday evenings. Anson explained to the parents that state accreditation for the school was still pending; however, the tutoring received at Schafer School would foster the children's progress until such time as they could return to the public school.

When Lark arrived in the office Monday morning, Anson showed her the names he'd added. "We're off to a fair start, don't you think?"

She perused the list. "Yes, definitely. I'm acquainted with some of these families. It couldn't have been easy convincing them."

"Daniel helped tremendously." Picking up another list, Anson blinked several times. He hadn't quite adjusted to the stronger prescription in his new glasses delivered in Saturday's mail. "We also expect two children for the Tuesday/Thursday sessions, and I still think Noah Jackson and his brother may change their minds."

"I hope you're right."

Anson didn't miss the hesitation in Lark's voice, and he couldn't keep the annoyance out of his own. "I've been warned a hundred times it's risky, but it's the right thing to do. We've already designated the smaller classroom for those lessons, and with meeting on the alternate evenings, there'll be no crossover. No reason for anyone to get up in arms."

Lark rose and stood before Anson's desk, her knuckles resting on the edge. "I know where your heart is, Anson, and what you're doing is truly a good thing. People will see that... eventually."

He frowned up at her. "And in the meantime?"

"In the meantime, we have to try very hard not to give our opposition any reason to retaliate."

"You make it sound like we're at war."

Lark sighed. "For certain factions, it *is* a war. The Klan isn't the force it used to be, but there are still a few staunch supporters around these parts, and they'd just as soon no black child ever got an education."

Anson rose and came around to her side of the desk. He leaned against it, his hand creeping closer to hers. "I don't want to fight with anyone. All I want is for every child to have equal opportunity to learn."

"And thanks to you, many of them will."

"Lark..." He slid his hand up her arm, a hunger welling up that refused to be contained. "Lark, I—"

"Don't say it." She touched a finger to his lips, her voice dropping to a shaky whisper. "Don't say it, or I'll never be able to do my work here as I should. What we have to do is too important."

Catching her hand, he pressed it to his chest. "Then at least tell me, am I imagining this? Because if I am, I'll never mention it again."

"No, no." Lark freed her hand and edged away. "I'm only being practical, that's all. We have important work to do here, and it requires clarity of focus. Unfortunately, I tend to see what I want to see, and not always very realistically."

"What's real—what's true," Anson began, wishing he could take her in his arms, "is that I knew you were special from the first moment I met you."

A weak laugh bubbled up from her throat. "You mean that silly, starry-eyed girl who landed on your front porch at Matumaini School so many months ago?"

"Starry-eyed? Yes." He found her hand again, cradling her slender, delicate fingers. "But not silly. Just young and innocent and refreshingly optimistic."

"Well, I'm not that much older now, and I'm still determined to keep my hopes up." With a sharp sigh, Lark drew herself erect. "However, I'd like to believe I left that innocent little girl back in Kenya."

"And I'd like to believe the best part of her is still around."

Lark hesitated, offering a shy smile. "I hope you're right, because there's something I've been wanting to tell you."

Her tone made him both curious and apprehensive. "Dare I ask what?"

She told him first about Mr. O'Neill's bequest, and while his heart prepared to hear the best news for her—and possibly the worst for him—she went on to explain about the correspondence course. "So you see? I can continue right here helping you get the school going and still progress toward my degree."

Anson slipped off his glasses and laid them on the desk, then gazed deeply into Lark's shining blue eyes. "Are you sure, Lark?

Because if I thought for a single moment you were staying out of obligation...or worse, pity—"

"Never! I'm staying because Schafer School has become as important to me as it is to you. I believe in what we're doing here." She pressed his hand to her cheek. "I believe in *you*."

Throat dry, he could barely swallow. "Lark, is there any chance, any chance at all—"

The partially closed office door flew open. "Anson, can you please—" Irwin gasped and gave an embarrassed cough. "Pardon me for interrupting."

Anson fumbled for his glasses as Lark skittered to her typing desk. "What is it, Irwin?"

"The Jackson brothers are asking to see you. They're waiting outside."

Following Irwin into the kitchen, Anson didn't dare glance back at Lark. He'd come so close to kissing her again that his pulse still raced. It was all he could do to tear his thoughts away and focus on putting one foot in front of the other.

Noah and Zeke Jackson waited on the back stoop. When Anson stepped out, Noah removed his hat and grinned. "We's decided. You still got room for our young'uns to come for schoolin'?"

"They'll be most welcome." Anson thrust out his arm, and this time neither of the two men hesitated in accepting his handshake. "We'll begin one week from tomorrow. Can you have your children here around six o'clock in the evening?"

* * *

Just as well Lark's desk faced the wall, because she didn't need Dr. Young noticing the blush heating her cheeks. She'd never moved so quickly as when he'd burst into the office moments ago.

On the other hand, his timing couldn't have been better. One more second and Anson would have voiced the question Lark was in no way prepared to answer. It was one thing to admit in her heart, and even to her sisters, that these feelings might be love. It was quite another to expose them to the very real object of her affection, because once spoken aloud, the words could never be taken back.

At least not without causing a world of hurt.

When Anson returned to the office with Dr. Young in tow, Lark whispered out a silent sigh of relief. Neither she nor Anson needed them to be alone again.

"Good news," Anson said, handing Lark a scrap of paper. "The Jacksons will be sending their children."

She glanced at the six names scrawled in Anson's large cursive, then looked up with a dubious smile. "All their children are coming?"

"Every one." Dr. Young crossed behind the larger desk and took a book from the shelf. "I need to brush up on high school curriculum. Those boys of Noah's should be graduating in the next year or two, but I suspect they're lagging far behind."

Anson eased into one of the straight-backed chairs on Lark's side of the desk. Hands folded, he sat forward. "Lark, if you're absolutely sure about what you told me earlier—"

"Of course I am."

"Then...perhaps we should discuss what your duties will be once classes begin."

She had to make herself look him in the eye and smile serenely, when her emotions as he sat this close were anything but serene. "You know I'll assist in whatever ways you need."

"What you've done in managing the office work has proven invaluable," Anson said. "However, beginning next week, I'd like you to assume a teaching role. With your level of education, you're more than qualified to tutor these children." He sat straighter, his jaw clenched as if his next words didn't come easily. "And the truth is, I—that is, Irwin and I are going to need you."

Anson's eyes, of course. Lark had tried hard not to be obvious in the ways she'd preserved his pride over the past couple of weeks, when it was plain his vision had grown worse. She could tell when she first arrived this morning that he'd gotten new glasses. The frames were almost identical to his previous pair, but the lenses were noticeably thicker.

With a decisive nod, Lark said, "I'm happy to help however I can."

"I'm grateful." Anson pushed to his feet. "Shall we get to work on some lesson plans?"

For the rest of the day, Lark joined Anson and Dr. Young at the kitchen table as they pored over arithmetic, reading, and history textbooks to design a curriculum appropriate for the various students they expected. Lark well remembered both the opportunities and the challenges of learning in a multi-grade classroom. She and her sisters had attended through eighth grade at the school housed in the church's tiny fellowship hall, and their teacher, the same prim, silver-haired woman for all the grades, had been adamant about providing the most comprehensive education possible for her students. Lark and her sisters had each passed their eighth-grade exams with flying colors.

Though neither Bryony nor Rose had gone much further in school, Grandpa had driven Lark to the bus stop every school day for the next four years so she could graduate from Brinkley High School with honors. Bookworm that she was, she'd had no interest in extracurricular activities. And besides keeping up with her studies, there were always plenty of chores waiting for her back at the farm.

Going to college and becoming a teacher was supposed to be her ticket out of Eden. Now, at least for the present, she'd committed herself to staying right here, dividing her time among Schafer School, the farm, and her correspondence studies. This wasn't the way she'd envisioned earning her degree, but she had no regrets.

The weekend had brought chillier temperatures, so Lark didn't refuse when Dr. Young made his usual offer to drive her home at the end of the day. They were barely out of town when he cleared his throat meaningfully and said, "My apologies again for this morning."

"Whatever for?" As if she had to ask. Lark kept her gaze riveted to the fence posts speeding past her window.

Dr. Young graciously didn't elaborate, just drove on in silence for another mile or so before murmuring, "I also wanted to thank you."

Lark shifted to look his way. Again, he didn't have to explain. "I would do anything in my power to protect Anson's pride. He's been so good to me."

More silence stretched between them as the car jounced over the bumpy dirt road. Dr. Young slowed to turn onto the lane leading to the farm. "Anson does have a lot of pride," he said. "Not hubris but simple human dignity, a need to show himself worthy and capable."

"He is, amazingly so. I admire him more than I can say."

Dr. Young cast her a fatherly smile as he braked beside the house. "Admiration? Is that all you feel for him?"

Lark's throat tightened. She reached for the door handle, then released it and laced her fingers in her lap. Her voice came out in a strained whisper. "It's all I dare admit to for now."

"I understand. But forgive me for saying I hope you will change your mind soon."

I hope so, too, she wanted to say. "I should go in. Thank you for the ride—" Just then noticing the empty space where Grandpa's old black pickup should be, Lark furrowed her brow. "I hope Grandpa or Rose didn't drive into town to bring me home."

"Surely we would have passed them on the road."

Then Lark noticed the tractor and plow sitting cockeyed at

the edge of the field, and a tremor started in the depths of her abdomen. "Something's wrong. Would you wait here while I find out what's happened?"

"Better yet, I'll go with you." Dr. Young shut off the motor and thrust open his car door.

Lark rushed through the screen porch to the kitchen. "Grandpa? Rose?"

No response.

She charged through the house calling their names. She returned to the kitchen to find Dr. Young snatching up a slip of paper that had blown under the table. "What is it—a note?"

"Seems so." He held it out to her.

Taking Grandpa to the doctor in Brinkley, Lark read silently. *Will try to send word when we know something.*

"It's my grandpa," she said, her knees going weak.

Dr. Young gave the note a quick glance, then slid his arm around Lark's shoulder. "Do you know which doctor they'd have gone to?"

"I'm sure the one we've always seen. Dr. Eddington."

"Then let me take you back to town. You can telephone from the school. And if need be, I'll drive you all the way to Brinkley."

"Thank you." Panic filling her, Lark allowed Dr. Young to lead her back to his car. "If anything happens to Grandpa—"

"Hold to your faith, my dear. Hold to your faith."

*   *   *

Rose paced the waiting room and wished the doctor or nurse or *someone* would come out and tell her what was going on. She and Grandpa had just gotten the plow hooked up to the old tractor to make sure everything was running like it should for spring planting. Then Grandpa suddenly clutched at his side and sank to his knees with a cry of pain. Scared half out of her mind, Rose rushed over to find him conscious and breathing but clearly in agony. She wrestled him into the pickup and drove as fast as she dared to get him to the doctor.

The bell over the clinic door jangled, and Rose spun around to see Bryony and Michael hurry in. Rose fell into Bryony's arms. "Praise God you're here!"

Bryony ran trembling hands up and down Rose's back. "What have they said? Will he be all right?"

"I haven't heard a word since they took him back to a room." Rose shuddered. "Bry, I'm scared."

"I know, honey. Me, too."

Michael steered them both toward some chairs. "Sit down and try to be calm. I'll see if I can find out anything."

Their fingers locked together, Bryony and Rose sat stiffly while Michael knocked on the glass partition at the reception window. "Hello? Anyone back there?"

"We barely made it in time," Rose said. "They were about to close. I think it's just Dr. Eddington and the nurse still here."

"What about Lark?" Bryony asked. "Does she know?"

"I left her a note. It was all I could take time for."

Minutes went by before the inner door opened and the nurse appeared. Rose and Bryony both jumped up, and only Michael's quick intervention kept them from talking over each other to bombard the woman with questions.

He sheltered them both with his arm. "What can you tell us, Mrs. Finch?"

The stern-faced woman seemed to appreciate Michael's cool-headed approach, a feat Rose would never have accomplished just now. "We've made Mr. Rigby as comfortable as possible. That's all I can tell you at this point."

A sob caught in Rose's throat. She twisted to bury her face in Bryony's coat collar.

"Is it serious? Will he be all right?" Bryony's grip came close to cutting off the circulation in Rose's fingers.

"Dr. Eddington wants to keep him here at the clinic overnight so we can run some tests." Mrs. Finch backed toward the door.

"We'll have more to tell you in the morning."

Rose jerked her head up. "That's all? Can't we see him?"

"It isn't a good idea." One hand on the knob, the nurse shook her head. "Go home and get some rest, yourselves. Especially you, Mrs. Heath, for the baby's sake. Call here first thing tomorrow, and we'll let you know how Mr. Rigby is doing."

"But—"

The door closed behind the nurse with a firm click.

Bryony turned to Michael. "We can't just leave. That's our grandpa in there."

"It doesn't appear we have much choice." With gentle nudges, Michael steered them toward the exit. "You'll stay with us tonight, Rose. The doctor knows how to reach us if anything changes."

"But Lark—she's going to be worried sick."

The telephone rang behind the reception window. Nurse Finch answered, spoke a few words, then signaled them over and passed the receiver through the opening. "It's your sister on the line. I already told her what I could, but you might want to reassure her."

Rose grabbed the telephone. "Lark, I'm sorry. Where are you?"

"At the school. Dr. Young brought me back so I could call." Lark's voice shook with worry. "Is Grandpa going to be okay?"

"I—I don't—" As more sobs erupted, Rose thrust the telephone at Michael. While he responded in soothing tones to the questions Lark must be pelting him with, Rose clung to Bryony with all her might. "I don't want Grandpa to die. Please, Lord, I need him! Don't let him die!"

*   *   *

Fearing she'd collapse, Anson stood right next to Lark. As she replaced the telephone receiver in its cradle, he locked his arm firmly about her waist. "What's the word?"

"They aren't sure yet." A hiccupping breath caught in her chest. "The doctor is keeping Grandpa at the clinic overnight. Rose will stay in town with Bryony and Michael."

"Then you must stay here with us."

From the other side of the desk, Dr. Young wagged a finger. "Not a wise idea, Anson. We're two bachelors, remember? Think of the young lady's reputation."

Lark pressed against Anson's side as her tears flowed. She seemed oblivious to their dilemma.

"We can't send her back to the farm alone," Anson whispered. "We have a perfectly good extra room upstairs—"

"And a town full of gossips who will spread the story far and wide before sunrise." Irwin tugged on his chin. "Perhaps she could stay with Pastor and Mrs. Unsworth. Or possibly Miranda Vargas."

"No, I can't." With a shuddering sniffle, Lark straightened but kept a firm hold on Anson's arm. "I have to go home. Someone has to take care of the livestock, and since Grandpa and Rose—" Another sob choked her.

"Then we'll go with you and help." Holding her closer, Anson dared a kiss to the top of her head. "It'll be all right, Lark, I promise."

Irwin started for the kitchen. "In the meantime, I shall attend to the practical matter of preparing our supper. We will all think more clearly with food in our bellies."

Anson guided Lark through the door and settled her into a chair at the kitchen table. All too conscious of the healing cut on his hand, he cautiously took a glass from the cupboard and filled it with water. "Here, Lark. Can I get you anything else?"

Holding the glass between two shaking hands, she took a tiny sip. "I just need to go home."

"Of course, of course." Anson gently squeezed her shoulder, then crossed to the stove, where Irwin heated up some canned soup. Keeping his voice low, he said, "We can take her home, but I'm not leaving her out there alone. I don't care what the gossips will say."

"I agree on your first point." Irwin stirred the pan of soup. "As for the second, if you want to preserve the school's reputation as well as young Miss Linwood's, you'd better care dearly about deflecting the rumormongers."

"Then what do you suggest?"

Lark came up behind them. "Don't talk about me as if I'm not present. And don't treat me like some frail hothouse flower in need of your protection."

Seeing her trembling lips and red-rimmed eyes, Anson bit down hard on his inner lip to keep his chivalrous impulses in check, because more than anything else in all the world, he wanted to hold her close and shield her from every hurt and worry.

Instead, he kept his hands at his sides and faced her squarely. "You are anything but frail, and if you thought we implied as much, it is only because we care about you and want to help in any way we can."

Arms locked against her ribs, she gazed up at Anson for a long moment, then swiped at a tear as it slid down her cheek. "I know. I'm sorry."

"There's nothing to be sorry about." Anson took her by the shoulders and turned her toward her chair. "But perhaps you'd allow a couple of bungling bachelors to do their good deed for the day and see to your well-being." Nudging her to sit, he added, "Now make yourself comfortable while Irwin and I get supper on the table."

With continual coaxing, Anson and Irwin convinced Lark to eat a few bites of the vegetable soup and warmed-over biscuits from breakfast. Afterward, Irwin fetched their coats.

As Anson helped Lark with her coat, she twisted around to look at him, panic filling her eyes. "If something happens in the night, how will anyone let me know?"

"I have an idea," Irwin said. "The Vargases have a telephone, don't they? We'll stop there on the way, and you can call your sister. Tell her if there's any urgent word to call Miranda. She can send Daniel out to the farm with the report."

Seemingly satisfied, Lark allowed Anson to help her into the car. They drove to Brookbirch Plantation and past the main house to the smaller brick Colonial where Miranda and Daniel resided. After hurried explanations and the Vargases' expressions of concern, Lark stepped into the foyer to telephone Bryony.

In the living room, Anson took Daniel aside. "To avoid any impropriety, I wonder if you'd permit Callie to accompany us out to the farm, and then stay with Lark until..." Glancing toward the foyer, he heaved a helpless shrug. "Until we know what happens next."

Daniel agreed immediately and sent Callie to pack a bag. A few minutes later, they were on their way.

By the time Irwin parked behind the farmhouse, an insistent banging sounded from inside the barn. In the backseat with Callie, Lark shoved open her door. "That's Daisy and Hermione. They must be starving by now."

Anson hurried after her. "What can I do to help?"

Lark was already scooping grain out of a burlap sack. "You can fill their water pails. The pump's out there, next to the vegetable garden."

Toting buckets didn't require perfect vision, and Anson was glad for something useful to do. On his way to the pump, he passed Callie as she instructed Irwin about tending the chickens.

"But chickens peck," Irwin said, and Anson almost laughed out loud at the trepidation on his friend's face.

"Move fast and don't give them any reason to go after you." Callie handed Irwin a tin cup filled with chicken feed and opened the coop. "Go on, nothing to be scared of. I'll be right behind you."

"*That's* what I'm scared of. I'd much rather you went in first and made the introductions."

Callie just shook her head.

With the four of them working together, they soon had the livestock fed, watered, and settled for the night. From Anson's perspective, it seemed Lark kept moving more out of desperation than necessity. Even after they'd gone into the house, she bustled about in the kitchen, twice washing and rinsing the same two coffee mugs, needlessly wiping counters, checking the pantry and icebox as if to be sure nothing had disappeared in the last five minutes.

"Lark." Anson blocked her next trip across the kitchen, holding her fast by her upper arms. "You're doing yourself no good flitting around like this. You'll only make yourself sick."

Her face crumpled. Fists clenched against Anson's chest, she allowed him to draw her into his embrace. "What am I supposed to do? What if—"

"No what-ifs, do you hear me?" She felt so good in his arms, so perfectly right. If only the circumstances were different. If only it hadn't taken a moment of need for her to let him hold her this way. He tipped her head back, cradling her messy bun and wishing he had the right to loosen the pins and lose himself in those silky golden tresses.

With a painful swallow, and knowing Irwin and Callie were in the next rooms making up beds, he kissed Lark's forehead instead of the dewy lips he hungered for. "I would give anything to promise your grandfather will get well and that everything will turn out fine, but I can't."

She nodded and clutched his lapels as more tears escaped.

"But I do promise you this," he said, his chest aflame with the ferocity of his love for this woman. "Whatever happens, I will take care of you. Always, do you hear? Always."

Chapter Fifteen

Lark never expected to sleep as soundly as she had. Long after Callie had crawled into Bryony's old bed and Dr. Young had slipped away to Grandpa's room, Lark had sat up with Anson in the parlor. Safe and secure in his arms, she'd listened to the soothing sound of his voice as he told her stories of growing up in Kenya. Lark didn't even remember when she finally drifted off.

She awoke the next morning to find a quilt tucked around her and her head on a pillow on Anson's lap.

He smiled down at her. "I tried to tell you how exhausted you were."

Lark sat up abruptly, the quilt falling to the floor. She straightened her skirt with one hand while attempting to corral her tangled hair with the other. "I slept here all night?"

"Since around one in the morning, actually." Anson stood and gathered up the quilt. "Hardly a full night's sleep, but at least you got some rest."

Unsure whether to be grateful or embarrassed, Lark took the other end of the quilt and helped Anson fold it. "And you?" she asked. "Did you sleep?"

"I dozed." He took the folded quilt from her and laid it on the settee. His glasses lay on the side table, leaving nothing between Lark's shy gaze and the love emanating from his warm brown eyes.

Today, she didn't have the strength to fight these feelings. She stepped into his arms and felt his surprised intake of breath. "Thank you for being here. Thank you for taking care of me."

"I wouldn't be anywhere else."

Dr. Young's exaggerated cough sounded from the hallway. "I do have an uncanny way of interrupting."

"Yes, you do, as a matter of fact." Anson's tone held both humor and annoyance. He kept his arms firmly around Lark, and she didn't resist. "Nothing untoward happened, I can assure you."

"I don't doubt it for a moment." Merriment sparked in the older man's eyes. "Why don't I go see what I can stir up for breakfast."

"Good idea. And take your time."

A distant bellowing drew Lark's attention to the window. She heaved a reluctant sigh. "That's Hermione, begging to be milked."

"Let me help. I've milked a cow or two in my day."

"Oh, really?" Lark noticed neither of them had made any move toward the kitchen and their coats. She liked the feel of Anson's sheltering embrace. She liked the smell of his starched shirt, wrinkled though it was after a long day and an even longer night.

Then remembrance came flooding back—why he'd stayed, why he'd held her all night long—and guilt throttled her. She should be thinking about Grandpa, not succumbing to feelings she'd fought so hard to keep in check.

With jerky breaths, she pulled away and started for the hallway. "The sooner we get the chores done, the sooner I can get to a telephone and find out about my grandfather."

By now, Callie was up and helping Dr. Young measure oatmeal into a pot of boiling water. Chicory percolating on the stove filled the kitchen with a pungent aroma. Lark offered only a terse "Good morning" before snatching her coat off the hook. She didn't wait for Anson to follow.

He did, though, catching up as Lark reached Hermione's stall. "I told you I'd help." His tone bore a hint of vexation.

"All right, but your hand is still healing, so I'll do the milking. You can let Daisy out into her pasture." Lark focused on setting up the milking stool and placing the pail under Hermione's udder. She didn't dare look at Anson just now. "Throw a flake of hay over the fence, and make sure she has water."

While the pail filled and the sweet scent of warm cow's milk soothed her senses, Lark leaned her forehead against Hermione's flank and took slow, deep breaths. She couldn't keep her thoughts from straying to Grandpa. What if he didn't get better? Rose certainly couldn't keep the farm going all alone. Lark could manage the simpler chores like milking, churning butter, and tending the vegetable garden. And she could pick cotton along with the best of them.

But plowing and planting? Fixing farm machinery? Understanding things like yield and crop rotation and irrigation? She'd be utterly useless.

"Stop," she softly chided herself. "Stop it right now." Grandpa would pull through. He had to, because what would they do without him? *Please, Lord. Please!*

Anson returned from tending to the mule and stepped inside Hermione's stall. He stood quietly while Lark finished filling the pail, then carried it into the house for her. By then, Dr. Young and Callie had breakfast ready.

Having eaten so little for supper the night before, Lark gave in to her hunger. The thick, hot oatmeal along with a steaming mug of chicory revived her, and as soon as they'd cleared the table, she was anxious to get to town and a telephone.

"I'll take care of things here," Callie said. "You just go on and don't worry about a thing."

Lark gave the girl a grateful hug, and a few minutes later, she darted out to the car with Anson and Dr. Young. When they arrived at Schafer School, Lark raced inside ahead of the men, went straight to the telephone in the office, and called Bryony.

"We're getting ready to leave for the clinic right now," Bryony said, her voice high and shaky. "Meet us there as soon as you can. And, Lark?"

"Yes?"

"Pray for all you're worth!"

She didn't have to be told. Hanging up, she turned to find Anson right there, ready to hold and comfort her. "I need to go to Brinkley," she said. "I hate to ask, but—"

"Of course we'll take you." Anson's arms encircled her. "We'll leave at once."

Dr. Young headed toward Brinkley at a fast clip, while Lark snuggled deeply against Anson's side, her eyes pressed closed and a constant silent prayer on her lips. Arriving at the clinic, Dr. Young parked next to Michael's green Chevrolet, and the three of them rushed inside.

Lark flew into Bryony's arms. "Have they told you anything? Anything at all?"

"We were waiting for you. Oh, honey, I'm scared, so scared!" Bryony opened her arm to include Rose, and the sisters clung together, their tears intermingling.

The inner door opened, and the girls separated as Dr. Eddington stepped into the waiting area. "Good, you're all here. If the immediate family would come to my office, please?"

When Bryony reached out for Michael, grasping his arm for support, Lark wished she could do the same with Anson. He'd been her rock these past several hours, and now, trudging after her sisters into the doctor's private office, she felt the emptiness of leaving Anson behind.

There were only two chairs on the front side of the desk. Michael urged Bryony into one of them and stood behind her, hands resting on her shoulders. Rose, looking as pale and scared as Lark had ever seen her, grasped Lark's hand before collapsing into the other chair. Lark held herself rigid in the narrow space between her sisters.

When the doctor had taken his seat behind the desk, he looked up with a bleak but sympathetic smile. "I know you're all worried, and I wish I had better news."

Bryony stifled a cry. Rose's grip clamped down even harder on Lark's hand.

She decided she'd have to be the strong one today. "Just tell us, Doctor."

The fatigue lines deepened around Dr. Eddington's eyes, evidence of the long night and his struggle to communicate the news they didn't want to hear. "Your grandfather has developed a cancer in his abdomen. It appears to be fast-growing. Otherwise, he would have exhibited more obvious symptoms before now."

Bryony clasped Lark's other hand as Rose sobbed quietly. Lark sniffed back a tear before asking the question she already knew the answer to. "Can you do anything?"

The doctor slowly shook his head. "I'm afraid not even surgery would avail at this stage. The best we can hope for is to minimize his pain until..."

"No!" Rose bolted to her feet. She hammered the desk with both fists while shouting in the doctor's face. "You fix my grandpa, do you hear me? Don't you dare let him die!"

"I'm sorry. I'm so very, very sorry." Dr. Eddington covered Rose's clenched fists with his own large hands and gently stilled the pounding.

Lark swallowed. "How...long?"

"Weeks. Perhaps three months at most." Rising, the doctor came around the desk. "My recommendation is to move your grandfather to a nursing facility I have connections with in Hot Springs."

Bryony jerked her head up. "Why so far away? Why can't we keep him here? I could care for him—"

"Out of the question, my dear." Dr. Eddington rested a hand on Bryony's shoulder. "You have your own health to think about, and the baby's. In Hot Springs they have the means to manage your grandfather's pain, see to his personal needs, and keep him as comfortable as possible until the end."

"But—but he'll be all alone," Rose protested. "Isn't there someplace closer?"

"The only other option would be Little Rock. If you'd prefer, I can look into availability there."

Lark chewed her lip. "There must be a reason you want to send him to Hot Springs."

"There is. This facility is where I took my own mother as her health failed. The care there is beyond excellent, and the setting is beautifully serene."

"Then that's where he'll go." Lark didn't know how they'd manage it, but Grandpa deserved only the best. Then a new worry assailed her. "Will it be expensive?"

Michael touched Lark's arm. "Don't concern yourself with cost. I'll personally see it's taken care of."

With a nod of thanks, Lark turned her attention to Dr. Eddington as he described their next steps. Grandpa would be moved by ambulance to the Hot Springs sanitarium later that afternoon. Since he would be heavily sedated with pain medication for the journey, there was no point in any of the family accompanying him. However, Dr. Eddington said they could visit as early as tomorrow. He recommended hotels nearby where they might find overnight lodging.

Once the details had been finalized, the doctor called for Mrs. Finch, who took the family down the corridor to the small room where Grandpa was being cared for. He looked so frail, so deathly pale. Their tears flowed unabated as they surrounded the bed. Rose begged him to awaken. Bryony assaulted the heavens with murmured prayers, while Michael held her close.

Lark trembled with shock and sorrow and confusion, and the certainty that the direction of her life was changing yet again.

* * *

When Lark and her family emerged, Anson saw the stunned look on her tear-streaked face and had no idea how to help, except to hold her. She stood stiffly in his arms, her chin quivering and her eyes unseeing. He glanced across the waiting room to where Michael comforted Bryony and Rose, who both appeared as devastated as Lark.

Excusing himself to his wife and sister-in-law, Michael approached Anson and quietly filled him in on what the doctor had said. As he spoke, Lark began to shiver uncontrollably.

"The girls are all in shock," Michael said. "There's nothing more to be done here. Let's go to my house."

Somehow they got everyone out to the automobiles. Lark wouldn't let go of Anson, so they climbed into Irwin's car and followed Michael across town to the little white bungalow where he and Bryony lived.

A purring calico cat greeted them at the front door. Bryony snatched her up and carried her to the living room. Lark and Rose followed, and the three of them huddled on the sofa, with Bryony hugging the wild-eyed cat as if she'd never let go.

Michael suggested the men join him in the kitchen, where he started a pot of coffee. While the percolator burbled, they sat around the table and stared at each other...or at nothing at all.

Finally Michael spoke. "Don't feel you have to stay. I'm sure you have plenty to do at the school."

"Nothing that can't wait," Anson said. "Anyway, I doubt I could think about anything besides Lark and her family."

Irwin tapped a fingertip on the table. "We must keep young Miss Vargas in mind. We left her alone at the Rigby farm, remember?"

"Oh dear—Callie." Michael rose to pour the coffee. "I'll telephone Daniel. He'll be glad to go out and see to the chores."

While Anson and Irwin sipped coffee, Michael went to the hallway to make the call. He returned a few minutes later. "All taken care of. Rose and Lark can stay here tonight. We'll drive over to Hot Springs first thing in the morning."

When it seemed there was no more reason to stay, Irwin subtly suggested to Anson that they say their good-byes. Anson hated leaving Lark, but she had her sisters now, and they seemed to have settled into a melancholy kind of acceptance. Bryony had found an old photograph album, and the sisters laughed and cried as they paged through scenes of their childhood.

As Michael handed Anson and Irwin their coats, Lark looked up from the sofa and rushed over. An anxious look clouded her expression. "You're leaving?"

Anson took her aside. "If you need anything—anything at all—" His heart climbed into his throat, and he reached up to caress her cheek. "You know where to find me."

She blinked several times. "The school—I feel like I'm deserting you."

"Nonsense. You need to be with your grandfather and your sisters. Don't give the school another thought."

When she wrapped her arms around him, the silky softness of her curls brushing his chin, he thought nothing this side of heaven could bring more bliss. Then, as if realizing other eyes might be watching, Lark backed away. "Thank you again, so very much. For everything."

On the drive back to Eden, Anson and Irwin spoke hardly a word. As they settled in for an afternoon of more office work and school preparations, Anson keenly felt Lark's absence. What would they do without her, and how long would they have to manage on their own? Selfish questions, to be sure. Anson mentally chastised himself for dwelling on his own wants and needs when Lark and her sisters dealt with the impending loss of their grandfather.

He made it through the day, and the next, and the next, only by force of will. But without Lark, the excitement and anticipation he'd felt as the first evening of classes approached had vanished.

By Friday afternoon, Irwin declared them as ready as they'd ever be. "Now we must hope that, come Monday evening, all those families we spoke with will actually send their children."

Anson laid aside the history book he'd been straining to read. "You don't sound at all convinced they will."

"Too many years in the mission field, I suppose." Seated behind the desk, Irwin twirled a fountain pen between his fingers. "You weren't there to see how long it took your parents to gain the Kenyans' trust when Matumaini School was first established."

"Hadn't considered it, but I'm sure you're right." Anson's eyes burned. He slipped off his glasses and massaged the bridge of his nose. "At the moment, I'd almost be happy for a small turnout. Otherwise, I don't know how I'll get through the lessons."

Outside in the driveway, a car door slammed. Irwin looked toward the window. "I think we have company."

They made their way to the back door as Miranda Vargas stepped onto the porch. Her toddler son, George, rode her hip. "Good afternoon, gentlemen. May we come in and visit for a few minutes?"

"Certainly." Anson showed her in and offered a chair at the kitchen table. "What brings you by?"

"A couple of things. First, I'm sure you're anxious for news about Lark and the family."

Anson plopped into the chair at Miranda's left. "Very. What's the latest?"

"For heaven's sake, where are your manners?" Irwin chided. "We should offer our guests some refreshments. Mrs. Vargas, would you care for some tea or coffee? And may I spoil this young lad with a cookie?"

"Nothing for me, thanks." She tousled George's dark curls. "But I'm sure my little man would be most grateful for a cookie—but just one, mind you. It's almost suppertime."

Impatient to get past all the social graces, Anson quietly tapped his heels on the floor while Irwin fetched the tin of sugar cookies Pastor Unsworth's wife had brought over a few days ago.

As the little boy munched, Miranda got to the point. "Michael and Bryony came home from Hot Springs earlier today. They also brought Rose. She's back at the farm."

"And Lark?"

Miranda cast Anson a regretful smile. "For now, she's staying with her grandfather. Under the circumstances—Bryony in her delicate condition, Rose needing to manage the farm—Lark felt she was the only one who could."

"Yes, that makes sense." For the family, at least. Anson still had no idea how he'd function without her.

"Which brings me to the other reason for my visit." Catching George's crumbs, Miranda deposited them on a napkin. "I'd like to volunteer my help. I don't have Lark's college hours, but I was a pretty fair high school student—the nuns at boarding school made sure of it—so if you need an extra hand with tutoring, I'm available."

This wasn't what Anson had been expecting. Open-mouthed, he glanced up at Irwin.

His friend chuckled. "I think the words you're looking for are *thank you.*"

"Yes, yes." Recovering his composure, Anson turned to Miranda. "Thank you very much indeed. Without Lark, I've been at loose ends. She's...she's been invaluable." A terribly inadequate word to describe everything Lark had come to mean to him.

"Then I'll see you Monday." Miranda gathered up her son and started for the door. "What time shall I arrive?"

Anson followed her to the porch. "Is five PM too early? We want to start lessons at six, and I'll need a little time to cover the evening's lesson plans with you."

"I'll be here." Halfway to her car, Miranda halted and glanced over her shoulder. "And don't worry," she said, her tone softening. "Lark will be back. She misses you as much as you miss her."

* * *

Grandpa's room was comfortable but small, barely wide enough for a hospital bed, a stocky metal bedside cabinet, and two chairs for visitors. The care facility seemed well managed, and the staff had been nothing but courteous, kind, and helpful.

Still, Lark had never felt so bereft as when Bryony and Rose left with Michael that morning. Her sisters had argued at first about staying, but Michael had finally talked some sense into Bryony about taking care of herself and the baby. Rose had required less convincing, because next to Grandpa, she knew the farm better than anyone, and she wouldn't let everything they'd worked for all these years fall into ruin. Such as it was, anyway, what with the damage the drought and dust storms had done.

Grandpa stirred. "That you, Larkspur?"

"I'm here." She scooted her chair closer and clutched Grandpa's bony hand. With all the morphine they'd given him for the pain, he continually drifted in and out of sleep. Every moment he was awake and aware had become a precious gift.

He motioned weakly toward the water pitcher. "Thirsty." After she'd filled a glass and helped him take a few sips through a straw, he closed his eyes again. Just when Lark thought he'd fallen back asleep, he murmured, "You shoulda gone home with your sisters."

"No, I'm not leaving you." She fought to keep her voice firm and steady.

"My girls…my dear, sweet girls." A whispery sigh slipped between his lips, and he slept again.

Lark had almost dozed off in her chair when a nurse peeked in, the same red-haired nurse who'd been so helpful when they first came to see Grandpa on Wednesday. Lark sat up. "Mrs. Ballard, isn't it?"

"Surprised you remembered." The woman spoke with a hint of Irish brogue, her kind eyes twinkling. She stepped to the opposite side of the bed and quietly took Grandpa's vitals, then jotted notes in a chart. "Holding his own, and the pain is controlled. That's a blessing."

Lark stood at the bedside, emotion welling up. "I still can't believe this is happening."

"I understand." The nurse circled the foot of the bed and came to stand next to Lark. "I spoke briefly with your family a while ago as they were leaving. Are you staying on by yourself?"

"I can't bear to leave Grandpa alone." With a shaky breath, Lark glanced toward the window and the Ouachita Mountains beyond. Dr. Eddington was right, the beautiful setting brought a measure of peace and comfort. "I should look for a less expensive place to stay, though. I can't ask my brother-in-law to continue paying the Arlington Hotel rates."

Mrs. Ballard pursed her lips. "Perhaps I can help. My shift ends in an hour. Will you meet me at the reception desk?"

Unsure what to expect, Lark agreed. When she slipped out of the room later, Grandpa was still resting quietly. She found Mrs. Ballard in conversation with the tall, fair-haired chaplain who had met with the family briefly the first day they'd arrived. Lark would never forget the look of surprise and delight on Michael's face when he recognized Pastor Vickary as the army chaplain who had ministered to him in the early days of his war injuries. Now retired from the army, the man pastored a small church

in Hot Springs and served as visiting chaplain at this and other
care facilities.

The nurse waved Lark over. "Miss Linwood, you remember
Pastor Vickary. This is his wife, Annemarie. They would be
delighted for you to stay with them as long as you're in town."

Lark snatched a breath. "That's so kind of you, but I couldn't
possibly impose."

"We insist." Mrs. Vickary clasped Lark's hand. "Do you need
to pick up some things from your hotel?"

Almost before she realized what had happened, Lark had
checked out of the Arlington and settled into the Vickarys' guest
room. She might have been more hesitant if not for Michael's
high regard for Pastor Vickary. And no one could have been
friendlier or more welcoming than his wife. Even before they'd
arrived at the couple's charming two-story Victorian, both had
insisted Lark call them by their first names.

When she went downstairs to offer her help with supper, she
met the Vickarys' two children, a girl of about twelve or thirteen
with ebony waves like her mother's, and a younger boy who
strongly favored his father.

The mouthwatering aroma of roast beef filled the kitchen. Lark
and her family hadn't had to tighten their belts quite as much
at the farm in recent months, but even so, she hadn't smelled
anything so good in ages. Her stomach growled in response.

Annemarie turned from the stove, a warm smile dimpling
her cheeks. "Before you even ask, the answer is no. You're our
guest. I won't have you lifting a finger."

Arguing did no good, and Lark found herself banished to the
parlor while Annemarie and her daughter finished preparing the
meal.

Pastor Vickary—Samuel, she had to remind herself—soon
joined her. "You've had a difficult few days. How are you
holding up?"

Her chin quivered as fatigue combined with myriad emotions. "I think I'm still in shock."

"Perfectly natural. It's good you're able to stay with your grandfather, but it can't be easy, coming to a strange place so far from your family."

His comment reminded Lark of her short-lived adventure in Kenya, which in turn brought Anson to mind. She couldn't help worrying about how things were going at the school, and she couldn't quell her guilt over not being there to help.

The next thing she knew, she was pouring out practically her entire life story in a rush, while Samuel Vickary listened patiently. When Lark's tears overflowed, he offered a handkerchief, and when her words ran down, he comforted her with scriptural reminders of God's unfailing love and hinted at his own journey through dark times. It helped somehow to remember that others had struggled through pain and grief and come out whole on the other side.

After supper, Lark used the Vickarys' telephone to call Bryony and tell her where she was staying. "I couldn't believe their kind offer. They've been so welcoming."

"Michael thinks the world of the chaplain. I know you're in good hands there." Bryony sniffled. "I wish Michael hadn't insisted we come home. He worries too much."

Lark almost laughed at the irony of her sister's words. "Seems only the other day *you* were the one doing all the worrying."

"Well, I—I know it was foolish, but—" Bryony's stammering reply made Lark wonder if she really had let go of her concerns about the baby.

"You can't dwell on maybes, Bry. Pastor Vickary reminded me of something Jesus taught, how we mustn't worry about tomorrow, because tomorrow will bring worries of its own."

"And today's trouble is enough for today." Bryony released a shaky sigh. "I know it's true. It's just—" Her voice broke. "Oh,

Lark, do you suppose all my scared feelings were a premonition about Grandpa getting sick?"

"How could you know? How could any of us?" Lark wished she could crawl through the telephone line and into her sister's embrace. "Not even Rose had an inkling, and she worked alongside him day in and day out. It's just Grandpa's way, carrying on without complaining. Besides, like the doctor said, it came on so fast."

"I don't want him to die, but"—Bryony choked on a sob—"I pray he doesn't suffer long."

"I know, I know." A tear slid down Lark's cheek, and she brushed it away. "I should go. Will you let Anson know I'm at the Vickarys'? I hate to run up the long-distance bill here."

"I'll tell him. And next time I'll call you. Maybe Sunday night?"

"Sounds good." Lark promised to get word to Bryony sooner if anything changed with Grandpa, and if not, Bryony and Michael would return to Hot Springs early next week for a short visit.

Next week had never seemed so far away.

Chapter Sixteen

As parishioners arrived for Mass on Sunday morning, all the talk was about Adolf Hitler's appointment as the new chancellor of Germany. It was more than Bryony wanted to think about— Nazis, communism, socialism. She didn't give much thought to politics in general. Even so, she sorely longed for March 4, when newly elected Franklin Delano Roosevelt would step into the presidency and they'd at last be rid of Hoover and his failed efforts to end the depression.

Bryony also prayed desperately that all the upheaval going on throughout the world wouldn't soon lead to another war on the scale of the one Michael had barely survived.

Yes, she was foolishly borrowing trouble again, and she couldn't seem to stop herself. Everything worried her these days. As Father Dempsey began chanting the liturgy, she slid one hand into Michael's and rested the other protectively over her abdomen.

He gave her hand a reassuring squeeze. "We'll light a candle for your grandfather after Mass."

With a quick nod, Bryony nudged her lips into a smile. Better for her husband to assume her anxiety was centered on Grandpa rather than the myriad other terrifying possibilities racing through her mind.

After worship, Bryony and Michael made their way to the small altar of votive candles. As Michael lit a candle, Bryony knelt to pray, but she couldn't focus her thoughts. A new worry crept in: Like her mother-in-law, Fenella, was she slowly losing her mind?

"Honey?" Michael set his arm around her shoulder and gently helped her rise. "Come on, let's get you home."

"But we were supposed to go to your parents' for dinner."

"They'll understand."

Bryony clung to Michael's arm as they exited into the bright February morning. After a brief word to Father Dempsey, they caught up with Miranda and Daniel at their car.

"We'd better pass on Sunday dinner this time," Michael said. "Bryony's still pretty tired after our trip to Hot Springs."

Miranda cast Bryony a sympathetic glance. "Mother isn't doing so well either. Dad stayed home with her this morning." Her lips creased. "Her memory's worse every day. She didn't even know me last night."

"Miranda, I'm so sorry." Guilt flooded Bryony. Instead of floundering in her fears, she should be spending more time with Fenella, doing more to help. The woman had been so good to her, even during her days as the Heaths' housemaid. Back then, Fenella often mistook Bryony for her grandmother, Violet. But now, if the woman didn't recognize her own daughter—

The anguish of it all suddenly tore through Bryony. With a pained gasp, she thrust a hand over her mouth and turned away. If Michael hadn't caught her, she might have fallen to the pavement.

"Is she all right?" Through the ringing in Bryony's ears, Miranda's voice sounded far away.

Bryony clung to Michael's arm. "Just take me home. I need to go home."

*   *   *

"That doesn't look good." From a vantage point a few cars over, Anson watched Bryony's husband help her across the parking lot.

Irwin clucked his tongue as he and Anson walked toward the car. "Poor dear. She must be worried sick about her grandfather."

"I wish we could do more. I wish…"

"That Lark weren't so far away in Hot Springs?" Irwin clasped

Anson's shoulder. "Maybe we should think about driving over to see her at the end of the week."

"Possibly." Anson pinched his hat brim. "We'll see how classes go."

"I'm sure she'll want a full report." Irwin's not-so-subtle chuckle suggested he knew Anson's desire to see Lark had nothing at all to do with the school.

Miranda Vargas waved and walked over. "I'm still planning to be there tomorrow evening. Callie can come, too, if you need an extra helper. Odette will watch George for us."

"We'd be most grateful." Anson hoped his smile seemed sincere. He wouldn't want anyone to know how nervous he was about the school's opening. Besides, without Lark at his side, his enthusiasm had waned.

Irwin stepped closer. "We couldn't help noticing as the Heaths left a few moments ago. How is Bryony holding up?"

Miranda glanced toward the street as Michael's green Chevrolet disappeared around the corner. "I'm worried about her. She hasn't been herself lately."

Irwin nodded. "All this stress can't be good for her health, or for the baby."

Daniel and Callie strode over, holding George's chubby hands between them, and they all spoke briefly about the plans for tomorrow. To make attendance even easier for the farm families, many of them several miles from town, Daniel had offered to make the rounds in his pickup and drive the children to the school, then take them home afterward. Knowing both Miranda and Callie would be on hand to greet the arrivals and help evaluate their immediate schooling needs, Anson released a portion of his anxiety.

Even so, as Monday evening approached, he found himself checking and rechecking every desk, chair, tablet, and textbook. By ten of six, dressed in a crisp white shirt, his best brown tweed suit, and a blue-striped bowtie, he stood on the front porch and strained his eyes down the street for any sign of Daniel's pickup.

Miranda stepped out to join him. "A little anxious, are we?"

He rocked on his heels. "I'm as nervous as I was the time my teacher called me to the front of the class to give my book report on *A Tale of Two Cities.*"

"Really, a smart man like you?" Miranda looked at him askance. "I would have thought you quite proficient at giving oral reports."

"Normally, yes. But in this case, I hadn't gotten around to actually reading the book." With a gulp, Anson added, "And to make matters worse, the teacher was my mother."

Miranda's laughter echoed off the porch roof. "Well, it's obvious you're much better prepared for tonight, so every-thing—" She leaned over the rail. "I hear Daniel's pickup. They're almost here!"

Anson snatched a breath and straightened his suit coat. A sudden memory of something Lark had said once about his looking "erudite" brought a quick smile to his lips. Much as he appreciated Miranda's encouragement, he wished more than anything that it could have been Lark at his side instead.

The sweep of headlights announced Daniel's arrival. By the time Anson and Miranda crossed the lawn to the driveway, Daniel was climbing out of the cab. Even in the dim light of dusk, Anson could read the apologetic tilt of the man's head. Looking past him, Anson counted only three children—a girl inside the pickup and two boys riding in the bed.

With a quick smile at the children, Anson drew Daniel aside. "We were expecting more. Where are the rest?"

"There is still uncertainty. Also..." Daniel spread his hands. "Some are not pleased that you have opened the school to... others."

Anger seethed in Anson's belly. He turned away from the children climbing out of the pickup and spoke in a rasping whisper. "I thought our alternating schedule and separate classrooms would keep these bigots mollified."

"Some people will never accept the intermixing of the races." Miranda nodded toward the children now standing awkwardly on the lawn. "Be grateful these kids came. The other families are only hurting themselves."

Anson knew she was right. Gathering himself, he faced the children and offered his most welcoming smile. "It's good you could come tonight. Shall we go inside and get acquainted?"

As Miranda and Callie situated the children at desks, Anson took in their tattered clothing and shoes with soles worn paper-thin. The two boys, brothers in their early teens, were gaunt. The girl, who said she was eight years old, had straight, stringy hair that looked as if it hadn't been washed in weeks. Anson remembered meeting these children's parents as well as each family's hope of breaking the cycle of poverty and illiteracy.

After visiting with the families over the past few weeks, Anson and Irwin had also surmised the children might arrive hungry, so they'd prepared a big pot of soup. The first order of business was getting some food into the children, because empty bellies weren't conducive to learning.

And once word spread to the other families that a hot meal accompanied the lessons, perhaps it would erode a little of these people's prejudice.

While Callie started the little girl on first-grade reading and arithmetic, Irwin tested the boys to see where their education was lacking. They'd need a solid review of grammar and spelling before much else could be taught, so Irwin and Miranda worked with them individually, sparing Anson the difficulty of pretending his eyes were better than they were. Instead, he made the rounds and listened in on the children's lessons, giving occasional suggestions on another approach to the problem at hand.

When it was time for Daniel to return the children to their homes, Anson felt much better about the success of their first evening of classes. Yes, they'd started small, but these children's eagerness to learn was evident. In the end, it was all that really mattered, making a difference in even one child's future.

"You did well," Irwin said as they set the empty classroom in order. "You should telephone Lark. I imagine she'll be quite anxious to hear how things went."

Anson had thought of little else since the Vargases left with the children. "You don't think it's too late? I wouldn't want to disturb her, or the people she's staying with."

"It's barely nine. Make the call."

His step lightening, Anson strode to the office. Seated at the desk, he pulled open the drawer and found the slip of paper where he'd written down the Vickarys' number. Taking a deep breath, he lifted the receiver.

Seconds later, Pastor Vickary answered, and Anson asked if Lark could come to the phone. "She's right here. I'll put her on."

Then Lark's sweet voice sounded in Anson's ear. "I was hoping you'd call. How did it go?"

When he told her about the small turnout, he could hear the disappointment in her long sigh. He tried to put into words how the children's eagerness to learn had buoyed his spirits and bolstered his faith in what they were doing. "I admit, I'd have been much happier if we'd had a few more students show up, but all in all, the only thing that would have made this night better is if you'd been here to share it with me."

"I wish I could have been there, too. I feel terrible about having to miss Schafer School's opening day."

Anson laid his glasses on the desk. "Forgive me, Lark. Here I am carrying on about the school when I should be asking about you. How's your grandfather?"

"He's very weak. He sleeps most of the time, but at least when he awakens, he knows he isn't alone."

"I wish I could be there, to help somehow. If nothing changes by the weekend, Irwin says he'll bring me over to see you."

"Really? That would be wonderful. Then you can tell me all about how the rest of the week went. I'm sure attendance will pick up. People will realize what a good thing you're doing."

"I hope you're right." They both fell silent for a moment. "Lark?"

"Yes?"

"I love you."

She didn't answer right away, and his heart began to pound. Had he spoken the words too soon?

Then, "I love you, too, Anson."

* * *

For Lark, the rest of the week dragged on with depressing sameness, brightened only by the memory of Anson's tender words in her ear: *I love you.* It had felt so freeing to reply in kind, to openly admit the love in her heart that sometimes made her want to cry out in sheer wonder of it all.

But she'd promised herself no more fanciful thinking. No more imagining her future in anything but the most practical terms. Everything she'd dreamed of in life, reached for, tried to make happen because she wished it so—why must she learn again and again to put her trust in God and not in her own efforts? Whatever came of the love growing between her and Anson, it would be God's doing and his alone.

After a week in Hot Springs, Lark had memorized every dip in the sidewalk between the Vickarys' house and the nursing facility. She'd counted each crack in the ceiling of Grandpa's room and knew almost all the nursing staff, day or night shift, by name. She'd discovered all the quiet walking paths around the building, the most comfortable pews in the small prayer chapel, and the best spots to study the correspondence lessons she'd brought along, though under these trying circumstances she wondered how much she'd retain.

On Saturday morning, as she sat by Grandpa's bedside reading to him from the Psalms, he lifted his hand toward something only he could see.

Lark laid the Bible aside. "What is it, Grandpa? Do you need something?"

"Wait for me, Violet." The words were barely a murmur, but a wan smile creased his cheeks. His eyes misted as he gazed into nothingness. "I'll be home soon, honey. I'll be home soon."

"No, Grandpa, not yet." Tears welling, Lark clasped his hand and stroked the papery skin. "Please, stay with us a little longer."

When a hand settled on her shoulder, she looked up to see Mrs. Ballard standing next to her. "Seems he's already seein' into the Great Beyond. You don't want him lingering to suffer, do you?"

Lark shook her head. "No, of course not. But this has happened so fast. How can we ever say good-bye?"

"It's that way sometimes. But think of it like this." The nurse smoothed the blanket over Grandpa's thin legs. "Good-byes are for the living. Your grandpa's going soon to a great heavenly hello, where there'll be no more pain or tears or want or worry, only inexpressible love."

"That's a beautiful reminder. Thank you." Sniffling, Lark edged closer so she could rest her head next to Grandpa's side.

Mrs. Ballard quietly went about her usual examination, checking Grandpa's pulse and listening to his chest. When she finished, she asked softly, "Will your family be returning for a visit soon?"

Lark sat up and dried her eyes. "It isn't easy for them to get away."

"Well, if they want to spend a little time with him"—empathy filled the nurse's expression—"they should come sooner rather than later."

Heart sinking, Lark squeezed her eyes shut. "I'll let them know."

The nurse excused herself from the room, leaving Lark to ponder her last conversation with Bryony. She'd expected Bryony and Michael to drive over earlier in the week, but Michael had telephoned Lark at the Vickarys' early Tuesday morning to say Bryony hadn't been well and he didn't think she should make the trip. Lark had heard the concern in his tone. Before he put Bryony on the line, he cautioned Lark not to ask too many questions, only to speak as reassuringly as she could.

Now Lark feared that if she told Bryony how quickly Grandpa was failing, it might endanger Bryony's health or the baby's. Yet if Bryony didn't get the chance to say her last good-byes, would she ever forgive Lark?

She'd just made up her mind to find Pastor Vickary and ask for his counsel when Mrs. Ballard stepped into the room again. "You have visitors waiting in the lobby."

Lark sat up with a start. "My sisters?"

"No, two gentlemen." The nurse winked. "And one of them looks mighty anxious to see you."

Anson!

Her pulse fluttering, Lark scurried along the corridor. When she rounded the corner and saw Anson watching for her, she practically flew into his sheltering arms. Neither spoke for several long moments as Lark melted into the healing comfort of his strength. Breathing in, she caught the musty wool scent of his overcoat. Eclipsing the medicinal hospital odors, today it was the most wonderful smell in the world.

She tipped her head back. "I'm so glad you came. Even as kind as everyone's been, I've never felt so alone."

Offering a crooked smile, Anson thumbed away a drop of moisture beneath her eye. "Never? Not even during those difficult days in Kenya?"

"This is different. There, I felt I had at least some semblance of control over my life. Misguided as I may have been, I was there by my own choice." Lark gave her head a helpless shake. "Here, it's as if all my choices have been taken away, and all I can do is wait and pray."

With a kiss to her forehead, Anson tucked her under his arm and led her to a sitting area near the front windows. Only then did she acknowledge Dr. Young's presence. He had remained quietly off to one side but now offered Lark a sympathetic hug.

"The receptionist told me there's coffee down the hall," Dr. Young said. "Why don't you two chat while I fetch us some."

Anson slipped out of his overcoat, and they sat together on a maroon jacquard sofa. Lark clutched his hand as she repeated what the nurse had advised her about Grandpa. "I understood he didn't have long, but I never expected it would happen this quickly. How will I ever tell my sisters?"

"Would you like me to make the call for you?"

"I couldn't ask you. It's my responsibility."

"But not one you have to bear alone." Anson cupped her chin. "Let me help, Lark. That's why I'm here."

It would be so easy to give everything over to him, then to collapse in a trembling puddle of tears and wallow in her grief and the unfairness of it all. With a shuddering sigh, she pasted on a determined smile. "Thank you—but your presence alone means more than I can say."

She looked toward the pay telephone booth across the lobby. This wasn't a call she could put off indefinitely, not if her sisters had any hopes of arriving in time. Still, she couldn't shake her concerns about Bryony.

Pushing to her feet, she held out her hand to Anson. "Would

you come with me to the telephone? It'll help just having you nearby."

He stood beside her in the open door of the booth while she placed the call. She breathed a quiet sigh of relief when it was Michael who answered. Her voice shook as she told him what Mrs. Ballard had said.

"I see, I see." Michael's impassive response suggested he didn't want to give anything away to listening ears. "Let me think it over and get back to you."

"She's close by, isn't she?"

"That's right."

Lark wanted to ask about Bryony's emotional state, but clearly Michael wouldn't be able to say much. She glanced at Anson over her shoulder and welcomed his encouraging smile. To Michael, she said, "Will you get word to Rose? Even if you decide you shouldn't bring Bryony, Rose will surely want to come."

"Of course. Thanks so much for calling." He paused, then added meaningfully, "Take care."

Hanging up, Lark leaned into Anson's embrace. "How long can you stay?"

"Until tomorrow afternoon. Irwin and I have rooms at the Majestic."

Knowing she could enjoy several more hours of Anson's company brought a lift to Lark's aching heart. They returned to the sitting area, where Dr. Young waited with three cups of coffee. While they sipped, Lark forced her thoughts away from her dying grandfather and listened while Anson and Dr. Young described the first week of school. She felt Anson's disappointment keenly when he described again the scant turnout on Monday night, but he reported with pride that all of the Jacksons' children had come on Tuesday evening, along with two more children of sharecroppers.

"Attendance continued to grow all week," Anson said. "I'm much more hopeful."

"I'm so glad." Lark cast a furtive glance at the wall clock. She hated to leave Anson, but she'd left Grandpa's room over an hour ago and was eager to get back and check on him.

Dr. Young gave a polite cough. "Well, well, look at the time. Anson, I believe I'll catch the trolley back to the hotel. You come along whenever you're ready."

They all stood as Dr. Young slipped into his overcoat. Anson turned to Lark. "Would you mind if I stay a while longer? Perhaps we could both sit with your grandfather for a bit."

Gratitude swelled her chest. "Yes, please. If Grandpa should awaken, I know it would cheer him to see you."

*   *   *

Rose had basically two choices: keep house or tend to the business of farming. Because she sure didn't have time or energy for both, not with Grandpa laid up and her sisters gone. And she knew for a fact that Grandpa would tan her sorry hide if she let the farm go to pot. It was their livelihood, but more than that, it was Grandpa's life's work and the pride of his heart.

"It'll all be here waiting for you, Grandpa." Rose brought the ax down on the end of another log on the chopping block. Kindling flew as the force of the blow reverberated up her arms. *Please, please, please, Lord, let him get better! Let him come home!*

She didn't care what the doctor had said. Doctors didn't know everything. They sure as all git-out didn't know how downright stubborn Grandpa could be.

As she set another log on the chopping block, Michael's Chevrolet rumbled up. Rose didn't see Bryony in the car, which surprised her. Michael rarely came out all this way by himself, and Rose hadn't seen her sister since they had gotten back from taking Grandpa to Hot Springs.

She laid down the ax and ambled over. "Hey, Michael. Where's Bry?"

"At home." His grim expression as he climbed from the car made Rose's insides jittery. He shoved his hands into the pockets of his tweed jacket. "She, uh, doesn't know I'm here."

Rose gnawed on the inside of her lip. "I don't think I like the sound of that."

"Can we go inside? There's something I need to tell you."

The jittery feeling became a jagged lump of pure dread in the pit of Rose's belly. "If it's about Grandpa, you best just spit it out. I ain't got time or patience for pleasantries."

"He's failing faster than anyone expected, Rose. Lark called. She says you should go see him while you can."

Blinking rapidly, Rose glanced away. "You go on and take Bry. I got too much work to do here."

"But don't you—"

"No!" she practically shouted, wheeling on him. "I do *not* want to go sit around a hospital bed and wait for my grandpa to die. Anyways"—angry tears clogged her throat—"I'm not gonna be the one giving up on him. I'm praying with my last breath for Grandpa to get well and come home where he belongs."

"Rose, honey—" Michael reached out for her hand, but she snatched it away. "Rose, don't be this way. Let me take you to Hot Springs. Daniel said he'd look after the farm till you get back. And then—"

"And then nothing! Just get on out of here and leave me to my work." Storming back to the woodpile, Rose seized the ax and raised it high over the log she'd been about to split before Michael drove up.

Then her arms set to trembling, and the ax clattered to the ground, inches from her boot. She collapsed at the base of the old stump that served as a chopping block and sobbed into her folded arms.

*   *   *

"Rose...Rosie, it's all right." Michael knelt and held her close against his side. *It's all right.* Such futile, meaningless words. He was useless to comfort his own wife, and now he felt powerless to help his sweet young sister-in-law face the inevitable.

When her tears let up, he eased her to her feet and guided her into the house. A few shaky sobs escaped as she tried to compose herself at the kitchen table. Michael wet a cloth at the sink and handed it to her so she could cool her reddened eyes.

"I'm sorry, I'm sorry," she murmured. "I'm not generally one to cry like that. I just..."

"You have nothing to explain or apologize for. We're all sad and hurting." Michael pulled out another chair and sat down tiredly. He couldn't stop thinking about Bryony, who still hadn't been told the latest about her grandfather.

But how could he add to the burden of worry she already carried? She'd been thrilled about the baby at first, but with each passing week of her pregnancy, she grew increasingly moody. For a while, she'd tried to hide behind a pretense of normalcy, but it never lasted long. She'd alternately wring her hands over unnamed worries or curl up under the covers in the depths of despondency.

And Dr. Eddington had assured them over and over again that there was absolutely no reason to be concerned about the baby.

Or there wouldn't be, provided Bryony didn't make herself physically ill with all this worrying. Between the morning sickness and the anxiety, Bryony seldom forced down a decent meal anymore. When Michael held her in bed at night, he could count each rib through her nightgown.

"Michael?" Rose peered up at him. "Are *you* all right?"

A weak smile disguised his inner turmoil. Rose didn't need the added strain of knowing how Bryony struggled. "Just thinking how hard this is on you and your sisters. I wish I could do more."

"You're doing plenty, and I appreciate it." With a determined sniff, Rose pushed up from the table. "I need to get after my chores, but you go on and take Bryony to see Grandpa. Give him my love and tell him the farm's in good hands."

Michael followed her outside, then stood to one side as she wielded the ax. He dodged a flying piece of kindling. "If you change your mind—"

"I won't."

"Then do you need anything? Can I send someone out to lend a hand? Daniel, maybe, or Caleb Wieland?"

"Thanks"—the ax came down and another log splintered—"but I'm managing just fine. Don't need anyone's help."

Michael gave a slow nod, said good-bye, and retreated to his car. Seemed each of the Linwood girls needed to deal with grief in her own private way. Something he should be familiar with, as he'd spent a full decade after the Great War trying to escape the agony of remembering.

Then Bryony had come into his life and shown him a way out of his self-imposed isolation. It was like awakening from a deep sleep. No, more like pulling back the curtains, letting in the bright light of day, and seeing once again how beautiful life could be.

If only he could find a way to bring Bryony back into the light.

Chapter Seventeen

Leaving Lark alone in Hot Springs was one of the hardest things Anson had ever done. He knew she wasn't really alone—the Vickarys and Nurse Ballard were taking good care of her—but the heartbreak in her eyes when she learned neither of her sisters was coming ripped a hole in Anson's chest.

"She's a strong girl," Irwin said after they'd been on the road awhile. "She'll get through this."

"If it weren't for the school—"

"Yes, and you'd have caused Lark even more distress if we'd stayed. Those children's education is as important to her as it is to you. She needs to know we're carrying on in her absence."

"That's all it will be—*carrying on*—because without her working alongside me, nothing's the same."

Irwin reached over to give Anson a pat on the arm. "She'll be back, my boy. Sadly for her and her family, it appears much sooner than anyone imagined."

They drove on in silence for the next several miles, then stopped briefly in Little Rock to refuel and get something to eat before continuing on to Eden. Darkness had fallen by the time they arrived at the house. The car's headlights swept the front porch as they turned into the driveway.

Irwin gasped. "Lord, have mercy!"

Body tensing, Anson grabbed the armrest. "What? What's wrong?"

"Be glad for your poor eyesight." Instead of slowing down, Irwin accelerated down the driveway to the back of the house, then slammed on the brakes and shut off the motor. Hands resting on the steering wheel, he stared straight ahead, the sound of each harsh breath filling the car.

"Tell me what you saw," Anson demanded. When Irwin only

shook his head, Anson thrust open his door and marched toward the front porch.

"Anson, don't." Irwin's footsteps pounded behind him. "It'll keep till morning. There's no sense—"

Rounding the porch, Anson halted on the lawn and squinted at the front of the house. As best he could make out with his faulty vision and a nearly full moon still low on the horizon, someone had streaked the walls and windows with black paint.

Irwin caught up with him. "Leave it, Anson. There's nothing to be done tonight."

"But what is it? Get a flashlight. I need to know."

Irwin's long, pained sigh suggested Anson might be sorry for insisting. "All right, but only if you promise to hold your temper and not try to do anything about it until after a good night's sleep."

Anson couldn't promise any such thing. Teeth clenched, he swung around to face his friend. "Either tell me what's been done to my school or get some light out here so I can see for myself."

After another slow breath, Irwin lowered his chin. "Suffice it to say that certain factions are not happy about our offering education to...all children."

Anson glared at the smeared paint. "What does it say, Irwin? Just tell me."

His voice barely a murmur, Irwin repeated the ugly, racist words.

Rage and revulsion boiled in Anson's belly. He shrugged out of his overcoat and threw it down in a wad, then set to rolling up his shirtsleeves. "Get soap and water, a bucket of paint, whatever it's going to take to get rid of this—this *filth*."

"Not tonight, Anson, please." Irwin bent to retrieve Anson's coat. "We can't see what we're doing anyway, and we're both exhausted from the trip."

"You think I can rest knowing those words are scrawled across the front of my school? No, I'm getting rid of them right now. I won't have half of Eden pass by tomorrow morning and see such ugliness." Anson started for the storage shed out back.

Irwin grabbed his arm and spun him around. "Calm down, will you? Odds are this was done last night while we were in Hot Springs, so I imagine too many saw it today already. The damage has been done."

Anson forced himself to breathe, to think rationally, when all he wanted was to find the cowards who'd done this and hammer them to a pulp. That anyone who called himself a Christian could abase another human being, much less deny innocent children the advantages of an education, simply because of the color of their skin—it was abomination of the highest degree.

He scraped a hand down his face. "After all we've worked for, all we've tried to do…"

"I know, believe me." Irwin draped Anson's coat around his shoulders and nudged him toward the house. "These are only scare tactics. Ugly words can't stop what we're doing here."

As they stepped into the kitchen, Anson halted and looked hard at Irwin. "What if they don't stop at words? What if—"

"One thing at a time. Please, let's get some sleep. We'll sort this out in the morning."

"All right, all right. Tomorrow." On his way upstairs, Anson could only think how glad he was that Lark hadn't been here to see this. He made up his mind to keep it from her for as long as possible.

* * *

Dawn's first light found Anson scraping and scouring black paint off the front windows. Cold, soapy water had long since numbed his fingers, but he took morbid delight in watching the hateful words turn to gray streaks and slide down the panes into oblivion.

The front door opened. Irwin, still in his pajamas and plaid flannel robe, stepped onto the porch. "I suspected you wouldn't wait for me to get started."

"The sooner this is gone, the better." Anson stooped to rinse the rag in the pail at his feet. He wrung it out with a violent twist and moved to the next pane of glass.

"Don't you think we should call the sheriff out before you go washing away the evidence?"

"What good would it do? If you've a mind to help instead of offering useless advice, you can start painting."

Irwin snorted. "Very well, but breakfast first. I don't perform hard labor on an empty stomach."

"And you might want to get dressed, too." Anson cast his friend a halfhearted smile of apology. "Bring me some coffee when it's made."

"Yes, your highness." The door slammed.

Anson's revulsion over what they'd come home to hadn't lessened, but at least the light of day had given him perspective. This was one act of cowardice. It had caused unnecessary work for them, but it wouldn't shut them down. Of that, Anson was determined.

He finished with the windows and was on his way around back to empty the water pail when he heard an automobile turn into the driveway. Pausing to look, he thought he recognized the beat-up old pickup Noah Jackson drove.

The driver's door opened, and a dark-skinned man stepped to the ground. "Howdy, Mr. Schafer."

"That you, Noah?" Anson set down the pail and strode over.

Noah removed his tattered hat and held it against his chest. "Yessuh, an' I'm mighty sorry about your trouble."

Anson couldn't even imagine the hurt those words had caused the Jackson family. "I'm the one who's sorry. I apologize to you on behalf of every white person who has ever disrespected you."

"You ain't the one who needs to apologize neither. They's hate in this world and ain't nothin' gonna stop it 'cept good people like you trying to make a difference." Noah ducked his head. "I'd rightly understand if you decided you ain't gonna teach our children no more, but all the same, I'm here to help."

"Your children are welcome here for as long as you are willing to send them." Anson firmed his mouth. "But I refuse to inflict further indignity by allowing you to clean up after these hoodlums."

"Honest, sir, it don't make me no nevermind. Maybe give me a bit of satisfaction, to tell the truth." Noah nodded toward the shed at the end of the driveway. "How 'bout I get the paint and get started? We'll have ever'thing back like it was, lickety-split."

Gratitude and admiration filled Anson's heart. How could he refuse such kindness, such Christian forbearance in the face of persecution? He stepped aside. "Thank you, Noah. You know where everything is."

Ready for the coffee he hoped Irwin had perking, Anson emptied the water pail at the far edge of the yard and then went inside. The pot burbled on the stove, and the aroma filled the kitchen. Anson was about to pour himself a cup when he heard Irwin speaking to someone on the telephone.

"Of course, Reverend Unsworth, I'm fully aware—Yes, but we were out of town over the weekend and—"

Anson moved to the office doorway. It sounded as if the pastor wasn't giving Irwin a chance to get a word in edgewise.

"Naturally, we're as put off by such vile sentiments as you are, but—" Irwin shot Anson an exasperated frown. "No, sir, it most definitely will *not* cause us to change our manner of operation. The school remains open to all!" He slammed down the receiver.

Braced against the doorframe, Anson crossed his arms. "What was that about, as if I needed to ask?"

"Just what it sounded like. The good reverend, along with half the town, so he says, is concerned we'll provoke racial violence if we refuse to make this a whites-only institution."

Anson glanced out the window as Noah emerged from the storage shed with a can of paint. With a defeated sigh, he sank into the chair at Lark's typing table. "I'm as certain as you are that we're in the right, but the last thing I want is to tear this community apart. Is it really worth the risk to those children?"

"Is it worth the risk to their futures if they're denied the education they deserve?" Irwin faced him squarely. "This school was your vision, Anson. Don't tell me you're now ready to throw in the towel?"

Anson's eyes fell shut, and instead of Schafer School in Eden, Arkansas, he saw his beloved Matumaini School on the slopes of Mount Kenya. He could still smell the rich, loamy dampness of the surrounding forest. He could hear the monkeys chattering in the treetops and the nighttime yipping of the hyenas.

He could still see Franklin Keene waving good-bye from the porch steps the day Anson and Irwin had set out for the train to Mombasa.

With a groan that was more of a growl, Anson slumped over and rested his forehead in his hands. "Nothing—*nothing*—has turned out the way I envisioned. Until my eyes got infected, I never intended to leave Kenya. Until funding didn't come through as hoped, I never intended for the work of the Schafer Foundation to be shunted to one obscure little town."

Another chair scraped across the floor, and Irwin plopped down in front of him. "And until we came home to racial epithets plastered across the house, neither of us intended to be having this conversation. But it is what it is, Anson, and we have to deal with it, either by caving to public outcry or standing our ground. Which is it going to be?"

"If you and I were the only two this affected, my answer would be simple. But we're not. We have to tread carefully, or we could be faced with something much, much worse." The coffee Anson had never gotten around to was beckoning. He pushed to his feet. "I need time to think."

*   *   *

Lark stayed at Grandpa's bedside all day Monday and into the night. Close to midnight, Pastor Vickary came looking for her.

"Annemarie was worried about you," he said, rousing her from a half-sleep. "Why don't you come home with me and get some rest. I'll bring you back first thing in the morning."

She gazed at Grandpa and counted each shallow breath. "But what if—"

"I spoke to the nurse on duty. Nothing's imminent." Pastor Vickary guided her to her feet. "Come on. You're going to need your strength when the time does come."

With a weak nod, Lark allowed the pastor to help her with her coat. Leaning over the bed, she smoothed the thin white hair at Grandpa's temples and kissed his cheek. His eyelids fluttered and his breathing quickened slightly, and then he settled into quiet sleep.

On the way out to the car, Pastor Vickary asked, "I take it nothing's changed with your sisters' plans?"

"It's for the best, at least for Bryony. Rose is...well, she's handling things the only way she knows how."

"Still, it's a heavy burden for you to bear alone. You're a brave young woman, Lark Linwood."

She smiled her thanks but didn't feel the least bit brave at the moment. Just...tired. Resigned. Hopeless.

A few hours' sleep in the Vickarys' comfortable guest bed revived her but changed her outlook very little. The aromas of coffee, toast, and eggs lured her to the kitchen, where Annemarie had breakfast on the table for Samuel and the children.

Annemarie motioned Lark to a chair and then set a cup and saucer in front of her. "Tea or coffee this morning?"

"You don't have to wait on me. You've done too much already, and I'll never be able to repay you."

"Nonsense." Cracking an egg into the skillet, Annemarie narrowed one eye in Lark's direction. "This looks like a coffee morning to me. Sam, will you pour Lark a cup, please?"

"Of course, my dear." Pastor Vickary rose and planted a kiss on his wife's cheek. "Anything for my Valentine."

The children groaned in unison.

Only then did the date register in Lark's mind—February 14. Since she'd never had a beau, her strongest memories of Valentine's Day were about the paper hearts she and her sisters had made every year for Grandpa. He'd exclaim over each one before fastening them to his dresser mirror, then leave them there to admire for several weeks afterward.

A long-forgotten image edged its way to the surface. One morning before school—Lark couldn't have been more than nine or ten years old—she'd hurried back to her room to fetch her spelling book. Grandpa's door stood barely ajar, and she'd heard his tearful sniff. Peeking in, she glimpsed him standing before an open dresser drawer, a faded red and pink card in his hand. Running his fingers tenderly over the front, he'd murmured, "Happy Valentine's Day, sweet Violet. I miss you, my love."

Lark put a hand to her mouth, a choked cry escaping as she recalled the vases of pink carnations the nurses had delivered to each patient's room yesterday. She'd thought it so kind of the staff to bring these small tokens of cheer to the ill and dying in their care.

Pastor Vickary stood over her with the coffeepot. "What is it, Lark?"

"It'll be today, I know it." Sudden urgency filled her. "I have to go back. Now."

The Vickarys didn't ask questions, just hurried to get her out
the door and into the car. Pastor Vickary wouldn't even consider
letting her walk, for which she was thankful. His calming presence was a balm to her shattering heart.

They found Mrs. Ballard at Grandpa's bedside. She looked
toward Lark with a sorrowful smile. "I was just about to have
someone telephone you. It won't be long now."

Lark pulled a chair close and cradled Grandpa's hand, the
knobby fingers icy beneath her touch. His breathing had become
irregular, shallower than yesterday and more labored. When he
didn't breathe at all for several seconds, Lark turned to Mrs.
Ballard with alarm.

"It's normal," the woman said, "just his tired, sick body
winding down." She lightly touched Lark's shoulder. "Would
you rather we leave you alone to say your good-byes?"

"No, please stay." Lark included Pastor Vickary in her glance.
"Maybe you could pray?"

"Unceasingly." Pastor Vickary knelt beside the bed, one hand
holding Lark's and the other resting upon Grandpa's head.
"Father, we commend this good man to your heavenly rest. Let
his passing be peaceful as you welcome him into your holy presence. Shower those left behind with the comfort only you can
give, and strengthen them in the days and weeks to come."

Six more quick breaths and then one deeper one, followed by
a shuddering sigh, and Grandpa was gone.

Chapter Eighteen

It seemed an unnecessary burden to expect someone to drive all the way to Hot Springs to take Lark and Grandpa home. Pastor Vickary assisted her in purchasing an inexpensive coffin from the local mortuary, then arranged her train passage to Brinkley. Michael met her at the depot, where a Brinkley mortician took charge of Grandpa's body.

"How's Bryony taking the news?" Lark asked as they left the depot.

"Heartbroken, as we all are. I wish you'd have let me come for you."

"And leave Bry alone? She needed you much more than I did."

Michael's silence confirmed her statement.

They stopped briefly at the mortuary to finalize burial arrangements. With no reason to expect out-of-town mourners, they had decided to hold the funeral service on the following afternoon. Michael had already contacted Pastor Unsworth, who would officiate at the family's church in Eden. Interment would follow at the adjoining cemetery, where Grandpa would be buried in the plot next to Grandma's.

When they arrived at Michael and Bryony's home, Lark hesitated to go inside for fear of the state she'd find Bryony in. How sudden this must seem for Lark's sisters—Grandpa alive and carrying on his tasks as usual, then scarcely two weeks ago, his collapse and the dire news of his illness. They'd all surely hoped for the miracle God hadn't chosen to provide. But spending hour after hour at Grandpa's bedside and watching his steady decline, Lark had given up on miracles. She'd been left with no choice but to face the inevitable.

Bryony's cat, Honey, met them at the door. The poor thing looked anxious and confused, and Lark scooped her up to nuzzle the soft fur. Behind the cat's ear, her fingers caught in a knotted mass, Honey's neglected grooming another sign of Bryony's despondency.

"She's probably in the bedroom," Michael said. "I tried to get her to sleep, but she's hardly stopped crying."

Lark set the cat on the carpet and tiptoed down the hall. She peeked into the bedroom and saw Bryony curled up beneath a blanket. "Bry?" she whispered. "It's me. I'm back."

Bursting out in a sob, Bryony sat up and opened her arms to Lark. "What will we do? What will we ever do without Grandpa?"

Lark had no answer. She already missed Grandpa horribly, but at this moment, she missed her sister more—the strong and determined Bryony who'd taken charge of the family after Mama died, who'd saved them from starvation by taking work as the Heaths' housemaid. *What's happened to you, Bry?*

After they'd held each other a while, Lark handed Bryony a handkerchief. "Here, dry your eyes, honey. You can't keep crying like this. And Michael says you're not eating or getting enough sleep. It isn't good for you or the baby."

"I'm trying, Lark, but everything's so hard lately. I—I don't know what's wrong with me."

"It'll be all right. We'll all be all right…in time." At least Lark hoped so, prayed so, with every ounce of her fragile faith.

Once Bryony had quieted again, Michael drove Lark out to the farm, where she encountered an entirely different reception.

Rose barely looked up from hoeing a trench in the vegetable garden. "I started some rabbit stew for supper. You might want to check on it."

Lark shot a glance at Michael.

He gave a halfhearted shrug. "As hard as Bryony's been crying, that's how hard Rose keeps working. I'm sorry, Lark, but it looks like you'll have to be the glue holding this family together now."

It was a role she'd never asked for or wanted. Heaving a long, slow breath, she waited while Michael fetched her suitcase from the trunk and carried it inside. She waved from the screen porch as he drove away.

The simmering stew filled the kitchen with a mixture of interesting aromas. Rose still wasn't much of a cook, and from the looks of things, her kitchen cleanup skills had also fallen by the wayside. More likely, she'd been too preoccupied with farm chores to care. Lark lifted the lid on the stewpot and sampled the concoction. Not bad, but a little more salt and a dash of pepper would help. While Rose finished outside, Lark washed dishes and wiped counters. It felt good to do something with visible results, something that served a practical purpose.

Lark understood now why Rose hadn't wanted to leave the farm. What could she have done in Hot Springs besides sit and wait with Lark? Here at least, Rose could keep things going just as Grandpa would have done. Here was life, purpose, meaning. Here was...

Grief stabbed deep and sharp. Lark dropped her dishcloth in the sink and doubled over with a muted cry.

Then all at once two strong arms surrounded her, and Anson's voice washed over her like sunlight on a winter's day. "I'm here, Lark. I'm here."

She turned within the circle of his embrace and leaned into him. "How did you know I would need you at exactly this moment?"

"Because I love you so much, and I knew what a hard day this would be." His lips brushed her forehead as he cradled her against his chest. "We met Michael on the road on our way here. He was worried about you. About Rose, too."

Lark scoffed. "He has enough to worry about with Bryony." Shifting slightly, she glanced around Anson's shoulder. "Where's Dr. Young?"

"Waiting in the car. He wanted to give us a few moments alone." Anson cupped her chin and looked deeply into her eyes. His glasses reflected the western sun angling through the window behind her. "How are you, really? Is there anything I can do?"

She straightened and forced a smile. "Keeping busy is helping. You can see what a mess Rose left for me."

Anson's soft chuckle warmed her as he slipped off his coat. "I'm a decent dishwasher. Let me help."

As they stood at the sink together, Anson washing and Lark drying, a sense of rightness enveloped her. She dared to imagine a life of preparing meals and doing dishes every night with him, of waking up beside him every morning. Heat rose in her cheeks at the shameless direction of her thoughts.

The back door opened, and Dr. Young stepped in. "I see you're making yourself useful. Need an extra hand?"

Anson passed Lark the last dish and turned with a grin. "Perfect timing—we're almost done."

"Yes, I'm good that way." The older man winked as he came toward Lark. "My dear, how are you?"

"Trying to be strong. Thank you for coming." She gave him a quick hug, only then noticing the covered dish he'd set on the table. "What's this?"

"A pie Mrs. Unsworth sent out with us. She sends her condolences. I believe they're also planning to serve a meal at the church following the funeral."

Lark lifted the cloth from the pie tin, revealing a golden-brown woven crust over plump apple slices. A lump rose in her throat as she recalled their neighbors' generous acts of kindness after Mama's death. Lark's family had also made a point of doing for others during times of grief, but she hadn't expected to be on the receiving end so soon.

Remembering the stew, Lark went to the stove to give the pot a stir. "You'll stay for supper and a slice of pie, won't you?" Almost immediately, she took note of the time. "But it's well past five. Shouldn't you be at the school preparing for students?" At Anson and Dr. Young's shared glance, Lark's stomach twisted. "What's wrong?"

"Nothing. Nothing at all." Anson's smile was only mildly reassuring. "I felt it was much more important to be with you this evening, so Miranda and Callie offered to tutor the children."

"But they'll surely need you, and I'll feel even worse if you stay." Rushing to the cupboard, Lark found a bowl large enough for two servings of stew. "Here, I'll dish up some supper to take back with you. Then you really must go."

* * *

It wasn't what he wanted, but Anson could see there'd be no changing Lark's mind. He accepted the bowl of stew and two slices of pie for the trip back to Eden. They arrived at the school a few minutes after six.

Miranda came through the house as they stepped into the kitchen. "Back already? We didn't expect you until much later."

"Lark insisted." Anson set down the dishes and shrugged out of his overcoat. "How many students do we have?"

Miranda lowered her gaze. "Only two, I'm afraid. Daniel tried, but…"

"But their parents are worried about more trouble." A gust of air whistled between Anson's teeth. "What can I say, when I'm uneasy about it, too?"

Irwin set out plates and silverware. "Give them time. This falderal will blow over eventually."

Arms crossed, Miranda remained silent.

Anson studied her. "You don't think so, do you?"

"Jobs are scarce enough for white folks. People are just trying to protect their own." She cast a quick glance over her shoulder as Callie's patient tones drifted from the classroom. "Believe me, Anson," she continued, lowering her voice, "I'm completely on your side. But Eden is a peaceful community, and no one here wants any part of a racial disturbance."

"Apparently that isn't the case, considering what someone in this *peaceful community* painted across the front of our school over the weekend."

"Anson." Irwin nudged his elbow. "Sit down and eat your supper. And in the meantime, have a little faith."

With a regretful sigh, Miranda excused herself to return to the classroom. Anson took his seat at the place Irwin had set for him but found he had no appetite. Down to four students on Monday, only the Jackson children on Tuesday, and now just the two tonight. They'd opened their doors barely more than a week ago, and already the school seemed doomed to fail.

All this for nothing, Lord? Why give him a heart for teaching, a dream of a better world filled with hope and opportunity for children of every color, only to take it all way—first with Anson's failing vision and now with hate and racism?

Though I was blind, now I see—the response given to the Pharisees when they questioned a man Jesus had healed. Had Anson been so blinded by his own plans and ambitions that he'd missed God's will somehow?

Irwin rose and cleared away the plate of stew Anson had barely touched. "I don't suppose you'll want pie either."

Shaken from his thoughts, Anson murmured, "Perhaps later."

"I'll save both your stew and your slice of pie for when you come down at midnight with a hole in your belly."

Anson offered a wry smile, the best he could do under the circumstances. If he could drive himself, he'd head straight back to the farm and find comfort in Lark's presence. Except he should be the one offering comfort to her. He wondered how Lark and Rose fared tonight, whether they were consolation to one another or hindered by their starkly different personalities.

Something else ate at him as well, the growing sense that Lark would feel compelled to leave Schafer School and defer her college degree even longer while helping to run the farm with Rose. As determined as Lark's plucky younger sister might be, how could she possibly operate a tenant farm on her own?

With a frustrated groan, Anson pushed away from the table. "I think I'll see how the lessons are going. May I leave you with the dishes?"

"Seeing as how you already have dishpan hands after helping Lark, how can I say no?"

Anson quirked a heartless smile and strode into the hallway. He paused outside the classroom and listened as Callie showed a young boy how to work an arithmetic problem. Her gentle tones encouraged even when the child made an error. With a college education, she would make a fine teacher.

The thought brought another stab to Anson's gut. Lark should be at Henderson State finishing her degree. Thanks to Franklin Keene's persuasion, she'd withdrawn from college to go to Kenya. Thanks to Anson, she'd delayed her return in order to assist with his foundation. Seemed having his own plans derailed wasn't enough. He'd contributed to the destruction of Lark's future as well.

* * *

Michael listened outside the bathroom door as Bryony lost her breakfast—what little he'd coaxed into her, anyway. She should be gaining weight with the baby, not wasting away. He well remembered the day Miranda had come home to Brookbirch two years ago, pregnant with George and near starvation. If Bryony hadn't taken her in, if the servants hadn't sent food over every day, no telling what might have happened. Michael praised God again and again for his sister's return to vitality, for the birth of a healthy little boy, and for the forgiveness their father had finally offered—years too late, in Michael's opinion.

He rested his forehead against the door. "Bryony? Please let me come in and help."

"No, I don't want you seeing me like this." A cough and a sputter. "I just need a minute more."

Two minutes passed, then five. At last, the door opened. Bryony looked pale, fragile, shaken. "I'm better now. Did you find my gray dress?"

"I laid it out on the bed. Honey, you don't have to go. Everyone will understand."

"And miss Grandpa's funeral?" One hand trailing the wall, she walked unsteadily toward the bedroom. "I have to go. My sisters need me."

If you only realized how much. And how much I need you, too.

While he helped her dress, Michael thought back to a conversation he'd had with Sam Vickary the day they'd admitted Bryony's grandfather to the care facility. In a private moment, Michael had confided his concerns about Bryony's health, his fears that if she didn't pull out of this despondency, she could lose the baby.

"Her doctor says it's an occasional complication of pregnancy, and there's nothing to be done but wait it out," Michael had explained. "But seeing her like this is destroying me."

After a thoughtful moment, Sam made an unexpected suggestion: "If and when you're ready, bring her here. The staff is competent and caring, and they can see to your wife's needs in the ways you're unable to. And equally important," the former army chaplain went on, "I'll be here to support you."

At the time, Michael hadn't given the idea much consideration. He should be able to take care of his own wife, shouldn't he?

If and when you're ready…

With Bryony leaning heavily on his arm as they went out to the car, Michael made a decision. This couldn't go on a day longer. First thing tomorrow, he would take Bryony to Hot Springs.

* * *

"Rose?" Lark shouted from the screen porch. "Rosie, where are you? We need to get to the church."

A fiery red mop of hair popped up from behind the tractor. "I need to finish here. Five minutes, okay?"

"No, it's *not* okay." Pushing through the door, Lark marched across the yard. "You've got to stop stalling, Rose. You can work on this pile of metal until the sky falls, but it won't change the fact—"

Rose's lower lip trembled. She tried to hide it by bending to get a wrench from the toolbox.

"Oh, Rosie, come here." Lark pulled her sister into a hug and felt every resistant muscle in Rose's body. "Crying isn't a bad thing, honey. Let it out."

"I can't." She gave a loud sniff. "Grandpa's counting on me. I have to—"

"No, you don't. Not today, anyway." Firming her chin, Lark steered Rose toward the house. "I want you cleaned up and in your Sunday best right now."

It took some prodding, but Lark finally got her sister into the only decent dress the girl owned, then brushed out and plaited her hair. "There. You look halfway civilized."

"I look like a sissy-girl."

"You look like the beautiful girl you are." Lark tucked a stray curl behind Rose's ear. "Grandpa might be counting on you to see after the farm, but I believe he's also looking down from heaven hoping you'll do him proud with all the friends who are coming to pay their respects. Now, get your coat, and let's be on our way."

Lark let Rose drive, figuring the responsibility would keep the girl's mind occupied. Rose had pulled herself together pretty well, but when they turned the corner and drove up in front of the church, Rose jerked the pickup to a halt. "Lord have mercy, looks like the whole county showed up."

Lark swallowed the catch in her throat. Considering how long Grandpa had been farming for Brookbirch Plantation, she'd expected a fair turnout, but this beat all.

Caleb Wieland strode over to Rose's door and helped her out. Wrapping his arms around her, he rocked her gently. "Mighty sorry, Rose. Mighty sorry."

The sight brought more tears to Lark's eyes. She stepped from the pickup to find Anson waiting for her. He handed her his handkerchief. "The church is full—standing room only, except for your family's pew up front." He tilted his head and offered a tenderly soothing smile. "You look like you could use an arm to lean on. May I walk you in?"

"Thank you." Lark wrapped her fingers around his coat sleeve, the wool scratchy against her palm yet comforting. "Please sit with us. I'm sure there's room."

He hesitated. "It wouldn't be right. Anyway, Irwin already has seats for us."

Lark started to insist, ready to invite Dr. Young to join them up front as well, but something in Anson's expression made her bite back her words.

Pastor Unsworth met them in the vestibule. "Your sisters have taken their seats. Are you ready, my dear?"

She nodded, reluctantly exchanging Anson's arm for the pastor's, and they started down the aisle.

It was one thing seeing all the automobiles and horse-drawn wagons parked outside, and quite another to be faced with this multitude—friends, acquaintances, even Sebastian Heath. Lark didn't see Mrs. Heath and wondered briefly at her absence. She knew how Michael worried about his mother's failing memory. Then she saw the coffin, and her steps faltered. Visions of Grandpa, alive and seemingly healthy only weeks ago, swam before her eyes. How could it be that they were gathered here today to commit his body to the earth?

Feeling numb and disconnected, she sank into the pew next to Rose. With a tremulous breath, she clasped Rose's hand, their fingers meshing. Rose gave her a shaky smile and then reached for Bryony. The three sisters clung to each other, tears falling unrestrained as Pastor Unsworth began the service.

Somehow they made it through. Still holding tightly to each other, they later stood at the gravesite as the pastor read from Genesis, "By the sweat of your face you shall eat bread until you return to the ground, for out of it you were taken; you are dust, and to dust you shall return."

And from John, "In my Father's house there are many dwelling places. If it were not so, would I have told you that I go to prepare a place for you?"

Rose leaned close to Lark's ear. "Do you think God will let Grandpa tend a farm in heaven?"

"Maybe after the angels have finished celebrating his arrival." Lark couldn't resist a tearful chuckle. "At least in heaven there are no droughts and the cotton bolls don't slice your fingers to shreds."

Caleb, Michael, and two neighboring farmers lowered the coffin into the grave. After Lark and her sisters had each tossed in a shovelful of dirt and Pastor Unsworth had uttered another prayer, the crowd of mourners meandered back to the church building. During the graveside service, several ladies from the congregation had laid out a potluck meal in the fellowship hall that served during the week as Eden's one-room schoolhouse. Funerals took precedence, though, so today the children had been dismissed early. Many of them still ran about the churchyard enjoying the mild February afternoon while their parents offered condolences to Lark and her sisters.

When all had eaten their fill and the last of the family friends had gathered up children and potluck dishes and left to return to their daily routines, Rose marched over and gave Lark's arm an impatient tug. "I've got farm chores waiting. Can we go home now?"

"Yes, in a minute." Lark glanced around the empty hall. "Have you seen Bryony?"

A dark look crossed Rose's face. "Michael took her to the sanctuary, where it was quiet. I don't like the looks of her, Lark."

"I don't either. Let's check on her before we leave."

They found Bryony in the last pew, where she wept softly against Michael's chest. Michael looked up as Lark drew near. His weary expression spoke more than words. With a kiss to Bryony's temple, he stood and stepped into the aisle, then motioned Lark and Rose toward the vestibule.

"I've made a decision," he told them. "First thing in the morning, I'm taking Bryony to Hot Springs and admitting her to the sanitarium where your grandfather was."

Lark's stomach clenched. "She's not—"

"No, no. I have every hope she'll pull out of this. But she needs more help than I can give." Running stiff fingers through his hair, Michael glanced back toward the sanctuary. "I've already talked to her about it. She agrees it's for the best."

"Will you stay there with her?"

"Yes. Sam Vickary has offered his guest room."

Rose swiped at a tear and edged away. "My whole family... I'm losing them all."

"No, you're not, honey." Lark set a comforting arm around her sister's shoulders. "Bry will be back when she's better"—she cast Michael a quick look for reassurance—"and I'm not going anywhere."

"I don't believe you. You might be working for Anson for now, but soon as you can, you'll go back to college, and then you'll go off to teach somewhere."

Lark squeezed her sister harder, giving her a gentle shake. "You're wrong. I meant what I said, Rosie Linwood. I'm staying with you at the farm for as long as you want to keep it going. And I promise I'll work right alongside you, even if it's for the rest of our lives."

No sooner had the words left her mouth than Lark looked up to see Anson standing in the open church door. His eyes narrowed, his lips flattened, before he lowered his head in silent understanding and turned away.

The rip in Lark's heart widened to a gaping chasm of grief, regret, and bitter hopelessness. Every dream she'd ever dreamed, all those lovely castles she'd built in her imagination...all of them were now in ruins.

Chapter Nineteen

A week passed, then two. With the certain knowledge Lark wouldn't be coming back to the school, Anson slogged through each day. It didn't help that student attendance had leveled off to only two farm families and the Jackson brothers' children. Anson, Irwin, and Daniel had gone out both together and separately to visit with the other parents, and the excuses varied only slightly. Farm chores were pressing. Spring planting season wasn't far off, and they needed every extra hand. High time the younger kids started pulling their weight.

Frustrated to the point of lunacy, Anson finally asked one father point blank: "Is it because the school isn't whites-only?"

The man wouldn't look him in the eye, but his firm jaw and stiff posture said it all. Anson had stormed out of the house ready to book passage on the next ship back to Kenya. He'd rather risk permanent loss of his sight than deal with the racial blind spots in these bigoted fools.

One afternoon as he prepared to sort through the mail Irwin had collected, Irwin plunked down on the other side of the desk. "How long are you planning on moping about like a lost puppy?"

"I'm not moping," Anson snapped. He rifled through the drawer for a letter opener.

"What would you call it, then? You wear a continual scowl, barely shifting to a mere frown in time for our students' arrival. You're going to bed earlier and sleeping later, and the last few times I've asked you for a chess game, you've turned me down flat."

"So I'm tired of chess. What of it?" Anson sliced open an envelope, almost taking off the side of his thumb in the process. He winced and fished in his pocket for a handkerchief to stanch the blood.

Irwin snorted. "Now see what you've done. Nearly cut off your hand again and ruined a perfectly good handkerchief in the process."

"It's mine to ruin." Shifting sideways, Anson fumbled to unfold the letter with his uninjured hand. It took his eyes a moment to focus, but as the typewritten words took shape, he let out a long, tired sigh and slapped the letter facedown on the desk.

"What is it?" Irwin snatched up the page. As he read it for himself, his self-righteous smirk faded. "Oh dear. The Fort Smith parish provided a sizable portion of our funding."

"So goes another nail in our coffin. Tell me honestly, Irwin, what are we accomplishing here?"

"We've been open barely a month. We have to give it time."

"While operating on a shoestring and failing to serve the children who need us most?" Anson shoved to his feet and paced to the window. "And with all these bank closures we've been hearing about, who knows when our accounts will be affected or how long this crisis will last? What little we have may not even be there when it's over."

Irwin didn't reply right away, and when he did, his tone had lost its bite. "The Lord has always provided whenever we've had need. He will again. And I thought we'd concluded that educating even one child toward better opportunities would be worth the effort. We're doing that, aren't we? So what's *really* eating at you?"

Anson hung his head. "I miss Lark. Miss her so much it makes my chest ache. Every day without her, it only hurts worse."

"I'm so sorry, my boy." Rising, Irwin came to stand by Anson at the window. "Would it help to drive out for a visit?"

"She made it clear when she came by the day after the funeral. Her first priority is Rose, and Rose is determined to keep the farm going."

"That can't possibly continue for long, can it? Two young women trying to make a go of it by themselves?"

"You've spent enough time around Rose to know how much the farm means to her. She won't give up without a fight."

Irwin stepped in front of Anson and arched a brow. "I sincerely hope you won't either."

"Give up? You mean on the school?"

"And on Lark."

Pinned by Irwin's sharp glare, Anson inched backward. "Appears the choices on both counts are out of my hands."

"See what you want to see." Irwin gave his head a quick shake and strode from the office.

It *wasn't* what Anson wanted to see, not by any means. He wanted to see his school thriving and filled with children eager to learn. He wanted to see an end to racial prejudice once and for all.

He wanted to see Lark again, hold her in his arms, tell her again and again how much he loved her. Tell her how he couldn't envision a life without her.

The telephone rang, startling him. He snatched up the receiver. "Hello, Schafer School."

"Hello, Anson. It's Miranda. I thought I should ask before coming over." He heard the hesitation in her voice. "Will you need Callie and me tonight?"

"Thanks, but no. It'll be only the Jackson children again, I'm sure." Anson paused. "I deeply appreciate how you both have pitched in, but considering how attendance has been..."

Miranda sighed. "We all hoped for more. I'm sorry, Anson. If things change, though, do call on us."

"I will."

After pecking out a tactfully worded response to the Fort Smith parish priest, Anson addressed an envelope to go out in tomorrow's mail. By then, Irwin had prepared a light supper, which they ate in silence.

Six o'clock rolled around, and then six thirty and seven, but the Jacksons didn't show. Anson stood on the front porch and stared across the darkened lawn for any sign of pickup headlights. Weighed down by disappointment, he trudged inside and began closing textbooks and gathering up pencils.

As he switched off the lights in the smaller classroom, Irwin ventured into the hallway. "Come to the kitchen. Now."

Too tired to ask why, Anson obeyed. When he turned the corner, he released a surprised gasp. "Noah?"

"Sorry 'bout not bringin' the children tonight, Mr. Schafer. Like I done told Dr. Young, we had a bit of a scare this week." Noah shot a nervous glance over his shoulder. "Didn't want nobody seein' me come here, so I snuck in from back yonder."

Anson edged closer. "What kind of scare? Was anyone hurt?"

"No, sir, praise God. But someone hung a headless chicken on our stoop last night, along with a warning 'bout schoolin' our kids." His sorrowful eyes speaking apology, Noah shuffled toward the door. "Me and Zeke appreciate all you's trying to do for us, but we ain't of a mind to cause you no more trouble. Ourselves neither. We gotta protect our families."

"I understand." It was a lie, but Anson had no other words. He wouldn't lay more guilt upon a good man who only sought the best for his children. "At least let me send some textbooks home with you. Your older children read well enough that they can make some progress on their own and also help the younger ones."

"I'd be most obliged. You's a kind and generous man, Mr. Schafer. I'm proud to know you."

With Irwin's help, Anson selected some arithmetic texts and reading primers and packed them in a cardboard crate along with writing tablets and pencils. Noah left as quietly as he'd

arrived, and once he'd gone, Anson collapsed into the nearest
chair.

"That's the end of it," he said. "I didn't establish this school
to serve only white children. If it can't be open to all, it won't be
open to anyone."

"Think of what you're saying, Anson." Irwin sat down and
looked him hard in the face. "It isn't those children's fault for
being born into a bigoted society. Don't they still deserve to be
educated? And who knows? God may be calling you to show
them how to live in harmony with their brothers and sisters in
Christ."

"I don't know." Anson slipped off his glasses and massaged
his eye sockets. "I just don't know."

"You'll figure it out, son. I have faith in you." Rising, Irwin
locked the back door. "I'm heading up to bed. See you in the
morning."

Anson sat at the table for a long time afterward. He knew his
friend was right—he wasn't being fair to the children he could
be teaching. And without the complication of the race issue,
more white families would probably start participating.

Two stanzas from a favorite hymn played through Anson's
mind:

> In Christ there is no East or West,
> In Him no South or North,
> But one great fellowship of love
> Throughout the whole wide earth....
> Join hands, then, disciples of the faith,
> Whate'er your race may be!
> Who serves my Father as a son
> Is surely kin to me.

Peace in Christ and the fellowship of all believers, no matter the
color of their skin—was such a dream even possible?

The longing to return to Kenya burned hot in Anson's chest. There, he'd felt at home. Yes, there'd been problems, but he'd believed he was making a difference. Here…his work had turned into a long, exhausting, and seemingly futile uphill battle. It would be so easy to walk away, to make his way back to Matumaini School and take up where he'd left off.

So easy except for one thing—no, make that *three* things. First, he'd never hear the end of it from Irwin. Second, he couldn't simply walk in, seize the reins, and send Franklin Keene packing.

And third, even with the fading prospects of a future with Lark, when he couldn't bear the thought of being separated from her by a few miles, how could he survive with the Atlantic Ocean and the whole continent of Africa between them?

* * *

No matter how laborious or loathsome the chores Rose gave her, Lark couldn't bring herself to work in overalls like her sister. Most of her dresses were already old and showing their wear anyway, and she preferred the swish of a skirt around her legs to the rough stiffness of denim.

And though she'd scarcely admit it even to herself, she didn't want to look *too* unfeminine should Anson venture out this way.

Not that she had any right to expect a visit considering the brush-off she'd given him after Grandpa's funeral. But what choice did she have? Rose couldn't manage the farm alone, and Lark wouldn't be much help if she spent the better part of every day at the school.

And now with Bryony convalescing in Hot Springs, Rose needed whatever sense of permanence and security Lark could offer. The girl might be strong of body and determined of mind, but emotionally she was still so young and vulnerable.

After milking Hermione and doing a little hoeing in the vege-table garden, Lark walked over to the edge of the field where Rose ran the plow. The old tractor rumbled and grumbled as the plow carved long, straight furrows where in a few weeks the green tips of new cotton would sprout.

When Rose headed back in Lark's direction, Lark waved and waited for her to stop at the end of the row. "I'm going into town for groceries and to mail our letters to Bryony. I'll be back to make lunch."

"Check at the feed-and-seed, will you?" Rose shouted over the roar of the tractor. "I need to know how much it's gonna cost us for cottonseed this year."

Money, always a sore subject. Worse since the drought. Grandpa had made scant headway with the farm debts this past year, and things were still too tight for comfort. Lark already missed the small salary Anson had paid her. Maybe she should ask if he could use her on a part-time basis.

No, that would only be playing with fire. Besides, wasn't she already working sunup to sundown trying to keep up with the never-ending farm chores? Seemed without Grandpa everything took twice the time and twice the effort. The work had been grueling with Grandpa and the three girls sharing the load. Now, with just Lark and Rose…she figured they'd both gone plumb crazy.

The drive into town gave her a brief respite. She made it a leisurely trip, enjoying the scenery along the way. Central Arkansas was beautiful in its own way, rolling farmlands everywhere you looked. Lark hadn't much cared for the farm when Mama had first moved them here, but today it was as if she saw the land with new eyes. It was her home, had been for most of her life. She could barely remember their Memphis home anymore, except every time she visited Bryony and Michael's cottage in Brinkley, flickers of familiarity tickled her mind. Reminders of another life were most likely why Bryony felt so happy there, at least until recently.

It hurt to think about Bryony too much right now. Lark hoped she and Rose could get away to visit soon.

After a quick stop at the feed-and-seed to get the price quote Rose needed, Lark parked in front of the general store. Shopping basket in one hand, her list and the envelope with their letters in the other, she went inside.

"'Mornin', Miss Larkspur." Joe appeared from behind one of the display shelves. "What can I do you for?"

"Just picking up some groceries and mailing a letter." Lark frowned as she scanned a shelf of canned vegetables. "Prices have gone up again, I see."

"Ever'body's gotta make a living. You pick out what you need, and I'll go fetch your mail." Joe slipped through a side door, and Lark could hear him rustling about behind the post office window.

A few minutes later, Lark had added cornmeal, dried beans, and four shriveled apples to her basket. After reading Joe's prices for ground beef and rump roast, she figured Rose would either have to kill another chicken or set more rabbit traps.

"Lark?"

At the sound of Anson's voice, she spun around and nearly dropped her basket. "H-hello," she stammered, her heart racing. "It's so good to see you. How have you been?"

He maintained a respectful distance between them. "Well. And you?"

"Fine." Such trivial conversation to avoid saying everything she wanted to say. *I love you, and I miss you so very, very much!* "How are things at the school?"

The abrupt change in his countenance told her she shouldn't have asked. His glance shot sideways. Hard knots appeared along his jawline. "It's been a difficult week."

"Is there anything I can do?"

"No, nothing." His forced smile didn't reassure her. "I just walked over to post a letter."

Noticing the envelope he held, Lark couldn't resist a peek at the address. "The congregation who's been so generous with donations?"

"Until now, anyway. Church finances no longer permit them to support us."

"Oh, no. What will you do?"

"That's yet to be decided." Anson gave a helpless shrug. "I should take care of this and get back to the school. Give Rose my best."

The defeated slant of his shoulders as he strode to the post office window brought a clutch to Lark's chest. His detachment hurt even more. They'd grown so close over the past several months, and now, to be treated like a casual acquaintance—

Joe stepped from behind the post office window and moved to the cash register. "No mail for y'all today, Miss Lark. You find everything you need?"

Her gaze followed Anson as he strode out of the store. "Yes, I think so."

Joe totaled her purchases. "Put this on your account like usual?"

"Please."

Hiking a brow, Joe handed her a receipt and pointed to the bottom line. "That there's what y'all owe as of today. I'll be needin' a payment soon, or I can't give you no more credit."

Lark read the figure and cringed. "I didn't realize how far behind we were."

"I ain't been wantin' to ask, seein' as how you've lost your grandpa and all. But business is business."

"I understand." With a crisp nod, Lark collected her shopping basket and trudged out to the pickup.

Seated behind the steering wheel, she lowered her head to her hands. How would they pay the grocery bill *and* purchase the cottonseed for next summer's crop? Rose might know farming, but did she have any concept at all for what her dogged determination could cost them?

After supper that evening, Lark made a point of finding out. "We need to talk, Rose."

"Did you get the cottonseed price?"

"I did." Lark reached into her pocket for the slip of paper the feed-and-seed manager had given her. She slid it across the table. "And that isn't all. Joe's asking for a payment on our general store account."

"Hmm. I'll give you some money to take over to him tomorrow."

"You'll give me some money?" Lark dropped her jaw. "What, did you go out and rob a bank while I was in town this morning?"

Rose looked at her like she'd lost her mind. Which, at the moment, it felt like she had. With an exasperated groan, Rose stood and walked out of the room.

"Where are you going? We need to—"

"To talk. I know. Be right back."

Lark didn't wait. Springing to her feet, she followed Rose into Grandpa's bedroom. "What are you doing?"

"I'll tell you if you give me five more seconds."

A rush of feelings overwhelmed Lark as she watched her sister light the oil lamp on Grandpa's desk. This had been his space, and the smells of old wood, musty papers, and Grandpa's favorite shaving soap still permeated the room.

A desk drawer screeched open, and Rose pulled out a ledger. "Just look here, will you? This shows exactly where our money's gone, and how much Grandpa had budgeted for this year's crops and equipment repairs. We'll make it, Lark. We can do this."

Lark leaned over the page, easily noting where Grandpa's entries had stopped a few weeks ago and Rose's had begun. "You've been keeping the farm records?"

"Grandpa's been teaching me for years." Pride etched Rose's cockeyed grin. "I may not be smart as you in reading and writing, but I got the eighth grade mathematics award, if you recall."

"I do." Lark looked at her sister in amazement. "I'm sorry, Rosie. I haven't given you enough credit."

"Ain't *that* the truth." With a roll of her eyes, Rose put away the ledger and opened another drawer. Shuffling some papers, she felt around toward the back, then produced a canvas drawstring bag. She emptied a wad of bills onto the desk. "Here's what Grandpa set aside from last year's cotton crop. It ain't near as much as it ought to be, but it'll buy enough seed for spring planting. And now the drought's letting loose of us, we're sure to do better this year."

Chewing her lip, Lark sank onto the edge of the bed. "Oh, Rosie, I'm just so scared. Can we really do this, you and me by ourselves?"

Rose put the money away in the drawer where she'd found it, then sat down next to Lark, their shoulders touching. She enfolded Lark's hand in her own. "Truth be told, I'm scared, too. But Grandpa gave his whole life to this farm, and I intend to do him proud and keep it going just like he would have done."

"You're so much stronger and braver than I'll ever be." Lark looked down at their entwined fingers and gave a squeeze. "And a right fine farmer, too. If this is what you want, I'll work alongside you the best I can."

A quick sniff was the only clue to Rose's tears. Her voice fell to a raspy whisper. "I should have gone to see him, though. I should have said good-bye."

"No, honey, I've been thinking about it, and you were right not to go. Better to remember Grandpa as he was, to picture him out there riding proud and sure on the tractor, or arguing with the cotton gin boss over what they'd pay him for a bale."

Rose gave a weak chuckle. "Boy, could he cuss up a storm when he didn't think they were giving us a fair shake!"

"See? That's what Grandpa would want, to hear you laughing again."

"And what about you, Larkspur?" Shifting slightly, Rose tilted her head. "I haven't heard you laugh for the longest time either."

"Well, it's been hard. Awful hard. But we'll make it. Nobody keeps the Linwood sisters down for long." Lark hoped her sister couldn't detect the false bravado in her voice. She stood. "I don't know about you, but I'm ready to have a hot bath and call it a day."

Rose snuffed the lantern, then followed Lark to the kitchen. As Lark lit the stove and set a kettle on to boil, Rose leaned against the counter, hands tucked into her overalls pockets. She stared for so long without speaking that Lark's nerves began to twitch. "What is it, honey?"

"You," Rose said. "You think I don't know how unhappy you are here? This isn't your life. This isn't what you were meant for."

"Don't be silly. I grew up a farm girl just like you, Rosie." Lark kept her gaze averted. "Sure, I've had my dreams, but family comes first. Always has, always will." Now she faced Rose directly. "I know where I belong now, and it's right here with you."

"But college. Anson's school. All those things you had your heart set on." Rose walked over and took Lark's hands. Holding them palms-up toward the lamplight, she rubbed her thumbs over the new calluses. "These weren't here a month ago."

Lark jerked away, remembering all too well how smooth her hands had grown those two years she'd been at college. How quickly the torn cuticles, rough spots, and broken nails had returned.

The kettle whistled. Lark grabbed a potholder. "Time for that bath."

*   *   *

Wrapped in a sweater, a blanket tucked around her legs, Bryony tipped her head back to the brilliant afternoon sunshine. A brief rain shower earlier had set the pine needles glistening on the tall trees surrounding the gardens. The fresh, cool smell, the sun on her face...Bryony began to feel almost human again.

The people here were so kind, especially Michael's friend Pastor Vickary and the cheery red-haired nurse with the Irish lilt. To know they'd been with Grandpa as he took his last breaths was a comfort to Bryony when her own weakness—this cruel melancholia that had drained her soul and body—had prevented her from being here herself.

Footsteps on the path drew her attention. Michael strode her way, smiling as always, as if the effort alone could lift Bryony from the dark abyss she'd fallen into. "Letters from home," he said, pulling a lawn chair closer. "One from your sisters, and another from Miranda."

"Read them to me." She settled deeper into the lounge and sent her husband a loving glance. He did cheer her, as much as anyone could these days. She loved Michael more than life itself.

He read Lark's letter first, words of assurance that she was looking after Rose and everything was running smoothly at the farm. No mention of Anson's school, which puzzled Bryony. She'd thought sure Lark would have gone back to work there by now. And the farm—was their baby sister really going to try to make a go of it on her own?

Rose's letter made it quite clear she would. *The north acreage is plowed and ready for cotton. I expect a good crop this year, and Caleb's already promised we'll trade off helping when harvest time comes.*

"See," Michael said, folding the pages, "your sisters are coming along fine."

Bryony twisted the corner of the blanket. "That's what they want me to believe, anyway. Rose may be content to stay on at the farm, but I know Lark isn't. I worry about her."

"You worry about everything lately." Michael's teasing tone didn't hide the truth of his words. "Your sisters are grown women, and quite capable of doing whatever they set their minds to."

What he didn't say was that Bryony was a grown woman as well, and she ought to be strong enough to shake these oppressive feelings and be the wife Michael deserved. She looked up at him, tears pooling in the corners of her eyes. "I'm sorry. I truly am."

"Nonsense." In one quick movement, he shifted onto the lounge next to her and scooped her into his arms. "I know you're trying, darling. I wish I knew how to help."

"You do, just by being here to hold and comfort me." She stroked the hair at his nape, relishing the way the curls slid through her fingers. With a sniff, she sat up and coaxed her mouth into a smile. "Did you bring your sketchbook? What have you been working on?"

"Hot Springs magnolia trees." His shy grin was one she'd seen often when anyone asked to see his drawings. He reached for a satchel beside the lawn chair.

Bryony could content herself for hours paging slowly through Michael's sketchbooks. His realistic colored pencil drawings of plants, trees, and flowers brought a foretaste of spring, of hope renewed. A breath of something warm and fragrant wafted across her spirit, and the veil of anxiety she'd been struggling beneath seemed to lighten.

She looked up at Michael, so much love in her heart that it hurt. "I really am getting better," she said.

And for the first time in a long time, she meant it.

Chapter Twenty

Within a week of the Jackson children's departure from Schafer School, white families started sending their children again. It was a mixed blessing, and certainly nothing Anson took any pride in.

He breathed somewhat easier about finances, though. Congress had passed the Emergency Banking Act, banks began reopening, and Irwin's repeated telephone calls to their Little Rock banker assured them the Schafer Foundation funds remained secure. Still, if they wanted to stay afloat for long, they'd need to seek out new donors, and they weren't likely to find many until the economy came out of its slump.

At least they were no longer budgeting for a secretary's salary— not that Lark had been paid anything near what her services were worth. Anson had discovered this the hard way when he'd taken over typing the correspondence to their supporters and potential donors. His hunt-and-peck system took three times as long to complete a letter, and by the time he finished, he had a headache from eyestrain and a pain between his shoulder blades.

When he hit the wrong key for the third time, he muttered a curse and tore the sheet from the platen. Crushing the page into a ball, he hurled it at the wastebasket.

"Temper, temper," Irwin chided from behind the larger desk. "Take a break, Anson. You've been hunched over that type-writer all morning."

"For all the good these mailings will do. They're costing us more in postage than they're bringing in."

Irwin slammed shut the farming journal he'd been taking notes from. One positive step they'd taken was to shape their lessons around situations the students dealt with in their daily lives. "Honestly, if you don't get control over your attitude—"

"You'll what, renounce our friendship?"

"Never our friendship, but possibly our partnership. I'm too old to deal with your mercurial moods day in and day out. You're exhausting me."

Much as he hated to admit it, Anson knew he'd been impossible to live with lately. He yanked off his glasses and tossed them onto the desk. "If I promise to work on my attitude, will you forgive me?"

"Done." Irwin stood and circled the desk. "Now get your coat. We're going for a drive."

"But what about—"

"Leave it. I know one surefire way to lift your spirits—that is, if you'll give her half a chance."

Anson lifted both hands. "Lark? No. I won't do that to her. I won't do it to *myself*."

"What are you afraid of, that the two of you might actually be right for each other?" Irwin's tone mellowed. "Anson, she's the best thing that ever happened to you. Don't let her get away."

"I haven't *let* anything happen. It's just...circumstances. She's committed to working the farm with her sister, and I'm going—"

"So help me, if you say you're going blind and no woman deserves to be saddled with an invalid, I shall haul you out back and give you a good lashing."

Anson turned away. "But it's true, isn't it? Lark has enough to worry about already without dealing with my failing eyesight."

"So it was all right while she was working here, arranging the classrooms, handling the correspondence, helping prepare lessons?"

"Would you stop, please?" Anson snatched up his glasses and began polishing them with a handkerchief. "Things are complicated. Messy. Confusing."

"I'll say." With a disgusted shake of his head, Irwin whipped his suit coat from the back of the desk chair and tugged it on. "Well, if you won't go to see Lark with me, then I'll—"

Before Irwin could finish his sentence, a knock sounded on the front door. Casting a withering look over his shoulder, he marched out of the office. Anson listened to the thud of footsteps through the house. He tried to tell from the voices who their visitor might be, but they spoke too quietly to be heard.

Curious, Anson started to the front hall. Before he made it as far as the classroom doorway, Irwin shut the door and turned, his face grim. "A telegram," he said. "It's from Franklin Keene."

Dread curdled in the pit of Anson's stomach. "What does it say?"

"*Situation untenable,* he says. *Closing school. Returning stateside next month.*" Dropping the slip of paper to his side, Irwin concluded, "*Letter with full details to follow.*"

Anson slumped against the wall. "How?...*Why?*"

"I suppose we'll have to wait for his letter." Irwin rested a hand on Anson's shoulder. "We must believe Frank had good reasons or he'd never have made such a decision. We knew already how the Kenyan school districts were pushing to educate their own children."

"Yes, but I thought we could work in cooperation with them." Anson slammed a fist into the wall behind him. "If I'd only stayed—"

"Enough!" Irwin gave him a brisk shake. "If you'd stayed, you most certainly would be blind by now. Whatever our opinions of Frank's conduct in his personal life, he was the right man to take over Matumaini School."

Head drooping, Anson gave a weak nod. He shoved away from the wall. "I need some air. I'm going for a walk."

God, why? It was the only question he could think to ask as he grabbed a jacket and lumbered out the door. Bad enough his hopes and plans for the Schafer Foundation were shrinking daily, but now, to see his parents' lifework come to an end—he didn't think he could bear it.

His long strides carried him through town, past the general store, and down a lonesome stretch of road. He didn't care which direction he headed or where he ended up. He didn't care whether he made it back in time for tutoring tonight. Miranda and Callie were helping again now that more students had enrolled, and between the Vargas women and Irwin, they'd manage fine without Anson.

He was a useless pile of bones anyway. A complete and utter failure at everything that mattered.

And that's the devil making you think such things about yourself. He could hear Sister Mary John's voice as clearly as if she walked beside him. What would she do now that the school was closing? She'd been serving at Matumaini since Anson was a boy.

He slowed his pace and released a cynical laugh. Sister Mary John, who must be in her seventies by now, might find this a welcome opportunity to enjoy a well-deserved retirement.

Reaching a turnoff, he halted to get his bearings. It would do no good to get so lost out here among the farms that he couldn't find his way back to town.

Then he realized the Rigby farm lay just down this lane to the right. Had he arrived here by accident...or by his own designs? Hands in his pockets, he stood there by a fence post for long moments, his gaze riveted on the distant and blurry image he knew to be the peak of Lark's roof. His logical mind told him he should turn around right now and walk away. His heart told him exactly the opposite.

His heart won.

* * *

The kitchen door burst open, startling Lark so badly that she nearly dropped a hot iron on her toe. Her mind had drifted a million miles away, easy to do while working her way through a laundry basket full of sheets straight from the clothesline.

"Company's coming," Rose blurted, a crooked grin skewing her lips. "You might want to fix your hair."

"Fix my—" Lark sucked in a breath, her stomach crashing as hard and fast as that iron would have fallen. The look on Rose's face left no doubt as to the identity of their visitor. Nearly two weeks to the day since Lark had run into Anson at the general store, and she'd counted every hour since, missing him so horribly that thoughts of him invaded even her dreams.

Dreams she hated to awaken from, because they could never come true.

Quick as a heartbeat, she composed her features into an impassive mask and set down the iron. "Invite them in. I'll brew some chicory."

"There's no *them*. It's just Anson. Looks like he walked all the way from town." Rose peered out the kitchen window. "I saw him ambling up the lane as I rode in on the tractor. He's almost here."

Lark's feet carried her toward the bedroom and her hairbrush and mirror before she could think of all the reasons her appearance shouldn't matter. She'd barely put the pins back in her bun when the sound of Rose's greeting carried from the back door.

"Hey, Anson. What brings you out our way?"

"I was, uh…"

From the hallway, Lark glimpsed the nervous shift of Anson's throat. She stepped forward, striving for a confident "Hello."

"Lark, I…" He swallowed. Lark had seen him mope about in frustration over problems with the school. She'd seen him try to hide his anger over his failing eyesight. She'd never seen him look so utterly bereft.

Shooting Lark a concerned glance, Rose edged toward the door. "I got some chores to finish up. Y'all have a nice visit."

"Anson, what is it?" Lark reached for his hand and drew him farther into the kitchen. "Sit down and tell me."

"I shouldn't have come. I don't want to burden you with this."

"With what?" A cold dread squeezed Lark's chest as she imagined all kinds of horrible news he might be holding inside.

He sank into a chair, one elbow resting heavily upon the table, his gaze fixed on something unseen. His tone as dead as his expression, he murmured, "Matumaini School is closing."

"Oh, no, Anson. No." Falling to her knees beside his chair, she wrapped him in her arms, one hand soothing the day's growth of beard along the curve of his jaw. She felt the heavy rise and fall of his chest beneath her cheek, heard each ponderous heartbeat. It was as if he had nothing left inside. No strength. No hope. No will to continue.

"I'm sorry," he murmured. "I know you didn't want to see me, but I—"

"Didn't want to see you?" Lark tilted her head back, seeking his gaze. "I've missed you until I thought I would die of the pain."

His lips parted. He drew his brows together as if he couldn't believe her words. Then with a choked breath, he pulled her onto his lap and buried his face in the crook of her shoulder. He clung to her so fiercely that she could hardly breathe, and she didn't care, because loving him—knowing he loved her—was all that mattered.

Slowly, his hold relaxed. He played his hands tenderly along her spine as his lips brushed her throat, searing each place they touched. She cupped his cheeks, gently lifting his head. One hand slid around to his nape as her mouth sought his. Their lips met, shyly at first, then building to an unquenchable hunger, and Lark poured into her kiss the full depth of her love.

Suddenly conscious of her shameless abandon, she shivered and pulled away. "I—I'm not like this, to be so forward—" Eyelids pressed shut, she covered her swollen lips with both hands.

"Please don't say it was wrong." Anson drew her hands away and enclosed them in his own. He pressed her knuckles with a long, meaningful kiss. "Only God knows how much I've needed you, needed this moment. I think it was God who led me here today, because I'd never have had the courage on my own."

Loath to leave the sanctuary of his nearness, Lark felt she must, or risk losing herself again to the ever-growing yearning inside. With her hands still locked in his, she edged backward onto another chair. From somewhere deep in the recesses of her mind, already so long ago, it seemed, she recalled what Anson had said about Matumaini School. She must think of this now, and remember it was why he'd come this afternoon. Not for passionate kisses and declarations of love, but for comfort.

Collecting herself, hoping he couldn't see past her façade of friendly concern, she tucked her hands firmly in her lap. "Tell me what happened. Why is Matumaini closing?"

He looked at her for a moment as if he didn't understand the question. Then his expression hardened, and the physical distance between them, no more than a few inches, seemed to widen. "I don't know the details yet, only what Franklin stated in his telegram."

At the mention of Professor Keene's name, long-buried emotions rose to the surface. She stifled them just as quickly and focused on Anson. "What did he say?"

He summarized the gist of the message. "We'll have to wait for his letter to know the rest." Looking away, he thumped the table with his fist. "Considering the rapid changes taking place in Kenya, I should have seen the end was inevitable. I just didn't want to admit it."

"Of course you didn't. It was your family's legacy." Lark wanted to reach for his hand, to offer more comfort, but she didn't dare. "You still have the Schafer Foundation, though. You can help so many children right here."

Resentment flashed. "Not as I'd hoped. Thanks to the floundering economy, we've lost a good deal of our financial support. And on top of everything else, I suppose you've heard we're now a whites-only school."

Lark nodded. "Daniel Vargas came out a few days ago to help Rose take down a dead tree. He told us what happened at Noah Jackson's place, said you'd given them some books so they could study at home."

"It was the least I could do. If I weren't—" Anson's lips flattened. He gave his head a brusque shake. Then, resolutely, he continued, "If I weren't losing my sight, I'd drive out to the Jackson farm every day and tutor the children myself."

Not surprisingly, Anson's passion for educating children far outpaced his concerns over lack of funding. Lark's guilt over abandoning him bore down upon her shoulders as if she carried the trunk of that old dead hickory tree. "If I could help somehow, I would. But Rose needs me now. Every day is"—her voice faltered—"so hard."

Anson muttered a curse and strode to the door. Hands low on his hips, he exhaled sharply. "This was the last thing I wanted, to upset you with my troubles. My...disappointments." He set his hand on the knob. "It's getting late. I'll be on my way."

* * *

Lark said little to Rose after Anson left, informing her sister only briefly about the difficulties he faced and deflecting further questions by going to bed early.

For all the good it did. All night long, Lark wrestled with her worries and regrets, all tangled up with an insatiable longing that only Anson could fill...and the devastating certainty that it would never happen.

One thing she could do, though, and by morning, she'd made up her mind. Up well before dawn, she'd milked Hermione and had oatmeal simmering by the time Rose awoke.

Rose took one look at Lark in her best Sunday dress and arched a brow. "Hope you're not planning to clean out the chicken coop wearing *that*."

Grimacing, Lark set a mug of chicory in front of her sister. "Can you manage without me until tomorrow? There's something I need to see to in..." She may as well spit it out. "Arkadelphia."

"Arkadelphia! What business do you have all the way over—" A sudden look of comprehension froze Rose's features. "You changed your mind. You're going back to college."

"No, honey, nothing like that. I promised you I wouldn't leave again." Lark took two bowls from the cupboard. "I—I'd like to visit Mrs. O'Neill, though." *Among other things.* But what if she was too late already? "I'll be back tomorrow afternoon, and I'll work to catch up on chores all night if I have to."

Rose chewed her lip. "I won't ever forget what you gave up, Lark. You go. I'll be fine."

After breakfast, Rose drove Lark into Eden in time to catch the next bus to Arkadelphia. The mild day made for a pleasant walk from the station to Mrs. O'Neill's house.

Answering the door, the elderly woman beamed a happy smile. "Lark Linwood. What a lovely surprise!"

"I hope you don't mind my coming unannounced. This was rather a spur-of-the-moment trip."

"Not at all. Come in, come in!" Mrs. O'Neill welcomed her with a warm hug before showing her into the cozy living room. "Have a seat. I'll put the teakettle on." Bustling toward the kitchen, she called over her shoulder, "How long are you staying? Are you planning to come back for the summer term?"

A pang of regret stabbed deep. "I can't. Things have changed... again." After Mrs. O'Neill returned, Lark explained about Grandpa's illness and death and the need to help her sister on the farm.

"But I thought you were working for your nice friend, Mr. Schafer. Wasn't he starting up a school out your way?"

"He did, but...he's encountered some problems." Lark decided not to mention the racial issues. Her reason for this visit involved another pressing matter. "With the economy so bad, many of the foundation's financial supporters have had to withdraw. Anson can't afford to pay me now anyway."

"What a shame. Yes, times are hard. The banking closures had us all in a panic." The teakettle whistled, and Mrs. O'Neill excused herself.

The break in conversation gave Lark a few moments to frame her thoughts. Was this the right thing to do? Would Mrs. O'Neill agree?

With cups of freshly brewed tea and a plate of sliced pound cake on the side table between them, Lark summoned her courage. "I've had a thought about the money Mr. O'Neill left me." She pressed her lips together. "I guess I should ask first if your bank survived the crisis."

"Yes, our accounts are intact, praise God." Mrs. O'Neill sipped her tea. "What is it you were thinking, dearie?"

The bite of cake Lark had taken lodged in her throat. Swallowing hard, she dabbed her lips with a napkin. "How would you feel if...if I were to use part of Mr. O'Neill's bequest toward helping the Schafer Foundation? I know it isn't what he stipulated," she rushed to add, "but the money could make a difference for so many children who might otherwise have few opportunities to learn."

Frowning thoughtfully, Mrs. O'Neill set down her cup and saucer. "I appreciate deeply what Mr. Schafer is striving to do. But wouldn't you be of much more value to him by completing your teaching degree?"

"I used to think so. But the need is immediate, and working the farm with Rose now, I can barely find the time or the energy for my home-study course. It'll be years yet before I could even hope to graduate." She swallowed the words *if ever.*

The woman exhaled through pursed lips. "The very thought just breaks my heart. Lark, dear, isn't there some way, some hope you can still do so, and sooner rather than later?"

Lark should be grateful Mrs. O'Neill hadn't chided her about the absurdity of two young women operating a tenant farm. "There's always hope, I suppose. Only God knows what the future holds." She glimpsed a Bible resting beneath a reading lamp. Taking it into her lap, she opened it to Matthew 25. "I can't help thinking of Jesus' words: 'Truly I tell you, just as you did it to one of the least of these who are members of my family, you did it to me.'"

Looking earnestly at Mrs. O'Neill, Lark continued, "These children, toiling every day alongside their parents just to make ends meet—surely they are the *least* whom Jesus would have us serve. I'm not asking to give the entire bequest to the foundation, only a portion to help Anson keep the school open while we hope and pray for better times."

The woman's gaze softened. "I don't suppose Benjamin would object at all to such a noble use of the money. Let's finish our tea, and then I'll take you to the bank to withdraw some funds."

"Thank you!" Heart lifting, Lark reached out for Mrs. O'Neill's hand. "I promise, the money will be put to good use."

"And promise me as well," Mrs. O'Neill said, eyes narrowing, "that as circumstances permit, you will do everything possible to finish college and earn your teaching certification."

Throat tightening, Lark answered with a nod. "As circumstances permit."

* * *

In town on Saturday to meet Lark's bus from Arkadelphia, Rose made a stop at the feed-and-seed to pick up some supplies. On her way out to the pickup, she saw Caleb Wieland striding her way.

Nearing, he grinned and tugged on the braid hanging across her shoulder. "How's it going, squirt?"

"Not too bad." Rose appreciated that Caleb hadn't come to her all sorrowful and sympathetic. She could do without the *squirt* business, though. She was a grown woman, after all. "How's your mama?"

He gave a thoughtful smile. "She's gettin' along all right. Like always, she has good days and bad. I'm hopeful this'll be a better year."

Clouds had rolled in, the smell of rain freshening the air. "Least it's not as dry. You about ready for spring planting?"

"Gettin' there. You?"

Rose stood a little taller. "Already got a head start on the plowing. Another couple weeks and I'll be ready to sow my cottonseed."

"Same here." A hint of concern sharpened Caleb's glance. "Remember, you need any help with anything, all you gotta do is ask."

"Me and Lark are managing just fine, thank you."

"Lark and *I*," Caleb corrected, showing off the little bit of college education he'd gotten before he quit to find work to help support his family.

Rose sniffed. "I didn't realize *you and Lark* were taking up farming together."

Caleb just rolled his eyes. "I mean it, Rosie, you need anything, anytime—"

"I said we're managing." She stepped off the feed-and-seed porch. "Nice seein' you, Caleb, but I gotta run. Lark's bus is due in any minute."

"Wait—where'd she go?"

Rose hesitated. "Arkadelphia."

"She's not—"

"No," Rose replied a little too brusquely. "Just visiting a friend. She'll be back. Today. Like I said."

"Rosie." Caleb's voice took on that sympathetic tone she'd hoped not to hear. "I know the farm's what you want, but you and I both know it isn't what Lark wants. And you know she'll stay anyway, because she loves you."

"You think I don't know that?" Rose balled her fists. "I think about it every single minute of every single day."

"Then you know you have to let her go, let her live her own life. Don't tie her to the farm with guilt and obligation."

Angry tears threatened, but Rose refused to shed them. "I'm not, Caleb, I swear. She could leave anytime she wants to."

"Does Lark know that? Because she won't move on without your permission." Caleb's fingertips grazed her arm. "Without your assurance you're gonna be okay."

Rose shifted sideways, teeth clamping down on her lower lip. She'd spoken so confidently to Lark that day in Grandpa's room, but now…"What if I ain't so all-fired sure, myself?"

Caleb laughed out loud, a warm and kindly laugh, not mocking or mean. "Rosie Linwood, if you weren't a little bit scared about what you've taken on, I'd be mighty worried. But when I look at you, I see strength and courage and stubbornness like nobody else."

His words lit a flame beneath her heart. She slid him a questioning glance. "Really?"

"Yes, really." He gripped her by the shoulders and looked deep into her eyes. "Just remember, I'll be here for you, too. If you ever need help, day or night, rain or shine, you only have to ask."

As everything Caleb had said sank in, as it melded with all the concerns eating away at Rose's heart and mind these past weeks, she knew the time had come to do the right thing. An idea began to form, and a tiny smirk crept across her face. "Did you mean it, Caleb? Anything I asked?"

He looked at her askance. "Why am I suddenly afraid I might regret those words?"

Chapter Twenty-One

Stretched out on the sofa in the upstairs sitting room, Anson rested his eyes while Irwin read aloud from Fitzgerald's *The Great Gatsby*. Every time Daisy entered the story, a vision of Lark came to mind—in her lightness and beauty only, because Lark certainly held nothing else in common with the frivolous, flighty Daisy Buchanan.

He couldn't stop thinking of the kiss they'd shared, the sweetness of Lark's mouth, the way she'd fit so comfortably against him as he held her in his arms.

He couldn't stop resenting the twists and turns of life that kept them apart.

Faith required that he believe the Lord works everything together for the good of those who love him—the subject of Father Dempsey's heartening message at Mass that morning—but why couldn't God allow Anson to see and experience those good results sooner rather than later?

"And so Daisy and Gatsby sprouted wings and flew to Timbuktu, where they happily survived on roots and berries—"

Anson's head shot up. "*What?*"

"Just seeing if you were listening." Chuckling, Irwin closed the book. "I wasn't certain whether you'd fallen asleep or if your mind was wandering."

Wandering far afield of East Egg, New York, no question about it. Rubbing his eyes, Anson shifted his feet to the floor and sat up. "Guess I've had my fill of the idle rich."

"Yes, we are rather far removed—"

A knock sounded on the front door.

Irwin checked his watch. "A Sunday afternoon caller? Who might it be?"

When Irwin made no move to rise, Anson gave a huff and reached for his glasses on the end table. "Since you're not budging, I suppose there's only one way to find out."

He found Caleb standing on the front porch. "Hey, Anson. Excuse me for interrupting your Sabbath rest."

"Not at all." Anson held the door. "What brings you by?"

"Wonder if you'd walk with me over to the church. There's someone you ought to meet."

"Is this school-related?"

"You might say that. Like I said, sorry to bother you on a Sunday, but this was the only time they could make it."

Anson hated to appear rude, especially if a parent wanted to ask about tutoring, but he couldn't help asking, "Is there some reason they didn't come straight here?"

"Uh, well...guess they were a little nervous about introductions." Caleb gestured to Anson and started down the steps. "It'll just take a few minutes."

"All right, let me slip on my suit coat."

"They're simple folk. Shirtsleeves are fine." Looking toward the shimmering afternoon sky, Caleb inhaled deeply. "And it's a right pretty spring day to be out and about."

Anson couldn't argue on that point. Besides, he couldn't afford to miss a chance to bring more students into the fold. If these folks had doubts or concerns, he must do his best to assuage them.

He turned to call upstairs to Irwin that he'd be stepping out for a bit, only to find his friend standing right behind him, ready to hand him his dark glasses. "Don't forget these, my boy."

"Eavesdropping, were you? I don't suppose you'd like to go along?"

"I'm sure they'd rather speak with you. You can fill me in when you return." With a dismissive smile, Irwin headed toward the kitchen.

"Have it your way," Anson muttered as he changed his glasses. Aloud to Caleb, he said, "Shall we go?"

On the short walk over to the church, Caleb whistled a carefree tune and didn't seem much interested in talking. At the sanctuary doors, he directed Anson inside. "Go have a seat. They'll be along presently."

Anson glanced around as he switched to his regular glasses. "But you said they were already here."

"Yeah. Uh, I'll just go hunt 'em up." Caleb waved a hand toward the nave. "Go on, now. Make yourself comfortable."

Anson suddenly felt very *un*comfortable. The odd nature of Caleb's request, and now the empty church building...something seemed off.

As he took a seat in a rear pew, a side door opened near the chancel. He stood, ready to meet whomever Caleb had sent over.

It was Pastor Unsworth. "Oh, hello, Mr. Schafer. Pardon the intrusion. Just tending to some business in the sacristy."

"You wouldn't by chance know whom Caleb Wieland sent me here to see?"

"Mmm. I'm sure they'll be along momentarily." The man disappeared through an inner door behind the chancel.

Settling into the pew, Anson angled his body so that he could watch both the main doors and the side entrance. Five minutes passed, then ten. Just when he'd decided to go in search of Caleb, the front door creaked open. Someone paused, a shadowy silhouette against the bright light from outdoors.

Again, Anson stood. "Hello, were you looking for me?"

A surprised gasp. "Anson?"

His heart spiraled through his chest. "Lark?"

She edged into the darker interior, her flaxen curls loose about her shoulders, the first time he could recall seeing her hair down. Casting a quick glance behind her, she said, "Sorry, I'm confused. Rose told me to meet Callie here to work on her studies."

"The only other person I've seen since I arrived is Pastor Unsworth. He's in the sacristy. Maybe he'd know—"

"Don't bother." With an annoyed huff, Lark sank into the nearest pew. "I'm getting the distinct feeling we've been set up."

After only a moment's thought, Anson realized she was right. Irwin had seemed rather too disinterested in Caleb's arrival, and Caleb had certainly been evasive about who would be waiting for Anson at the church.

"So." Anson stood at the end of Lark's pew, his fingers aching with the desire to comb through her satin tresses. "What do you suppose this is all about?"

"I hate to imagine. But Rose has been acting strangely ever since I got back from Arkadelphia yesterday."

"You went to Arkadelphia?"

Lark scooted over to make room for Anson to sit next to her. She left far more room than he needed, much to his disappointment, but he respected the distance, knowing it was safer for both of them. She twisted the strap of her handbag. "I didn't plan to tell you like this."

"You're going back to school?" He shifted, covering her hand with his own. "Lark, I'm so glad!"

"No, that isn't why I went. I wanted to—" She released a flustered breath. "Just listen, all right? And don't refuse my offer out of hand or lecture me about all the reasons I shouldn't have done this."

He studied her face. "What are you trying to tell me, Lark?"

"I went to see Mrs. O'Neill to ask about using a portion of her late husband's bequest as a donation to your foundation. I was planning to bring the money to you in the morning"—she smiled up sheepishly—"after I had time to prepare a list of all the arguments why you had to accept."

Anson's heart was so full that he struggled to find words. "I'm grateful beyond measure, but you could never have enough arguments to convince me. Lark, that's your college money. I can't—"

"You can, and you will." Her fingertips grazed his cheek, sending a shiver through him. "Please, Anson. Let me do this for you. For all the children you'll be helping."

He gazed at her for so long that time seemed to stop. His arm slid along the back of the pew until his fingers found her hair and wove deeply into its silkiness. Her lips parted, and he slanted his head to brush them with a kiss. "I love you, Lark Linwood. I love you so very, very much."

Lashes lowered, she murmured, "Then you must surely realize how deeply I've fallen in love with you."

"Why, Lark? Why have we fought this for so long?"

"Because we both have responsibilities we can't shirk." Her longing glance slashed through him. "You have the foundation; I have Rose and the farm."

He drew her close and rested his forehead against hers. "Every day we're apart is torture."

"For me, too. You don't know how badly I wish..." Her voice trailed off, and she lifted her head to glance around the sanctuary.

"What is it?"

"I can't help but wonder...if we really are the unwitting victims of a setup, what could Rose and Caleb have had in mind?"

Anson twirled one of her curls around his finger. "Maybe exactly what's happening here, the two of us together, acknowledging the feelings neither of us can deny."

"But Rose would have no reason to encourage this. She needs me too much on the farm."

The sanctuary doors flew open, and Rose marched in. "There you go, treating me like the helpless baby sister again."

Both Anson and Lark leapt to their feet, and Lark whirled to face her sister. "How long have you been listening?"

"Long enough." Rose signaled to someone behind her, and Irwin walked in.

Anson snorted. "I guessed you had to be in on this." He slid a protective arm around Lark's shoulders. "Toying with people's emotions is a dangerous game."

"And don't we know it!" Rose's expression turned solemn. "Larkspur, I'll be grateful till my dying breath for everything you were willing to give up for me. But how long do you think I could live with myself if I kept you from the future you were meant to have?

"And you, Anson," she went on, "why, you two are peas in a pod, both of you bound and determined to put every other thing in your lives ahead of your own happiness. You're doin' a right good thing with the school, but if you don't marry my sister and—"

"Excuse me—*what?*" The words hit Anson like a punch in the belly.

"You heard her," Irwin piped up. "And it's about time, because frankly, I've grown tired of your whining about how lonely and meaningless your life is without Lark in it."

Lark jerked her head up. "Is that true?"

Forcing a swallow, Anson dipped his chin. "Which part—the whining, or how much I miss you?"

"Both, I suppose." A loving twinkle lit her blue gaze.

"And glory be," Irwin raved, "here we are in a church, and there's the parson right behind you, ready to schedule your wedding date."

Heat rose in Anson's face as he twisted to look.

"Hello, there." Pastor Unsworth stood in the aisle, his smile obsequious and a pen and notebook in his hand. "The church is available tomorrow. We can hold the ceremony as soon as you return with your marriage license."

Feeling Lark stiffen beside him, Anson drew her closer. "Let's just slow down here. You can't manipulate us this way. We need time—"

"Time?" Irwin clucked his tongue. "How much more time do you need to face the fact that the two of you are meant to be together? You *do* want to be together, don't you?"

Something cracked deep in Anson's chest, like a padlock snapping open and setting free all his hopes and dreams for a future with Lark. Each precious image soared upward, swelling his heart, filling the very air around them. He couldn't have forced words out just then if his life depended on it.

Lark, bless her sweet soul, found words enough for both of them. "You two are incorrigible! Rose. Outside. Now."

* * *

With a firm grip on Rose's elbow, Lark marched them both around the side of the church building before jerking to a halt. She spun her sister around. "Rose Catherine Linwood, what in the name of all that's holy are you trying to do?"

"Should be obvious," Rose shot back, shaking off Lark's hold. "Especially to a college-educated woman of the world like you."

"I am not—" Infuriated, Lark slapped a hand to her forehead and forced a series of deliberately calming breaths. When she could speak without shouting, she said, "Do you have any idea how embarrassing that was? Anson and I had both accepted our circumstances, and now..." Her throat tightened. "Now..."

Rose's upper lip curled with a knowing smirk. "Now you're stuck with the bald truth that you're madly in love with each other, and you're scared silly."

Lark's mouth fell open, her sister's quiet assertion cutting to the quick. "Yes," she said, her voice shaking. "Yes, I'm scared. I feel like a ship on a stormy sea, tossed this way and that, with no idea where, or if, I'll find anchor again."

"It's these crazy times, that's all." Rose caught Lark's hand and gently held it. "I've felt much the same, only I've already dropped anchor, right there on Grandpa's farm. It's where my heart is, where I feel safe, where I find my purpose." She looked earnestly into Lark's eyes. "But you have to find your own harbor, and we both know it's not on the farm. It's with Anson."

"Rose—"

"No, just listen. I know you're worried about me, how I'll manage on my own. Yeah, I'm scared, too. But with God as my strength, I know I can do it." She offered a misty smile. "Anyway, didn't I have the best teacher ever?

Lark whispered out a sigh. "Grandpa."

"I feel his presence every day, right here." Rose laid her hand over her heart. "I feel him with me in the sunshine on my back, in every furrow I plow, and in every cup of chicory so bitter it makes my mouth pucker."

They both laughed.

"Still don't know how he could stand it so strong." Lark flicked away a tear. "Oh, Rosie, I do love you for what you're trying to do, but how could I ever leave you all alone out there? It's too much for one person, even a woman as strong as you."

"Help will be there when I need it. Caleb's been persistent about offering, and frankly, I'm concerned he'll become a downright nuisance. There's Daniel, too, always willing to lend a hand. And plenty of the other tenant farmers around to call on. Haven't we always pitched in when needs arose?"

"I know, but—"

"But nothing." Rose gave Lark's hand a quick, hard shake. "Your place is with Anson at his school. And when the time is right, you'll go back to Henderson State and get your degree, like you always dreamed. You'll be the best teacher ever, Lark, mark my words—Oh, for pity's sake, dry those tears, woman!"

Rose fumbled around in her overalls pockets and brought out a handkerchief, none too clean, from the looks of it.

Lark accepted it anyway and found an unused corner to dab at her cheeks.

"Alrighty," Rose stated, "now that we've settled this business, you'd best get back inside. Pastor Unsworth might have better things to do than wait around all afternoon for you to pick a date."

It took a full second for understanding to dawn. "Rose. You didn't honestly think we'd marry this quickly."

"The sooner, the better, that's what I'm figuring." Rose grabbed Lark by the wrist and tugged her toward the front doors. "We can get it all legal first thing tomorrow—I'll even wear a dress if it'll make you happy—and then if Anson feels the need of his priest's blessing, y'all can head over to Brinkley afterward and do it all again at the Catholic church."

"Rose!" Face aflame, Lark tried in vain to free her arm from her sister's grip.

Then they rounded the corner, and Lark found herself toe to toe with Anson at the bottom of the church steps. Squinting against the bright sun, he clutched her hands, and his cockeyed grin suggested he must have recently finished a similar conversation with Irwin.

Breathing hard, Lark shook her head. "This is crazy. We can't—"

"Why not? What's stopping us?"

She opened her mouth intending to provide a dozen or more reasons why they shouldn't rush things, but with her heart lodged in her throat, no words could escape.

"If you need more time to plan, I understand." His gaze turning soft and solicitous, Anson caressed her cheek. He released a tender chuckle. "Besides, I haven't even properly proposed yet, have I?"

Lark couldn't help smiling. "Well, there is that."

Still holding her right hand, Anson stepped back and dropped to one knee. "Larkspur Linwood, I love you more than words can say. Whether it's tomorrow, or next month, or whenever your heart allows, please tell me I can look happily forward to the day you'll become my wife."

A sob caught in Lark's throat. The only answer she could give was a quick and emphatic nod.

Laughter bursting from his lips, Anson thrust to his feet and wrapped her in his embrace. He kissed her soundly, insistently, joyfully, and she trembled in his arms. It seemed like an impossible dream, too wonderful to be true, but the heat of Anson's mouth upon hers, the taste of his salty tears mingling with her own—and then the cheers and applause suddenly exploding all around them—assured her this moment was so very, very real.

Pastor Unsworth's voice rang out. "So, are we having a wedding tomorrow, or not?"

Still locked in Anson's arms, Lark tilted her head to peer up at him. A sad smile pinched at her lips. "I can't, not without Bryony here."

"Of course not." Anson kissed her forehead. "We'll wait until she's better."

Rose came close and rested her cheek on Lark's shoulder. "She'll be back with us real soon, I just know it."

Reluctantly freeing herself from Anson's tender hold, Lark shifted to wrap her sister in a hug. "I should probably tan your hide for interfering like this, but my heart isn't in it. Thank you, Rosie. Thank you for making me see the wondrous gift that was right before my eyes all along."

＊　＊　＊

When Lark awoke Monday morning—not that she'd slept all that soundly—she had to remind herself all over again that Anson had proposed and she'd said yes. Doubts continued to niggle: anxious thoughts about abandoning Rose, worries over Bryony's health, concern for Anson as he resisted prejudice and strove to bring education to deserving children no matter their race.

With the morning chores done and the breakfast dishes washed, Rose handed Lark her sweater and handbag. "Come on, we're going to town."

Lark scowled. "I don't need any more surprises, little sister."

"No surprises, just taking you in to work." Rose started for the door. "Let's go. Anson'll be waiting."

Though Lark and Anson had talked a good while longer yesterday, they hadn't gotten around to the subject of Lark's returning to the school. Mostly they'd been numb with shock, plus there'd been quite a bit of kissing. Running her tongue across her lips, Lark could still taste the sweetness of those kisses.

Rose tapped her booted toe. "Are you just going to stand there looking all love-struck? Get a move on, girl!"

"But don't you need me here? There's so much to do—"

"I thought we already settled that issue. I'm well ahead on getting ready for spring planting. I'll manage fine from here on out."

Lark crossed the kitchen and stood before her sister. "Rosie, I saw the mess this house was in after I got back from Hot Springs."

Looking sheepish, Rose ducked her head. "Yeah, I let it get out of hand. Mostly 'cause of how upset I was about Grandpa. I can do better."

"Even so..." Lark firmed her mouth. "The thought of you out here all alone—it scares me silly."

"If it eases your mind any, I was talking to Bo Jorgensen after church yesterday. He just got one of those party lines hooked up out at their place. It's a huge relief to his wife, let me tell you, though I'm guessing she'll spend more time jawing with the neighbors now than seeing to her chores."

"A telephone line?" Lark had hoped for years that they could someday afford one. "Is it in the budget?"

"I'll make do." Rose winked. "Shouldn't be hard with one less mouth to feed around here."

Then they both winced, sharing a moment of sadness over the huge hole left when Grandpa passed.

"Well, I'd sure rest easier knowing you could call if you needed help." With a sigh, Lark slipped on her sweater. "All right, then. Let's go to town."

After Rose dropped her at Schafer School, Lark let herself in through the kitchen door. Anson stood at the counter pouring himself a mug of coffee and nearly dropped it when he saw her.

His mouth spread into a surprised but happy grin. "Lark, what are you doing here?"

"Apparently, I've come to work. That is, if I still have a job with the foundation."

"Of course, if you want it. But I thought..."

"My little sister can be very persuasive." Lark set her handbag on the table and nodded toward the coffeepot. "Got enough for another cup?"

Slipping into the office routine felt like coming home, if Lark didn't count the teasing twinkle in Dr. Young's eye as she settled in at the typing desk. Judging from the stack of handwritten notes and correspondence waiting to be handled, they'd missed Lark more than she had imagined.

Once she'd made some headway, she pushed her chair back from the typewriter and stretched. Anson looked up from the letters he'd been signing, and his smile brought a clutch to her chest.

"Things feel back to normal with you sitting there," he said. Then his smile wavered. "I promise you, Lark, someday soon I'll take you back to Henderson so you can finish your degree."

"There'll be time. For now, this is where I need to be. And in the meantime, you can help me study my correspondence lessons." She gave Anson a reassuring smile before her glance fell to the telephone on the corner of his desk. "Do you suppose I could call Bryony? It would be so good to hear her voice, and maybe if we tell her our news…"

Minutes later, Lark reached the reception desk at the convalescent home. She was told Bryony's husband had taken her out for a stroll around the grounds, but the receptionist would have her return the call as soon as they returned. It seemed a good sign if Michael had coaxed Bryony out for a breath of fresh air. Lark tried to keep busy for the next hour while waiting for the telephone to ring.

When it did, Anson nodded for Lark to answer and then stepped quietly from the room.

"Bryony?" Lark pressed the receiver to her ear. "How are you, honey?"

"So much better." Lark could hear it in her voice. "Hot Springs is a lovely place, and the people here have been so nice. I'm glad…" Bryony's words faltered. "I'm glad Grandpa's last days were spent in such peaceful surroundings."

"Me, too…. Bryony, I have something to tell you, and I hope you'll be happy for me. Anson and I—we've become engaged."

"Oh, Lark! I couldn't possibly be happier!" Bryony's sniffles sounded through the telephone line. "When's the wedding? Are you already making plans?"

"He only proposed yesterday. We've hardly had time to think about it." Lark wouldn't mention Rose's little scheme. "Anyway, I can't get married without both my sisters in attendance, so until you're well enough to come home—"

"Then I have some good news for you, too. I've been seeing the obstetrician Annemarie Vickary recommended, and he says I'm not his only patient to suffer through anxiety and sadness during pregnancy. He says I'm doing all the right things now to feel better, and he promises it won't last."

Lightness filled Lark's chest. "That *is* good news, Bry. And you do sound better. Happier. More yourself."

"My visits with Pastor Vickary have helped, too. We've been reading through Philippians, especially chapter four, where St. Paul reminds us to keep our thoughts on those things that are true, honorable, just, and pure." A peaceful sigh whispered across the miles. "Lark, I'm seeing everything so much more clearly now. I still struggle, but when I turn my eyes to my Savior, all my fears and cares and worries start to fade."

Barely able to speak over the lump in her throat, Lark looked heavenward and whispered a heartfelt "Thank you, Lord Jesus!"

"So set a date and start planning your wedding," Bryony said. "Nothing could keep me away."

"I love you, Bry."

"I love you, too, my dear, sweet sister."

As Lark ended the call, Anson came up behind her. His arms encircled her, his lips caressing her neck. "I couldn't resist listening. You sound encouraged."

"I am." She rested against him, cherishing the moment and feeling more hopeful than she had in months.

"Then can we talk about a wedding date? Because if we don't marry soon, I shall have increasing difficulty remaining a gentleman in your presence."

Warm and tingly and very womanly sensations swept through Lark. She swiveled to look up at him, her hands pressing firmly against his shoulders. "And don't you dare kiss me again, or I shall have a terrible time keeping my mind on typing correspondence or reviewing this evening's lesson plans with you."

"You mean like this?" Anson dipped his head, his lips searing hers with a kiss that stole her breath away.

"Exactly," she forced out over the pounding of her heart.

"Or this?" Grinning, he slanted his mouth over hers once again.

Her whole body went limp. "Anson...about that wedding date..."

Epilogue

"You look fine, darling." Anson paced behind his lovely wife as she tucked a tortoise-shell comb into her newly bobbed hair. He personally preferred it long, but she did look sassy with those flaxen curls skimming her neck. "Let's hurry. Irwin's already in the car."

She winked at him through the mirror. "Honestly, I'd almost think *you* were the one about to become a father."

A pang shot sideways through his belly. "Lark. You're not—"

"No, dearest, I'm not." She turned with a smile and pinched his cheeks. "Relax, will you? Miranda told me first babies always take longer. We have plenty of time to get to Brinkley before Bryony delivers."

Anson couldn't help feeling the tiniest bit disappointed that his wife wasn't yet carrying their child, but they both knew things would go easier if God didn't bless them with children until after Lark finished school. At Anson's urging, Lark had registered for the first term of summer classes at Henderson, but she adamantly insisted on being home the rest of the summer so she could spend as much time as possible with Bryony and the new baby.

It certainly hadn't been easy to spend those weeks apart while Lark was at school, but if they could survive the next couple of years, they'd have the rest of their lives to enjoy each other's company, both as husband and wife and as teachers for the Schafer Foundation.

Anson also harbored cautious hope that as the depression eased and financial contributions picked up again, he could establish a second school in Arkadelphia so that he could be near Lark while she finished college. Irwin could handle the

Eden school just fine, especially with the increasing likelihood of recruiting local county schoolteachers to assist with tutoring.

Bringing education to nonwhite children continued to be a challenge. Even with Anson and Irwin making weekend visits to those families for private tutoring, undercurrents of opposition remained. Anson refused to be thwarted, though. He believed with heart and soul that God had given him a mission to bring hope and encouragement to all children through education, and if God had called him, God would provide both the knowledge and the means.

He still carried regrets about the closing of Matumaini School, but Franklin Keene's letter of explanation had eased his mind somewhat. In the months after Anson's departure, Frank had nurtured good working relationships with the local school board, and a number of Kenyan teachers had enhanced their skills thanks to the training programs Frank developed. But with the Kenyan schools' increasing independence, the cost of keeping Matumaini open outweighed the further good they might have done.

The school had lived up to its name, though, offering hope where before there had been so little.

"Now who's stalling?" At the top of the stairs, Lark glanced back with a gently chiding look. "Your mind's wandering again. What this time?"

Grinning, he caught her around the waist. "Just counting my blessings."

She leaned away. "Don't you dare kiss me, Anson Schafer, or we'll never get to Bryony's before the baby comes."

"So suddenly you're in a hurry?" Anson teased her nose with a quick brush of his lips, then gave an exaggerated sigh. "Very well. Not to mention I'd have a hard time explaining to Irwin why we've kept him waiting in the car while we—"

"Anson!" With a playful slap to his arm, Lark flounced downstairs.

Anson decided it was worth her refusal just so he could admire the saucy twist of her hips.

Riding in the backseat with Anson, Lark found herself pushing her right foot hard against the floorboard, as if by doing so she could make Irwin drive faster. She might have appeared calm to Anson, but inside, she was a quivering mess of anticipation, and no small amount of worry. Bryony had chosen to have her baby at home rather than in the hospital, and even though Dr. Eddington would attend the birth and Dancy would be there to assist with her midwifery experience, there could still be complications.

By the time Irwin pulled up in front of Michael and Bryony's house, several other vehicles were parked either on the street or in the driveway. Even Rose had already driven in from the farm. Lark plunged from the car and darted up the front steps.

"Finally!" Rose hopped up from the parlor sofa and threw her arms around Lark.

Over Rose's shoulder, Lark glimpsed Miranda and Callie. On a chair across the room, Sebastian Heath wore a distracted expression as he bounced young George on his knee.

Lark twisted to look down the hallway toward the subdued moans and groans coming from the bedroom. "Any word yet?"

"It's close, that's all we know. Oh, Lark, she's makin' the most awful noises. For the last few minutes, she's been screamin' like a banshee—"

Another shriek from the bedroom made them both jump.

Then laughter and Dancy's shout, "Hallelujah, Miss Bryony, you got yourself a baby girl!"

Lark and Rose hugged each other fiercely. "A niece," Lark sighed. "We have ourselves a precious little niece!"

It seemed forever before Michael emerged, a tiny bundle swaddled in his arms and a mile-wide grin splitting his face. "Meet Iris Miranda Heath."

"Mama would be so proud." Lark gave Rose another squeeze, then stretched out a hand to Miranda, who'd succumbed to happy tears.

Misty-eyed, Sebastian inched forward, George on his hip. "Look here, you have a brand new cousin."

The toddler extended one finger to touch the baby's tiny hand. "Pwetty."

Sebastian blinked several times. "Yes, indeed. She's beautiful."

"When can we see Bryony?" Lark asked.

"A few minutes more. They're finishing up." Michael had no sooner said the words than the bedroom door opened again.

Dancy peeked out. "Miss Bryony's asking for her sisters. Y'all come on back."

Clasping hands, Lark and Rose scurried down the hall. In the bedroom, Dr. Eddington finished packing away his instruments. After a few words of instruction, first to Bryony and then to Dancy, who'd be staying the night, he excused himself, promising to check back first thing tomorrow.

As the door closed behind him, Bryony reached out to her sisters. "Did you see her? Isn't she precious?"

"The most beautiful baby ever." Lark eased onto the edge of the bed as Rose circled to the other side. They took turns giving Bryony gentle hugs, all of them sharing tears of joy.

Bryony breathed out a tired but contented sigh. "What a year this has been."

"A year of changes, that's for sure," Rose agreed.

A wistful smiled played at Lark's mouth. "Some sad ones, and some happy ones, but we've come through stronger and wiser." Her gaze drifted along with her thoughts. "Exactly one year ago I was in Kenya, a starry-eyed girl dreaming of doing great things in the world."

Rose reached across to poke her in the arm. "And now you're an old married lady like Bryony."

"*And*," Bryony added with a pointed look, "doing all kinds of great things in the world. Your dreams are coming true, Lark, just like I always believed they would." She shifted a little higher in the bed. "Now, y'all go fetch me my baby girl. I'm already missing her something awful."

With Michael and the baby back with Bryony and Dancy in the kitchen preparing a meal, the rest of the family began to disperse. When only Lark and Anson remained, Irwin gave them a little time alone on Bryony's porch swing.

"You do want a baby someday?" Anson ventured.

"You know I do." She could see the longing in his eyes, the hope, the need. And beneath it all, the worry that his sight would fail before he ever had the chance to gaze upon the faces of his children. "Anson, if you want me to postpone college a while longer—"

"Absolutely not." Holding her close, he pressed a long, tender kiss to her forehead.

She nestled beneath his chin. "How about if we leave the decision to God? He's so much better at seeing what lies ahead than either of us." A quiet laugh bubbled up from her chest. "After all, he saw how much I needed you."

"I think you have it backward, because I don't even want to imagine where I'd be without you, my love."

As the swing swayed gently and the golden rays of the setting summer sun warmed their backs, Lark looked toward the pink clouds drifting across the sky. Then she closed her eyes and smiled, because her happiest dream wasn't somewhere high up in the clouds but sitting right here beside her, holding her in arms so strong and solid and sure that she need never again look elsewhere for what only God's merciful love could provide.

Author's Note

Once again, I sincerely hope my story has honored the history of this difficult era of America's past. The Great Depression hit hard everywhere, but as William D. Downs Jr. explains in *Stories of Survival: Arkansas Farmers during the Great Depression*, the 1920s had already brought hard times to the state. Lives and property were lost to a series of tornado outbreaks in 1926, then the great flood of 1927. The drought of 1930–31 inflicted more crippling disaster as crops burned to a crisp and the bottom fell out of the cotton market. As Downs states, "The Wall Street crash in faraway New York City was the least of their worries."

Yet even as drought conditions in Arkansas began to abate in the early 1930s, the Plains States' struggle was only beginning. Overzealous farming and scant rainfall turned the Oklahoma and Texas panhandles and sections of Kansas, Colorado, and New Mexico into what became known as the Dust Bowl. Storm fronts kicked up high winds, whipping topsoil into massive walls of dust, and the particles could be carried for hundreds of miles. In 1932, there were fourteen reported dust storms. The number climbed to thirty-eight the following year. For a fascinating look at the causes and struggles of the Dust Bowl years, I recommend the video *Black Blizzard*, which originally aired on the History Channel.

The national financial crisis certainly played a role in Arkansas's economic woes. According to the *Encyclopedia of Arkansas* (www.encyclopediaofarkansas.net), the state entered the 1930s with 420 banking institutions. Between 1930 and 1933, 283 Arkansas banks shut their doors. Then on March 6, 1933, only two days after taking office, President Franklin Roosevelt issued a proclamation ordering the suspension of all banking transactions, effective immediately. Congress quickly labored to enact legislation to avert the crisis, and on March 9, the Emergency Banking Act was passed. Beginning a few days later, banks were allowed to reopen. Yet even with banking operations stabilizing, Arkansas ended the decade with only 234 banks in operation. Nationwide, more than four thousand banks would remain permanently closed. For a more in-depth examination of the 1930s banking crisis, visit the Federal Reserve History website (http://www.federalreservehistory.org).

As in *The Sweetest Rain*, book one in the Flowers of Eden series, the Arkansas towns and cities mentioned in this story actually exist. Even so, an Internet search for Eden, Arkansas, will bring up only a "populated place" in Monroe County, pinpointing the location on country roads south of I-40 and about twenty-five miles southwest of Brinkley. Thus, the 1930s version of Eden as described in these novels is entirely from my imagination. "Rich, flat delta farmland" is how the Monroe County website describes the surrounding landscape. If you're interested in learning more about Arkansas's tenant and share-cropping systems of the early twentieth century, refer to the Encyclopedia of Arkansas website referenced above.

Larkspur's sojourn in Kenya was inspired in part by the August 2013 Kenyan photo safari my husband and I enjoyed with our church tour group, as mentioned in the acknowledgments. As our Kenyan guide drove us across this beautiful land of contrasts, he pointed out the many schools while giving us a brief oral history of the establishment of the independent school districts. These schools owe their beginnings to the escalating conflict between Christian missionaries and the Kikuyu (the largest ethnic group in Kenya) over the cultural tradition of female circumcision. This controversy reached a turning point in 1929, when large numbers of Kikuyu Christian converts, refusing to denounce their centuries-old tribal customs even at the risk of excommunication, began boycotting the mission schools and churches. Throughout the 1920s and 1930s, more and more schools and churches free of missionary or government control were established in Kenya. For further reading, I recommend *Facing Mt. Kenya*, by Jomo Kenyatta, and *The Beautiful Tree*, by James Tooley.

On a side note, if you're interested in the views Lark and her companions would have enjoyed while their ship traversed the Suez Canal, go to YouTube and search "Suez Canal 1930."

In rural America, schools adjusted schedules so as not to interfere with planting and harvesting times. Even so, it wasn't at all uncommon for children to drop out after eighth grade, and sometimes much earlier. Many were needed at home for chores or caring for younger siblings. Others had to find work to help support their families.

Jim Crow laws prevented whites and blacks from attending the same schools, and naturally, the white schools received much more public funding. As a result, black teachers didn't receive the same level of training as white teachers, and schools for blacks were often run-down and overcrowded. In Downs's *Stories of Survival*, William Edward Delamar, who dropped out after third grade, describes his experiences attending a segregated school: "When white children were riding school buses to their schools, we had to walk. I didn't know what a raincoat was. If it was raining, I just kept on walking."

Henderson State Teachers College, now Henderson State University, began in 1890 as Arkadelphia Methodist College. The bulletin published in 1929 upon the school's establishment as Henderson State Teachers College reads in part, "Henderson State will stand for thorough scholarship, as well as for professional training. Its graduates will know *what* to teach as well as *how* to teach.... It wants students earnest in preparing for effective service in the field of teaching and in the world without." I like to think that's exactly the kind of education Lark received there.

The eye infection Anson contracted is a disease called trachoma, or granular conjunctivitis. Endemic to most of the African continent, including Kenya, this bacterial disease is spread through contact with eye or nasal discharge from an infected person. Trachoma causes a roughening of the inner surface of the eyelids, which can lead to scarring of the cornea and, with multiple reinfections, eventual blindness. The application of a copper sulfate solution remained the most effective treatment until the late 1930s; today, antibiotics like tetracycline are prescribed. More information can be found on the World Health Organization website (http://www.who.int).

A note about Bryony's prenatal depression, a very real condition that experts believe affects as many as one in ten pregnant women. Warning signs include chronic anxiety, loss of energy, weight gain or weight loss, difficulty sleeping or sleeping too much, lack of interest in activities once enjoyed, and recurring thoughts of death or suicide. One source describes this condition as "a nine-month tunnel of doom, anxiety and despair."

While prenatal depression can happen to any woman no matter her circumstances, upsetting life events such as family problems or the death of a loved one may contribute. Bryony's issues were compounded by worries over her sisters' well-being, her mother-in-law's worsening dementia, and the sudden loss of her grandfather—and all this during a time of nationwide economic strain.

As with depression of any origin, there is no telling the sufferer to "just snap out of it," and failure to take prenatal depression seriously and treat it appropriately could present a higher risk of birth complications. Cognitive therapy—talking through the issues with a professional—can often prove helpful. For more serious cases of prenatal depression, the option of carefully monitored antidepressant medication may be advised. In Bryony's situation, the combination of hospital care, family support, and her strong reliance on faith finally brought her through.

The main thing is not to suffer alone. You aren't going crazy, and this isn't "all in your head." If you think you may have prenatal depression, or if you recognize the signs in someone you love, seek help.

I've learned so much during my explorations of this time in history as I imagined what these characters' lives might be like, both the struggles they would face and their triumph in overcoming them. I hope you enjoyed getting to know Lark, Anson, and their friends, and if you haven't yet read *The Sweetest Rain*, that's where you'll find Bryony and Michael's love story. Rose gets her turn for romance in book three, coming next year, and you can be sure there'll be sparks aplenty!

Again, thank you for sharing this time with me. As always, please forgive any historical discrepancies you may find and chalk them up to liberties taken for the sake of storytelling. I do love to hear from my readers, so feel free to contact me through my website, www.MyraJohnson.com, where you'll also find my social media links and information about my other books.

With blessings and gratitude,
Myra Johnson